And We All Bled Oil

And We All Bled Oil

Abigail C. Edwards

To Donna :)

And We All Bled Oil by Abigail C. Edwards

acedwardsbooks.com

Cover by Sarah Tharpe.

ISBN: 978-0-578-33582-7 (print)

First Edition

to Claudia

who heard it first

and listened till the end

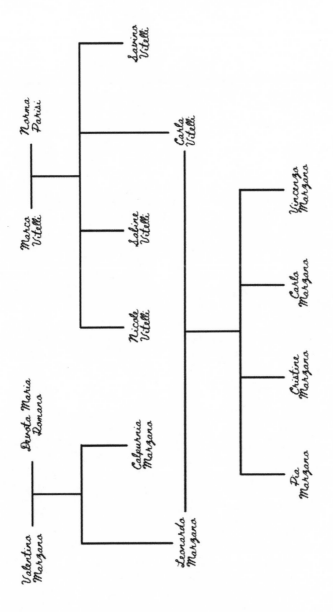

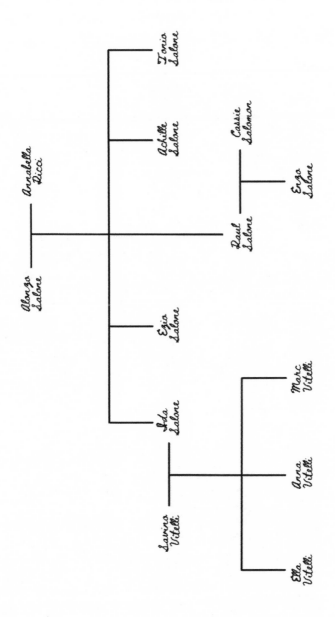

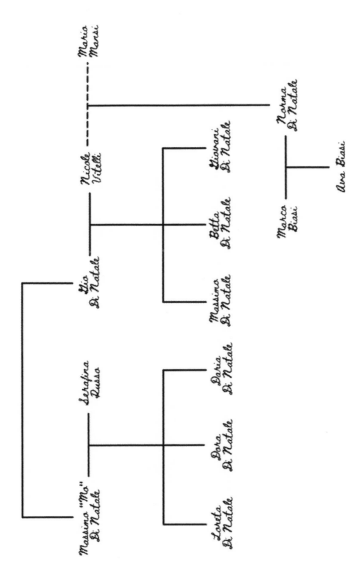

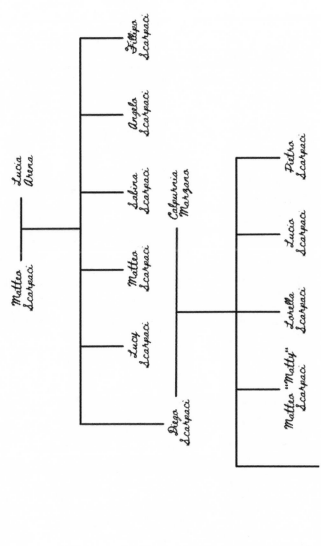

PROLOGUE
The Infinite

Lorel once told me that fate is a poet, organizing beauty out of chaos. I believed that for a long time—that life happens *to* a person, buoying them along on its tide whichever way it pleases, instead of bending and shaping itself around my will. And even now I'm not sure that I can entirely discard the idea, because God knows my life has spiraled into gothic prose, and even in the depths of my insanity I could not have thought up the repeating rhythms of horrible motif. Blood as oil, oil as sacred chrism, the suffocating paradox of its sacred and sensual nature, and can oil really run in a person's blood? Because when I think of one, I think of the other—they are inseparable in my mind. When I think of the times I dipped my fingers in green-gold oil, memory calls forth the image of blood on a warehouse floor, and blood mixed with oil in the creases of my hands.

I don't know much about poetry—I didn't pay much attention in those classes—but Papa had a favorite poem. It's the only one I know: "*L 'Infinito*" by Giacomo Leopardi. He talks about losing himself in the infinite, the future, and he paints it so beautifully that the longing and fear become muddled.

While I cannot entirely exclude the idea of fate as an artist, I prefer a different image: one of humans as the poets of their own destiny, a pen in a shaky hand, ribbons of cursive ink punctuated by sweat and blood. Poets, and we are abysmal at our craft.

I know nothing of the infinite. But I do know something about losing myself.

PART 1

"But as I sit and gaze, there is an endless
Space still beyond, there is a more than mortal
Silence spread out to the last depth of peace,
Which in my thought I shape until my heart
Scarcely can hide a fear."

- "The Infinite", Giacomo Leopardi

I

Marzano

i.

Two weeks after the funeral, and I was still trying to figure out what to do with my life. I'd always sort of flirted with the idea of planning my future, but it hadn't felt imminent until then, with no direction, very little money, and a whole lot of life staring me in the face. I suppose these things sort of catch up to you, when the world comes crashing down around your feet.

I remember sitting on the back step, smoking. My bare feet planted in the moss. Staring out past the garbage cans and the old play-set towards where the scrubby yard ended and the woods began.

The door squeaked open behind me. The shades clattered as it slammed shut behind a big whiff of dinner smells and my aunt.

"Oh, Pia, don't do that, you'll kill your lungs." Sabine smacked the cigarette out of my fingers. She dropped down on the step beside me, a blur of dyed-blond hair and fuchsia lipstick. "Look at me, *cara*."

I looked at her. I looked down at the cigarette in the grass. I picked it up and set it on the step beside me. "Please don't do that."

She brushed me off. "Okay, look, we need to talk about this. What are we gonna do, huh? We've gotta do something at some point, the kids need to get back to normal."

Normal. I rubbed my temple and watched the sun slink below the treeline. *Normal.* "They can catch up on school. I'll catch up. Then...I can take the summer to figure things out." Things such as: my parents were dead and my part-time job at the bakery was now our only source of income; my aunt could hardly help because she was a "writer for a fashion magazine" and didn't exactly rake in the big bucks; and any plans I might have had for my future had just spiraled down the drain. Good thing I didn't have many plans.

Sabine sighed, ran her hands through her hair. It wasn't just blond, her hair. It was platinum-blond. She was dark-complected Italian lady. I figured that someone, at some point in her life, would tell her she couldn't pull it off, but it certainly wouldn't be me.

My aunt pursed her lips. "Pia, you aren't finishing school."

"What?"

"Look, you can't. Exams are what, two, three weeks away? You gonna catch up that fast? Or are you gonna have to retake the semester? No, it doesn't work, you aren't finishing. The kids, maybe—they have more time. But not you."

This seemed uncharacteristically mean. "Why? What are you talking about?"

"You can take a pass or something, yes? Don't community colleges do that thing, like *pass or fail*, that sort of thing?"

"I'll catch up this summer." *When? How?*

"Look, I talked to Savino. I called him, we talked, he's gonna work something out."

I pushed back my hair, appraised her in the gray dying light. The cicadas crackled in the grass, and my siblings stormed about inside the house, but otherwise the yard was quiet. Sabine breathed loudly—she wore really tight jeans, it tended to make her pant. "Who's Savino?"

"You know, Savino, my brother, your mamma's brother. You know."

"No. I don't. What? You have a brother?"

She shrugged. She *shrugged.* "Yeah, you didn't know that?"

"How could I know that? You never—Mamma didn't—*what*?"

Sabine didn't get rattled, she just got mildly annoyed. She chewed a red thumbnail, looked at me sideways, like this was somehow *my* problem for not knowing. "Calm *down,* Pia. Don't get excited, huh?" She rubbed my arm, as if it was soothing or something. "Look, I called him—"

"Your brother. *Savino.*" *I* got annoyed. My patience ran short.

"Yeah, my brother. I called him, I talked to him, him and his Ida, they run the *panificio* in Manhattan, the *Zeppole.* You know what *panificio* is?"

"Bakery?"

"Yeah, okay. Well, I think you should go up there. You stay with family, you live with Savino and Ida. They'll take care of you. You finish school up there and you work in the bakery. I'll take care of the kids here, you can send back money for the kids—whatever, we'll figure it out, okay?"

We lived in Augusta, Georgia. More accurately, we lived in the rural outskirts banding Augusta, where you had to stop your car to let a farmer herd his cows across the road, and where there were more abandoned barns and sprawling corn fields than there were houses. It was April and the air was already hot, the soil was arid, the only sound was distant traffic and a violent chorus of seasonal insects. I lived in Augusta, and she wanted me to go to New York.

"I can't do that." I reached in my pocket for the lighter, pulled out another cigarette. I held up a finger. "Please, don't smack it out my hand."

Her fuchsia lips twisted in a displeased way, but she sighed. "Yeah, okay. Just don't let the kids see, huh? Especially Carlo, he'll copy you."

"That's fair."

The scent of smoke mingled with the flowering gardenias the Rondolfos had dropped off—the Rondolfos from down the road. They had way too many plants obscuring the front windows of their ancient farmhouse. They'd uprooted a three-year-old gardenia bush, thrown it in a big-ass urn and deposited it on our back porch like nobody's business. Some people sent flower arrangements, but the Rondolfos sent the most cloyingly sweet tree on their property. I thought they were just looking for an opportunity to get rid of it, actually. I refused to put it in the ground, yet it insisted on flourishing in its clay urn beside the back step.

"I've got to finish school," I said.

"I know, Pia, I know. That's why you should go stay with Savino and Ida, the Vitellis—they'll take care of you, you'll finish school, and honestly *cara*"—she squeezed my knee—"you need space, you need to breathe, you need to let someone take care of you before you come back and have to take care of all of *this*. Here, with the kids? You won't finish school. You won't. So I'll put you in a community college in Brooklyn, you work part time, you learn part time. What you want to do, you want to be a baker?"

I hadn't thought about it too much. I mean, sure I'd thought about the fact that I *needed* to figure out what I was going to major in, but that was about as far as I'd gotten. "Maybe…computer science."

"You know a lot about computers?" Why did every question have to sound like an attack?

"A little bit." I knew next to nothing about computers. "But everyone's looking for people good with programming and coding. And stuff. There are a lot of jobs available, people are always hiring, I know a lot of kids—"

"Do you *want* to be a computer scientist, Pia? You want to be a nerd sitting at a big computer in a basement, telling people to turn their electronics on and off and put them in rice?"

I snorted. Choked on smoke. "Is that what they do?"

"I don't know, it's all the same. What you want to do?"

"I don't know, maybe Italian—"

"Your Italian is atrocious, you want to speak Italian? You've got to care, you've never cared that much, why care now? Want to make you poor aunt's ears bleed every time you speak? That's not what you want to do. VINNY!"

I tucked the cigarette under my leg and waved off the smoke seconds before the back door crashed open. Vince, the youngest, stuck his head out. "Yeah?" He looked down at us through his hair—I needed to cut it, I didn't know how to cut hair, Mamma had always done that. He was ten, but his eyes were older.

"What does your sister want to do, huh? What's Pia want to do when she grows up?"

He spoke slowly, every word thoughtful. "I don't know. She's talked about food. Food science."

Sabine waved him away. "Thank you Vinny, go away *bambino*, please check my *lasagne. Grazie.*"

My brother disappeared. Sabine raised a dark eyebrow. "You get your AA, then you learn food science. And you be a food scientist, yes? That's what they would want, is for you and Cristine and the boys to be happy. And this would make you happy."

"Are you telling me or asking me?"

"I'm telling you. I call Savino tonight, I tell him you're coming for the summer semester, you'll stay with the family, and tomorrow we transfer your schooling to New York. Yes?"

The cigarette burned my fingers. "Shit." I switched hands, aware of her eyes on me—careful, concerned, yet openly judgmental. I shook my head—"What family?"— ground my knuckles into my temple, and again—"What *family?*"

"Pia—"

"There's more?" I exploded. "More than a brother?"

"What do you mean? What are you talking about?"

"Do we have cousins? Do we have grandparents?"

"Of course you have grandparents, where do you think *I* came from? Everyone has grandparents." She shook her head.

"Alive?"

"Yes, alive. Yes."

"Well, how come we've never met them? Where are they? *Why didn't they come to the funeral?* How come Mamma didn't talk about them?"

Sabine blew out her cheeks, ran a hand through her hair. "Pia, I don't know. They were probably busy, they found out too late, I don't know! They're just family, you know?"

"No!"

"Hey, you don't have to get excited."

"Look—"

"What?"

"—I didn't know any of this, five minutes ago. We don't know them—*I* don't know them—and apparently they never cared enough to know *us*, they didn't even

10

come to Mamma and Papa's funeral. I can't go live with them. I can't go to New York."

"Carla and Leo decided to move away, it was their choice—"

"I can't leave them, Sabine." My voice broke.

I couldn't abandon the kids and run off to what might as well have been a foreign city. And I couldn't make plans—I was shit at planning, I didn't trust myself to not screw everything up. I couldn't even remember what my parents 'plan had been for when I got my AA. Had Papa mapped it out? Had we ever discussed it?

I ground my palms into my eye sockets. "None of this was supposed to happen."

"Hey. Look." Sabine wasn't the huggy type, and I didn't normally like to be hugged, but she held me while I cried. She ran her hands through my hair and held me on the doorstep. And she carefully pried the cigarette from my fingers, flicked it away. "Look, Pia. Let me help. Let other people help, let your family help you. You'll live again—we'll all live again. But we need to keep moving forward, yes?"

ii.

And so, a few weeks later, I stepped off a plane and into New York City.

I guess I expected it to feel different than Georgia right away, but I didn't detect a noticeable change at first; the world didn't have an altered tint to it, the place smelled very much like any stale and subtly disgusting airport atmosphere, crowded with unwashed bodies and sweat and sleep-deprived eyes staring out of tired faces. And it was loud—the moment I stumbled off the plane, garbage jazz and screaming announcements rained down from hidden speakers.

I gripped my backpack straps like they might anchor me. I stepped to the side to collect myself, and almost got mowed down by a herd of speed-walkers with rolling suitcases pounding the tile.

"Ross, if you don't walk fasta, I swear—"

"Well, get a cab, get two cabs, we'll make it fit, we'll meet back up at the hotel—"

"You can't leave ya bag unattended, can't ya read the fucking signs, they're screamin 'at ya everywhere ya look, yer gonna end up with a bomb in your suitcase—"

"—*you can't say bomb in an airport*—"

"—well I gotta take a piss I haven't pissed in twelve hours I'm gonna get a UTI and I can't fit the bag in the stall, what was I supposed to do?"

I *felt* different, and not in a good way. I felt remarkably small, and slow, and it hit me then that I was far away from Sabine and the kids and the only home I'd ever known.

I was their official guardian. I knew how to be their older sister and take care of them, but I didn't know how to be a parent. Sabine didn't either, but at least with the two of us at home, the kids had some amount of constancy in their lives. I hadn't even had the guts to tell them the plan until my aunt and I had the whole thing settled, till we'd worked it out with the community college in Manhattan and gotten my records transferred. By then, it was too late to go back.

I still hadn't talked to my uncle, but Sabine assured me that she'd dealt with it. I'd asked if I should see about a recommendation letter for the bakery job. Sabine had waved it off. "You're family, Savino doesn't care, his Ida doesn't care, they won't care at all."

I hadn't been to work for weeks, but I'd finally called in to officially resign the day after I talked to Sabine. The bakery owner was a sort of gruff, impersonal guy named Donny, who said he'd kind of seen this coming, and had actually already replaced me. Which stung—I was a good worker, I'd been there for three years, and I'd miss the place. "So they don't care if I can bake?" That seemed like a bad way to run a business.

"Hey, I tell him you can bake. He trusts me. I say you can bake, he knows you can bake, he hires you. And if you don't know how to bake, he teaches you, *si*?"

"But I do know how. To bake."

"Are you trying to be difficult, Pia?"

I wasn't. I was just confused and a bit scared. *A lot* scared.

I finally detached myself from the airport wall. I needed to find the baggage claim. Although the thought of leaving the airport felt terribly final, as if I was cutting off my only path to escape, like there was no going back from this thing I'd done. I joined the flow of travelers exiting the gate; I got swept up and jostled between a couple men in suits and a large family all wearing Mickey Mouse ears. I pulled my backpack tighter, tucked my chin to my chest, and plowed on through. Conversation rose up around me, announcements echoing through the airport.

"Well I gotta get to the bathroom before the next flight—"

"You got twenty minutes, you don't got time—"

"ATTENTION TRAVELERS, NEVER LEAVE YOUR BAGS UNATTENDED—"

I followed the scavenger hunt of signs to the baggage claim. Then I stood there for what felt like a small eternity before my suitcase came around.

When we'd gotten to the airport in Atlanta, Sabine had rattled off instructions, prancing ahead of me and the kids in her heels—Vince close to tears, Carlo deadpan, Cristine with moody teenage betrayal in her eyes. "Okay, Savino said he's gonna have someone pick you up from the airport—make sure you know who they are, okay? Yes? Don't go off with a random stranger, this isn't Augusta, this is New York City, okay? Pia?"

"Okay."

I still hadn't talked to any of Mamma's family, and here I was stepping off a plane and going to live with these people in an unfamiliar city. I didn't think I was supposed to be nervous—they were family, right? What did that mean anyway, *family*? We were blood related, but that was all I had in common with these people. They could be horrible. I didn't have a clue what to expect.

My heart raced as I dragged my suitcase towards the terminal exit. I didn't know who was waiting for me, or where they were waiting, and I was starting to sweat worrying I'd passed up my ride—had they been waiting at baggage? Or the gate? *Calm down.*

There was a man standing by the doors, gripping a little cardboard sign with my name scrawled with marker: *Pia Marzano.* He was stout, with a wide face that looked like it could be friendly, but at the moment was scrunched up and irritated. He had a set of expensive-looking sunglasses propped on his dark, curly head. He was also on the phone. I caught a snippet of conversation as I approached.

"—well, I don't care, I talked to Stefano already, and he told the guys—hey, talk to Raul, okay? Well, Raul deals with that kind of thing, that isn't my department if you know what I mean..... Okay, but you've got to talk to Raul before you—" Then his eyes locked on mine and he stopped. His mustache twitched. "Hey Johnny, we'll deal with this later. I've got to go." And apparently without waiting for a response, he hung up the phone and clipped it onto his belt. "Pia Marzano?"

"Yeah. Hi."

He folded up the cardboard sign and tucked it into his waistband. "I'm Gio Di Natale, I'm Nicole's husband. Is this all you got?" He motioned at my luggage, but he eyes were fixed on me, sweeping and curious, as if checking to make sure I was the person I said I was.

"Uh, yeah. Yes sir." Did they say *sir* in New York? "This is it. Sabine said I wouldn't need much."

"I'm not sir," he said, "I'm just Gio." He moved to take my suitcase—I let him. He tested its weight and nodded for me to follow him. "We had a Mass said for your parents, at Thomas Aquinas in Brooklyn. Made a donation, lit some candles, had a Mass said that Sunday after your aunt called with the news. What's with the casts? Broken wrists?"

"Uh, tendonitis." I wore wrist braces when I wasn't working.

"Is that a bone thing?" He led the way through the exit, out into the parking lot.

"It's a tendon thing. I don't really know much about it. I just get these shooting pains up my forearms, in my elbows. From work."

"Yeah, you work in a bakery, right? Savino told us you work in a bakery, you're gonna hang around the *panificio*, is that right? Can't do that with broken wrists."

13

I didn't know who Nicole was. And that felt like something I *should* know. I'd rifled through the leather-bound photo albums in the attic after my conversation with Sabine, but they didn't go back very far, just to my parents 'wedding. There were only a couple photos of the day: the two of them running down the church steps in a flurry of rose petals; cutting an enormous cake with a few old men smoking fat cigars lurking in the background. But no evidence of an uncle. No evidence of Sabine either, for that matter. No evidence of Gio Di Natale or anyone named Nicole.

I followed him between cabs idling on the curb, around families packing their luggage into hotel vans. I was in a hoodie for comfort's sake, but New York in May was warmer than I'd expected, and the asphalt just reflected the heat right back up at me. I also felt strangely underdressed; Gio Di Natale was in khakis and a collared shirt, like he was about to go to church or a work meeting. Papa only wore khakis to Sunday Mass, never on a weekday. Carlo and Vince only wore them when forced.

Gio flicked down his sunglasses. My suitcase bounced along behind him. He wasn't tall, but he walked fast and I struggled to keep up.

"So—" I cleared my throat. "Are we related? Sorry, I don't know—"

"Nah, I'm just married to Nicole." Gio kept glancing at me as we walked out across the parking area—curious, furtive glances.

"Nicole is…?"

"Oh, Carla's her sister." Neither Mamma nor Sabine had ever mentioned having a third sister. He stared straight ahead while he spoke. "Hey, we're all really sorry we couldn't make it down to the funeral, it happened really fast and we couldn't up and leave like that. But like I said, we had a nice memorial service, had a Mass said for her soul, her's and Leo's."

As if any of that made up for the fact that no one had showed up to the funeral. No one. It had been Mamma's and Papa's work friends, some church folk, Sabine, a couple of my coworkers. But no New York relatives. No Vitellis *or* Marzanos. "Does she talk to Sabine much?"

"Who?"

"Nicole. Sabine didn't mention a sister—I mean, I didn't know we had family up here to start with, I didn't know I had an uncle, but Sabine didn't mention Nicole at all when she told me. I didn't know she or Savino existed."

"Oh, yeah. They don't really talk."

"Her and Savino?"

"Her and Nicole. Savino talks to her sometimes, but not much. She does her own thing, you know?"

We were halfway through the lot when a huge black BMW pulled out a parking space up ahead, like it had been watching for us. It swung around and crawled forward, slowing to a halt beside Gio. There was a young man at the wheel.

Gio waved at the driver, and the back popped open. He walked around the car, opened the door for me, and shoved the luggage up into the trunk. "Watch the step."

It would be hard to *not* watch the step; I wasn't tall, so I really had to climb up into the vehicle. It had that leather-and-new-car smell. I settled into a seat and buckled myself in, supremely uncomfortable, because this car was surely worth more than my house back home, and I'd learned to drive on a fifteen-year-old minivan.

The driver twisted around to look at me. "Hi."

Gio climbed into the passenger's seat and shut the door behind him.

"Hi," I returned, as the BMW started moving again.

The kids and I didn't look completely exotic back home, but we were also clearly not from Georgia—I'd even been asked before, at Carlo's soccer practice, if he was adopted from the Middle East or thereabouts. So it was a strange feeling to be surrounded by people with similar features: this boy had dark hair and black eyes and a big Roman nose—"That's Italians," Mamma always said, "unnecessary amounts of nose and eyebrow"— and he and I had the same darkish olive skin. But it all suited him much better, I thought. I felt blended in, like a raven in a murder of crows.

"This is Massimo," said Gio. "He's my kid, number two. He just graduated and he's working with me this summer. We've got Norma, then we've got Massimo and the rest. So, you're cousins."

"I have cousins?"

Massimo snorted. He look at his dad—a quick glance that I didn't understand, almost as if he was asking for permission to speak.

Gio ignored him; he rubbed his nose. "Yeah, a few." Which meant: *quite a lot.*

I guessed it made sense, our family being Italian Catholics and all. Breeding like we were trying to repopulate the planet. But I didn't know anything about cousins, I didn't know how to act around relatives of my own age. Were we supposed to be friends? Siblings? Or was it just a sort of mutual acceptance of the other person's existence, a cursory nod in public, casual acknowledgment?

I looked like these people, and I didn't even know them.

iii.

I sat back and watched out the window for most of the drive. Gio and Massimo didn't talk much, and they didn't listen to music either—they just drove in silence, staring straight ahead. I felt like I should say something, but I didn't really have anything to say, so I sat there on the slick leather seat, feeling awkward and a bit like baggage being carted from one place to another.

I didn't like cities. At all. The towering buildings and narrow, crowded streets were suffocating, blocking me in like a cage. Too many people, too much noise, constant overstimulation. Our house back home was sandwiched between farms and orchards; I

15

was used to sky, and lots of it, and silence but for the passing interstate traffic. I hated cities, and here I was in New York.

The Vitellis lived in Brooklyn, and Savino lived in Fort Greene: a row of books packed tight into a shelf, their spines in shades of red and brown and yellow. Elegant windows and great big doors, intricately designed handrails leading up to the steep doorstep, but they were packed in there all the same. Later, I'd learn that the Vitelli house was actually a million-dollar home, it just didn't look like much from the outside. Apparently this was how big cities worked: they called a couple streets a neighborhood, pretty much all of them were rife with crime, and most were outrageously overpriced.

Cars lined topiary that lined the spotless sidewalk. Massimo parallel-parked between two other BMWs and opened the back door for me while Gio got the luggage.

I stepped carefully down out of the car, inspected the building before us—shuttered windows, more crawling ivy than red brick, a hefty black door and a silver knocker. I craned my neck to see the third-floor level. "This is where Savino lives?"

Massimo shut the door. He dressed like his dad, khakis and a button-down. I wondered if they were going to a meeting after this. "Yeah, Savino and Ida and the kids."

More kids. More cousins. More names to learn and add to that rapidly-growing family tree in my head.

He looked at me curiously. I looked back. Massimo had a lot of hair, like Carlo—thick, dark, hard-to-manage hair, but it was perfectly combed and gelled in a way I'd never been able to fix my brother's bedhead. I figured he was sort of classically good-looking, like an old Italian movie star, just clean-cut and upstanding.

"Do you like theater?" he asked.

I lifted the hair off my neck. Tugged down my hoodie. "Musical theater?"

"Stage plays."

"It's okay." I wondered what about me screamed *theater* that he'd thought to ask.

Gio rolled my luggage around the car. He handed it off to Massimo and waved a hand at the place. "The Vitelli house." With that, he marched across the sidewalk and up the steps. I followed, and Massimo dragged the suitcase behind. Gio rapped twice on the door, but didn't wait for anyone to answer before throwing it open. He waved me inside.

Again, what might pass for the upper end of wealthy where I came from was actually outrageously posh, by Brooklyn standards. My family with its four kids had always been a bit at the lower end of middle class—not really struggling, but never fancy.

The Vitellis were *fancy*. The front room was spacious, full of natural light from the windows facing the street. The floor was nice wood, the back wall was a dusty green color like sea foam. You could tell just by looking at each piece of furniture that nothing came second-hand, it was all fashionable and spanking new, black leather without a single rip in the cushions. A collection of sepia photos clustered above the fireplace mantel. To my left, stairs led to the upper levels. Behind that, another staircase spiraled down into what I assumed to be the basement. The Vitellis overstepped *well-off* and bordered on *pretentious*.

If Gio's khakis had been a bit much, this definitely was. I felt like a dumpster person in my hoodie and flour-dusted sneakers. My throat was dry. This wasn't a house—this was a showroom at IKEA, this was a place staged for real-estate.

Massimo pulled the front door shut behind him. "I'll bring your stuff up," he said in a low voice. He disappeared upstairs with my suitcase.

I looked at Gio sideways. "Savino's a baker, right?"

"Huh? Yeah, he owns the *panificio*."

I wasn't sure how to vocalize it politely, but food service workers aren't known for their considerable incomes. Maybe his wife was an heiress or something. "What does Ida do?"

"Uh, she's a dental hygienist."

"Gio?" A woman's voice called from the room beyond the living area.

"Hey, Ida, I got Pia Marzano from the airport!"

He nodded across the room, and I followed him into the dining area. It was just as big as the front room, with black-and-white framed photos and newspaper clippings crowding the walls, an impressive glass-fronted liquor cabinet, and the lingering scent of cigar smoke.

A woman sat at the wide table, her back to the window. She stood when I walked in; she swept a jumble of papers into a neat stack and set it aside. She had a wide smile, a wide mouth, but it suited her face.

"Pia, hello." She walked around the table and hugged me, which I hadn't expected—maybe a handshake, a touch on the shoulder, but a full-body hug hadn't been on the list. She held me out by the shoulders and looked me in the eye while I sweated and tried to not look too terribly nervous. "I'm Ida, we're so happy you're staying with us, and we're sorry about your parents, it's tragic—you, your sister and brothers, so young. I didn't know Carla or Leo, but the whole family was extremely upset at the news."

I blinked, overwhelmed by...everything. "Thank you. Thanks for...letting me stay."

She looked like a runner, lean and compact, big strong hands. I wouldn't have been surprised if she was the type to get up at four AM and run ten miles before work. "We had a Mass said for your family."

"I told her," said Gio.

Ida acknowledged him. "Is Nicole going to be here for dinner? Nicole, the kids, are they coming?"

17

"Yeah, Nicole and Massimo—the boy drove me, he's upstairs now—but Norma's still out of town. Betta and Giovani might come by for a while, but they work early tomorrow, you know, so it'll be an early night. I think Mo and his wife are coming."

"Okay, well, thank you Gio. Tell Massimo thank you. We'll see you later, yes? Eight o'clock? Tell Nicole."

"I'll tell her."

Gio left. Massimo waved at me from the front room, then he followed his dad outside.

"Come on Pia, I'll show you your room. How was your flight?"

"It was fine. I haven't flown before, but it wasn't bad."

"Are your wrists okay? What is this? Are you hurt?"

"Tendonitis. It's fine."

I was shaking. I stuck my hands back in the hoodie pocket, but I wasn't cold and it wasn't just in my hands anyway—my arms and shoulders trembled, my legs felt like jelly. Everything was too new, too fast. I was positive I was infringing on these people's privacy, on their family. What had Sabine been *thinking*? This was insane.

But I followed Ida upstairs.

"How old are you, Pia?"

I thought maybe she was trying to establish trust or be welcoming or something by saying my name over and over again, but it wasn't working. It just made me painfully aware that she was trying to gain my trust because she didn't know me because for some reason my entire family lived in Brooklyn and no one had bothered to mention this or even attempt contact. "I'm nineteen."

"Aww, you're all grown up. And you're the oldest, yes?"

"Yes."

"My brother Tonio is the baby, he is twenty-four, twenty-five, I can't remember. He doesn't go to the school you'll be going to, but he tutors there sometimes--I'll introduce you, you'll know someone." When she wasn't repeating my name, Ida had a soothing timbre to her voice, a low musical quality. She held a finger to her lips as we passed a closed door—I heard a fan going, a noisemaker. "That's Marc, he's eighteen months. Nap time."

We passed another room with the door wide open. It was painted pink and the floor was covered with toys. A big rumpled bed with floral blankets, stuffed animals and pillows askew. "And Anna and Ella, the twins—they're at preschool, they'll be home soon, this is their bedroom."

More closed doors (how far back did this place go?), an alcove with a huge fake fern and a painting of a stern man in an orchard. At the end of the hall Ida opened an arched, wood-paneled door into an empty bedroom.

18

It was cozy. Actually, it was a bit more than cozy, only I couldn't quite wrap my mind around how nice it was at the time. I didn't realize the intricate iron bed-frame was shipped over from Italy, or that the bookshelf was packed with first-edition classics, or that the big window with its blue stained-glass sparrow in flight was a commissioned piece probably worth one of the cars stationed out front. I did like the wallpaper, though—it was a green and gray pattern like ivy.

Massimo had parked my suitcase at the foot of the bed.

"Is this alright?" Ida watched me anxiously. "The bathroom is through there, by the closet."

I swallowed. "It's wonderful. Thank you."

"Let us know if you need a different room, or if you want to change anything at all. We didn't know what you would like, so we didn't decorate..." She waited, as if expecting me to say something.

I swallowed again. Why was my mouth so dry? "I brought some photos. And some books."

"Well, talk to me Pia, tell me if you need anything else, okay? We're gonna take care of you, you're family, so just let me and Savino know if you need anything, alright? We're gonna have some family over later for supper, you'll get to meet everyone, and Savino will be back by then."

"Thank you."

"I'll let you settle in, yes? I'll be down in the kitchen. Just be careful coming down the stairs, they echo a bit and Marc will wake up and the baby is a monster if he doesn't finish his nap. "

I nodded. Ida left; she pulled the door shut behind her.

I dug around in the front pocket of my carry-on, then I levered open the expensive window and perched on the window seat. The mid-afternoon sun shone through the blue sparrow, casting my legs in an aquamarine glow. There was a courtyard below—a bright square of grass, an oak tree and a bench, surrounded by a brick path.

The oak reminded me of home. Papa and I would go on walks around the countryside, we'd park the car on a dirt road and wander until the mosquitoes got bad and it was time to head home and more often than not we'd end up at the same oak-lined path leading up to the abandoned pecan orchard down the road. Ancient oaks, far older and huger than this one, but it made me homesick all the same.

I lit a cigarette and thought about how Sabine would roll her eyes if she could see me. Sitting up here in a fancy house in Brooklyn, in my own fancy room, smoking cheap-ass cigarettes and killing my lungs while I had a low-key panic attack.

Smoke trickled down my throat. I shut my eyes and rested my head back against the window frame.

19

I heard people arriving downstairs, but I didn't budge from the sill for a long time. When I finally shut the window and got up, it had gotten dark outside. The blue sparrow was black.

I switched on the overhead light and started organizing my things. The closet was ridiculously large for what I'd brought with me, so I took this as an opportunity to hang pretty much everything I owned, including underwear. *Anything to avoid ironing clothes.* I dumped everything else on the bed and sorted through it slowly.

Toiletries went in the bathroom, which had an elegant china washbasin and big glass knobs for the faucet and the softest bathmat in the world. I'd never had my own bathroom. I'd always shared with Cristine and the boys, so there was a permanent spray of toothpaste and saliva across the bottom of the mirror, and a lot of hair-gel cramming the cabinet.

I left the window seat bare, but I arranged my photos on the desk and bedside table. There were polaroids and old family pictures of me and the kids, a few of my parents. I had a little wood carving of the Virgin Mary from Papa, some necklaces and an assortment of saint medals (for any occasion) from Mamma. She'd always worn an excessive number of medals on a single chain, so she'd jangled everywhere she went— "I want to remember my brothers and sisters in heaven, so they'll remember me and they'll talk me up pretty to God, so what, Pia? Sounding like a bell when you walk is a small price to pay for an eternity partying in heaven with Mama Mary and Jesus ' friends, *sì?*"

I got a shower. I ran a towel over my hair—I'd cut it to my shoulders around Christmas, and it dried fast. I changed into jeans and my least-wrinkled shirt, but I left off the wrist braces; I didn't want any more questions or unnecessary pity surrounding my minor tendonitis.

I put on Mamma's medals. They were heavy.

When I opened the door, the sound hit me like a physical force. I took a step back. The roar of voices—too many voices—echoed upstairs, amplified by the stairwell.

I shuffled down the corridor in socked feet. The twins 'room was dark now, the baby's door was open as he'd apparently been retrieved from his crib. As I descended the stairs, my heart in my throat, I frantically ran through the list of names I'd had thrown at me. *Nicole is married to Gio, Massimo is their son, but there are more than just him...Ida and Savino have Marc and the twins (I need to remember their names)...someone named Betta, someone named Mo....*

I realized, halfway down the stairs, that I had no reason to freak out. I mean—okay, sure, I had pretty much every reason. But I shouldn't feel bad about not knowing these people or remembering their names, or what they did for a living, or who they were married to. Because they'd never tried to meet me either. I hadn't even known I had an uncle until a month ago, but they'd always known I existed. Or so I assumed.

20

For the millionth time, I wondered why Mamma and Sabine hadn't talked about their family before.

A bit later—and I mean a good bit, I was slow on the uptake—it started to make sense.

iv.

There were people sitting at the base of the stairs. I recognized one of them as Massimo, his khaki-clad legs stretched out across a step. There was another young man around his age, thin with a wide smile, and a girl in overalls with brown hair down to her waist.

Massimo saw me first. He waved a wine glass at the others, and they cleared off the stairs. "Hi." He moved out of my way.

"Hi."

"This is Tonio, he's Ida's brother. And this is my sister Betta."

Betta, who looked to be around my age and was therefore definitely too young to be drinking wine, raised her wine glass at me from the bottom step. She'd scooted against the wall to let me pass. "Cheers."

"Pia, do you like theater?" That was Tonio. His dark hair was slicked back with liberal quantities of gel.

I glanced at Massimo, who leveled his gaze at Tonio, though his expression didn't change. "I guess."

Tonio shrugged at my cousin, in an unintelligible sort of way. It might have meant "Well, that's okay then", but it also very easily could have been something more like "Told you so". "Pia *Marzano*," he muttered into his wine glass. *"Mar. Saw. No."*

Betta grinned.

I looked at Tonio. "What?" Something about his face reminded me of an oil painting—shadowed and a bit unreal. His words were careful and intentional enough that he had to know just how pretentious he sounded, like he was trying to get under my skin, like he was laughing at a joke reserved for a superior few.

"You look more like a *Vitelli* than a *Marzano*," he said.

I didn't know what that was supposed to mean. Massimo licked his lips, cast a furtive glance in my direction, and was about to say something when Ida appeared around the corner. She wore a black sundress, and she'd twisted her hair up into a big silver clip.

"Pia! Good, I was looking for you. Nicole wants to meet you, come on—Betta, don't drink too much, you've got to drive Giovani home later, okay?"

"Yeah, okay."

Ida had less of an Italian accent than Sabine and Mamma did, but it was still there, under a heavy layer of *New York*. The kids all had Brooklyn accents until they said a name—*MAR-SAW-NO*—then they slid into a thick Italian. The combination reminded me of old mobster movies, and seemed weirdly intense—cinematic—for people so young.

I followed Ida into the front room, through a crowd of dark-haired adults. A gaggle of children were playing with action figures by the lit fireplace—over the din, I could make out fight sounds—*swish, bam, AHHHH*—reminiscent of Carlo and Vince. The adults in the house ranged from silver-haired to late teens. Most were drinking, all of them were talking at once, and there was not a single blond hair to be found. I'd never seen fewer blonds in one place, actually; I felt camouflaged as Ida led me through the room, into the dining area, and from there into the big white-tiled kitchen.

A group of women stood around the expansive kitchen island. An elderly woman with silver hair and wide hips held a dozing baby on her shoulder. On the other side of the room, an older boy carefully applied almonds to what looked like lumps of cookie dough, his features scrunched up in disproportional concentration.

A woman who looked startlingly like Sabine and Mamma threw up her hands, rushed around the counter—"Oh, Pia, oh, I'm so sorry"—and threw her arms around me.

I didn't like it. But I supposed I'd have to get used to the hugging.

This was Nicole. Her chestnut hair was streaked with silver, and it was soft around her face, like a cocker spaniel's ears. It was Mamma's face—a bit older, and with different eyes, but it was Mamma all the same. My throat choked up when I looked at her. *Calm down.* "Hi."

"Oh." She pulled me in for another hug. "Oh, God, you look just like her, you know that? Just like Carla. Horrible, tragic. We had a Mass said for them, you know that? For Carla and her Leo and all you kids. So her soul's up in Heaven with Jesus now."

The other women were Nonna Annabella (Ida's mother, with baby Marc on her shoulder), Zia Serafina (Gio's brother Mo's wife) and Serafina's daughter Daria Di Natale. The boy with the almonds, who barely looked up when introduced, was Giovani, Massimo's little brother.

"He works at the *panificio*," said Nicole. "Betta and Giovani, you'll work with them and Savino and my Norma's husband Marco at the bakery."

"Where *is* the bakery?"

"Manhattan," said Ida. "The college isn't far, you could probably walk. We'll figure out your commute once school starts—you could drive in with Savino, but I don't know that you want to go in that early. Or one of the kids could pick you up on their way to school...."

Nonna Annabella put a hand on her cheek, watching me. After a long silence, she said, "She looks like Savino."

"She looks like Carla," said Nicole. "Savino looks like Carla, it's the same, they're all Vitellis. Pia, how many siblings do you have? You have brothers? Sisters?"

She didn't *know*? She didn't know how many kids her sister had? Clearly she hadn't spoken to Mamma in a long time. I remember what Gio had said, about her and Sabine not talking. "Three. Cristine is fourteen, Carlo is thirteen, Vince is ten."

"Oh, *bambini*—they're *babies*."

I was in danger of seriously freaking out, now. It was loud and I was surrounded by strangers and they were talking about my dead parents and the siblings I'd left behind. I swallowed hard. "Where is Savino?"

Nicole looked at Ida.

Ida shrugged. "He's dealing with business. He'll be here soon. You want a drink, Pia? You drink?"

A little. We were Catholic, after all—it's not like I'd never sipped wine by the age of nineteen. But I had enough bad habits to manage stress, I didn't need to add alcohol. "I'm okay, thank you though."

"Okay," said Ida, clapping her hands, "dinner will be ready in an hour"—it was already nearly nine—"it's time to say a Divine Mercy for the departed souls. Everyone into the living room—Giovani, Raul and Ezio are out back, call them in, yeah? Everyone else, let's go."

I found myself shoved out of the kitchen, into the dining room, and from there followed the crush of bodies into the front room where everyone was collecting on sofas and the stairs, perched on the edges of coffee tables. The kids were still playing action figures.

I didn't mind praying a Divine Mercy—I'd said plenty of chaplets, over the past month. But there was a difference between crying myself to sleep with a rosary in my fingers and having to pray for my dead parents 'souls in front of a bunch of strangers that also happened to be relatives. No one really noticed me, and I was able to slip into the back of the room by the spiral staircase, where I commenced to have a quiet panic attack in the shadows. Everyone twisted around in their seats to face the fireplace, where Ida sat with Marc on her lap and passed around rosary beads from a hat box.

The room was huge. This house was huge. This family was bigger than I'd ever imagined, but I didn't feel like I was a part of it.

I found myself standing beside Massimo, leaning up against the spiral staircase. He didn't even look at me, just passively handed over his half-empty wine glass.

I took it. Waited a second. But he still didn't say anything, so I tossed back what was left and handed it back.

When the hat box got to us, he gave me a rosary and took one himself, then passed the box on again. I fingered the beads, fought to find peace in the motion, but I was clammy and my hands shook.

Eternal Father, I offer you the Body and Blood, Soul and Divinity of Your Dearly Beloved Son, Our Lord, Jesus Christ...

...in atonement for our sins and those of the whole world.

Dinner was a spread: two types of risotto, *falsomagro* (prosciutto and sausage wrapped around boiled eggs) sliced and swimming in sauce, roasted fennel bulbs, and a pile of focaccia with an assortment of hard aged cheeses. Heaping *affettati* lined the buffet—trays of prosciutto and soppressata, surrounded by figs, olives, and seasonal fruit. People loaded up plates and grazed. Later, Giovani added a tray of *biscotti di mandorla*, golden and studded with almonds.

I didn't have the stomach for food right now—and that was saying something, seeing as I loved food and everything looked and smelled amazing. Still, the thought of eating made my stomach clench. So as adults migrated to the dining room table and the younger people lingered around the front room, I parked myself beside the fireplace and did the only thing I could think of that might clear the panicked fog in my skull: I played action figures with a bunch of little kids.

Anna and Ella were easy to pick out, because they were identical and looked a lot like their mother. They were three. Despite their strawberry-covered hands and faces—I didn't know where they'd gotten the strawberries—they wore pristine, frilly pink dresses covered in bows and roses. There was a fat-faced toddler the twins called Ava (I didn't know who she belonged to), and Marc the baby, who was in a pleasant mood after his many afternoon and evening naps. There was also a five-year-old named Enzo—not to be confused with Ezio, Ida's oldest brother, who I'd been introduced to in a flurry of greetings. I didn't know whose kid Enzo was, either, but I thought he was somehow related to Ida.

Playing with little kids is easy. You just let them beat up your toys and make distressed sounds, they love it. This was something familiar and comforting, a constant in the upheaval of the day: wherever I went, I could always let a velociraptor pummel my Power Ranger, and the kids would lose their minds every time.

One of the adults wandered in at some point—a younger guy, probably in his thirties. He planted himself in an armchair near the fire and watched me with the kids for a while.

His hair was short, cropped close to his head, and he had a great knob of a nose and smallish eyes. The line of a tattoo crept above the collar of his shirt. His stare was open and borderline rude.

"So," he said at last, "Carla Vitelli, huh?"

I shrugged. The fire was warm on my back, but my feet were cold.

He shrugged and sipped something amber from a glass—scotch, maybe. There were more tattoos on his hands. "Didn't know she had any kids."

"Yep."

"Never met Leonardo *Marzano*, either. Everyone says he was *something* else, huh?"

I didn't answer. He sat forward and extended his hand. "Achille Salone." He was short, but strong—thick shoulders and arms tight in his sports coat, like he knew how buff he was and felt immensely proud about it, really wanted the world to know. "So you're a Marzano, huh? You ever been over there?"

I shook his hand. "Over where?"

"*Sicilia*, you know."

I didn't know. "No. I haven't been anywhere but Georgia, really."

"Yeah? You ever been to Atlanta? I've got friends went to school in Atlanta."

"I've been to the outskirts. But I'm from Augusta."

"Yeah? So what'd your dad do, then?"

I set my Power Ranger on Marc's head—he fell over laughing. "Uh. He was a mechanic, he worked at a garage in town. And Mamma worked at the hardware store next door." The folks at the store had sent over a fruit basket, after the funeral. We'd gotten something like five bouquets of lilies from the garage. And then those stupid gardenias from the Rondolfos.

"A hardware store, huh? A Vitelli woman in a hardware store. That's a good fucking laugh."

I decided I didn't like Achille Salone very much, and I wished he would go away. "How come?" My voice came out cold.

He ignored the question, gazed out over the top of my head. "And a Marzano in a garage, huh? Can't believe it. Genuinely can't believe it." He seemed like he was trying quite hard to be suave and all-knowing, like a character from a movie, sipping his scotch in his suit beside the fire. But it was just uncomfortable and insulting.

"Well," I deadpanned, "believe it." I hoped he wasn't anyone terribly important that I'd just pissed off.

His eyes flicked to me. "So, why'd they leave, huh? Up and left the life of luxury to work in a Podunk Georgia town. I heard the old man had got them a place in the Bowery. You remember that?"

"I don't think I was born yet."

"God. How old are you anyway?"

"I am nineteen."

"God. They just get younger and younger."

I narrowed my eyes at him. The kids squirmed and rolled around in front of me, but I'd blocked them out at this point because I got the sense there was something loudly dangerous about Achille. Maybe it was because I'd just realized his name was tattooed on his knuckles, and I felt like that said loads about a person's character and the sorts of life choices they made.

Achille sipped his drink, watching me over his glass. "You know anything about boats?"

"What?"

25

He didn't answer. His eyes snapped up behind me, fixed on something over my shoulder. "*Buonasera*, Chief."

I turned. A man in a long dark overcoat had slipped in the front door and was shutting it softly behind him, as if trying to not attract attention. He raised a hand to Achille as he shrugged off his coat, scanned the room before his eyes settled on me. There was something cat-like about his dark, narrow face. His hair, black as pitch, was combed back like Tonio's and slick in the firelight. He was lean like a runner, like Ida, but under his coat he wore a flour-dusted t-shirt, and he had what I call Baker's Arms—muscular forearms slashed with criss-crossed burn scars, strong shoulders, cut-up and calloused hands.

He glanced at the youths hanging out on the stairs. Then he crossed the room to the fireplace, taking long, slow strides, as if he had all the time in the world. Like he owned the place, which I guess he did.

He stopped beside me and scooped up Marc into his arms. "Pia Marzano."

I stood. I wasn't sure if it was the right thing to do, but it hurt to keep looking up. My head didn't reach his shoulder; the kids and I had certainly missed out on those genes.

"PIA'S STAYING WITH US PAPA," one of the twins shrieked.

Savino shifted the baby onto his hip. He held out a hand, and I shook. "I'm sorry about Carla and Leo. I talked to Sabine. We're gonna take care of you and the kids."

I didn't know what that meant. So I just nodded.

"She looks like a Vitelli, huh, Savino?" Achille sat back, finished his drink. I hated that he was still there.

"Nah." Savino held my eyes. "She's a Marzano."

Achille wasn't listening. "They say she looks like you and Carla, do ya see it? Hey, you won't believe this shit, she said Carla worked in a hardware store, can you believe it? Your sister Carla." He swung to his feet and clapped my uncle on the back. "Do you wanna drink? I'm getting another drink. Whiskey?"

Savino shook his head.

Achille disappeared into the dining room. Marc was wriggling, so Savino set him down and took the armchair. "You're a baker?" he asked.

"I bake." I thought it generous to call myself a baker—I was more of a baking *assistant*. *Baker* sounded too much like *chef*, like someone who was actually in charge and knew what they were doing.

"Then you're a baker." He said it like it settled something. "What do you bake?"

"Bread. Pastry."

"Focaccia?"

"I've done it before. We mostly made bagels and bread, back at the bakery, but I like to be in the kitchen at home too. I just mess around with stuff, mostly."

"Who taught you? Carla?"

I wondered if he'd known Mamma at all. "She doesn't bake. Didn't, bake." I took a deep breath. "I taught myself."

"Hmm." He watched the kids play. "I talked to the folks at the school, they're gonna make the transfer real easy. Nicole's kids take classes too, so you'll have some guys there. How early do you wake up?"

"I got up at five, for work. Seven for school."

"I walk out the door at four. You can drive in with me and do the early shift first thing, or you can wander in around six like Marco and the kids. If you have morning classes, you should come with me so you can get in some hours before school."

"Okay."

"You okay with that?"

"Yeah."

Savino nodded, like he'd figured. "We'll start you off easy. You can come in tomorrow for a later shift, and we'll see how it goes when school starts next week. You worried about your brothers? Your sister?"

I shrugged. "Sabine's got them."

"You worried?"

How could I not be? They were far away, Vince was probably crying himself to sleep right now, and Cristine and Carlo hid their grief so well, I knew it was going to bounce back and bite them in the ass one of these days. All I saw in their futures was years and years of therapy.

"Don't be. Our family's taken a lot, we keep moving forward because we take care of each other. We're gonna take care of you." He stood. "You want a drink?"

"I'm nineteen."

He didn't miss a beat. "We don't care."

Mamma and Papa hadn't cared, either. "I'm fine, thanks."

He wandered off into the dining room. Shouts greeted him—"Eh, Savino!" "Chief!" "*Hey*, where's the *bambino*? You seen your son?" ("Pia's got him, Ida.")

I sat there for a while in front of the fireplace, letting the twins talk at me. The adults were exclusively in the dining area now, sitting around the wide dark table and drinking over enormous platters of cold food. I realized I hadn't eaten, and I was only just now getting hungry, but I didn't have the guts to walk in there and try to serve myself at this point.

I didn't know what to make of Savino. I'd wondered what a male version of Mamma would look like, and I hadn't pictured this: because his eyes were all Mamma, they were pure black like pools of ink—and we had the same big Roman nose, which definitely suited him more than it did me—but where Mamma's face softened around

27

these harsh features, there was no softness in Savino. He was all harsh lines and hollows, and soft even breaths. While my mother was abrupt and bossy and loud, Savino had a quiet confidence that commanded no less respect—a calmness that assured the room that he had everything under control, he sat in this armchair and surveyed his kingdom. And I sensed that if Achille was loudly dangerous, there was something quietly dangerous in Savino's presence.

I wasn't sure how I felt about him, or Ida, or Nicole with all her enthusiasm, because none of them had ever made an effort to know the Marzano siblings—not until our parents were dead and we were truly pathetic.

And Mamma had never mentioned them, not once.

I watched Giovani and Betta leave, slipping out the front door. I took that as my cue. I extricated myself from the twins and Marc, Ava and Enzo, and I tried to slip away upstairs.

Massimo and Tonio were still sitting on the lower step. Massimo didn't say anything, but as I skirted past, Tonio shot me a thin, sardonic smile.

"*Mar-saw-no,*" he said.

I narrowed my eyes at him, but that only made Tonio grin wider.

My bedroom was quiet at the far end of the house. The heater had clicked on, and although the floorboards were cold under my feet, the room was warm. I thought about calling Sabine and the kids, but it was almost midnight and I doubted anyone except Cristine was awake. Vince would be furious if I called and he didn't get to talk to me.

I pulled on my pajamas and climbed into bed. I read a couple pages of *The Silmarillion,* which usually put me to sleep right quick (no offense, Mr. Tolkien, but it's sawdust-dry stuff). It didn't work; the voices were loud downstairs, my nerves were on high alert, and I was wide-awake. So I lit up a cigarette and cracked open the sparrow window, sat on the window ledge in the dark and stared out at the night.

Maybe I should have had a drink, after all—I got sleepy after a drink, even a small one. Everyone had tried offering me drinks, and I'd brushed it off each time because I just didn't want to pick up any more bad habits. But I thought some people drink because they want to feel something. And other people drink because they want to feel nothing at all. I thought I was in the latter group.

Way below, there was a figure in the square out back. The porch lights were dim, and they just barely illuminated a man standing beneath the oak tree, beside the park bench. A faint orange glow told me he was smoking too.

It could have been anyone—I didn't know their faces well enough to name everyone yet, and it was pretty dark. I wondered why they were standing out there alone. Then again, the only person I'd ever smoked with was Papa. I couldn't imagine doing it with anyone else around. There was something vulnerable about it, showing a weakness, flaunting a character flaw on your sleeve—unless you were the sort of person who enjoyed that. I wasn't, but I guessed Achille Salone was.

Something crashed downstairs in the kitchen. The back door slammed.
I blinked again, and the man beneath the oak tree was gone.

II

Panificio

i.

I woke to knocking.

For a second, I forgot where I was—no one *knocked* at la casa Marzano, we just busted into rooms and started yelling. But I wasn't in Augusta. I was in Brooklyn, and apparently the Vitellis practiced common courtesy like respecting privacy.

I was only half-awake when I sat up. "Come in." The blankets puddled in my lap, hair in my eyes, the blue-stained sparrow window still black with predawn gloom.

Ida poked her head into the room, illuminated by the hallway light. "Betta and Giovani are downstairs, they're gonna drive you to the bakery. Did they not tell you?"

I shook my head. Blinked at the opposite wall. "Okay. I'm...I'm coming."

She shut the door. I rolled out of bed and stumbled to my feet.

I tugged on some leggings and an old paint-flecked soccer jersey. Socks and sneakers, a headband (my hair was still too short to pull back properly, so I managed with lots of kerchiefs and clips). I did a rushed job of brushing my teeth, splashed water on my face, then grabbed my backpack and hurried downstairs.

The house was strangely quiet after last night, big and empty, with ghosts of the previous evening blurring across my vision. Distant clinking echoed from the kitchen, but I didn't see Ida. Shadows stretched across the front room.

Betta stood beside the door in overalls, her hair pulled back tight in a braid. "Ready?" Her arms were crossed, eyes wide and sharp without a hint of sleep.

I nodded.

It looked strange now that I thought of it, that line of shiny black BMWs queued up on the walk outside the Vitelli house, like a Congo line of beetles. Betta's car could very well have been the same one Massimo and Gio had driven yesterday, because I couldn't tell any of them apart.

I took the passenger's seat. Giovani, still blinking awake, sat slumped in the back with a thermos cradled in his hands. He was lanky and awkward-looking, a mop of dark curls over exhausted eyes and a moody scowl—like Carlo, his joints were too big and knobby, his skin was stretched too tight as he struggled to grow into his skeleton. He seemed put-out over it. Put-out over everything, maybe.

Betta pulled out and barreled down the street. "Ida said you didn't know we were coming." It sounded a little aggressive, but maybe that was just how Betta spoke—Cristine was like that.

"No," I said, "sorry to keep you waiting."

"Nah, I thought Savino told you, it's fine. Wednesdays are light, he thought it would be good to get you in there on a calmer day. I mean, not that any day is calm—it's always insane. Savino's got all these orders out lately, these charity donations to soup kitchens and shit, and it's just too much work. But you can't argue with him, right? Because it's Savino. I tried telling Marco—he works up front, Marco's a bitch—but you know what he said?"

"What?"

"He said to get over it, I'm paid above minimum wage but that could change. What a bitch. Savino wouldn't let that happen. Dad wouldn't. Marco knows that, but he likes to lord his managerial stuff over everyone, makes him feel powerful. Did you have breakfast? Hey, Gio—"

Giovani leaned forward and passed me a piece of cold pizza wrapped in a napkin.

For it being so early (ten till six), the streets were crowded. It took nearly a half hour to navigate through Manhattan and into the area they called Little Italy. Betta parked on a back road behind a cluster of buildings, on the curb by a row of dumpsters.

"Okay, let's go, we're a few minutes late." Betta kicked open the door and slid out.

"I hate being late," Giovani muttered into his thermos. I followed him and Betta up to the building.

"Well, we had to wait for your coffee."

"I was waiting for the coffee while *you* did your hair."

"I only did my hair because we had time because you were—oh, forget it." Betta rolled her eyes. She unlocked the back door and let us in.

It looked even smaller than the kitchen in Augusta, but I guess it was probably bigger than it seemed; a huge wood-fire oven took up a lot of space, plus a long row of proofing racks covered in plastic sheets. There was a deep-fryer, several long metal shelves and racks bolted into the brick walls, piles of five-gallon buckets bursting with expanding dough. And a flour-covered Savino with oil on his hands.

He barely glanced up from the bench where he was portioning dough. "Betta, the fryer's heated, start on *zeppole*. Giovani, check the pastry case and fill the cannoli, I already did the shells. Pia." He motioned me over. "Focaccia."

I washed my hands, took the apron Betta threw at me—a soft gray thing with bleach stains and a fuzzy old hem—and stood beside Savino. He looked a bit less intimidating in the harsh bakery lights, when he wasn't sitting beside a fire in a huge expensive armchair.

32

He had a bowl of oil, a stack of greased quarter sheet pans, and one of the five-gallon buckets tipped over on the bench. I could smell the dough from here, tangy and sour. Huge bubbles dappled its surface.

"Is it sourdough?"

"Always. Look"—he used his bench scraper, separated a chunk of dough from the rest and tossed it on an oiled scale—"forty-three ounces. And then...this." He tossed it on a pan, dipped his hands in the oil, and stretched the dough gently but firmly into all the corners. He pressed his fingers into the dough all the way down, dimpling it for the brine. "Just like that." He pulled a towel over it and slid the tray onto a rack; he'd already done at least a dozen before we'd arrived.

Savino handed me a towel and motioned for me to take his place. He stood over my shoulder while I worked.

It was good to be back in a bakery, even if it was an unfamiliar bakery in Manhattan. The bench scraper felt nice in my hand. I weighed the dough, spread it on the pan, dimpled it. Easy.

"Stiff," he said. He took the tray and put it up to proof anyway, but he came right back. "Have you done this before?"

"Only at home."

"It's the same at home and in the bakery, it doesn't change. Don't think about the bakery, just think about the dough. Do it again. Loosen up. Dough knows when you're scared of it—it'll tear."

I did it again, but it was hard to pretend that I was at home when Savino was staring over my shoulder, watching me like a hawk. I tried to loosen up, I even rolled my shoulders to *show* that I was loosening up. My wrists decided, at this moment, to start hurting.

Savino tapped the bowl of oil—it shimmered green-gold in the glaring light. "Can you smell it?"

I could. It was slick over my hands. Earthy, almost grassy notes drifted up from the oiled dough.

"Isn't deodorized, or diluted. This is the good stuff—not *great*, but good, from Liguria—we get it shipped over straight from the *oliveto* in Italy, they mill it on the property." He rubbed it between his fingers. "Good olive oil yields a good product. We use it fresh, we use it quickly, we use a lot of it." Apparently through with his olive oil spiel, Savino nodded back at the pile of dough. "Do it again."

But clearly what I'd done wasn't *that* bad, because he added it to the other trays on the rack.

I didn't know what he wanted. I'd just walked into the kitchen ten minutes ago. He'd given me the job because Sabine said I could bake, he hadn't known anything about me before that, this was the first time he was seeing whether I was *all that*. Or not.

33

My fingers tensed up. I rolled my neck. *Don't mess this up, Pia.* What if he decided I couldn't bake? I needed to finish school, I needed a job and a place to stay....

"Hey Savino, should I change the oil?" That was Betta.

Savino walked off across the kitchen to check the fryer.

I'd taught myself to bake, without any supervision or guiding hands from my parents. I'd watched the folks at work, saw how the bakers treated the different doughs—when they were firm, when they were delicate. That's how I learned bagels and bread, doughnuts and pastry. But with the Italian stuff, I had to teach myself everything.

Like this: the dough was soft, but elastic. It was sourdough, so it was more delicate, even if it had gluten strands binding it all together. It was alive, and it didn't want to be bothered. So when I portioned the dough and slipped it onto the scale, I kept my wrists loose—I didn't want to disturb the culture, the frothing activity webbed through its structure. The dough wasn't sticky, but it was soft and oiled and I wanted to keep my hands close to the same consistency. With yeasted doughs and pastry, you flour your hands; with sourdough, you wet them. I dipped my hands into olive oil and transferred the dough to the pan.

Focaccia isn't like pizza dough, turned on the knuckles, checking the thinner spots to prevent tearing—I knew this. It was always a game of knowing what the gluten was doing, sensing when it tensed up and needed to rest. Like an injury: if you over-stretch it, you tear something. So instead you push the dough out on an oiled pan, using palms and fingertips. You find the thicker spots and gently coax them into the corners of the pan, leaving the thinner bits to relax. *Use your fingertips. Use your intuition.*

And when it had reached as close to the edge of the tray as it would go, I oiled my fingers again and dimpled the dough all the way down, pushing at a slight slant, until my fingertips nearly touch the tray. Because once it proofed a second time and rose to the lip of the pan, the dimples were deep enough that they'd stay through the bake. And when I poured on the brine and oil, it would settle into these indents, it would pool there. You bake the bread, and the flavor hides in those spaces—the salt, herbs, oil.

I frowned, covered the tray with a towel.

I hadn't baked focaccia in months. Last time I'd made it, Mamma had constructed a prosciutto sandwich that was two enormous slabs of focaccia and about one-and-a-half slices of prosciutto arranged between.

I stretched my wrists, took a deep breath.

A hand reached around me and flipped back the towel. I jumped.

Savino took a good long look. I stared at him as he stared at the focaccia dough, paralyzed for an instant, awaiting his verdict. He raised his eyebrows and dropped the towel back into place. "Good." He slid it off the counter and put it with the rest.

I started to relax.

ii.

34

Up front, Marco Biasi—a tall, bald man who perpetually lived in suits and wire-rimmed glasses—worked the counter with Dora Di Natale, the eldest daughter of Gio's brother Mo. I wasn't sure what that made either of them to me, but I was learning more and more that no one actually cared. First or second cousins, removed or not, uncle or great-uncle or whatever—the Vitellis and beyond made no distinction. They were just "family", and were treated as such.

That didn't really help me, trying to figure out how to navigate this new family tree. Were aunts and uncles authority figures? Savino certainly seemed like someone who I was supposed to listen to, someone who had everything in control, but I wasn't sure about Nicole or Gio. I still didn't know how to deal with cousins. I supposed it was sort of like siblings: you can't choose who you're related to, but you're stuck with them and you have to love them, whatever happens.

"It's not that bad, really," Betta informed me over break.

We sat on the back step while she drank coffee and I ate fresh focaccia, still hot from the oven, with sun-dried tomato baked into the crust. And I pretended I wasn't itching for a cigarette.

The smoking thing had actually gone further than I'd meant it to. It had started a few months ago, with Papa smoking every now and then, and school stressing me out; it had become a habit to sit with him outside in the evenings, and relax and talk and smoke. I guess sometime around the funeral it had gotten really bad without my noticing.

"Does it just start making sense?" I forgot I wasn't wearing an apron and I dusted off my fingers on my leggings.

Betta shrugged, put her feet up on a crate. She had thick athlete's calves. "You just stop caring. It's all the same. They're all brothers, sisters, aunts, uncles. You'll see a lot of them this week, but they'll get busy once school starts. And they'll leave you alone." She sipped her coffee. "Everyone's just nosy and up in everyone's business, but they don't really care. It's just *family*."

That was the core of my discomfort. "It was always just me and the kids. I didn't realize we had such a big family."

"Oh, God, it's like everywhere you look there's another one popping up. I don't even know some of them, Mom's and Savino's cousins are spread out all over the globe, some of them are still back in Italy. And everyone's always pregnant and getting married, you can't keep track." She tossed back the rest of her coffee, wiped her mouth on the back of her hand. "And you're a Marzano," she said suddenly.

I looked at her. "Yeah."

"So that's something."

"Is it? Why?"

35

"Because, you know." Betta crumpled up her paper cup, glanced at me sideways. "The *Marzanos*. I mean. You know. That's something."

"I don't get why it's such a big deal. People keep saying that name like it means something." Papa was a good man, and a wonderful father, but there was nothing particularly impressive or mysterious about Leo Marzano—nothing that would cause people to act this weird about my last name.

"Well, okay. You know, I shouldn't talk about it. Hey, Savino says you're going to Fortuna, it's kind of a shit-hole but I can show you around."

"Is that the school?"

"Fortuna Community College."

I wanted to push the whole Marzano discussion, but I really didn't think I could get her to say anything I didn't already know. "What are you studying?"

"Psychology."

I wondered if she was the type who actually had a passion for the science, or who used it as a fallback because they wanted a degree but didn't care too much about the actual subject matter. Betta didn't seem like she'd end up a counselor or clinical psychologist. "Don't psychoanalyze me."

She flashed a condescending smile that reminded me, uncomfortably, of Tonio from the other night. "Nothing to psychoanalyze, you're an open book."

Before I could come up with a suitable response to that, the back door slammed open and bounced off the wall. Giovani stuck his head into the alley. He had the look of someone permanently displeased.

"Hurry up, I want to go on break." He glanced at me. "Savino wants to show you how to fill the cannoli, he's up front."

He ducked back inside. Betta and I heaved ourselves up and joined him in the kitchen. I pulled on my apron as I headed up front. The bakery, while narrow, managed to pack in five tables beyond the counter. The front window spilled morning light across the scuffed wooden floors, and a couple ivy plants crawled the old brick walls. In a way, the inside of the bakery reminded me of the Vitelli house-front.

Dora stood at the register talking to customers; Savino had his back to her while he worked at a sliver of counter space sticking out from the kitchen, a piping bag in one gloved hand and a cannoli shell in the other.

Dora Di Natale, I thought, looked like the picture of a classic Italian model. She was thin and long-limbed, perfectly tanned, and she had a lovely nose of a more reasonable size than my own. Her burnt-caramel hair was piled atop her head, showing off hoop earrings and a slim neck. She looked a bit like an older Cristine—and I thought about it for a moment, but I couldn't puzzle out their relation enough to decide whether the similarity was coincidence or not.

Savino showed me how to fill the cannoli, handed me a pair of gloves, then disappeared into the back.

I don't know how long I stood there for, filling shells with ricotta, before the front door crashed open and the bell went crazy.

"The *hell*," said Dora. "Hey, what the hell?"

I swung around. The door slammed shut. The shop was empty but for Ida's brother, the older one, the one whose name I couldn't remember because I'd only met him in passing last night. He stormed up to the front with wild hair and wild eyes. He slammed his hand on the counter.

" Where's Savino?" He panted like he'd ran to the bakery—sweat soaked the front of his shirt under the sports coat. "Where is he? He won't pick up the phone."

"Hey, Ezio. You know he never answers the phone at work, what—?"

Betta poked her head out of the kitchen to see the commotion. I'd paused, transfixed, a half-filled cannoli shell and the piping bag in hand.

Ezio waved at her. "Hey, Betta—get your uncle, get Savino, it's bad—" His voice was loud.

Betta's brow furrowed. She disappeared, and a moment later Savino ran up front. "What happened?" He took in Ezio, dripping sweat and gasping for air, and his face hardened. "Who?"

"Achille—nah, he's isn't, you know…. He was drunk, he wandered into the wrong side of town—you know where—and he got picked up by a couple guys—"

"Where is he?"

"They dumped him in Chinatown, we picked him up and we've got him at the house, but we don't know what he told them—"

While Ezio was still speaking, Savino took off his apron; he balled it up and tossed it on the counter by Dora. "Giovani!" He shouted. "Bolt the back door!" He pointed at me. "Stay here. Dora, lock the front, get everyone into the office and stay there till I tell you. Don't move, don't answer the door for anyone, *stay here.*"

He grabbed his coat from a hook on the back wall, yanked something out of a drawer behind the counter, and stuffed it under the coat before I could see. Then he and Ezio were out the door. They sprinted past the front window, and they were gone.

The bakery was silent. Dora shut her mouth. She fumbled for a key chain and ran around the counter to lock the door.

Giovani stepped out of the kitchen. "What happened?"

Dora shouted back at him. "Where's Marco?"

"He's in the office, what happened?"

"Get Betta, everyone get in the office."

Giovani's eyes widened. It was the first sort of real emotion I'd seen on his face, fear. "Is everyone okay?"

37

"For now." Dora herded us back into the kitchen, around the corner and into the office. Marco shut the door behind us and locked it.

The office was small with four people crowded inside. The enormous, hand-detailed mahogany desk seemed out of place in the back of a bakery, especially with Marco's laptop and a Starbucks cup sitting atop. Dora sat back against the file cabinets, Betta and Giovani crouched by the desk as if sheltering from gunfire. Marco stood against the door, strangely calm, his thumbs playing across his phone screen—the *plinking* texting sound was loud in the silence. It was an eerily normal sound.

What the hell. I looked at Dora. "Was that a gun? Did Savino have a gun?"

She just pressed her lips together and shook her head.

"Okay." Marco adjusted his glasses and spoke without looking up from his phone. "I'm texting Gio and Mo. It's okay, we're just going to stay in here for a bit while Savino sorts it out."

The silence panned out for what felt like hours. I finally tucked myself into a corner of the room with my knees pulled to my chest. This felt like a school shooting. I'd never experienced a school shooting, but I'd heard enough stories to have thought through this scenario a thousand times—*lock the door, stay quiet, pray*. And that was when I was living in Georgia. This was *New York*, this was *Manhattan*—what had I expected? Betta seemed composed, but she gripped Giovani's arm with white knuckles. A vein pulsed spastically in Dora's temple.

"Achille had an accident," said Marco. "An *incident*. They're assessing the—"

"Was Tonio with him?" Betta's voice was choked.

Marco rubbed his neck. "No. Just Achille. The Salones locked down the Vitelli house, all the Di Natales are home and safe. But Savino and Ida and Gio are assessing the situation."

I swallowed. "What's *the situation*?"

Betta's eyebrows shot up. She glanced at Dora, who looked at Marco, who didn't so much as glance up from his text chain. Behind the glasses, his eyes followed each new message as it popped in. "It's just precautionary."

"But the situation…?"

Dora pressed her lips together and shook her head.

I gave up after that—a little angry that I was clearly being kept in the dark, but mostly anxious. Bakeries weren't supposed to be dangerous places. Working with family wasn't supposed to be this terrifying. And suddenly—stupidly—my mind grasped on to the idea that a cigarette would fix most of those problems. I screwed my eyes shut. The bakery hummed from the water, the fridge, the ovens that were still on full-blast (but hopefully empty). The air conditioning clicked on at some point, and the vent by my feet roared to life. *Plink plink plink* went Marco's phone, on full volume.

I'd forgotten to put on my medals that morning. I missed them not so much for their saints and prayers, but for the feeling that Mamma was watching me from where she partied in Heaven.

It dawned on me just then, in a terrible moment of foreshadowing, that perhaps there was a very good reason why I'd never known the Vitellis.

Marco got a call maybe an hour later. His ringtone blared to life, startling Dora—she shot upright and squeaked. Marco answered, listened while we all watched, but all he said was, "uh huh," and "yeah, alright," a couple times before hanging up and putting his phone away.

"Betta, you take Dora and Giovani, you guys go to the Di Natale house, your family's waiting. Nicole's got Ava from the preschool, I have to go pick her up. Savino sent a car for Pia." He unlocked the office door and moved over to the desk, where he shut his computer and started putting things in a briefcase. "Out the back door, guys."

Betta went first. She cast a perturbed glance towards the front of the shop, then grabbed her things and hurried out the back. Giovani and Dora followed.

Marco trailed behind me, shutting off lights and ovens and the fryer as he went. We stepped out into the alley and he locked the door behind us. Betta's BMW was already peeling away. A low, charcoal-gray Lexus idled across the alley. Marco pointed it out to me, then turned and without another word got into his own car—something sleek and red.

I hurried across the alley, head bowed, shoulders hunched like I was bolting through a rainstorm. The Lexus 'driver reached around and opened the back door—I slammed it behind me as I climbed inside.

Massimo put the car into drive. The bakery slipped away behind us.

I leaned forward. "What happened?"

He kept his eyes fixed straight ahead, but I noticed he was sweating. Why was everyone *running* today? Later, I'd think it was strange how different this Massimo was from the cleaned-up, hair-gelled version from the night before—wrinkled khakis and sweat-soaked shirt, his jaw tight—but at the moment I just found an ounce of relief in the fact that his face was calm. I needed one person besides Marco to be calm.

I climbed into the front seat over the console. I plopped down and dropped my backpack at my feet, turned to Massimo so he couldn't ignore me. "Do you have a gun?"

His head snapped around. "What?"

"Savino had a gun, do you have a gun? Are there gunfights in the streets, was there a terrorist attack? What's happening?"

Massimo scratched the back of his head. He probably had a gun. "Tonio's brother Achille Salone got in a fight with a couple of guys, they messed him up. We want to make sure it was just Achille being stupid and not a targeted attack on the family."

"Why would someone attack the Salones?"

"Well...an attack on the Salones," said Massimo, evenly, "is an attack on the Di Natales, the Biasis, the Vitellis...the Marzanos. They could have issue with any of us. Or Achille might have just been drunk and stupid."

"He was drunk in the middle of the day?"

"Yes." A muscle twitched in his jaw.

I sat back, realized I hadn't put on my seatbelt. That should have been simple habit, putting on a seatbelt—back home, any one of my siblings would have jumped on me immediately like I'd committed a felony. I strapped myself in as we flew over the East River. Either there was much less traffic than earlier, or Massimo was really gunning it for Brooklyn. I didn't know where Betta was headed, but I'd lost sight of the black BMW far ahead. "Why did Savino send you?"

He glanced at me. "We're trying to be safe."

"Well, why didn't I ride with Betta and Giovani?"

"They're going home."

That didn't add up. "But they picked me up this morning, it must be on their way—"

"Do you have a problem with me, Pia?"

I looked at him. "No."

"It just really seems like you don't want me driving you."

"No. That's not—sorry. I just...." It just felt an awful lot like Savino was splitting us up, like he was worried we might be followed, and that chilled me. But it seemed like a paranoid thing to vocalize. I didn't want to come off as paranoid. And I didn't have a problem with Massimo, I actually liked him and his calm, calculated demeanor, even if he seemed to be collaborating with the rest of the family to be outrageously vague. "Just...is it always like this?"

He tapped the steering wheel absently. "Like what?"

"I mean, how many times a week will I have to lock myself in the bakery office? Is Manhattan really that bad?"

"No," he said, "it's not."

The bridge ended. I'd thought Massimo was staring straight ahead, but I noticed now that his eyes kept flicking back to the rearview mirror. Not in a checking-the-next-lane sort of way, either—it reminded me of the times I'd be driving home from work, and I'd become paranoid because that same red truck had been on my tail since downtown.

I glanced back behind us, but I didn't see anything suspicious. We were getting into the neighborhoods; we'd left most traffic behind.

A couple minutes later, we pulled up in front of the Vitelli house.

"I'm sorry it happened," said Massimo, throwing the car into park. "On your first day here."

"Yeah."

"See you later, Pia."

"Seeya."

The front door was locked. I jiggled the doorknob, then I hit the silver knocker a few times.

The curtains at the front window rustled. I caught the faintest glimpse of something moving behind them, then the knob clicked and the door opened.

It was Ezio. He ushered me inside—waved Massimo on—and locked the door behind me.

Nonna Annabella and a portly older man with silver hair sat on the couch together. Tonio stood with his back against the mantel, arms crossed, his dark eyes fixed on some faraway place. He wore a dress shirt and slacks, but he looked like he'd either rolled out of bed in them, or else he'd gotten himself into a fight. Maybe both. A young woman with short blond hair—she stood out in the room like a tropical bird—sat in Savino's armchair. A bespectacled man who looked a bit like Tonio and a bit like Ezio stood behind her.

I froze in the foyer. The sound of kids playing and laughing drifted downstairs, but the party in the front room was solemn. The tension was palpable.

"Is he here?" My voice sounded small.

"They're in the basement," said Ezio.

They, meaning Savino and Ida and maybe Gio. I glanced at the spiral staircase. "Is he alright?"

The man behind the armchair glanced at Tonio, then at Ezio. "He'll be fine."

I waited, but no one offered up more information, they just shared secret looks or stared at the floor and sat in the suffocating silence. Like they were grieving someone. The atmosphere reminded me of a wake.

I went upstairs. I shut the door to my bedroom, kicked off my shoes, and put on the wrist braces. Then I opened the sparrow window and stood looking out at the square below.

I wanted this to work out. I *needed* this to work out. Because the honest truth was that I couldn't stand the thought of going back to Augusta and trying to live my life in that big house empty of Mamma and Papa. I would do what I needed to do to take care of the kids. But if I tried to live the same as before, the absence of those two pivotal characters would haunt my every moment, and the only way to fight that was to abruptly change my course in life.

That's what I was doing here, in Brooklyn. Sabine knew it. I knew it. What had Savino said last night? *"Our family's taken a lot, we keep moving forward."* Like a shark. If I went back to Georgia, I'd whither away into something that no longer resembled Pia Marzano. I had to keep moving forward, or I would die.

III

Macbeth

i.

I didn't go back to work the next day. Or for the rest of the week, for that matter. I thought Betta and Giovani might be working, but then Ida told me Savino had closed the bakery for a few days and only he and Marco were going in.

That was all she told me. Getting information out of anyone was like pulling teeth, except the teeth never ended up coming out and I just expended a lot of energy for my efforts.

I called home on Thursday night, and Cristine immediately jumped on me, always on the offense. "Why didn't you call yesterday?"

"Things have just been kind of crazy. It got late, you know?"

"I would have answered."

"Yeah, but Vince..."

"Yeah, I know, he didn't have to know. You could have called." She was quiet for a moment. Music played in the background—synthesized pop music, the occasional synthesized animal sound. "So. What's it like? Are they nice?"

Nice wasn't the word I would use. *Familiar* seemed a bit closer to the truth, but still couldn't quite sum up the Vitellis and their welcome. "They are...very Italian. They're like Sabine." Except not. "Imagine the most awkward, overwhelming family reunion ever, and it's like that but a lot more hectic. Everyone's loud. No sense of personal space.... It's a nice house."

"Do you have your own bedroom?"

"And *bathroom*."

"Wow." She was quiet again. Cristine did this thing where she liked to talk on the phone, but she didn't like to invest in the conversation; she'd rather draw or scrapbook or edit something on the computer while she barely kept up the conversation on her end.

"Cristine? Is Carlo there?"

"No. He's in his room."

I fit myself onto the window seat and cracked open the sparrow window. "Can you give him the phone?"

She sighed, like I was asking the world of her. "Sure."

I waited. Out back, Ida walked laps around the square with Marc in the stroller. I'd been right about the running thing—she had the runner's apparel and a visor and everything, and she did indeed wake up at an insane hour for her workouts. "Carlo?"

"Hey, Pia, Sabine's making us eat Brussel sprouts. Mamma didn't make us eat Brussel sprouts."

"Did you tell her that?"

"No."

"Maybe you should talk to her." I fought the urge to roll my eyes, but it was a relief to hear his voice. "Tell her Brussel sprouts make you gassy, it's the fiber, she'll understand."

"What if she doesn't?"

"Carlo, are you guys doing alright? Is Vince alright?"

"We're okay…it's just weird."

I wanted to tell him it would get better. But I didn't know that. "Hey, the Vitellis have BMWs."

"Whoa."

"Yeah. Like, at least three, I don't know what they use them for. There are just…so many BMWs. And our cousin Massimo has a Lexus." Car facts never failed to get his attention.

"What year?"

"I don't know, Carlo, I don't pay attention to that stuff."

"Well, find out. I wanna look it up. Hey, Vince is here, he wants to talk, is that okay?"

"Yeah, put him on."

Carlo had started sounding older on the phone a few months back. But Vince's voice was still soft, still made me melt. "Hi, Pia."

"Hey Vince. I love you, I miss you."

"I miss you too…Sabine made us eat Brussel sprouts."

"I heard, I'm sorry. I'll talk to her."

"She put balsamic vinegar on them. I almost threw up."

I didn't doubt that; Vince had a sensitive gag reflex. Also motion sickness. He was a pretty sickly little kid. "Cristine and Carlo are being good, right? You guys are okay?"

"They're okay. It's just quiet. I made waffles this morning. Sabine sleeps in a lot, and Cristine just stays locked up in her room a lot. Me and Carlo put peanut butter and bananas on them. I burnt them a little bit, but they still taste good. What's New York like?"

"It's big, really big. And crowded. I'm not a fan. But the neighborhood's nice. I saw Spiderman."

"Pia…"

"Hey, I'm just telling you what I saw." I smiled out the window. The stained-glass sparrow painted the bedroom floor with blue spangles of light. Below, Ida had broken into a jog, which I'm sure Marc was enjoying immensely. "Is Sabine around?"

"She's downstairs."

I waited. "Can you…bring her the phone?"

"Oh, yeah. I think she's making cookies or something." He sighed. "She uses box mixes."

"I'm sorry I turned you into a food snob."

"No, it's okay."

"Box mixes are okay."

"They taste like cardboard," he said. "Cardboard and sugar. It's not real baking, is it?"

"You can make them taste better. Use browned butter instead of oil, add almond extract or something. Hey, I left a bunch of cookbooks in my room, why don't you go through them and pick something out? Carlo can help you."

"Yeah, okay. Maybe. *Hey, it's Pia, she wants to talk to you.*"

"Love you, Vince."

"Love you. Bye."

Summer was just getting started, but I needed it to finish up so I could go home and hug that kid, hug all of them. "Sabine?"

"Pia, *cara*, how are you? Hey, how was the flight, it was bad, huh? The turbulence, I tell you—last time I was on a plane, a man (he must have been two-hundred years old, this man), he had a heart attack because of the turbulence, and then we had to make an emergency landing at another airport, and then my flights got all screwed up and it's a mess, Pia, I'm sorry you had to go through that, that's how it always is. And don't get me started on that crap they call food, if I ever have to eat another stale croissant with obnoxious little marmalade packets—"

"The flight was okay," I said.

45

She plowed ahead. "Hey, is Savino being nice? I told him, the family better be real welcoming, because you aren't used to New York and it's a big city, Pia, don't wander around alone, okay? Hey, have you got any pepper spray? I'm gonna send you some mace or something, yeah?"

"It's fine." Not sure what I was responding to—dialogue with Sabine functioned in the form of large chunks of her talking at someone and asking several questions, and the other person trying to answer at least one of those questions before the next topic change. "Hey, uh...the kids mentioned Brussel sprouts."

"Yeah, I put balsamic vinaigrette and toasted pistachios on them—oh, Cristine *loved* them, Pia, she—"

"So," I interrupted, as gently as possible, "Carlo and Vince have really sensitive stomachs, and they *will* vomit if something doesn't agree with them."

There was silence on the other line.

I cleared my throat. "Uh. Just, thought I should warn you."

"Okay, thank you."

I'd probably offended her. "Also, uh, I've got a question. A big question. Several big questions. You might want to sit down."

"Oh no, Pia, what's happened? Are you okay? Did something happen with the school? They did the transfer, right? I talked to the people—"

"No, the school—it's fine. I haven't been yet, but I'm sure it's fine. I just...wondered why you and Mamma never talked about your family. I don't think you ever explained that."

Sabine was quiet for a long moment. "What do you mean?" she said at last, like she knew exactly what I meant. "I talk about them."

"I mean, not really." I ran a hand through my hair, let the black strands fan out through my fingers. "Not at all. It's a big family, I didn't know I had cousins, I didn't know—hey, Zia Nicole? I didn't know you and Mamma had another sister."

"Oh, you see, Nikki and I don't really see eye-to-eye—she settled down, I didn't want to, it was a big scandal."

I could tell she liked the idea of being *a big scandal*. Everything about Sabine, from her dyed blond hair to the fact that she was over forty and had no intention of "settling down" screamed *rebel child*. "No one even mentioned her, though. Or the fact that I have *cousins*."

"Oh, I haven't met them."

"When's the last time you visited?"

"Oh, gosh, Pia, I don't know—hey, my cookies are burning, *cara*, can I call you back in a bit?"

"Sabine?"

"Yes?"

I had more questions. But I had no way to voice them politely; I didn't even have words for most of them. This whole family was one big question mark and I didn't know how to communicate that to my aunt, who was hundreds of miles away and burning her cardboard sugar-cookies.

"I love you," I said instead.

"I love you too Pia—hey, tell Savino to call me sometime, yes? I'll talk to you soon. Okay, okay, bye-bye."

ii.

Friday morning, I went out for school supplies. The twins were at preschool, Ida had taken Marc along on some errands, and I hadn't seen Savino in a while, so I locked the house behind me and walked to a convenience store a couple blocks away. The shock of the week had worn off a bit, and I thought I was fine—until I was heading back to the house, arms laden with plastic bags of notebooks and pens.

I paused at a crosswalk, waited for the light to turn. And I got this crawling, spine-tingling feeling that someone was right behind me.

There wasn't. I checked. There were pedestrians a ways off, but no one was following me or even looking in my direction. I adjusted my grip on the bags and sped across the street.

Sometimes that happened, the random rushes of paranoia. I tended towards anxiousness, sure, but there was a difference between feeling stressed and unnecessarily concerned in the safety of my home, and the sense that I was being followed on an unfamiliar Brooklyn street.

I glanced back again, but I was alone on the sidewalk.

Suspiciously alone, said my brain.

Something flashed behind me—the swish of a coat, maybe a passing car, *something*. My heart skipped a beat.

I started running.

It was the stupidest thing, looking back, and I must have looked insane (or maybe not—this was New York, after all). But that same feeling that had possessed me upon leaving the bakery the other day, sneaking out the back door like there might be snipers on the roof, had tracked me down again and latched on. My feet pounded the pavement.

I didn't notice the extra car parked in front of the Vitelli house—I wouldn't notice until later. I unlocked the front door and slipped inside, threw the bolt, and stood panting on the threshold. What was *happening*?

Get it together.

"—and it's quality, you can tell just by looking at it. Have you tried it?"

I jumped. I wasn't alone in the house anymore; voices drifted in through the dining room, from the kitchen. I stood in the foyer and waited to see who it was. They'd

47

moved Achille out of the basement last night—I hadn't seen him go, but Ezio had picked him up and I'd heard them talking downstairs.

"Hey, don't be bringing that stuff here, don't bring that around. You know the rules."

"It's fine, Raul, take it easy." That was Savino's voice. Something clanked around in the kitchen. "I told him it was alright, better here than the bakery, especially right now. And Johnny—you can't tell by just looking, don't let them tell you that." A brief pause, silence thick with anticipation. "It's fine. I'll let them know."

"Hey, but Achille—went and ran his mouth at the casino, man, we can't trust--"

"I dealt with it." Savino's voice was low.

"Yeah, but the guy—"

"He dealt with it, Johnny, now shut up about Achille."

"When are you gonna tell the guys, Savino? Yeah? We're all fumbling in the dark here, we're going into this blind. You can't just change the time, we set the plan in stone months ago, we can't just change that."

"Well," said Savino, "we're not gonna change it, we're shifting the location. I want you to get in contact, you tell them—no middleman, you tell Valentino himself."

"Yeah? And what about the folks across town?"

"Geez, Johnny," Raul snapped, "watch it. We've got it under control."

There was a pause. More clinking, like glass against glass. "I'll deal with the other guys," said Savino, "got it?"

"Fine. But these guys, they've got families too, I gotta look out for them. The old man knew that, it's why my dad stuck with him—you take care of the people, too, right? You keep them happy, they keeps their mouths shut—consistency is the key to the game, that's what you've always said, yeah? We need to know by tonight."

"I don't like ultimatums, Johnny."

I held my breath; I was positive they could hear my heartbeat from across the house. My pulse was still rapid from the run.

"You'll know by tonight," said Savino, finally. "I'll talk to Valentino's guys about it, we've got an understanding. And I keep my people safe, Johnny, you know that. I keep this family safe."

I couldn't risk staying around any longer. I crept up the stairs—softly, I remembered how the steps squeaked and echoed—and shut myself in the bedroom.

I tossed the shopping bag on my bed. I didn't bother taking off my shoes or emptying my pockets before I threw open the window and fished a cigarette out of my backpack. I hadn't smoked in a couple days, and it didn't feel as good as I remembered, but still my body relaxed and my heartbeat slowed and I immersed myself in the comforting smell. It smelled like Papa, who was an honest mechanic, who read Charles Dickens and invited me out on long hikes around the countryside.

When I finished that cigarette, I lit another.

The back door slammed. Below, a short figure strode off across the green, someone with an athletic jacket and a backpack. He disappeared around the next block.

We hadn't taken Cristine or Carlo or Vince on those walks. It had just been me and Papa. Sometimes we didn't even talk, we just hiked through damp bahiagrass and red clay soil, walked in silence until the sun got low and the mosquitoes emerged. I really think he only took me and not the others simply because he knew I needed that time— no, he wanted that time too—and not just because I was the only one who really wanted to go. He could have forced everyone to go on a walk with him, like he forced Carlo to bike to IGA with him sometimes, just because he wanted the company. This was better than that. All those times we'd disappeared for the evening and hiked down some lonely dirt road bordered by orchards and dilapidated barns, and all the times we sat outside after dinner and smoked together, it was because he genuinely wanted to spend time with me. Mamma preferred Vince over everyone, and we all knew it and understood—Vince was my favorite, too. But I think I was Papa's favorite.

I shut my eyes. That hurt. I wasn't anyone's favorite anymore—we'd gone on our last hike, smoked our last cigarettes together. And that was that. And life was shit.

Vince and the kids didn't have Mamma. They didn't have me, either. I needed to become something bigger that could fill that enormous hole in their lives, and I was trying, but I was terrified, and I didn't know how to do it.

There was a knock at my door.

It opened before I could call out or lose my cigarette. Savino seemed surprised to see me there. "When did you get back?"

Something in me whispered, *He can tell if you lie.* But I didn't want him to know I'd overheard the conversation downstairs. I don't know what I thought might happen, and I didn't want to follow that train of thought any further. "A few minutes ago. I went out to get school supplies."

He glanced at the CVS bag on my bed. Then he fixed his pitch-black eyes on me. "What's that?"

It took me a moment to realize he meant the wrist braces, not the cigarette, which he was graciously ignoring. "Tendonitis."

"They don't work," he said.

"What?"

"I've tried them, they don't work. You have to rest up for over a year with no strain to get it right again." He put his hands in his pockets. "Don't like to rest, Pia?"

I shook my head. Resting meant thinking, thinking meant grieving and dwelling on the past. *We move forward.*

49

"Me neither." Savino stood in the doorway. He wore a polo and khakis, the unofficial Di Natale dress code, and his hair was unkept like he simply hadn't had the time to deal with it today. When he was outside the kitchen, when he wasn't surrounded by all the other Vitellis and Di Natales, I saw more of Mamma in him—just a glimpse, and it hid behind a shield. It was more comfortable dealing with him like this. The sun filtered in through the sparrow window, I was relaxed, and it was easier to humanize him when he was standing here in front of me, instead of some disembodied voice from across the house. "You talk to your aunt?"

"Which one?"

"Sabine."

"Yeah, I talked to her. And the kids. I asked her why she never talked about you guys."

He didn't react. He just stood there, still as a statue on the threshold, watching me. Waiting for me to go on.

I did. "She said you guys didn't see eye-to-eye. Because she was a bit of a scandal."

"Yeah, I bet she said that."

He didn't smile like Mamma, but it was familiar, and I wondered where I'd seen it before. A voice in the back of my mind had the answer, but the answer made me uneasy. *That's you.* It was a slippery slope, all this *you remind me of Savino, you look like a Vitelli*, and me not knowing him well enough to identify how I felt about that.

I hung my cigarette out the window, out of view. "So," I said, "what's the truth?"

He rubbed his neck. "She went to school out of state. Never came back. We all thought she was gonna marry Nic Tabone from the Bronx, but she got involved in some cult out of college and apparently forgot about him."

I choked on my own smoke. "A *cult*?"

The smile stayed. "That's the story. She always acted like we'd make her settle down with some guy and make Italian babies, if she came back. So I'm sure she does consider herself a scandal. I'm sure that makes her very happy."

It rang true. All this was totally in character for my Aunt Sabine, even if it was new information. "And Mamma? She never talked about her family."

Savino's smile disappeared. I felt like I was getting dangerously close to a touchy subject, something that shouldn't be broached. "I liked Carla," he said. "And Leo Marzano. But I didn't understand them."

I waited, but that's all there was. Again with the teeth-pulling—getting information out of anyone was a futile struggle.

Savino narrowed his eyes out the window. "You look like her, but you're not a lot like her, you know?"

I knew. Cristine was more like Mamma, proud and aloof, and I prayed she grew into the nurturing parts of our mother's personality. "They say I'm like you."

His eyes glanced over me, the useless wrist braces. "Maybe. I don't like to rest, either. We've got people to take care of, who has time for rest?" He turned away, one hand on the doorjamb, and pulled the door shut as he went. He called back over his shoulder. "There are pain-killers downstairs, if you need them."

iii.

Massimo and Betta showed up after breakfast the next day. They were going to the park to play soccer, and wanted to know if I'd come. I would. I liked soccer—I hadn't played in months—and I needed to get outside and do something that didn't feel like house arrest.

Giovani sat in the back seat of Massimo's charcoal Lexus, slumped and sullen. I sat beside him and tried to not annoy him by breathing.

"Ignore him," said Massimo, when Giovani refused to acknowledge my greeting. "He thinks he's going through something."

"He's just a moody bitch," said Betta. "Right, Gio? He's listening to a lot of Green Day. Right, Giovani?"

In response, Giovani flipped her off.

Betta was loud. She bordered on obnoxious, but she seemed just self-aware enough to rein herself back from full-blown *annoying*. I assumed it had something to do with growing up with lots of brothers and cousins. She complained to us about the teacher she'd been stuck with for Spanish—Joshua Puck, a lame nerd who answered every question with an overlong explanation and read all the course material word-for-word off Powerpoint slides. She was also taking some bullshit class called "Creating Experiences", because it satisfied an extracurricular requirement.

Giovani was only taking one class, and that was because he'd failed calculus the previous semester. Betta announced this to the car.

When asked about my own schedule, I became uncomfortably aware that I was, apparently, behind in school. I'd never been academically inclined—I more preferred to do things with my hands than sit and study—but never finishing the spring semester had put me in a tight spot. Taking summer courses should get me back on track, but at the moment my college roadmap was a miserable sight.

"Calculus," I said, "chemistry and lab, Greek history, biology, Christian ethics. That's it."

Betta's eyebrows shot up. "Wow."

I cleared my throat. I wanted to make it abundantly clear that I wasn't a genius or an overachiever or anything, just a loser forced into a horrifying semester's load of coursework. "I didn't finish last semester."

"Oh." Betta glanced at Massimo, who didn't react.

I decided to turn the conversation away from me. "So, how's the school?"

"Oh, it's fine, I guess. Massimo finished, he did stuff with his life, if he did it any one of us can."

"What kind of stuff?"

"Chemistry," he said.

I couldn't tell yet whether he was the type of person I could ask for study help from. But it was good to know. "Wow."

Betta waved a hand. "Oh, it isn't a big deal, he just went to a good school."

"What school?"

"Columbia," said Massimo. "I did two years at Fortuna, then I went to Columbia." He said it casually, but there was a stiffness to it, an air of discomfort that said he really didn't want to talk about it.

I understood that. I looked at Giovani, again anxious to change the topic. "What do you want to do?"

"Sleep."

"He's just upset," said Betta, "because Savino won't let us back at the bakery. And he doesn't know how *not* to work because he's horrible like that."

I leaned forward against the seatbelt. "Why aren't you allowed back? To the bakery?"

"I think it's just Savino going in, right now. To finish up orders and stuff, but he doesn't want us there because—well, he just doesn't, the thing with Achille"— Massimo glanced at her—"I mean, who knows, it's his bakery, I guess he can do what he wants with it. But I bet Marco's going in, to work in the office. Isn't Marco the worst?"

I wasn't fond of Marco and his cellphone, but he certainly wasn't *the worst*. "I haven't really talked to him."

"Exactly. He just texts and talks to customers and sometimes Savino, he doesn't even talk to Dora, he just walks around in his suit and bosses people around. I'd be super depressed if I was Dora and I had to work up front with him all day, that sounds miserable."

"Tell us how you really feel, Betta," Giovani mumbled at the window.

Massimo flicked on the turn signal and rounded a corner. "Don't let Dad hear you talk about Marco like that."

"Bleh."

"How are we related to Marco?" I asked. "Am *I* related?"

"Marco's Norma's husband," said Massimo.

"Okay." That didn't help. "Who is Norma?"

"She's our sister," said Betta. "And she *sucks*."

Massimo did not refute this point. "Marco and Norma got married, Ava's our niece."

"She's pregnant again." Betta chewed on the end of her braid. "But we don't know what it is. I think we need another girl, there are too many guys in this family. Look at the Salones, it's ridiculous."

"Uh huh." I leaned against the headrest, narrowed my eyes at the back of Massimo's seat. I'd thought I'd have put together a rough family tree by now, but it seemed like the more people I met, the more branches I had to tack on. "How are the Salones related?"

"They married in, too," said Massimo. "Ida's a Salone."

Betta ticked them off on her fingers. "Annabella and Alonzo are her parents. They've got Ezio, Raul, Ida, Achille, Tonio. In that order, I think." She looked at her older brother. "Am I missing anyone?"

"Raul married Cassie."

"Oh, Cassie *sucks*. Oh, funny story." Betta twisted around in her seat to look at me. "So, Ezio—he's the oldest, he's the guy who came into the bakery the other day—he had this thing with a *Napoletano* lady a few years back, he went over there on a business trip, and he came back and he didn't really talk to her again, but she ended up getting pregnant—"

Massimo furrowed his brow. "This is *not* a funny story."

"—*but*," Betta plunged ahead, "but he went back to visit her last year. In Naples. And it turns out she's married, but he didn't know that. So it's nighttime, he's at her house or apartment or whatever, and there's a knock on the front door at like midnight—"

"Two AM," said Giovani, with his eyes shut and head lolled against the window.

"Or two AM, whatever, the point *is*, he's walking to the front door and he realizes there's someone else there, in the apartment—we don't know what the knocking was about, but it turns out her husband was hiding in the kitchen and he shot Ezio in the stomach. But Ezio sleeps with a gun because he's a badass, so he ends up shooting this guy in the head. But it was self defense, so he got away with it. So now he sends money back to his kid in Naples—or, I think they moved, to, uh…."

"Sapri," Massimo supplied.

"Yeah, Sapri. But he sends back money and visits the kid and the lady—what's her name?"

"The baby's name is Marina."

"No, the uh…Ezio's Naples bitch."

"Betta—"

"What, she is! I bet she just did it for the money, and then she was gonna have her husband get rid of Ezio. That's what Achille says."

"You shouldn't listen to anything Achille says."

"Well, Ezio told him stuff."

"Her name was like…Natala or something," Giovani muttered.

Massimo sighed. He glanced back at me through the rearview mirror. "You getting all this, Pia?"

"Some of it." I already knew way more than I'd ever hoped to learn—more than I probably needed to know about certain people. Yet, at the same time, I felt like there was something significant I was missing at the core of this family. I didn't know much about aunts and uncles and cousins, extended family and all that, but there was something curious about the way everyone hung so closely together, both at home and at work, running errands for Savino. Maybe it was an Italian thing. "It's…a big family."

"Well." Betta smirked. "It really isn't that complicated."

We kicked around the soccer ball for a half hour, warming up with keep-away. Then Massimo went back to his car and reappeared with some green plastic cones to mark goals. We were just getting ready to start when I saw a figure striding towards us across the park, cleats dangling from one hand by their laces.

Tonio dropped to the grass nearby and grinned thinly as he yanked off his sneakers and pulled on the cleats. "Hello," he said.

Betta flipped him off. Massimo looked up briefly, waved, and went back to his cones.

"Hello, *Marzano*."

I nodded. I could tell already he was yanking my chain, and I refused to get caught up in it.

Tonio clambered to his feet and jogged over to where Betta and Giovani and I stood. It was strange seeing any of them out of their normal clothes—Massimo sans his khakis, Betta without her overalls—but it was especially jarring to see Tonio in a tank and black ankle socks. "Giovani," he said, "hello."

"Hey."

"Chipper as usual."

"How's Achille?" asked Betta.

There was something strange about Tonio's face, like his skin was drawn too tight over his bones. His eyes and brows were dark and distinct, and his mouth was a wide, attenuated slash, but they were all too big for his narrow face—as if God had simply copied Ida's features onto all her brothers, without concern for the final result. There was something slightly skeletal about it.

54

"Oh, you know Achille," he said, "he's drunk as usual and rearing for another fight. Hasn't learned his lesson, sharp as a marble—isn't that the definition of insanity, doing one thing over and over again and assuming it won't bite you in the ass every time?"

Betta shrugged.

Giovani shuffled his feet and said nothing.

Tonio turned on me. "Settling in, Marzano? Not too much like *Georgia*, is it?"

"Not especially," I said.

"So we haven't scared you away yet, huh?"

Massimo sent the soccer ball hurtling towards Tonio, saving me a response. Tonio stopped it neatly with a lime-green cleat. "Let's play."

As the youngest of Ida's brothers, Tonio Salone resembled less a youngest sibling, and more a privileged only-child whose siblings were much older, therefore affording him a special, favored spot with his parents. He was an intern with a local literary agency, as well as an English tutor at Fortuna, where I hoped to never encounter him on campus. He was twenty-five and might go back to school for his doctorate, if he felt so inclined. Despite this busy schedule of assorted part-time jobs, he somehow had time to turn up at every family function, drink loads of expensive wine, and harass everyone present through a lens of eloquent prose.

I didn't like him.

Betta pretended not to like him either, but I think she found his presence—with all its sardonic, sideways jabs and suspicious innuendo—amusing at the least. Inspiring, at the most.

Giovani didn't seem to care either way. He lived in his own world, and anything going on internally never manifested on the outside. Everything I learned about him came from other people—he was seventeen, he took the bakery very seriously, and he was quiet not out of self-consciousness, but purely due to a sense of superiority.

In between games, while the Di Natales righted some upset cones and I brought the ball back to center field, Tonio sidled up and said, with his signature unsettling grin, "And what's your deal, Marzano?"

I fought back a grimace. "Be more specific."

"Coasting through life? Got any goals, aspirations? How do you feel about Fascism?"

"I'm not a fan." I tried not not react. "I'm just trying to get through school so I can get a job. That's all."

"Oh, you're one of *those* types." He laughed.

"What type?" asked Betta, wandering over. She flipped back her braid and planted her fists on her hips.

"The type who sees education as a stopping point in life, a diving board into the abyss of adulthood and employment."

I stared at him, failing to see his point. "Well. What else is it?"

His eyebrows shot up. His strange, strange face restructured itself into something like overwhelming condescension, and I hated him. "Employment is a path to continuing academic endeavors. Academia is a lifelong journey, a lifestyle, not an expensive slip of paper to frame and flaunt on the wall of your study."

"I don't have the luxury of loafing around college and...being a student as a job. I don't have *money. Most* people don't have that kind of money. I'll never have a home office, or a study, or multiple degrees."

"Not with *that* attitude."

I wished I were more cool, when angry. I wished I could spit out a calculated response, stare him down, and move on. But I was royally *pissed;* I spat when I spoke. "I *literally* can't afford to make my career *academic endeavors.* My parents are dead, I have siblings I have to support, and I'm just trying to get by. So you can take all your opinions about my life, and you can shove them up your ass, *Tonio Salone.*"

Betta's eyes widened. An impressed smile crept across her face.

Giovani was still too far off to have heard, but Massimo stood right behind Tonio, and he looked deadly serious.

Tonio narrowed his eyes. His grin didn't waver. "She says my name just like *Savino* does, right?" He spoke to no one in particular.

"Shut up, Tonio," said Massimo, in a tone that almost made me feel bad for the guy. Almost.

I swallowed. I'd been having a good time, out here playing soccer with my cousins, and then this stupid English tutor had to show up and ruin everything. His smile made my skin crawl; his words curled up and made themselves comfortable in my skull. "Why do people keep saying that about Savino?"

Massimo shook his head, grabbed Tonio's arm and dragged him off a ways. Tonio tripped and laughed, but went with him. So I turned to Betta, who chewed her thumbnail and smiled.

"Betta. Why?"

"Oh," she said. "It's just that some of us are firecrackers."

"What?"

She shrugged. "That's what Mom said, she and Dad talked about it last night. *You.* They were talking about you. Some people are firecrackers, but you and Savino are time bombs, you know?"

"No. What does that mean?" They were talking about me?

"Unapproachable, I guess, even if you aren't sure why. Don't really know what it is until you get too close. Then..." She closed her fist. *"Boom."*

I still didn't understand. I shifted on my feet, passed her the soccer ball. "What's Massimo, then?" Because he struck me as neither a time bomb like Savino, nor the firecracker personality of Betta and Tonio.

Betta's smile wavered, for the briefest moment. She glanced towards her brother, who seemed to be in the middle of a lecture directed at an unrepentant Tonio.

"Massimo's a grenade," she said. "You throw it. Then you run."

Savino was at dinner that night. While he and Ida juggled the kids and tried to keep soup out of everyone's hair, I watched the two of them in silence: Ida, with her quick, very *Salone* smiles, her fast hands and constant, rotating surveillance of each child; Savino, somehow softer and less intimidating a figure beside his wife, untangling Marc's fat fingers from the baby's own hair and placing them back on the highchair tray with his cereal.

He caught my eye at one point, after another attempted hair-wrangling by his son. "You like theater, Pia?"

I hadn't heard *that* line in a while. "I guess," I said, cautious. "Why does everyone keep asking me that?"

Ida looked up and squinted across the table. "Who's everyone?"

"Massimo, Tonio."

She rolled her eyes. "My brothers are fools."

Savino shrugged one shoulder. "The school's putting on *Macbeth* tomorrow night, the whole family's going."

By "the school" I assumed we were talking about Fortuna Community College, which apparently considered itself adept in the world of stage performance. By "family", I assumed that included me as well. For a brief moment, I wondered what might happen if I refused to go. Everyone was acting rather suspicious and pushy about the whole theater thing, which naturally made me want to buck up against it a bit. But this general attitude towards the long-awaited *Macbeth* also gave me the sense that my dismissal of the event might not be met well. "Is someone in it?"

"Hmm?"

"Someone in the family?

"No."

I didn't say anything more about it. Sure, I knew there was something cagey going on, but that didn't mean I was ready to confront anyone about it. I was, after all, new to Brooklyn. I was new to the Vitellis and Salones and Di Natales.

Maybe, I thought, with one last misguided braincell struggling to assume the best, *maybe there's a simple explanation for everything. For Achille and the gun in the bakery and the men who came to talk to Savino. Maybe it's something reasonable.*

Somehow, I doubted that.

But I still didn't have the guts to say anything.

iv.

The next morning, Savino drove us to Mass at a small Catholic church in Brooklyn. It was called Thomas Aquinas. The building was outfitted with exposed rafters, creaky floorboards, an altar rail, and a disproportionally enormous baptismal font at the entrance.

The rest of the family was waiting—the entire family. Gio and Nicole Di Natale sat in the front pew with Massimo, Betta, and Giovani. Right behind them, the dreadful Marco Biasi from the bakery balanced Ava on his knee. A woman I assumed was Norma knelt and prayed beside him. Filling up the rest of the pew were Mo and Serafina and the girls—Dora flashed me a smile.

The Salones occupied the next pew, Nonna Annabella and her husband Alonzo. Ezio frowned at the altar—I thought about the story Betta had rattled off, like it was some hilarious anecdote of misadventure and mischief. But it had been a bit horrifying, and was made even more so by Ezio's presence, his brooding gaze drilling into my back; he'd killed someone, maybe in self-defense, maybe not, and no one seemed too terribly concerned about it. I was. Or maybe I just felt that I should be.

Raul sat beside him. Raul was the one I'd heard the other day, talking to Savino in the back of the house. He'd also been in the room when they'd brought Achille to the Vitelli house. He had his arm around the blond woman from that day, and held little Enzo sprawled across both of their laps.

And then there was stupid Tonio, whose face spread into a wide, amused smile when he caught my eye. He even had the audacity to wink.

I shuddered and quickly looked away.

The only family member missing, as far as I could tell, was Achille. Which was a shame. Because I was curious.

Savino and Ida took the front pew beside the Di Natales. I slid in behind them.

I'd heard that, in some countries, Catholics were a bit more conscious of not going up to Communion when they didn't feel like they were in the proper state to receive the Eucharist, when they hadn't been to Confession in a while. Places where cultural Catholicism was more common, where there wasn't as much judgement for staying behind in the pew.

About half the family didn't go up to Communion.

I assumed it was an Italian thing.

It wasn't.

v.

I tried calling Sabine that morning, but she didn't pick up. I tried Cristine's phone, and the home phone, and then I remembered that they were probably at Mass. So I gave up on communication and dedicated the rest of the afternoon to organizing my things for school tomorrow.

I didn't know where Savino was. The bakery wasn't open Sundays, but he'd disappeared again and no one was offering up any information.

That evening, I helped Ida get the kids into one of the BMWs. The twins and Marc were all in car seats at this point, so I strapped them into the back and rode up front with Ida, who was more pleasant to drive with than Massimo—she played soft classical music, hummed along, and occasionally supplied pleasantries about the weather and NYC trivia.

"Where do the Di Natales live?" I asked, as we sped over the Brooklyn Bridge.

"Nicole and Gio have a house in Brooklyn Heights, it's close. But Massimo lives in the Financial District, he's got an apartment with my brother."

I looked at her, startled. "Achille?"

"Oh, no. No, Tonio."

That was slightly less bad. Maybe. I wondered how Massimo, who worked for his dad, and Tonio, an English tutor, afforded an apartment in the Financial District. I wondered.

Fortuna Community College was bigger than my school back home—bigger and newer, probably with fewer AC problems and possibly with a parking lot that was more tarmac than pothole. I knew I'd gotten a scholarship, and I knew my parents 'savings would help, but seeing the brick arches and great big windows set against the backdrop of New York City...it made my throat tighten.

The auditorium doors were already open. The wall beside the ticket booth was plastered with old sun-bleached posters, newer ones tacked on over the top: *Macbeth* was scrawled across a black background in blood-red script.

Ezio Salone was waiting for us by the entrance, hands in his pockets—grave and dark, his mouth permanently unsmiling, looking distinctly dangerous even while doing nothing at all. "Savino will be along in a bit," he told his sister. "Had something to take care of. Said to get seated and he'll be here before it starts."

"He'd better," Ida muttered. She shifted Marc on her hip and followed Ezio into the theater.

Savino hadn't exaggerated about the whole family coming. They filled the back center row, a whole line of dark heads that turned when Ida and I wandered in behind Ezio with the kids. Bodies shuffled. I ended up wedged between the twins and Betta.

I was barely in my seat before she threw her elbow into my ribs and leaned over. "You see the drummer?" she whispered.

I held my side—she had bony arms. "What?"

She cast a furtive glance around. Beside her, Giovani grimaced. "The drummer." She nodded towards the corner of the theater, where a small ensemble in halfhearted costumes—big lumpy hats with feathers—hunkered in the shadows with their instruments. There was a harp, something that looked like a thin guitar, and a box drum with a boy perched atop.

"What about him?" I whispered back.

"Do you think he's cute?"

I didn't. Although, between the oversized hat and the lack of light, I couldn't see much of him either. "Do *you*?"

Betta blushed—*blushed*—and snapped, "Stop smiling."

"I'm not."

"Stop smiling or he'll think I'm talking about him." I doubted he could see us in the back row, but I didn't want to dash her hopes. Betta leaned closer and said, out of the corner of her mouth. "He was in my Spanish class, last semester. He's in Spanish 2 with me."

"How do you know?"

"I checked the class list, *obviously*, stop smiling. His name is Alec and he's beautiful and he drives a sports car."

"*Mar-saw-no.*"

I slapped the back of my neck. By the time I spun around, Tonio was settled back in his seat and grinning thinly at me.

Raul thumped Tonio in the chest. "Watch it."

Achille sat a few seats down from them. I might not have recognized him apart from his brothers if not for the ugly yellow-green bruise, as if someone had taken a fistful of paint and dragged it across his face. His chin had a couple stitches, and his lower lip was healing from a split. He looked like shit, like someone had dragged him here out of a pain-killer induced stupor.

I faced front before he could meet my gaze. What had *happened*? And why *had* they dragged him here when clearly he should have been lying on a sofa somewhere with an ice pack on his face?

The lights dimmed. The whispers fizzled out. A loud, crackling announcement came on over the speakers; it instructed everyone to shut off their phones and take crying children far, far away from this incredibly important performance, and to under no circumstances take photos with the flash on, or photos at all for that matter. Signed posters and professional photographs of your student are available for purchase in the lobby.

The band started playing. Beside me, Betta caught her breath.

As the curtain drew back from the stage, the auditorium door cracked open and someone slipped inside. The sliver of light disappeared. The end of the row shuffled— Ida got up and switched seats with someone, maybe Ezio—and Savino took the end seat. I watched as he turned down the collar on his black overcoat, situated himself with his eyes fixed on the stage. Savino Vitelli gave the impression of always being serious, but in that moment his jaw was clenched and he seemed especially tense.

Ida leaned over and whispered in his ear. He shook his head, brows drawn, whispered back. They went on like that for a while—I missed the first bit of *Macbeth,* I wasn't really paying attention—something about witches and prophecies and kings, but all I could think was *something is wrong.* It was almost the same feeling as when I'd been walking back from the CVS the other day.

A chill crawled down my spine. And this time it wasn't because stupid Tonio was breathing down my neck.

I liked *Macbeth.* I didn't really understand it, and I hated the overall atmosphere of *dark crowded room*, so maybe it isn't right to say I *liked* it exactly. I guess I respected it. The actors were all very good and the music was creative at best. I especially liked Lady Macbeth—the girl who played her had flowers woven into her hair, even in the scene with the blood all over her hands. I thought that said something interesting about...something. Blood and flowers. Maybe something about innocence. Whatever.

I escaped at intermission and followed the flood of people heading to the restrooms. By the time I made it down the line and had started heading back to the auditorium, the lobby was already clearing out and the ensemble had begun retuning.

"Hi, Pia."

Massimo stood in the lobby, tucked away in the shadows by the water fountain.

"Hi." I stopped, watched him from a distance. Shifted on my feet. He waited patiently as I turned the words over in my head. "How is...Achille."

Massimo crossed his arms. He looked thoughtfully over the top of my head, as if calculating his response—his eyes cut to the auditorium doors. Then he waved me over.

I leaned back against the wall beside him, stuck my hands in my pockets. "What *happened?* Really?"

"Like I said the other day: some people don't like the Vitellis. They've got problems with Savino and the rest." Voice low, dark eyes actively scanning the lobby as he spoke—just like Betta, worried someone might overhear her confessions of love.

"Achille is a Salone," I pointed out. "Ida's brother, right?"

"These guys don't like the Salones by association. Or Di Natales or Biasis. Like I said, an attack on one is an attack on all of them. Only most of the issues are with the Vitellis, if you ask me."

"How come?"

"Lots of reasons. Anyway." Massimo half-turned to me, his voice dropping even lower. "Achille wandered into their territory and got recognized. Raul and Tonio were out looking for him, they picked him up on a backstreet in Chinatown. They got him good."

"I saw him."

"He looked worse, last week."

"You saw him?"

"Yeah, Tonio and I drove over to the Vitelli house. I didn't see you. But we saw Achille on the day after, and he was rough."

I stared at Massimo. The way they spoke about Achille, about *some guys* not liking their—our—family, the way Betta had told that story the other day about Ezio and the lady from Naples—there was something unnaturally calm about it. It struck me that they were numb to this sort of thing. That didn't bode well.

"Does this happen often?" I'd asked him something similar that day in the car. I didn't think he'd actually answered.

"It does happen."

"That isn't a real response."

He smiled. "I responded. It *happens*. Being part of this family is a full-time job and it comes with occupational hazards."

That was the wrong thing to say. I hadn't asked to be part of this family and its hazards. Sabine hadn't told me about this, whatever *this* was, and I definitely wouldn't have gotten involved if I'd had even the foggiest idea that there was something wrong here. I still didn't have a clue what was going on, and I already wanted to run. I hadn't asked for this, and I'd be damned if I got my siblings involved. The Marzanos didn't want any part in this Vitelli nonsense.

Except. I needed to finish school, I needed work, I needed a place to stay. And I couldn't go back to Augusta. Not now.

I shifted on my feet. "One of these days, I'll figure out what's going on."

"You're sharp, Pia. But I doubt that. I think eventually someone will tell you."

I narrowed my eyes. I wondered what Betta had meant, about Massimo being a grenade. About me being a time bomb. I wondered about the difference. "Would *you?*"

His smile wavered. "Maybe me. But not now."

The remainder of the show was dramatic. I didn't completely understand Macduff's motives or the thing about the trees, but the rest of Fortuna Community College seemed to appreciate it. As the cast commenced their final bows, Savino slipped out of the auditorium as quietly as he'd come.

The lights came on slowly. Seats slammed shut and echoed through the hall like rapid gunfire. The auditorium started emptying into the lobby, chattering voices rising up above the thin strains of music. Ida held a sleeping Marc slumped over her shoulder, her back to me while she talked to Ezio. Ella and Anna had fallen asleep too.

Betta elbowed Giovani awake. She stood and stretched.

"Are you going to go talk to him?" I asked.

62

She caught herself craning her neck around to get a glimpse of her drummer boy. "Who?"

"Spanish 2."

"God, no, Pia, gosh." She looked horrified. "In front of *my family?* No!"

The twins were still drowsy. Ezio swooped in and picked up Anna, so I grabbed Ella and hoisted her onto my shoulder. She was hot and sweaty in the way napping kids often are—I brushed her hair off my neck and followed Ida and her brother straight through the lobby, out of the building. We strapped Marc and the twins into the back of the BMW in the middle of the dark parking lot. Ezio said goodnight—I watched him walk back to the auditorium, square shoulders hunched under his coat.

"Ida," I said.

"Yes?"

"What happened to Achille?"

Ida started the car, squinted through the headlights. She brushed a strand of hair off her neck and threw the car into reverse, determinedly avoiding eye contact. "Achille's an idiot, don't pay him any mind. He's fine. He's the middle child, he gets into trouble for the attention."

"It isn't because of the Vitellis?" She didn't answer, just reached around back and tugged Marc's seatbelt to make sure he was secured. "Ida. Are we safe?"

There was a long pause, and I thought she might continue ignoring my questions. She sighed as we pulled out of the parking lot, into the brightly-lit streets of Lower Manhattan. It was only once we'd left the lights of Fortuna Community College behind that she finally answered.

"Everything we do in this family, Pia, we do to keep each other safe. We take care of each other. You're safe."

She said it with such sincerity and poise, I wanted to believe her. But for some reason her words made me more anxious than before.

IV

Fortuna

i.

Here was my summer schedule:

Mondays, Wednesdays, and Fridays, I was supposed to drive in to the bakery with Betta and Giovani. At 8:30 I had to leave and walk a few blocks to Fortuna; I couldn't take the car, since Betta only had Tuesday-Thursday courses.

At 9:00, I had Biology in an auditorium. At 10:30, I walked across campus to the liberal arts building, where I took Greek History. I had a short break when I planned to scarf lunch, before the dreaded Calculus at noon. After that, I had Chemistry back in the biology auditorium. Then I would either walk back to the bakery, or someone would pick me up, or I supposed I could take a cab or something, but I really wasn't comfortable with having a stranger drive me—probably something I should get over, living in New York.

One time, when I mentioned this thing about the cabs to Betta, she made a face and said "Oh, we don't *do* taxis." I'd thought that was a bit pretentious, as if the Di Natales with their billion BMWs and Massimo's flat in the Financial District were simply too good for public transportation. They didn't do cabs and they generally didn't take the subway when alone.

Later, I'd come to realize she'd meant something else entirely. Something like *"we don't trust taxis"*.

This family didn't trust many people.

Someone they did trust was a guy named Oscar. Monday morning, when I arrived at the bakery with Betta and Giovani, there was a long-legged guy with ratty brown hair and a ratty green jacket lounging in a seat by the window, reading the newspaper and drinking a coffee from the place across the street. He didn't budge all morning, though he did switch to a Consumer Reports magazine on Tuesday, and on Wednesday I saw him eat a croissant.

This was Oscar. I didn't know his last name till much later on, everyone just referred to him as *Oscar* or *that guy*. Dora was slightly fascinated by him, but Betta and Giovani ignored him for the most part, and Oscar ignored us right back. Every now and then Savino or Marco Biasi would speak with him, but other than that he simply sat by the window and read.

"What's he doing here?" I asked, that first Monday.

We weren't even open yet; Betta and I were filling the pastry case with cannoli and fresh *zeppole*, sliced focaccia topped with whole green olives, ricotta-stuffed *sfogliatelle*. The bakery didn't open for another twenty minutes, but already Oscar was immersed in his paper, his booted feet propped on the opposite chair at the little circular table.

"Nothing, really," Betta murmured. "He's just security, I guess."

"The bakery has security?"

"Sometimes."

From 7:00 to 8:00, Savino had me working on focaccia and cannoli. For the last thirty minutes, he had Betta walk me through restocking ingredients in the pantry. Then I took off my apron, dusted off as much flour as I could from my shirt, shouldered my backpack, and got ready to leave.

Savino looked up when I walked up front. "Class?"

"Yeah."

He eyed my wrist braces. Wiped olive oil off his hands, onto a threadbare kitchen towel. He wore a black bandana around his head, though his hair was short enough that he probably didn't need it. This was simply how Savino did things: slightly over he top, taking every precaution. Betta told me Giovani had tried growing a goatee last year, and Savino had forced him to wear a hairnet over his chin, which had prematurely aborted the experiment.

He nodded at the front window. "Oscar will walk with you."

I looked at Oscar, at his grungy boots and ratty green coat and stylish sunglasses propped in his hair.

I didn't like the idea of wandering unfamiliar streets on my own while I tried to find the best route to school—for days I'd been haunted by anxiety over that short walk. But now I weighed that against the discomfort of having to interact with Oscar, Savino's one-man Bakery Security Team, and I wasn't so sure.

Savino was still looking at me, and it took me a second. It took me a moment of comparing the two options before I realized that it hadn't been a suggestion, or even an offer. My uncle was simply stating the way it was going to be. I could have fought it, probably—I didn't like being told what to do—but it came down to this: I didn't know the Vitellis well enough to take advantage of their hospitality and simultaneously challenge their house rules.

So I walked to school with Oscar.

When I rounded the counter, he raised himself from his seat, tucked the folded newspaper into his back waistband, and zipped his jacket to his chin. He opened the door for me and threw back a salute to Savino and Dora.

I shouldered my backpack. I always felt short, but walking with Oscar made me feel shorter. "You work for Savino?"

"Don't we all?" We reached the end of the block and he hit the crosswalk signal, then stood on the curb with his hands in his pockets. "Actually, I'm a student. I'm at NYU for computer tech, but I take night classes so I can help Savino during the day."

"Help him how?"

"Errands and stuff. Sometimes I help out with Johnny. Drive the trucks." He flipped his sunglasses down and pushed back his hair. There was a lot of it, curly to his shoulders, streaked brown and gold, and he didn't look much like anyone else I'd met since moving up here. He looked like he was into a lot of indie music, maybe hiking and essential oils.

"Are we related?"

"Nah. Nah, my dad's friends with Savino and Ida. My dad goes way back with Savino and the Moriondos."

"Who?"

"You know, Johnny Moriondo. He's got the trucking business in Queens. And you're a Vitelli, right?"

"No. Marzano. Savino's my uncle."

"Oh, you look like him."

"That's what I've heard."

I asked him about computer tech, and he confirmed that he'd already gotten several job offers for when he graduated in the spring. He said coding was like learning another language, but he'd been practicing for a long time and he was nearly fluent—he didn't sound pretentious about it, just factual. He also said you really had to have a *thing* for computers; it was like engineering in the way that you had to possess that nameless attribute, that sort of passion for the field, or else it wouldn't click and you might end up terrifically unhappy.

I didn't know how much of that I believed. I'd seen unhappy engineers who were good at their jobs, I'd seen useless IT people with decent jobs. Sabine was insistent that I follow my dreams, but whatever hazy ideas about my future I might have entertained before the spring seemed ridiculous now.

Oscar left me at the school entrance, with a salute and a "seeya". He ambled off back to the bakery.

So began my first day at Fortuna Community College.

ii.

On my way to class, I managed to run by the bookstore and pick up my textbooks. Greek History in particular called for several course texts that I probably could have found in the back of a thrift store, stuff like *The Iliad, More Plays by Sophocles,* Thucydides *'History of The Peloponnesian War,* and *Mycenaean Tholoi: A Complete History.* Every one of these books was rented from the campus bookstore, and every single one of them looked like it had been used to sand down a table at some point in its life.

This class also apparently required advanced writing. I wasn't so sure about that; I had barely scraped by in high school English. It was like my note-taking thing: sitting down and focusing long enough to organize everything right was too much of a challenge for my brain to handle. Every now and then I'd get close to the proper balance of zoomed-in focus and a wider view of the project, then my brain would say *Hey! Here's some other stuff to think about!* And I'd lose the moment.

The liberal arts building was built like a book on a shelf, real narrow and tall. It towered over most of the other buildings on campus, but it also had several levels of basement that were not immediately apparent. What looked like the first floor was not, in fact, at ground-level; you had to walk up a flight of stairs to get into the building in the first place. To make matters worse, the room numbers were all messed up, with random letters thrown into the mix to further complicate the layout.

Greek History was in room 5B. That, to me, said *basement.*

So I took the stairs down to the basement, found the fifth room, and entered.

It was a narrow classroom, only four desks wide. The ceiling was low, the lights flickered, and the projector pulled down over the whiteboard had marker graffiti. It was a claustrophobic, highly-uncomfortable place. A lone figure occupied a seat in the front row—a blond head bowed low over the desk. And when I let the door click shut behind me, and I made my way to the front of the room, I found that she was bent almost double with her face inches away from a wide-open book, reading unblinkingly, apparently oblivious of my presence.

I checked the clock. Ten minutes till class.

I dropped my backpack beside a desk in the second row. "Excuse me."

The girl started. She straightened, blinked a couple times at me, and arched her eyebrows in surprise. "What? Sorry, what's that?" There were flowers in her curly bobbed hair—a combination of dandelions and clover, most of them wilted.

"Are you here for Greek History?" I asked.

"Yes! I am. Are you?"

"Yeah. Should people be here already?"

"Are we not people?" She slapped her book shut. "Yes, they probably should. How much time have we got?" Dandelion petals had come loose and were caught in her hair. There was something familiar about her face, though I couldn't quite place it—heart-shaped, soft and pale, with distracted blue eyes.

I craned around to find the clock. "Six minutes."

She nodded, but didn't seem too concerned. "That is strange, isn't it? Huh. Maybe he rescheduled, did he send an email?"

"I don't know."

"I'll check." She dug in her satchel and fished out a phone.

I leaned back in my seat and stared at the projector. Someone had written *EBOLA*, all capital letters, in permanent marker.

"No," she said. "No email, I dunno. Weird, huh? Like the beginning of a horror movie, right?"

I looked up at the flickering lights, barked a nervous laugh. "Yeah."

"Is he always like this, I wonder? Who's the teacher—Harlock? Have you had him before?"

"No. This is my first semester here."

"Oh, are you a freshman?"

I shrugged, fiddled with my braces. It was too complicated to explain fully. "A rising junior, I think. I went to school in Georgia, but I only just moved here last week."

"Oh, that's fun! How do you like it?" She tilted her head and narrowed her eyes like she was genuinely interested.

I suddenly realized why she seemed familiar. "Were you in *Macbeth* last night?" I asked.

She grinned, tossed her hair. "Indeed, I *am* Macbeth! The Lady. Although I've enjoyed spreading rumors that the play is actually named after Lady Macbeth after all, which suggests that we should refer to that impossible Scot as something like Mr. Macbeth."

"Yes. That seems like the sort of thing Shakespeare would have done." As if I knew anything about Shakespeare.

"What's your name?"

"Pia."

"I'm Lorel. I like your medals."

All fifty of them. "I like your medals" was code for "I am Catholic and I am acknowledging that you too are Catholic". I appreciated it.

"Thanks. It was a great performance, the other night. I don't know much about theater, but I thought you did great."

"Thank you *very* much." She crossed her legs and faced me at her desk. "It's something of a dream role of mine. It's rare, in classic plays, to find such an active female character like Lady Macbeth. It reminds me of Clytemnestra almost, from the *Agamemnon*. She stands there with blood on her hands and no remorse in her eyes—it's powerful stuff, it sticks with you, and it is *so fun* to perform."

"Are you studying to be an actress?"

"Oh, no, I'm studying English. Because, you know," she waved a hand, "that's a *lot* more useful. My dad hates it, my sister says I'm gonna end up working at Starbucks. How long till class starts?"

I checked. "It's time." I tapped the desk. Then I slipped the purple notebook into my backpack and got to my feet, slowly. "I feel like we're in the wrong spot."

"This is a confusing building," Lorel admitted. She stood too, with the satchel over her shoulder and the book under her arm. She wore a white wrinkled blouse tucked into a green skirt, and oxfords. It was exactly the sort of outfit I'd expect an actress/English major to wear, including the wilted flower crown.

"Are we supposed to be in the basement?" I asked.

"Oh." Her eyebrows shot up. "Are we in the basement? I thought this was the ground floor."

"I guess it is, technically. I don't know, I thought that was what the *B* in 5B stood for."

"Is it 5B? I thought it was 105B."

The lights flickered again. *EBOLA* glared at us menacingly from the front of the room. She was right about the horror movie thing. "No, it's 5B."

"Oh, well, that makes sense then. We *are* in the wrong room." She shrugged the satchel higher on her shoulder. "We need to be on the fifth floor, second room."

"Shit," I said.

We ran for the stairs.

iii.

AJ Harlock was curiously self-important for a man who taught Greek History. He was balding, straight out of his doctorate program, and incredibly severe about the reading list for his course. As if anyone at Fortuna was going to be the next great Greek scholar. Or the next great anything.

Lorel was fascinated. Later, she'd explain that the teachers at Fortuna were wonderful character studies, and Harlock was a glowing example. While I scowled at our teacher and wondered how easily I could switch classes, she made clean bracketed notes in the margins of her textbook: *constantly straightens his tie and shirt cuffs; paces back and forth at an uncomfortably aggressive speed.*

We ate lunch in the green outside the liberal arts building. That was Lorel's last class for the day, but she said she liked hanging around campus because it gave her wonderful studying inspiration. That led into a rant about the poor state of the library, which segued into a lengthy discussion about books. I'd always thought I was quite the reader, but Lorel made my reading list look pitiful; we were both fans of Tolkien and Dickens, but she'd read an overwhelming number of classics that I simply did not have the courage to attempt.

70

Lunch concluded with me rushing off to Calculus, and her declaring that we should form a two-person book club—highly exclusive, of course, and she'd provide a long list we could choose from.

I hadn't had many friends back home. There were the kids at school, and then there was me, who scraped by with mediocre grades and homework crammed at the end of the workday. I didn't participate in school events. I worked early in the morning, I made time for a few hours of learning amongst strangers, then I went home and helped coach Vince's soccer team. I wasn't a particularly lonely person, but I was used to being alone. Maybe I was just too busy to be lonesome, just like I was procrastinating mourning and thinking about death. Just like I was too busy to figure out what the hell was wrong with my family.

But I liked Lorel. She was easy to be around. Over the next few weeks we learned each other's schedules and met up between classes and my shifts at the bakery. We worked on Greek History readings and homework. We spent an inordinate amount of time discussing the weather—arguments, really, with me complaining about the heat and her romanticizing the idea of summer and the "scent of baking tarmac". We did not, after all, have time for an exclusive book club, between my own class schedule and her habit of putting off assignments till the last minute.

Lorel somehow got the idea that I was an intimidating person. Or, as she put it: "You look like you won't take shit from anyone." I was fairly certain that she was the only person who found me remotely tough, but she used this to her advantage and forced me to help her get into the Fine Arts Library, which was unofficially only open to grad students. This feat involved walking past the front desk without cowering.

Massimo was a puzzle. Whenever I thought I had him figured out—tied to the apron strings, helping chauffeur his daddy's friends around town, level-headed Columbia alumnus—he'd lower another shield and I'd have to do a double-take.

He joked about arson a lot. We'd have a normal conversation about weekend plans, and he'd suggest we burn something down, sandwiched between soccer in the park and a stop to get hoagies. I'd ask him about some chemistry concept I was struggling with, and he'd wind up giving me one of the three theoretical formulas for Greek fire.

He had a really dark sense of humor. He was, to some extent, the calm and collected boy I'd first met, but he wasn't perfect—I'd realized there was a certain facade about him, and I caught it slipping on more than one occasion.

Case in point.

Every now and then, Betta would join me and Lorel on campus. She would sit nearby while we studied and regale us with tales of woe surrounding her "Creating Experiences" course, the stupid Powerpoints she'd had to piece together detailing her experiences of the week, etcetera. I didn't mind it. In fact, I liked that Betta sought me out, as if she actually preferred my company.

71

Lorel found her fascinating. "She's so intense. Every emotion is so dramatic, it's like stage acting. Is she always like this?"

"Pretty much."

One Tuesday, Betta joined us for lunch on the green. Lorel had a lengthy paper for her English course due the next night, only she really didn't feel comfortable with the final result—despite having read it to me twice—but she was on the fence about going to the tutoring lab because…well, it was Lorel.

Betta looked up at me between bites of her sandwich. "Didn't you tell her about Tonio?"

I almost choked. "Of course not."

There was a mischievous look in her eye." Oh, come on, he isn't all that bad."

Lorel leaned forward, intrigued. "Who is *Tonio*?"

"He's our Aunt Ida's brother," said Betta. "He works in the tutoring lab here, but he lives with my brother. Pia, have her talk to Tonio—he'll help, he's *family*."

"I know he's family. He's also a pretentious prick."

"Oh, he'll be civil." Betta said this with all the confidence in the world. I was becoming increasingly sure that she secretly idolized Tonio Salone.

Lorel was in the middle of a clover chain—it draped around her shoulders and pooled in her lap. "I must meet Tonio," she announced.

"You'll eat those words," I warned her.

But Betta went ahead and texted Massimo, letting him know we'd swing by after school. She had to get to soccer practice—she played with a city league—but she gave Lorel the address.

I had chem lab, then Christian Ethics at 3:00. After my last class I met Lorel out by the parking lot—she was still wearing the clover chain wrapped around her hair—and we took her car down to the Financial District, against my better judgement.

Here was the thing: I'd thought before how weird it was that Massimo and Tonio had their own apartment—a kid working for his dad, an English tutor, having a flat in *New York City?* They were probably dealing with student loans on top of everything else. But it was worse than I'd thought. The apartment was enormous, and shaped a bit like the liberal arts building—tall and narrow and solid brick. There was a coffee shop downstairs. I repeat: the lobby of the apartment building was furnished with a *personal coffee shop*. That was the first big red flag for the shock awaiting me upstairs. Their apartment was on the top floor. In fact, the entire top floor was their apartment.

Tonio had known we were coming, but he still answered the door in flannel pajamas and a bathrobe. He had a scotch glass in one hand and a cigarette in the other. It was 4:00 PM.

"Hi," I said. I stared hard at his cigarette—I hadn't smoked in days, and this was the first real threat to my fast.

"Oh, hey, *Marzano*. Greetings and salutations." He waved his glass at Lorel. "Damsel in distress?"

"Only mildly distressed," Lorel returned. For a moment, I was impressed by how well she was taking the fact that Tonio was Tonio and he was horrible. Then I remembered that this was Lorel—of course she thought this was some sort of character study.

Tonio opened the door to let us in.

I looked around and said, "Oh."

It was big. Really quite big. It had that sort of open, ugly, modern architecture so common to new apartments, only it had been decorated with tapestries and antique furniture. Like a library. It felt like stepping into another world, or at least another time—some time with tobacco-smell and candle smoke, with dark woven rugs on the walls and soft light filtering through the floor-to-ceiling window and spilling dust motes across the living space.

"Is this for Adriana Corkey's English class?" Tonio wandered across the living room and kicked back in an unreasonably large armchair. Despite his dusty bathrobe, his hair was neatly slicked back and perfect as always. He lazily put out his cigarette in an ashtray. "Corkey always makes the kids do this insipid analysis on Frost's *The Road Not Taken*, and if I have to power through one more juvenile theory, I might kill myself." He swirled his scotch.

Lorel was absolutely delighted. "Is that so?"

He raised his razor eyebrows. "Yes. It is." His eyes swept over Lorel, taking her in, his gaze amused—and, by the time it reached me, patronizing. He tossed back the rest of his scotch. "So is it? Corkey?"

"Chester, actually," she said. "We're breaking down parallels between *Frankenstein* and Shelley's own life. Bonus points if you include a commentary on how the patriarchy has suppressed and influenced female voices."

Tonio's eyes brightened. "Well, that's comparatively refreshing. Let's see it then."

Lorel plopped herself down on the sofa and dug around in her satchel.

I stood on the threshold. Tonio's second-hand smoke was getting to me—I shifted on my feet, supremely uncomfortable. "Is Massimo around?"

He pointed with his glass. "He's doing nerd things in the breakfast nook."

I wandered off in that direction, around the corner, through an unnecessarily spacious kitchen—*butcher-block counters, a gas stove, an enormous kitchen island perfect for rolling out tons and tons of pastry*. I had kitchen envy for Tonio's bachelor pad.

I found Massimo in a space between kitchen and hallway. A semi-circle of windows shed light on a mess of papers scattered across the scratched tabletop. Massimo was slumped back in a chair, a large coffee mug in one hand and a dry-erase board in the other. He was frowning at the board, but he looked up when I came in.

73

"Hi." He quickly set his mug aside.

I paused in the doorway. His hair was unkempt and his eyes were red, and I felt like I'd walked in on something. "Everything alright?"

"Sure." He rubbed his temple and slid the dry-erase board onto the table. "I...forgot you were coming, sorry. Betta said something about you bringing a friend by. What's going on?"

An excellent question. "Lorel needs English tutoring. She's scared of the tutoring lab, but apparently not of Tonio." I shouldered my backpack. "Are you busy? I don't want to interrupt you if you're in the middle of something—"

"No, I'm just messing around." The dry-erase board was covered in his narrow, slanting handwriting—formulas, molecular geometry, fragments underlined in red. *Messing around?* "What do you need?"

"Do you know anything about electrochemistry?"

Massimo stood carefully. "I know many things about electrochemistry." He faltered for a moment, caught his balance on the edge of the table.

"Are you sure you're alright?"

"Of course." To prove it, he walked past me into the kitchen. I followed him. "You want coffee? Or tea?"

"What are *you* drinking?"

"Uh." He paused, looked over my shoulder at the breakfast nook and his coffee mug resting on the table. "Uh, sambuca. Want some?"

My eyebrows shot up. "I'm nineteen."

"We don't care."

"Massimo. It's four o'clock, you know that, right?"

"I know." He rubbed his eyes. "Sorry. Tea?"

"Coffee."

"Have you seen Savino today?" he asked, as he pulled milk from the fridge.

As a matter of fact, I hadn't. Dora had said he'd come in extra early to the bakery, just to get things started, but he'd been gone by the time everyone else arrived. Betta told me that happened sometimes, and he'd come in later to close up. No explanations. It just *happened*.

I repeated this to Massimo. "Why do you ask?"

"Did you see him last night?"

"No." I'd helped Ida put the kids to bed, and retired early. Savino hadn't been at dinner—Ida had said something about him meeting with Marco or Raul or someone. "Just business things" is what she'd called it.

"We were out," said Massimo. "Last night."

I slid onto one of the bar stools against the kitchen island. Across the counter, Massimo carefully leveled out three scoops of coffee grounds. He slapped the coffee maker lid shut and pulled a mug down from the cabinet above the stove. The cabinets were navy blue. I loved that. I'd always loved the idea of blue cabinets in a spacious kitchen, full of natural light and herbs on the windowsill.

"*Who* went out last night?" I asked. "Just you and Savino?"

"The Salone brothers," he said, his back to me. "My dad and Uncle Mo. Tony Malone, Savino's cousin Stefano. Oscar and Johnny and the guys."

Of course. A full entourage. "How come?"

He watched the coffee drip into the pot. "Family business."

A shiver ran up my spine. "And what did you do?" Because he looked like shit. I could easily picture Tonio drinking this early in the day as a habit, but Massimo?

He topped off the mug with milk and set it in front of me. "Business. What's your grievance with electrochemistry?"

And just like that, the discussion had moved on. I knew by the look on Massimo's face that no matter how hard I pressed, it wouldn't come back around.

iv.

June crept into July. There were fireworks, but the Vitellis didn't celebrate the Fourth—they'd all come over from Sicily recently enough that American holidays didn't mean much.

July crept into August. The summer heat dulled. Whenever I wasn't in the bakery, I was studying like mad, getting ready for finals. AJ Harlock had assigned a real whopper of a research paper, chem lab required a titration practical, ethics had a presentation, and both calculus and chemistry lecture were notorious for killer final exams.

Every chance I got, I hunted down Massimo to help with chemistry. Lorel and I poured over Greek History—we traded off reading aloud from the textbooks we were supposed to have studied all summer, and we slaved over that research paper. Every now and then Tonio would wander past us on campus, and Lorel would enlist him into some off-duty English tutor work, much to my distress. She still refused to go into the tutoring lab, but she stood by the fact that Tonio was an upstanding and immensely interesting asset.

I talked to Sabine and the kids. I'd thought for a while that my aunt was simply hard-headed and unwilling to dish up about her family, but it became increasingly apparent that Sabine didn't actually know any more than I did. She was strangely egocentric for a person who'd uprooted her life out west to live in a dumpster house and take care of her niece and nephews; as far as she was concerned, her life was the most riveting story, and that plot didn't have a backstory including her family and early life. The story probably picked up sometime in college, with the cult she refused to talk about.

"Was there Kool-Aid involved?" I'd pressed. "Hoop skirts? Did someone blackmail you?"

"Oh, it was a phase, I was finding myself," came the cool, dismissive response.

Sabine's life was a chapter-book about her and her scandals. She'd been oblivious to anything odd about her childhood, and she simply hadn't cared enough to look into her family's business once she got old enough to notice anything strange.

It was incredibly frustrating. Even more concerning was the idea that my siblings were getting on with their lives in my absence; a week would go by between phone calls, and when next I heard from one of the kids, something had changed that I wasn't aware of.

"Carlo started gymnastics," said Cristine, one Sunday after Mass. I could tell she was distracted, either browsing online or drawing.

"What, really? When? How?" I was sitting on my windowsill, chewing the end of a cigarette.

"He asked, he's been asking for years, Sabine signed him up at the place downtown by the park. The warehouse place with the chalk sidewalks. He's got a lot of bruises, but I think he likes it. He won't shut up about it."

I hung one leg out the window. My back teeth ground together. "*How?*"

"What do you mean, how? Sabine drops him off and runs errands, that's how."

I was silent for a beat. I knew that if I pursued this I wouldn't be satisfied with the answer. But I needed to know. "Cristine, we don't have that kind of money. He's wanted gymnastics for years, but Papa said we didn't have the money. Mamma and Papa are gone—"

"I know they're gone." Her voice was hard.

I wished she'd cry or something—I'd never wished for an encounter with dramatic human emotion, but at least I'd know how to deal with tears better than I dealt with bottled-up emotions.

"I know," I said. "Look…is Sabine paying for gymnastics?"

"I don't know. Why?"

What were we but charity cases, at this point? I worked for family, lived with family, got rides from Lorel and Betta and Massimo because I didn't have a car. Sabine looked after the kids and apparently ran errands. Why did it matter so much if she paid for gymnastics lessons that got Carlo's mind off death and Brussel sprouts?

"Oh." Cristine didn't wait for a response to her last question. "I forgot to tell you. We've been getting your mail."

"I get *mail*?"

"Checks and stuff. Sabine deals with it."

I stopped chewing my cigarette. Kicked my leg against the outside of the building. "Who's it from?"

"*Il forno.* That means bakery, right? Or *panificio.*"

"Yeah." I leaned my head back against the window frame. "Why are you getting checks from the bakery?"

"I don't know. Ask Sabine. I'm just telling you."

I did ask Sabine. Her response was less than satisfactory.

"Oh, you know, Pia, it's just part of your salary is all. You're working at the bakery with Savino, yes?"

"Yes." I only needed money for textbooks and the bit of coursework my scholarship didn't cover. I'd been planning to send my paycheck to the kids, anyway, but Savino hadn't asked me about splitting it up. "How much are they made out for?" I'd discarded my unlit cigarette by now, so I chewed my lip.

"Sure, sure, let me find it. Are you alright, Pia, are you okay, *cara*? Hey, did Savino get you a flight back for the end of the month? The kids are excited, I'll clean out your room, you can show us all the fancy stuff you've been learning at the *panificio.*"

"I have a flight."

"Oh, I found it, here." She rattled off an astounding number.

"Oh."

I thought about it. I gnawed my lip and clenched and unclenched my jaw. I'd gotten deposits in my bank account since I started working at the beginning of the summer, deposits that didn't match up to the hours I'd been working. Those numbers, plus the numbers Sabine repeated in my ear at my request, added up to something uncomfortably substantial.

I was okay with Sabine helping with the kids—I was more than okay, I was *grateful.* But the Vitellis giving away money like we didn't have a cent to our name sparked something in me.

I asked Betta how much she was paid. Betta was the sort of person who didn't take issue with that sort of question—she was blunt most of the time anyway, I think she appreciated people being straight with her.

She told me. It didn't add up. Savino was definitely throwing money at the Marzanos.

So I talked to him about it. It was, strangely enough, the boldest thing I'd ever done, and it scared the hell out of me. But I did it all the same. I cornered him in the back of the bakery one morning before opening, except when you spoke to Savino on his own turf, it felt a lot more like he was cornering *you.*

"I talked to Sabine."

He nodded. He had his hands deep in *levain*. I had my hands deep in lard for the *sfogliatelle.* "What scandals has she been up to?"

I didn't laugh. I didn't think he'd meant it as a joke, anyway. "She said she's getting checks in the mail. Stuff addressed to me. From the bakery. Do you know anything about it?"

He glanced at me. Somehow, seriousness clung to him like a personality. It wasn't a mood; he could be casual and at-ease while fixing you with a stare that said he was thinking more deeply about this thing than you ever could. I wondered if he knew he was doing it.

"Some of it's me," he said. "Some of it's Marco Vitelli."

I thought I'd misheard him. "Marco?"

"Marco Vitelli, our dad."

My grandfather. "Why? Where is he?"

"New Orleans. Some of it's me, some of it's him. Some of it's the Marzanos."

I stopped with the lard. The filo was something that needed to be done quickly or it would melt, but I'd forgotten it for the moment. "The Marzanos. Where are *they*?"

The silence stretched. Savino dipped his hands in a dish of water and scraped the leaven into the bowl of a stand-mixer. "Your filo, Pia."

Frustrated, I slapped on a layer of lard and rolled the layers into a sausage shape. I dragged the cling film over and wrapped the dough, winding the plastic at the ends to make it tight. Then I set it aside. "Where are the Marzanos?"

"Sicily."

And they were sending us money from *overseas?* I didn't know what to say. We were charity cases, but I didn't want handouts from grandparents I'd never met. Maybe I did need the rest of the family—even I could admit that, at this point, we'd drown without Sabine and Savino. I was dependent on these people, dependent on whatever they did at night with "Oscar and Johnny and the guys", dependent on that gun kept in the front counter, dependent on Massimo in his Lexus and whatever Ida and Savino whispered about in the middle of a Shakespeare production.

Lorel was moving out at the end of the summer, to an apartment in Manhattan.

"I need space," she told me. "Space to breathe. I've been living with my aunt, but I need a space of my own so I can grow like a goldfish in a bigger bowl."

Lorel didn't talk about her family often. All I knew was that she didn't have the best relationship with her parents. She had a sister named Sara who she barely spoke to, and a few other siblings I figured were younger; she talked about them like they were still tied to the apron strings while she attempted to cut herself loose. And Lorel wasn't a particularly bold person, so moving out was a big step for her.

She made me do some apartment tours with her—she was worried the real estate people would pressure her—and she finally settled on a modest two-bedroom place a few blocks from Fortuna. It didn't have a view, and it may have had black mold in the corners, but she said it was perfectly within her budget. Her budget came from scholarships. Lorel had enough scholarships that she didn't need a job—she was virtually being *paid* to go to school, a position I envied but could never hope to obtain in my wildest dreams. She was brilliant and studious. I was decidedly *not*.

"It's a two-bedroom," she said, meaningfully, as she browsed fun curtain designs on IKEA's website. "You know what that means."

I sat beside her in the back of the library, watching her scroll through page after page of patterned drapes on her laptop. I needed to finish my calculus study guide for the final, but it made me want to cry. And I needed to finish my chemistry study guide as well, but I needed to talk to Massimo about salt hydrolysis shit and I hadn't found the time. And I kept wanting to cry over that, as well.

I didn't wear stress well.

"I don't know," I said. I pointed at some blue butterfly curtains. "Those are nice."

She clicked on them. They were on sale. "The other bedroom is yours."

I paused. "What?" It set my teeth on edge. Not charity again, not from *Lorel*—she was one of the only people who didn't treat me like a delicate, pitiful orphan, even though she knew about my parents and my siblings and all about this past spring.

"It's cheap," she said. "It's close to campus, you wouldn't have to get rides from Betta, we could study together all the time." Her fingers hovered over the keyboard—she didn't look at me. "Unless…you don't want to move in with me. I'd understand. We've only just met."

"I do." I sat up straight. "I'd pay for my room," I hedged.

"Oh, yeah, sure. We'd split utilities and stuff, I could even get you a car key."

Move out of the Vitelli house? Not that it was stifling there, just that…it was a bit stifling. Everyone was watching my every move in Fort Greene, and at the bakery, and on the walk to Fortuna and everywhere else. This would cut down on that. This would get me one step towards *independent*. And I certainly had the money.

I hesitated a moment, the words, "I'll ask Savino," on the tip of my tongue. I swallowed them.

I didn't need to ask Savino. I'd be twenty in December: I was an adult. I'd worked for some of this money, at least, and I didn't have to ask my uncle or even Sabine before I spent it. "Alright."

"Really?" Lorel's face lit up. She had dandelions in her hair, the last dandelions we'd managed to find on the campus green.

"Yeah, really. Yes. Let's do this."

So she ordered two sets of curtains—one with blue butterflies, the other with gray sparrows flitting across white canvas.

79

I'd miss the blue sparrow window in my upstairs bedroom. But I was getting my own window, something with less stained glass and a lot more *Made in China*. I was fine with that.

v.

Massimo got me through my finals. Not that I cheated or even *needed* to cheat in order to pass the semester, it was just that he explained things better than any of my teachers.

Right after I got out of my Calculus final, Lorel picked me up and we signed off on the apartment. We celebrated with buying real flower bouquets from outside a corner store, and making fabulous flower crowns on the green outside the liberal arts building. We turned in our research essays, after Lorel said a complicated prayer/spell over them. I did my ethics presentation, then I walked back to the bakery and told Savino about the apartment.

Yes, I know. I did the entire thing behind his back. It was less of a gutsy move, though, and more inspired by fear because I didn't want to confront him and Ida about it until the thing was finalized.

I started off with what was probably a really poor intro. "I did something."

Dora looked up from the register, face guarded. Behind her, Savino turned slowly, a piping bag in a half-filled cannoli shell.

I ripped off the bandaid. "I got an apartment. With a friend."

"Ooh." Dora seemed impressed. "Exciting."

Savino turned back to the cannoli counter. He finished what he was doing and wiped off his hands, tossed the towel over his shoulder. Then he leaned back against the counter, crossed his arms, and looked at me long and hard.

The bakery was in the middle of closing for the day. I'd only stopped by to tell him, before Betta and Giovani and I drove back to Brooklyn. The Di Natales were cleaning up in the back. Dora was finishing with the register, counting up tips. I stood on the wrong side of the pastry case, the side for customers; it felt weird, like a wall between me and my family.

By the window, Oscar had looked up from his book—clearly this was the most exciting development in his day. I shifted my backpack straps. I couldn't tell whether Savino's expression was disappointed or suspicious. Furious or thoughtful. He had a confusing face.

"Who?" he said.

"My friend Lorel, from school. She was in that *Macbeth* performance, at the beginning of the summer. Lady Macbeth. Remember?" I didn't know why I was spilling so much information.

Dora nodded. Savino just watched me.

Betta ducked out of the kitchen. "Pia, we're heading out. Car's in the back."

Savino held up a hand. "Pia's riding with me."

For some reason, I thought he might drive us to a graveyard or an abandoned dock. Somewhere he'd make a point, maybe tell me about all the family members who'd died because they'd moved into apartments in Manhattan with their college friends. Or maybe he'd tell me what was going on. Or maybe he'd stick my feet in wet concrete and tip me into the Hudson.

It turned out, he really did just want to drive me back to Brooklyn. Savino didn't speak as he locked up the bakery, or even as he climbed into the BMW and navigated out of the Little Italy district. We were nearly to the Brooklyn Bridge when he finally spoke.

"Did we do something to you, Pia?"

It wasn't a guilt-trip. He was genuinely curious. "No. No, you guys have been wonderful. I just..."

"Did *someone* do something to you?"

That irritated me for some reason. "No." Did I really need to justify to him why I, a nineteen-year-old young woman, had decided to move out with a friend?

He stopped at a light and looked over at me. "If someone does something, I want to know."

"Okay." I didn't like the way he said that. There was something distinctly threatening about it—not to me, but to that *someone*. I stared straight ahead. "I'm fine. I appreciate everything you've done, but I need a bit of...independence, I guess."

"You don't strike me as a Sabine type."

It was an odd thing to say, given that everyone I met rather aggressively compared me to *him* at every given opportunity.

"I'm not," I said. It was easier to talk to him while the car was moving, when he wasn't looking at me and I fixed my gaze at some distant point. "Sabine didn't leave because she wanted to distance herself, she doesn't care about independence. She didn't come back because she just *doesn't care*." I wondered, if we'd grown up amongst family in Brooklyn, if we'd ever have known her. Because this place, these people—it was backstory to Sabine's dramatic life, and she'd done a marvelous job forgetting about it.

I glanced at Savino. A smile twitched at the corners of his lips. "You're not wrong."

"It's nothing about you or Ida or the kids. If you hadn't helped, I don't know..." I didn't know where I'd be if I hadn't come to Brooklyn—mentally or emotionally *or* physically.

"How's security?"

"What?"

81

"The apartment's security. Where is it?"

I hadn't thought about it much. I probably should have, considering my impression of NYC so far. "It's near the school. Clinton, I think. I don't know about security, but it's an upstairs apartment. It's got a fire escape."

"Hmm." That wasn't what he wanted to hear. "I have some guys who can put locks on the windows. An alarm system."

The logical part of me was grateful. I was learning to distinguish *help* from *charity*. "That would be great."

My flight to Atlanta was booked for the next night. I would only be gone a couple of weeks, but I met up with Lorel one last time before summer break. The thing about hanging out with Lorel was that I could pretend, for however brief a period, that I was someone else entirely: I was the sort of person who made flower crowns and debated classic literature. I had a separate life from the Vitellis, a life on campus where all I had to be was Pia—not *Marzano*, not *Savino's niece*, just a student with normal student responsibilities.

"The curtains came in the mail," Lorel told me, as we wandered down a tree-shaded path in Central Park.

"Are they fabulous?"

"They *are* fabulous," she said. "I'm going to start moving my things, next week. Do you have any boxes you'd like me to keep for you?"

"I don't really have much." I kicked some dead leaves off the path.

"Hey," she said. "The theater department is doing *Wicked* this fall." Because, on top of everything else, of course Lorel could sing and dance as well as act. "I'm going to audition, first week back."

"That's fun," I said. "For who?"

"A starring role—aim high, right? But I'm trying to pick. Elphaba, Galinda…. I think I'm more of a Galinda, but I've got to think about it. Do you know who reminds me of Fiyero, is Massimo. Not Fiyero when you first meet him, with the parties and stuff, but later on. Scarecrow Fiyero. Just…very calm and collected, but I bet he could cut loose."

I thought about Massimo buzzed at four in the afternoon. "Maybe he could."

We walked for a bit. I mulled over the fall, about how I needed to iron out my schedule and make sure I wasn't overloading myself, because I really needed to keep my scholarship. And I was taking Organic Chemistry in the fall, which was going to be a nightmare.

A few minutes passed. "So what's his deal?" said Lorel. "What's his…thing."

I raised my head. The mid-day sun shone down through the trees and turned her hair vibrant gold. "Who? Massimo?"

"Mmhm." She looked straight ahead, rigidly casual, trying hard to look like she wasn't trying hard to act natural. For such a wonderful actress, she was remarkably easy to see through.

It reminded me of Betta. Of Alec the drummer boy. "He's...single."

That did it. Her face tinged pink.

"Oh, Lorel." I couldn't fight back the smile. "Oh, you're in love with Massimo Di Natale." Because it was impossible for someone like Lorel to have a crush. She always dove in headfirst, arms wide, and she was undoubtedly head-over-heels in love with my cousin.

She didn't deny it. She threw herself down on a park bench instead—her floral skirt fluttered down around her. "Oh, I suppose so." She grinned at the treetops. "Goodness. Chivalrous. And he has great hair."

It occurred to me, in a flash, that I should say something. Something about getting involved with my family. She'd spent lots of time with me at Tonio's and Massimo's apartment, pouring over homework, and she'd interacted with Betta on a regular basis, but she hadn't the slightest clue that anything might be a bit *odd* about any of them, besides the obvious quirks and flaws. And I didn't know how to say it, or actually what to say, so I ended up empty of words.

I sat beside her in silence.

"You're going back to Georgia tonight," Lorel pointed out.

"Yeah."

"Ready?"

Physically, yes. I was packed, my suitcase was at the bedroom door. And I was ready to see my siblings, ready to hug my aunt. But I'd left a part of myself behind in Augusta, and I was going to have to reconcile with something when I went back. An earlier version of me. A version from last spring.

Lorel squeezed my hand. "It'll be alright. You can always call me, you know. I'll be here when you get back."

I'd said goodbye to Betta in passing, the day before at the bakery. She'd passed her summer courses with flying colors—she was a better student than she let on, with all that complaining—and she was back to a full load of coursework in the fall. Despite the loss of our morning drives to the bakery, we'd be seeing a lot of each other between work and campus and being a part of this family that apparently did everything together.

I didn't say goodbye to Giovani. I didn't think he cared. I was probably right.

An hour before we left for the airport, I was out back of the Vitelli house, in the square. There was a hush on the afternoon—an uncanny quiet before the flurry of departure and airport insanity, a window of time for sitting and overthinking. I sat on a bench under the big oak tree and I smoked my last cigarette; I'd decided to not bring any back to Augusta, but this last smoke couldn't do any harm. Maybe those two weeks on break would help me quit for good.

A figure appeared around the side of the house. I straightened—the calm was broken, an intruder had entered the bubble of quiet aloneness, but it was only Massimo and his naturally serene demeanor did little to disrupt the moment.

He was back in his khakis and a white button-down. He strode across the path that circled round the square, across the green, and sat down hard on the bench beside me.

"I didn't know you smoked."

"I don't." After a moment I added, "I'm quitting." I put out the cigarette.

He shifted, reached into his back pocket. "Here." He handed me a business card.

"What's this?"

"There's a lab at Fortuna for food science, it's attached to the chemistry department. They mostly do research, but there are some grad students who take courses there."

I turned the card over in my fingers. "Who's Grace Burnett?"

"Chem faculty, I worked with her for a while. I told her about you. She said if you applied, she might consider letting an undergrad join the lab for the fall."

My heart kicked in my chest. "Really?"

"Yeah."

"What kind of application?" I tucked the business card into my pocket. "My grades are...not the best. Not *bad*, but not impressive."

"Maybe an essay or a meeting. I don't know." He tilted back his face to the light, like he was drinking in the sun for photosynthesis reasons. Just like Lorel in the park.

"Thanks, Massimo. You didn't have to do that."

"I like to help."

I didn't bother with a segue. "What do you think of Lorel?"

He tensed up, cut his eyes at me. "Why?"

"She's great, right? I mean, she's smart and she's kind, and talented—boy, she's talented—and she looks like a fairy princess in Oxfords."

He shut his eyes and stretched his arms back behind his head.

"I mean," I hedged, "you probably haven't noticed."

"I noticed," he said, too quickly. He narrowed his eyes at me again, like he could definitely tell what I was doing.

"So talk to her," I said. I stood, my burnt-out cigarette tucked between two fingers. "She thinks you have great hair."

He frowned a bit—the sort of frown that desperately wanted to turn into a smile—and rubbed his head, which I took for his version of a blush.

"I've got to go. Seeya in a couple weeks."

"Bye, Pia. Be careful."

84

Looking back, those parting words were loaded. He could have said "take care of yourself" or "have a safe flight" or literally anything else. But he hadn't.

Be careful. It had an ominous ring to it.

Gio and Savino drove me to the airport. I wasn't sure why it required both of them, until Gio parked and Savino got out with me. He took my luggage and walked me all the way to baggage check-in, and then to security, silent and mildly intimidating in his long black overcoat. This experience played out in stark contrast to my first day in New York: I didn't have to barrel through any crowds, and no one slammed into me or ran over my feet with their suitcases—Savino cut a path through the airport without even trying.

"Tell Sabine we said hi," he said. "Tell her to call me, yeah?"

"I'll do that," I said. "Thanks again, for everything."

He nodded. He glanced over his shoulder, then over mine, his eyes distracted, as if he wanted to say something but wasn't sure if he should.

He opened his mouth. But he seemed to change his mind at the last moment, and all he said was," Be careful." Innocent enough, if it wasn't coming from someone like Savino or Massimo.

"I will."

He reached out and dragged his thumb across my forehead, quick, up and down in a cross. I didn't even blink, I was so used to it; Mamma used to do that, before we went to bed or as we were leaving the house. I still did it for the kids, but no one had done it for me since Mamma had gone. I wondered if Nicole did it. I wondered if all the Vitellis did it. I wondered what else in my life was a product of family habits—a little reminder that, even before this summer, even before I knew they existed, this family's reach had bled into my life.

Savino left. I swallowed—my throat had choked up—and I took a deep breath.

I was going home.

V

Oliveto

i.

I felt like I'd stepped back into an earlier chapter of my life.

When my family greeted me at the airport, it was in stark contrast to Gio Di Natale and his little cardboard sign—they screamed and tackled me as I left the gate; Sabine grabbed my face and planted a thousand kisses on my forehead. Vince held my hand tight and didn't let go till we'd driven all the way out of Atlanta, all the way home.

Carlo showed me his tumbling tricks on the front lawn. We went inside and ate lasagna and I tucked my suitcase into the corner of the living room. Sabine said she'd sleep on the couch; I said, nonsense, she'd been in my room for months, she might as well stay. I'd only be home a few weeks, anyway.

This sobered Vince. So we baked cookies and forgot about it.

Once the kids had gone to bed, I sat out on the back doorstep. Sabine pushed open the screen and joined me.

"They're real happy you're back, Pia, they missed you bad."

I nodded. I chewed a strand of bahiagrass, because I didn't have a cigarette. Last time we'd sat here together, Sabine had told me I'd kill my lungs if I kept smoking, then she'd sent me up to Brooklyn with her brother.

"They're real nice," I said, picking up in the middle of my train of thought. "Your family."

"Yeah, they're your family too." But it didn't really feel like that, and I think she knew it.

"What was the cult like?"

She looked at me. Her dark roots were growing back, and I noticed she was wearing less lipstick. Maybe she was trying to go more natural. Did she have eyelash extensions? "No. I'm not talking about that, no."

"Oh, come on."

"No, Pia, no. *Punto e basta.*"

I chewed the grass and looked off across the yard at the old play-set. Papa had built it. It was probably a hazard, all PVC pipes with jagged edges, a burning-hot slide made from a single sheet of rust-skinned metal. It was beautiful, but it sat abandoned like we'd forgotten how to be children. I wondered about the last time I'd gone down that slide. I wondered when Vince had last risked his life on the tire swing. Once upon a time, there had been a day that the last of us stopped playing on it. That made me sad.

"It's gonna rain tonight."

"Oh, I don't know," said Sabine, "the weather said no."

"But it is," I said. I knew this place, I knew the smell, I knew when it was going to rain around the same time the insects did. Me and the animals sat low during a storm. "What was Savino like, as a kid?"

"Oh, he's seven years younger," said Sabine. "Your mamma, she knew him better."

"I'm almost ten years older than Vince," I pointed out.

"I left when I was seventeen."

"Why?" There it was, the big question: *why?* What was so wrong with her family that she'd moved across the country, broken off connections, and never rebuilt those bridges?

She shrugged. "Nicole married young. I didn't want to. I wanted to travel and try things, I didn't want to get stuck in New York with Nic Tabone."

"Did you like Nic Tabone?"

"No, but he was Italian."

"You realize we live in the twenty-first century, right?" I smiled and nudged her with my elbow, but she didn't smile back, just raised her eyebrows. "They couldn't have forced you to marry some guy just because he's Italian, like an arranged marriage. They wouldn't have done that, they're family."

Sabine looked amused. "What, Pia, you're not gonna marry a charming Italian guy from the Bronx?"

"No," I said, staunchly, "I'm not."

"How come?"

"There are more non-Italians than Italians, the chance I'll end up with some Italian guy sometime far—*far*—in the future is real slim." I didn't like the way she was looking at me. "What?"

"How many non-Italian marriages do you see in this family, Pia?"

I thought about it—not many. Savino married a Salone, Nicole married Gio Di Natale, and even Massimo's sister Norma was married to Marco Biasi from the bakery. The more I thought about it, the more uneasy I became. I spat out the bahiagrass. "Are you saying marriages *are* arranged?"

88

"I'm saying, there's a way things are done. You don't even realize you're thinking like a Vitelli until you're at the altar in a veil, and next thing you know you've got ten *bambini* and more on the way."

I didn't like that image. At all. "That's why you got out."

"I didn't want to get stuck." She played with her hair, tucked it back into her bun, pulled out another strand and chewed it. Then she straightened and looked at me seriously. "And I didn't get stuck, I got out, I'm not gonna marry some guy my papa likes just because that's what Nicole did."

"Don't you miss them?"

She shrugged.

I picked a new blade of grass and ground it between my back teeth. I chewed on thoughts, too; Sabine and her siblings, they weren't like me and the kids—they talked big about *family* and taking care of each other, but there was something missing. If I up and left at seventeen, I'd miss the kids terribly. I'd have to come back. "So why did Mamma and Papa leave?"

"I don't know, Pia. They just left, I don't know, they didn't talk to me about it. But once they left it was nice because I could see Carla again, I didn't want to visit when she was in Brooklyn, but this made it easier. Maybe she didn't want to have twelve kids, I don't know."

I spoke around the bahiagrass. "And why do people keep saying I'm like Savino?"

Sabine looked me up and down. "Oh, I see it. You look like him and Carla, and you've got that *thing*."

"What *thing*?"

She fussed with her hair again, the stripes of blond and dark brown, and I wondered if it was a nervous thing. Was she nervous? "The humidity, oh, this humidity—it isn't like this out west." She sighed and tossed back her hair. Focused back on me. "I don't know, whatever the thing is Savino's got. I haven't seen him in forever, we rarely talk, but you both do what needs to be done, you don't think too hard about it, you just do it."

Moths populated the area around the back porch lights. Moths and beetle-like insects and probably a load of spiders, too. Spiders were smart like that. They knew where to be at the right time. They knew where the moth parties were held.

"I don't get it," I said.

Sabine patted me on the back. "That's the best I can do, *cara*."

The next day, Carlo had gymnastics in the morning. I went with Sabine and the kids. We watched him practice—he was actually alright—and then we picked up groceries and restocked the kitchen. I made *zeppole* for them. Sabine demanded cannoli, but I didn't have any molds, so she promptly ordered some online (express shipping) for the next evening. She must really have been hurting for Italian pastry.

When the boys were out of earshot, Sabine and Cristine told me the plan for that night, after the boys went to sleep. We were going to tackle Mamma and Papa's room.

Mamma and Papa's room, with its door shut tight and an invisible *no trespassing* sign plastered across the front. Holy ground. Special ground. Don't move a thing, don't breathe the air, just let it rest in peace.

We watched *The Andy Griffith Show* until Vince fell asleep. I carried him up to his and Carlo's room, and the two of them went to bed.

Someone had run through our parents 'room and done a quick clean, probably in the flurry of activity around the funeral. Maybe it had been Sabine, maybe one of Mamma's friends from the hardware store. The sheets and blankets were stripped off the bed, the laundry basket was empty. Cristine took a good look; she did a once-over, walked a circle around the perimeter, then immediately left.

I heard her footsteps on the stairs. *Fine.* If I was going to cry, I'd rather it be without Cristine present.

Sabine had cardboard boxes. We went through clothes and belongings—sweaters and pictures and jewelry, seashells from vacations, books and toiletries. I cried. My aunt pretended not to see. Some of the clothes would probably end up donated, but not now. Not for a few years, anyway; Carlo would grow into dad's stuff soon, and then so would Vince. And Cristine and I might go through Mamma's clothes at some point. But not now.

I was halfway through the closet when Sabine kissed me goodnight and went up to bed. "Close the door when you're done for the night," she said, before she left. "I don't want Vince in here."

I didn't either. *I* didn't want to be in here.

The clothes in the back of the closet were older, some of them I couldn't remember Mamma or Papa ever wearing. There was a polka-dotted dress with flowing sleeves, a dusty pin-striped suit, a pile of sunhats in garish colors. And there were a few forest-green polos draped over a hanger, in the very back. I pulled them down and spread them out on the bed to fold.

Oliveto Marzano, said each of the breast pockets. An embroidered sparrow in gray, an olive branch in its beak, and those two words encircling the bird in cursive: "*Oliveto* Marzano." My Italian was atrocious—Sabine was right about that—but I knew what an *oliveto* was. Olive orchard.

I took one of the polos and went back into the living room. My computer was on the coffee table; I opened it and put that into the search engine: *Oliveto Marzano.*

It came up with rolling hills of olive trees, branches draping down a mountainside spotted with ruins. Great stone buildings and ancient warehouses, old mills, all built low to the ground. Sicily. There was a page on the website for *About the Orchard,* translated into rough English from Italian. A line of black-and-white photos trailed down one side of the page—workers in the trees, hand-picking the fruit, heaving up great nets of olives; mechanical stone mills; men and women bottling oil and celebrating a harvest. Rows of gnarled, twisting olive trees, sprawling up the hillside. I found myself scanning the pictures for Papa's face; I didn't find it.

The orchard was run by Valentino Leonardo Marzano.

I recognized that name, *Valentino*. I recognized it from the day at the beginning of the summer, when I'd just come back in from the CVS with my school supplies. Savino and the guys talking on the other side of the house, the clinking of glasses—it was all engrained into my memory. *Valentino.*

Maybe it was a different Valentino he'd been talking about. Hell, we had three Marcos in the family, two Giovanis, and even Massimo was named after his Zio Mo. It could very well have been a different Valentino.

But there was some connection here. There was something with the *oliveto*, with Valentino, with the Marzanos and the Vitellis. And Leonardo was Papa's name.

I slept on the couch, with the green polo tucked under my pillow. I dreamt of rolling hills and flower crowns, cigarette smoke clouding my vision till all I saw were hazy silhouettes of distant figures. They danced beneath the olive trees.

The next morning, I found a sponge and bucket and sandpaper in the garage. I dragged them all out into the backyard. Then I dragged Vince and Carlo away from the breakfast table.

"What are we doing?" Vince was excited.

Carlo was crabby in the morning, but my presence at home was still fresh enough that he was aiming for politeness. Or at least civility. "I didn't finish my pancakes," he said, carefully. He cast a glance back at the house.

"Pancakes are forever," I said. "This play-set will fall apart with the next strong wind."

"We had a hurricane last year, it was fine."

"If Vince burps, *it will collapse.*"

Vince laughed. Carlo smirked. "And if he *farts*—"

"Okay, yeah, that's enough." I waved a hand; I didn't want to hear the end of that. "I want to sand down the PVC edges. Carlo, there's sandpaper in the bucket. Vince, start scrubbing. I'm going to look for tubing in the garage."

Vince ran off to grab the hose.

Carlo folded over the sandpaper. "Tubing for what? What tubing?"

"For the edges of the slide."

"The slide's fine."

"Someone's going to die on it, Carlo. I'll be right back." In the back of the garage, I found an old hose coiled atop the push-mower. I took a pair of shears to it, cut it down lengthwise, and construction-glued the lips down both sides of the slide.

91

We were out back for about an hour while the sun rose golden over the roof. The grass was dew-wet. Carlo cut himself on a pipe—proof, I think, of the need for sanding—so we took an intermission to get bandaids and ointment, check with Sabine to confirm he'd had his tetanus shot, and reassure Carlo he wasn't going to die. Vince and I had a short water fight with the hose, then we got back to work scrubbing grime and lichen off the play-set.

At some point, the screen slammed open against the side of the house and Cristine stepped out. She held my phone above her head. "YOU HAVE A CALL."

I straightened, a brown-dripping sponge in one hand. There was green streaked down my capris. "What?"

"YOU GOT A PHONE CALL, PIA."

I never got phone calls. Mostly because I never turned on my ringer, because I didn't *want* phone calls. "Who is it?" *And why did you answer my phone?*

Cristine rolled her eyes. "I'm not wearing shoes, come get it." She didn't want to step off the back porch in her socks. She held out the phone at arm's length, unhelpful.

I dropped my sponge into the soap bucket. Then I walked across the yard and took the phone from her. I stared at the screen for a moment, but I didn't recognize the caller—not that I would have recognized most phone numbers. "Who is it?"

"I don't know. Some guy."

She turned and disappeared back into the house. The screen slammed in my face.

Some guy. I didn't get calls from guys. I didn't know any *guys.* I stood on the step and faced the yard—Carlo and Vince had paused, watching me. "Hello?"

"You didn't tell anyone about Lorel, did you?"

The words came fast and urgent. I blinked—it took me a second to place the voice—and once I did, the greeting still seemed terribly out of character. "Hi, Massimo, I'm good, how are you?"

He exhaled on the other line. "Sorry. Did you tell anyone?"

"How did you get my phone number?"

"Betta." I didn't know how Betta had gotten it, but I wasn't surprised either. "Did you say anything?"

"About you and Lorel?" My hand was grimy. I used my wrist to scratch my chin. "Is this about you and your hair?"

"No!"

My smile faltered. He actually sounded concerned. "Are you alright?"

"I don't know, Pia. You didn't tell anyone about Lorel, did you?"

"You mean about her existence?"

"Yeah."

What a strange question. I sat down on the step. "Like...Savino and Dora, and probably Ida...they know she *exists*. Because she's my roommate. And Betta, they've met a few times on campus. But no one else has actually seen Lorel, I've just mentioned I'm moving in with her. Why? What's wrong?"

"Nothing's wrong, I just—" He caught himself. "No, everything's wrong. This whole family's wrong."

This sounded so terribly unlike Massimo that it really kick-started my imagination. Maybe he'd been drinking. It was only half-past ten, but that didn't mean much. "Where are you?"

"In my car."

"Where's Lorel?"

A long pause. "I was just helping her unpack stuff. She's at her apartment." I heard his blinker turn on, a soft click-clack in the background hum of New York traffic. "I'm fine."

"Okay." I squinted across the yard. Carlo was bossing Vince around, and Vince wasn't happy.

"I'm fine," Massimo said again, insistent, like maybe I didn't believe him. I didn't. "But, Lorel.... There's a reason our family sticks close to *family*. There aren't a lot of outsiders in our circle. Did Savino tell you..."

"Tell me what?"

His voice dropped low, though I assumed he was alone. "You know about the Scarpacis, right?"

Scarpaci was Lorel's last name. "She doesn't talk about her family."

"Savino's got an issue with them, Pia. The whole family...has an issue with them."

Why did this always come back to the Vitellis and their weird rules? Why did they have to ruin the simplest things—a great roommate, a new apartment, simple relationships outside the family? "This isn't about Savino."

He laughed. I jumped—the sound was harsh, strangely cynical. "Pia. *Everything is about Savino.*"

Unfortunately, that was probably true. I understood it, really—I understood why people listened to Savino, why they always asked him before making a move. He had that *something*. He was charismatic, confident, level—he gave off that air of *I know things*. "It doesn't have to be. *This* doesn't have to be." *Lorel is mine,* I wanted to point out, *I found her first, this isn't the Vitellis 'business.* That just sounded petty. But it was how I felt.

He sighed. "It does."

"She doesn't really have anything to do with her family, anyway. What did they do to Savino?"

Massimo was silent for a beat. I heard the turn signal click on again. "What did Savino do to *them*?" he returned. "It's the same thing. It doesn't matter. Just...be careful, I guess, and don't tell anyone about her, okay?"

"Okay," I said, slowly. "Does Lorel know?"

"I don't think so. Have you thrown the name *Vitelli* around recently?"

"No. I won't." I rubbed my neck—I was hunched up on the step, but I couldn't be bothered to correct my posture. The bakery had ruined my back, it was probably too late at this point anyway. "Is this an issue that could be resolved over a beer and a family dinner or something?"

Massimo laughed, again. This laugh seemed a lot less forced, as if he found what I'd said really humorous. "I don't think so. Maybe a public brawl. A firing squad. And a fire."

I rolled my eyes at the sky. "What's with you and the fire?"

"Just don't talk about her or use the name *Scarpaci* around the Vitellis, okay? Or my dad. Or—God, don't tell Betta her last name, Betta can't keep her mouth shut. Don't act like we're hiding anything either, okay? Or she'll sniff it out."

"Alright, Massimo," I said, with suppressed irritation. So many rules, and from Massimo Di Natale of all people. I suddenly remembered last night. "Hey, have you ever heard of *Oliveto Marzano*?"

I heard keys jangle. The gentle hum of his Lexus shut off. "Why?" He said it slowly, cautiously.

I lowered my voice so the boys wouldn't overhear. "I was cleaning out my parents' room last night. My dad has an old polo shirt with the name—several polos. I looked it up. Who's Valentino Marzano?"

Again, Massimo sounded careful when he spoke. "I guess...Carla Vitelli's father-in-law. Your dad's dad."

I'd figured that much. "Is he still alive? Does Savino know him?"

"Why?"

My jaw clicked. "Because...he's my grandfather. I think I deserve to know whether he's alive, if nothing else. Why do you know this and I don't?"

Again, Massimo's keys jingled. I heard the car door open. "What you deserve," he said, "is to not be caught up in all this—" He didn't finish his sentence, he cut off abruptly, but the following silence was loaded with contempt. "Anyway. He's alive, Pia. But I've got to go."

Did he really? Or was he just done talking? Had he reached his daily quota of information he'd impart upon me? "Well. Bye," I said, unenthusiastic.

"Bye."

94

I dropped the phone from my ear. My brothers were fighting over the hose, sponge abandoned—this had turned into a water party. The play-set was forgotten. But from this distance, it already looked loads better than it had first thing in the morning. Maybe Vince would play on it again.

I didn't get up off the step. I scrolled through my contacts and called Lorel.

"Pia! How are you? How is Georgia? Oh—you'll never guess what just happened, Massimo—your cousin, Massimo—offered to help me move into the apartment. He put bolts in the walls and helped me hang curtain rods."

"How is it?"

"Oh, it's—uh—I mean, it's like those writers in their dusty attics, pumping out all sorts of inspired art."

Which meant it was mediocre and we might die from black mold, but she was making the best of it. "I'm glad you feel that way. Hey, you haven't bumped into my family, have you?"

"Just Tonio and Massimo. And Betta. Why?"

"I just got a weird call from…Tonio." I thought it might be a bad idea to explain that, right after leaving their first "date," Massimo had called me with concerns. "He…um. You know what, just avoid anyone I'm related to, okay? Except the guys. Massimo and Tonio. Actually, you should probably avoid Tonio too, because he's a real heck-wad."

She was silent on the other line. But I heard her breathing—she was still there. "What's wrong?"

"Honestly, I don't know. I think my uncle has an issue with someone you might be related to." That was the best I could do.

"Oh!" she said. "Well, I'll just avoid your uncle, then. Is he a heck-wad too?" She was making fun of me.

"More like…" *Dangerous.* That was the word on the tip of my tongue. But she wasn't looking for a real answer. "Yeah, a regular heck-wad."

"I'll stay clear, then. I try to minimize the heck-wads in my life. Why did Tonio call you, again?"

I pulled up a bahiagrass stem and stuck it between my back teeth. "Heck-wad business."

"Well, this has been an informative phone call."

She had to go soon after. So did I—Vince had wet the slide and the glue on the cut-up hose was coming loose; Carlo was flipping out because he thought someone might cut off a limb on the edge.

I left my phone on the step and walked over to fix the hose. Carlo hovered at my shoulder, nervous as he watched me reapply the glue. "Who was that?"

"Cousin. Massimo."

"From Brooklyn?"

"Yeah." I held down the cut-up hose against the side of the slide, just until the glue got tacky.

"He's the one with the Lexus," Carlo recalled. "Do you remember what—"

"I don't know the year, no."

Carlo and Vince went back to scrubbing the pipes. I crouched by the slide until the glue had mostly dried, then I stayed crouching there while the thoughts turned over in my head.

Savino had said that Marco Vitelli, Mamma's dad, was in New Orleans. He hadn't said anything about my dad's side. I didn't know anything about either of my grandmothers. But he'd also told me that the Marzanos were still in Sicily.

What business did Savino have with Valentino Marzano, all the way over in Sicily?

ii.

Talking to Massimo reminded me of Grace Burnett, and her phone number on that business card. I unearthed it from the bottom of the backpack and gave her a call.

She was nice, very to-the-point. They didn't let many undergrad students into the food science lab, but she'd worked with Massimo at Columbia and she respected his referral. She'd checked out my academics before the call. She made it clear that she wasn't overwhelmed by my GPA.

I explained about the past spring. I explained that I was in a transition phase, but that this was something I was really passionate about. I channeled my inner Lorel and really leaned into my *passion* about this topic.

She said she'd discuss it with the other faculty. I thanked her for her time.

It would be fantastic if it worked out. Except for one small detail: my scholarships didn't cover the lab, or the extra textbooks. I hadn't been cutting it this close mid-summer, when I'd carefully selected the perfect number of fall classes that would be covered by scholarships and my dwindling college funds, when I'd researched rented textbooks and poured all my extra pocket money into the apartment with Lorel.

I was okay. I was going to be alright. I'd have to be real careful about keeping my scholarship, and I might have to talk to Savino about picking up more hours at the bakery.

But I was okay.

A week passed, then another. August crept to a close.

Sabine and I emptied Mamma's and Papa's room. She moved in quietly—I could tell Vince noticed, though he didn't say anything about it. I explained to Carlo that he could have my room now, but he was curiously against the idea of having his own space. I didn't understand why until I really pushed him to talk about it.

"It's Vince." He was uncomfortable in the way teenage boys are when they don't want to show emotion or general humanness. "Sometimes he cries at night. He doesn't want to be alone."

Like the mature oldest sibling, I sobbed at this news. Then I forbade Carlo from telling Vince that I knew, and I proceeded to absolutely wreck myself over the course of my last week at home. It was the same struggle I'd fought through before: how could I *leave* them? What kind of monster abandoned her parentless siblings and ran off to New York City? *Twice?*

I did go back, though. I got a flight. Ida had booked it with me, actually, before I'd left; I wasn't sure, but I thought she might have secretly paid for it without telling me.

I didn't mind so much when it was Ida who did things for me. It was somehow different—not pity, just a mother being a mother. An aunt being an aunt.

Dr. Burnett called me back, the day before I left Augusta.

"Alright, Pia. I can fit you in." She had a sharp New York accent—none of this smooth, dense Italian stuff—it cut right to the point with clipped words.

My heart kicked in my chest. "Really?"

"Yeah. Let me know if you have any questions. See you in class."

That was all. I was in.

I left the last week of August. Sabine and the kids drove me back up to Atlanta, we all cried, and I spent the whole flight regretting my decision. Every decision, actually; I should be disrupting my life in every way possible, just so I could stay at home with the kids, just so that there was one more constant thing in their lives.

Ida had texted me the day before, asking if I wanted to come over for dinner my first night back. But I'd politely declined—I wanted to get settled first. I wanted to plant my feet and reorient myself before diving back into the everyday madness.

That meant no Gio or Savino or even Massimo picking me up from the airport. That meant, when I grabbed my luggage and headed towards the parking lot, I called Lorel and she swung around in her car, blasting show-tunes on the stereo.

The apartment was a few blocks north of the Financial District. The bedrooms were the size of my closet back at the Vitelli house, there was a single shared bathroom, and the minuscule kitchen took up half the living room. It was simple, the appliances weren't in the best shape, and it was definitely a downgrade from Savino's place. But Lorel had worked her magic. She'd taken a page from Tonio's book and hung cheap floral tapestries across the badly-painted walls. She'd brought her cozy lamps and throw pillows to decorate the new IKEA furniture. And she'd even done something about the musty smell—she explained how she opened the windows every evening and lit every single candle in the place, so by now the apartment smelled less like mold and dust and a lot more like Eucalyptus Daydream and Old Leather Oxfords (an actual candle scent that is sold to people like Lorel).

It came partially furnished with bed-frames, dressers and desks in the rooms. I didn't have a mattress, but Lorel had explained that she owned a trundle bed, and I could have the bottom pad since she wouldn't be using it otherwise.

She'd already hung the gray sparrow curtains in my room. I stared at them as I unpacked my luggage into the dresser. I'd always liked sparrows, and now I wondered if it was some subconscious thing from my childhood. Maybe I remembered Papa wearing the green shirt with *Oliveto Marzano* and the sparrow with the olive branch. Maybe Papa had said something about sparrows, once upon a time, and I'd latched on to the idea. Had he worked in the *oliveto* back in Sicily? Maybe that was why he'd liked the pecan orchards on our hikes. Maybe, just like me with my Italian pastries, he'd been trying in his own way to stay connected to his heritage.

What would I ask him, if he was still alive? I'd take him on a walk up the country roads. I'd walk barefoot in the dust with my sneakers in hand, dangling from their laces. I'd pry up pebbles with my toes and kick them down the path. I'd ask him about olives and Valentino Marzano. I'd ask him why he and Mamma had left the Vitellis behind in New York, severed every tie, cut us off from our family. Or maybe I wouldn't have spoken at all—because if Mamma and Papa had still been alive, that would have been enough, no questions asked. I would have been content. I would have gone on more hikes and made more focaccia for Mamma. I wouldn't have been thinking about *oliveti* at all.

I'd left the polo behind in Augusta; I'd packed it into a cardboard box with the rest of Papa's things. But I couldn't get it out of my head.

Lorel ordered Chinese food. We sat on the narrow balcony with its rusted, paint-flecked rail—sat in cheap folding chairs and watched the sun set between buildings.

"Elphaba or Glinda?" I asked.

"It's *Ga*-linda," she corrected. "As much as I'd like to try for Elphaba, I think I'm more of a Galinda. Not the book Galinda. But the show."

"It's a book?"

"It is. *Don't read it.*"

I looked at her sideways, eyebrows raised. "Does book-Galinda end up with Fiyero?"

Lorel smiled, but waved a hand dismissively. "Oh, enough about Fiyero."

When the food arrived, we locked up the apartment and sat on the floor in the living room, where we watched a BBC series of *David Copperfield* on her laptop.

Around ten, there was a knock on the door, and my heart skipped a beat.

Reality set in: two young women, living in a dinky apartment in New York City. Sure, Massimo had put extra locks on the windows, and sure, Lorel had a butterfly-patterned baseball bat leaning up beside the apartment door. But we were alone.

Lorel wasn't concerned. "I couldn't fit my rocking chair in the car," she explained as she clambered to her feet. "My brother's dropping it off. It's fine."

This was the first I'd heard about a brother. I sat up and pushed aside some takeout cartons as Lorel checked the peephole. Then she removed the chain and threw open the door.

A young man stepped inside, dragging an ancient rocking chair behind him. He didn't look much like Lorel; he was blond, but it was a dirty blond, and a lot curlier than her hair. He was tall and built like the sort of person who spent a lot of time in a gym.

"Pia, this is my brother Matty. Matty, say hi to Pia."

"Hi, Pia." His eyebrows were dark and thick, low over his pale eyes. He thumped the rocking chair down between them. "Where do you want it?"

"My bedroom, please. Thank you, dear!"

He disappeared down the hall. I watched him go.

So this was a Scarpaci. This was the family Lorel never talked about. "I didn't know you had a brother."

"I have three," she said. She settled back down on the floor beside me, cross-legged "And a sister. But I only really get along with Matty." She called back over her shoulder. "MATTY, do you want some fried rice?"

"How old is it?" he called back. He stepped back into the living room, liberated of the rocking chair.

"Maybe an hour."

"She always tries feeding me her leftovers," he told me. He stared at my face while he said it. I looked away.

Lorel sat back on her heels. "I don't want them to go bad!"

"Most of the time, they've already gone bad. Do I know you?"

"Probably not."

"She's from Georgia," said Lorel.

"Huh." Matty was still watching me closely. "You look familiar."

Lorel held up the carton of rice. "We're watching *David Copperfield*."

"Is that Jane Austen?"

"You're a disgrace," she said, and pointed at the door. "Get out."

He took the rice. "I know it's Dickens. Are your arms okay?" This was directed at me.

"It's tendonitis," I said. Whenever people said that, I always felt like hiding my arms behind me, which probably would have looked stupid and been slightly offensive.

"She works in a bakery," Lorel elaborated. "It's a baker thing, bad wrists."

99

Matty sat on the arm of the couch behind Lorel. He picked through the fried rice with the plastic spoon his sister procured. "What bakery? In Manhattan?"

"Little Italy," said Lorel.

I wished she'd stop answering questions for me. Right about now, I was wondering how much I'd told her without thinking. She was my friend—I shouldn't worry, right? And this was her brother—of course it was alright.

Matty put down his spoon. *"Zeppole?"*

A lump materialized in my throat. I nodded. "I've only worked there a few months."

"You a Vitelli?"

Lorel looked at me. She looked at her brother. And when I didn't say anything, she did. "No. Marzano, like the tomato. What's going on, what are you saying?"

"Marzano," Matty repeated. He rolled the word around in his mouth, just like Tonio, but a lot less condescending and a lot more suspicious. Then he said, "Alright," and went on eating his rice.

"Matty, why are you being weird?"

"I don't know, maybe I have *food poisoning*."

"Pia's a food scientist, she'd know if it was bad, right Pia?"

"Not a food scientist," I said. "Just…studying. I don't know anything yet."

"When's your audition?" Matty asked his sister, mouth full.

Lorel laid on her back, sprawled across the carpet. She squinted at the ceiling. "Tomorrow night."

"Don't sing anything from *Les Mis*." He set the empty carton aside. "I'm out. Seeya. Also"—he paused at the apartment door—"don't talk to Dad, if he calls. Just let it go to voicemail, *capisce?* He might use Pete's phone, ignore it."

"Yeah, okay. Thanks."

He nodded at me as he ducked out. His pale eyes still had a suspicious look to them. "Seeya, Pia Marzano."

Lorel turned to me once he'd gone. "What was that about?"

"I don't know."

"Do you know the Vitellis?"

I stared at the door. "I don't know." It was one of those times I was terribly glad that Lorel was passive—she wasn't going to pursue something like this, since I definitely wasn't comfortable talking about it. And I wasn't going to ask about her dad, either.

She army-crawled her way over to the laptop and hit *play* on *David Copperfield*. "Let's see if Daniel Radcliffe ends up on the streets of London, then. That poor child needs a bath."

iii.

The next day was Monday, and my first week back at school. My schedule was similar enough to the summer that I could keep my morning routine of opening the bakery and walking to Fortuna. At quarter to six, Betta and Giovani picked me up outside the apartment in their dad's BMW.

"How's the place?" asked Betta, without preamble.

"It's nice."

"It looks…" She pulled off the curb and didn't finish the statement.

Giovani finished it for her. "Like a dumpster fire."

"Oh, it's fine," I said.

"Why'd you leave the Vitelli house?" Betta asked. "The Vitellis live like *kings*. The bathroom is bigger than my bedroom."

"I don't mind the apartment," was my only response.

We parked around back of the bakery. As Betta and Giovani donned their aprons and wandered off to their various tasks, I sought out Savino—he was already thoroughly flour-dusted and stocking the front case with *sfogliatelle*.

He straightened when I appeared. Eyed me up and down, as if checking for broken limbs. "Pia. Good morning. How's Sabine?"

"She's Sabine," I said.

"Right." He tapped the counter idly. "Ida wants you at dinner tonight."

I pretended it was an offer, instead of a demand. "Sure. What time?"

"Eight. I'll send someone to drive you."

I spent the rest of the morning laminating *cornetto* dough, working in layers of cold butter before folding the rectangle of dough and re-rolling. The bakery bustled—Betta and Savino fought to keep the front cases full, while Giovani pumped out a steady stream of cannoli shells and *zeppole* at the deep-fryers.

At half-past nine, I pulled the last pan of the focaccia from the big wood-fire oven and shrugged off my apron; I bundled it up in a fist as I ducked up front.

The bakery was full. Betta was bagging pastries, Marco was on the phone, and Dora was at the cash register, shouting to be heard over the other voices. Savino stood, calm and collected—almost serene, I'd say—carefully filling cannoli with ricotta. His face gave no indication that he was even aware of the ruckus.

I held up my apron. "I have to get to school."

He didn't look up. "Is the bread out?"

"It's out."

"Take Oscar."

"I really have to run," I said. I tried to keep the annoyance out of my voice; I was already running late.

Savino slowly raised his head. He blinked. "Oscar has long legs," he said.
So I brought Oscar.

Organic chemistry was a nightmare. We hadn't even started in on the subject matter, but I was already sweating just looking at the syllabus. Immediately after, I darted across a courtyard and climbed three sets of stairs to the physics classroom. That was slightly less nightmarish. Around noon, between classes, I found a park bench where I forced myself to eat lunch. And I thought long and hard about my decision to quit smoking. My stomach was all turned-over. I wanted to call Cristine, I wanted to talk to Lorel, I wanted Sabine to hug me close and tell me everything would be fine, even if I didn't completely believe her.

Instead, I hiked across campus and found the food science lab. It was a low brick building built into the back of the STEM faculty offices. This was the sort of place I could easily imagine being one of the oldest parts of campus; spiderweb cracks and twisted plastic shades over the windows, chipped paint on the doors. There was a keypad and card slot by the door. It was locked.

I knocked. A guy with too much hair crammed under a backwards baseball cap opened the door. He wore a bleach-stained *Slipknot* shirt and a wrinkled lab coat, buttoned wrong. "Yeah?"

"I'm here for Dr. Burnett's lab."

He blinked. I couldn't decide whether he was high or falling asleep. Maybe both. He kicked the door the rest of the way open and held it there with his knee.

I'd expected the lab to smell like formaldehyde, like my high school bio lab with its jars of preserved hagfish and sheep's eyeballs. Instead, it smelled vaguely of bleach and bread. The guy in the baseball cap rejoined the group of about a dozen students in lab coats, at the end of the room.

"Pia?" A short woman with frizzy red hair waved me over.

I joined the others. I felt like a small child, surrounded by all these white-clad figures. "Hi."

"Pia." She checked her clipboard. "Marzano?"

"Yes."

"Like the tomato," someone said under their breath.

"Yep," I said, without looking.

I needed a cigarette. But I didn't think those were allowed in lab anyway.

Lorel and I met up after school—I waited outside the liberal arts building and studied on the green until she got out of British Literature.

"I've got Harlock again." She held back the golden hair from her forehead, squinted into the sky. It was hot enough that she'd forgone her usual floral skirts and oxfords for shorts and sandals, but she still looked like an angel standing there, haloed by late-afternoon sun.

"Rest in peace," I said.

"He doesn't like how I do my footnotes. I can tell he's going to get on me about that, this semester—he hated it this summer, but I think they're technically correct."

It was so trivial: the textbooks, my stress over class locations and times, footnotes. I think what was really bothering me was that school wasn't the issue at all: my stressors were outside the scope of Fortuna.

"Are you alright?" We were in the parking lot. Lorel pressed her key fob, and a car chirped nearby.

"Yeah." I swung into the front seat. "Are *you?*"

"Oh, I'm fine." She turned on the car and blasted the AC.

"I mean, you have auditions tonight."

"Oh, no. No. I'm not okay, never mind. People talk about butterflies in their belly, but really it feels more like a vulture or something. I need chocolate and probably some Beethoven."

I spent the rest of the afternoon organizing my school things at the apartment, and helping Lorel get ready for her audition. She sang her show-tune twice, drank loads of lukewarm tea with honey, and then refused to speak for the last hour because she was on vocal rest (that's what the post-it note on my bedroom door said, anyway). She hugged me goodbye and dashed out the door in a pink romper and a beret.

Afternoon crawled into evening. I'd expected Betta or Massimo to pick me up, maybe even Gio.

I hadn't expected Achille Salone.

"Hi," I said, surprised. I slammed the passenger side door.

"Hey, how's it going." The car thumped with the base from some bad Italian rap. He had the decency to turn it down when I got in, before peeling off the curb and executing a death-defying U-turn that left me clenching the armrests and questioning his sobriety. "Hey, you really got a shit deal with this place, it's kind of a dumpster fire, you know? Now Tonio, he's got a real nice place—I found it for him, down in the Financial District—just a few blocks off Broadway." He rubbed his jaw with a thick, tattooed hand. "You been to Broadway yet, Georgia?"

"No, I haven't."

"Not Broadway, not Sicily. You've really lived in a bubble, huh?" He said it in such a ridiculously self-important way, I couldn't help responding.

"We don't get our faces smashed up in Augusta," I muttered.

He was silent for a beat. I thought I'd offended him, but he just chuckled. "Sounds boring."

Maybe I did hurt his feelings, because he didn't talk again until we got to Fort Greene. He cranked up his music and cracked the windows so the car was full of wind and whiny rap.

I was actually relieved when we finally pulled up outside the Vitelli house. "Thanks."

"Oh, well, yeah. Anything for family."

I got a good look at his face, then. The last time I'd seen him, it'd been the beginning of the summer and he'd looked like someone had taken a brick to the bridge of his nose. That was still a bit crooked. And there was a pale scar on his chin, where the stitches had come out. Otherwise, he looked just like an older, broader, shorter Tonio—a Tonio with black eyes like dull stones, instead of magma.

"Thanks," I said again. I slammed the door and turned my back to the BMW. It shot off down the street.

There were a lot of cars, lining the sidewalk. That only sort of prepared me for what waited inside. Because here's the thing about my family: even if you only invited the Di Natales to join for dinner, that meant an additional eight people between Nicole and Gio, Massimo and Betta and Giovani, Norma Biasi, plus her husband Marco and their little Ava. But Ida and Savino didn't just have the Di Natales to dinner—they had Oscar (who was in an actual *dress shirt*), Nonna Annabella and Alonzo, Ezio and Tonio, and several other men and women I didn't recognize, but assumed I was probably related to in some way.

After the sort of day I'd had, I didn't need this. I went in anyway.

"Pia!" Nicole found me the second I walked through the door—she had a glass of wine in hand and she slapped my cheek with the other. "Good, good, you're back—I want you to meet someone, we were just talking about you."

Oh, God, I thought. I was already rattled. "Oh, hi, who?"

"Here, come here—*hey, Vittoria!*" Nicole led me by the elbow through the front room.

I ducked around Marco and Gio, who were in a heated debate with Raul—skirted past four kids piled into a single armchair, rocking it back and forth dangerously— almost slammed into Ezio, who stood in the middle of the room and watched the kids while moodily eating a plate of what looked like an entire stuffed artichoke.

"Sorry," I said, but he barely glanced at me, and Nicole dragged me on through the room.

"Look, Pia, this is Vittoria Gaglione." My aunt finally stopped in the dining room doorway, tapped a woman on the shoulder and basically thrust me into her face. "Vittoria, this is Pia, this is Carla's *bambina!*"

"Oooh, Pia!" This woman I'd never met wrapped her arms around me—I let her, kind of patted her on the back, uncomfortable, wondering when it became rude to not throw your entire body at a person you'd only just met in this family. She held me back and I got a look at her face: heavy blue mascara, blonde hair ironed so straight it was surely fried; lipstick, laugh lines, neck and chest marked with sun damage, and the most bulbous earrings I'd ever seen. "Oh, she's so big," Vittoria told my aunt.

"How old are you, Pia?" asked Nicole.

She didn't know how old I was. "Nineteen."

"She's *nineteen*." Nicole squeezed Vittoria's arm. "Long time, she's grown up—the kids, they've grown up, Pia, you've got to show her pictures of the kids—*I* haven't even seen pictures, I bet they're huge, right?"

Deep discomfort wormed its way into my chest. The kids felt like a secret, something I had to keep private and far away from this part of my life. I had pictures, but I wasn't going to pass them around. "Yeah, maybe. I mean, they're grown." I waited for someone to tell me who Vittoria was.

The blond woman patted my cheek—I flinched. "You look so much like Carla did, when she was young—I remember, she cut her hair one summer, remember?"

"Yeah, she did—it was shorter back home, she grew it once we got here—"

"Her and Savino, they had hair the same length, remember?"

Nicole laughed. "Pia, Vittoria is your godmother, when Carla and Leo got you baptized."

Here was yet another person who hadn't known me since I was a baby, another person who acted like I owed them attention and explanations. Apparently I wasn't interesting until I was conveniently placed back in Brooklyn. She and Nicole got talking, and after a few minutes I managed to slip away. I wandered down the hall to hide in the bathroom and I slammed into Betta.

"Oh!" She grabbed my arm. "Sorry. Hey—" She was wearing perfume, a lot of it; I tried to not make a face when she leaned close and lowered her voice. "Hey. I'm *leaving*."

I narrowed my eyes at her. "Okay."

She glanced behind me. Satisfied that we were alone, a wicked smile spread across her face. "I'm going to a *party*," she said, out of the corner of her mouth.

"This is a party."

Betta scoffed. "This is a family dinner. I'm going to a *real* party, with the Fortuna kids."

"Are you sneaking out?"

"I'm going home early to"—she made air quotes—"*do homework.*"

She didn't look like she was going to a party. Although, on second thought, I was pretty sure she was wearing extra layers of clothing. And the perfume was pretty suspicious. "Will drummer boy be there?"

"Who?"

"Drummer *Macbeth* boy."

"Oh." She waved a hand. "Alec. No, I don't care about him, that's behind me. You want to come?"

I tugged on my braces. "I don't like parties." In fact, I hated parties, and this family dinner was already just a bit too close to a party for my taste. In fact, by any other family's standards, this was probably a real shindig.

"Are you sure? It's fun, they've got drinks, you look like you could use a drink." She punched my shoulder. "C'mon, Pia, live a little."

"Sorry. No."

Betta shrugged. "Well, don't tell anyone I'm gone, alright? That's the least you can do." Without waiting for my answer, she disappeared in a cloud of perfume.

iv.

Ella and Anna were excited that I was back. They dragged me into a corner of the front room to show me a dance they'd come up with (probably on the spot).

Dora Di Natale showed up at some point. She brought her new boyfriend. He was some outrageously good-looking Italian guy who spoke minimal English yet seemed to earn a seal of approval from everyone in the family—possibly for this very reason. They made a glamorous couple. I experienced a fleeting spark of envy until I recalled the conversation I'd had with Sabine about Nic Tabone. Then the jealously disappeared pretty quickly.

Ida and Nonna Annabella were in the kitchen with wine and a platter of *bruschetta*. They both gave me huge hugs and asked after Sabine and my siblings. But they couldn't have cared too much—just like Vittoria and Sabine, if they'd really cared, they would have called to talk to the kids themselves. They'd have reached out to Sabine and asked if she was okay since her sister had died, ask if she needed help. I struggled to focus, to pull myself back into the physical location. But there were so many people and it was so loud, my brain started shutting down.

Giovani was in the back of the kitchen. I watched as he lifted a simmering pot from the stove—brow furrowed—and drained a mountain of *orecchiette* into a strainer. He took a step back from the steam and scowled into the sink.

I felt that. "Where's Massimo?" I asked, when I finally managed to detach myself from my aunts.

Giovani didn't look up. He nodded towards the back door.

I stepped outside.

It was abruptly quiet when I shut the door—just the hum of distant traffic, crickets, the rustling oak tree in the square. The air was already getting cooler at night. In Augusta, it would be October before we got down to these temperatures.

Massimo sat on the back step. I settled down beside him.

He glanced at me. The porch lights cast a dull orange glow across his face, which seemed more hollowed than I remembered, but perhaps it was just the strange evening shadows." Hi."

"Hi." I noticed the wine glass in his hand. Then I noticed the bottle of Cabernet, nestled in the grass beside the step. But I didn't say anything.

The kids were probably getting ready for bed, it was almost nine o'clock, they had school in the morning. I imagined the play-set out back of the house, the swing swaying in the warm breeze, the groan of tree branches punctuating the night. Crickets in the bahiagrass, fireflies in the distance.

"It's quiet," said Massimo. He sipped his wine and stared off across the square. But I didn't think he was actually seeing the tree, the million-dollar homes—his eyes were somewhere else. "Quiet as it ever gets."

I wrapped my arms around my knees. "Outside Augusta, at night, you can't even hear the cars. We're too far from the highway. It's just cicadas and wind and leaves. Papa would take me on hikes in the evening after school and work, we'd wander down old dirt roads and hike across abandoned pecan orchards. All of it, quiet."

"That sounds nice."

"It is. This is all loud." I pulled on my wrist braces. Even a tipsy Massimo was, I thought, an improvement over the circus going on inside the house. Somehow, Massimo with some alcohol in him was just as easy to be around as sober Massimo. Maybe easier.

He handed me his half-empty wine glass. "You understand," he said. "You don't like this family either."

Did I dislike them? I wasn't sure. I also didn't argue his point. I took the glass, but I didn't drink. "You're out of college. You're an adult. You could leave."

"So could you."

In some fantasy world where my parents were still alive, I'd finish school and a world of opportunity would open to me. And I could make choices, I could go places and do things. Sabine and I didn't have a lot in common, but I understood why she'd run away from Nic Tabone—in the peak of her youth, she didn't want to get saddled with a husband, with kids. She didn't want to lose those years of spontaneity and probably bad decisions. If I thought about that too hard, it was depressing. Because I was trying to make all the right choices, get through school, stay disengaged, but I could never have those years back: I already had people to take care of, I didn't get to be a kid.

There was no one to blame for that. But it put a bitter taste in my mouth.

I shook my head. "I have to finish school."

"Do you?" Massimo took a swig from the bottle and frowned at the pavement between his feet. "Be careful, Pia," he said, his voice low. "Or you'll just end up

107

working for this family. That's how it goes—they push you through school, you feel independent, you don't realize you've been roped into the business until it's too late. Just a worker bee in the hive."

"Is Savino the queen?"

"Savino is everything. And everywhere. And we'd all die without him." I couldn't tell if he was exaggerating. He rubbed the neck of the bottle between his hands. "Some of us signed our lives away willingly. Some of us, our parents did it when we were young. You don't realize how deep you're getting until you've got your feet in wet cement and you realize you're planted in this place forever. A fixture in the Vitelli museum."

He took another drink. I still hadn't touched my wine. "I can't leave," he said.

"You could. *I* could." I didn't want to be sucked into this *stuck* mindset.

"Leave like Sabine left?" He shook his head. "That isn't the way to do it."

"What about my parents?"

"It always catches up," he murmured. "Look at you. Back here again, working for Savino Vitelli. Living with a Scarpaci." He rubbed his eyes.

Across the dark square, something flickered. A lighter. Just a hint of flame, then it was gone. I kicked his foot. "Is someone out there?"

"Where?" I pointed. "Maybe." He took another drink.

I thought about the person smoking in the square. When I'd lived in the upstairs bedroom, I'd seen someone out there in the evening—under the oak tree, looking up at the blue sparrow window, before they disappeared into the night. My skin crawled.

Massimo set the bottle down. "How's Lorel?"

"She has an audition tonight. Fortuna's doing *Wicked*."

"She told me about that."

"She's good." Very good. Better than me, for sure, and probably even better than Massimo.

"I want to go to Montana." He looked at me, curiously intense. "It's big, but it's quiet. You could get lost out there in the mountains. Just, miles of nothing."

I was unfazed by the topic change—this was something Cristine did, her thoughts speeding ahead faster than the conversation. "Have you ever been?"

"No."

"It's cold."

"Have *you* been?" he asked.

"No."

"I want to go," he said.

For the first time, I was actually worried about him. It took me a moment to realize why: I recognized that look in his eye. He needed to get out, he needed to run away, and even if he was never going to do it, he needed to at least act like it was a possibility. "You should go sometime," I said, hollowly.

"Yeah." He ran his thumb over the wine bottle label. "Where do you want to go?"

"I don't know." I didn't make life plans, they just happened to me. I figured I'd end up somewhere where I wouldn't be happy, but I wouldn't be miserable either—somewhere like Augusta. "You know, I've never belonged anywhere. I say I'm from Georgia, but I'm not really, am I? It's like school, I was never a normal student, I was always working and helping Mamma with the kids. I went to school, but I didn't *belong* there. We didn't grow up like other kids. And we didn't have family around, we didn't have people or traditions to belong *with*. Like the Fourth of July."

Massimo sat in silence, listening.

"It's like the Fourth," I repeated. I wondered if that person was still in the darkness of the square—lingering, listening. The hair on the back of my neck stood on end. Behind me, buried in the depths of the Vitelli house, someone's kid screamed a laugh. "The Fourth of July. Everyone else did cook-outs and fireworks, but not us. We celebrated the Feast of the Immaculate Conception and All Saints Day. Then I come up here, and you guys do the same thing. It wouldn't have felt so lonely if we'd had that. If I'd known."

"Your parents made the right choice."

"I don't think there is a right choice," I said. I'd never thought about it, but saying the words aloud and having someone to listen suddenly made it all so simple. "Whether you stay or leave, it gets you in the end. It's like an addiction."

I thought about my smoking. Massimo looked down at the glass in my hands.

"That's a good way to put it," he said, as he tipped back the bottle. "This family's an addiction."

v.

Tonio ended up driving me back to my apartment. Betta had left long before and none of the other Salones or Di Natales were going that way, so Ida put the task on him. And, curiously enough, he hadn't had anything to drink that night. It was almost as if he'd expected it.

I said bye to Ida and Nicole. I managed to dodge around saying goodbye to Vittoria, who'd disappeared. As I passed down the hallway, Savino's office door was open—he sat on the edge of his desk, surrounded by several other men, all of them with cigars and pipes. I nodded at him. He nodded back.

"Pia Marzano," I heard him say to the group, by way of explanation.

And, as I left the hallway behind, one of the men echoed, "Ah, *Marzano*."

Tonio drove a green Mercedes convertible. It looked ridiculous, and it was too cold to have the top down, but I'd be damned if I was going to complain or show any sign of weakness in front of Tonio Salone. He'd just give me endless grief.

"*Mar-saw-no*," he said, as we pulled off the curb. "Enjoying your blip of academic experience?"

Massimo sat in the back seat, arms crossed, staring pensively out into the passing night.

"Screw you," I muttered.

"What's that?" A narrow grin stretched across Tonio's face—his weirdly skeletal face, with all the features too deep-set, the sharp jaw and cheekbones, the dark eyes too big and suggestive of empty sockets. His hair was slicked back and it barely moved in the wind.

"How's the happy damsel with the literature problems?" he asked.

"Her name's Lorel," I said.

"He knows," said Massimo, tired, from the backseat.

"Lorel *Scarpaci*," said Tonio, under his breath.

I looked at him sharply. "What?"

"He *knows*," said Massimo.

"What a scandal," said Tonio. We sped over the Brooklyn Bridge, below flashing lights—chaotic cello music drifted from the car speakers. "You're a scandal, Massimo!"

Massimo didn't react. I think he'd mastered dealings with Tonio Salone, by now.

"Here's the thing, Marzano, is—I don't know if anyone's pointed this out to you yet—but your flat's a real dumpster fire. Security is abysmal. Speaking of fire, a fire escape is more a hazard these days than it is a quick escape. Quick escape? I say quick entrance into the building. And have you got mold? I imagine there's quite a bit of mold in a place like that. Although"—he was still grinning—"I imagine your Scarpaci friend finds the idea romantic. Very *Little Women, Little Princess*, one of the *littles*. A writer's hovel, am I right?"

"It does the job," I murmured.

"What job? Lead poisoning?"

"There's no lead in the paint," said Massimo.

"Oh, I forgot, Di Natale is a *scientist*." Tonio cranked up the music. Violin shrieked through the night.

They dropped me off on the curb.

"Should I walk you upstairs so you don't get mugged on the way?" Tonio leaned back in his seat. His smile widened when I slammed the car door too hard. "Or would you rather take the fire escape? It might be an easier entrance."

I flipped him off. He laughed.

"Bye, Pia," said Massimo.

"Bye."

I was all in the my head as I stomped up the stairs. Massimo of all people was getting to me—Massimo, who was a calm, calculated anchor in the insanity of this existence. He was breaking loose and I didn't know why. Deep down, somewhere buried beneath loads of trauma and bottled up emotions that only manifested as ridiculous tears and terrible anxiety, I knew that I needed someone stable to lean against. The problem was, I got the feeling we were both leaning against each other, but neither of us was really as pulled-together as we seemed. It was like Lorel thinking I was tough and intimidating—I gave off that nameless "Savino *thing*". Maybe it had fooled Massimo too. But we were both threadbare humans bent on self-destruction by a variety of means.

Massimo was accessible, approachable. I *wanted* to lean against him, even if I knew it was a bad idea. Even though I knew that I needed someone more solid and permanent, someone like Savino.

I unlocked the apartment door and shut it gently behind me. It was dark—Lorel was still at auditions. I wondered how long they'd go, and whether we still had Chinese food in the fridge. I wondered if she was leaning against me too. The thought made my stomach clench. I wanted to call Cristine, but it was nearly midnight and the kids had school in the morning.

I headed for the hallway. I'd try to sleep, and I'd talk to Lorel in the morning. I'd pray for her audition. I'd pray for Massimo. And I'd pray Tonio's car got wrecked.

Out of the corner of my eye, something moved in the kitchen.

I froze.

There was someone at the end of the hallway—a figure in the shadows by my room.

Nothing moved. The world held its breath. The moment was frozen in my memory, a snapshot, every nightmare caught in flesh.

Something slammed into me. I stumbled. Lorel had a baseball bat beside the door— I turned to get it.

Hands knocked me to the floor. Something pinned me down—fabric pressed over my face—they were going to suffocate me. I inhaled something sweet and I choked.

Then. Then blackness crept in, and then—

VI

The Family Business

i.

I came to slowly. A headache pulsed against my skull, and my throat scratched. My eyelids fluttered.

The room was dark. It wasn't my apartment—towering stacks of cardboard boxes lines the walls on either side, pressed into my back, filled the corners. A sliver of yellow light seeped under the door in front of me. It was less of a room and more of a closet.

The sharp edge of a box pressed into my hip. I shifted my weight, scooted up on my butt. My arms wouldn't move. They were duct-taped at the wrist.

I sat there for what felt like forever. I stared at the streak of light and dust across the floor. I wasn't at the apartment. I'd gone to the apartment, but I wasn't there anymore—someone had taken me somewhere else. They'd knocked me out—my head still ached from whatever they'd used—and they'd bound my wrists and thrown me in a closet.

I had been kidnapped. And clearly, I was about to die.

Shit. Shit. Shit shit shit. This was like the crime films Cristine and Carlo watched, with bodies turning up in basements and skeletons buried under tomato patches. Lorel didn't know where I was. Tonio and Massimo, they'd left, they didn't know there had been someone in my apartment. Savino might realize something was wrong when I didn't turn up at work in the morning, but Lorel could get up early and go the whole day at school and expect to see me in the evening, except I'd just never show up.

Fuck. My chest ached—I didn't know whether that was dust or fear. Probably fear. This wasn't the same anxiety that made me sprint down a crowded Brooklyn street in broad daylight, because I had a hunch I was being followed. This wasn't the shiver up my spine when I stood at the sparrow window and looked out at the square below.

This was real. I spiraled. I dug in my heels to the uneven wood floors and my back teeth ground together and I tried—I tried—I really fought—to keep it together.

113

I heard footsteps, and I felt sick. Shadows paused outside, the knob rattled, and the door swung open.

Three figures shuffled into the room. They shut the door behind them, and the lights flickered on. I was momentarily blinded. Then my eyes adjusted.

The man standing front and center reminded me of a pit bull—dark, intense eyes; short, thick with muscle, and standing like it would take a truck to knock him down. The man behind him had the same curly dark hair, the same wide shoulders. He was taller and wore glasses.

The third person was a woman. For some reason, that was the most disturbing thing to me: that a young woman was in on this, whatever *this* was. Her blond hair was braided back away from her face. They all wore dress clothes—slacks and button-downs and ties, all very professional and tidy.

"Here's what we need," said the man in the middle. He was talking to me, but his eyes were distracted, wandering. His voice sounded like crunching gravel—stone against stone, deep and harsh. "Here's what we need, is we need you to say"—he turned to the bespectacled man—"have you got the camera? Fine, we need you to say you're alive and say your name and date of birth and then we'll get on with this." His eyes finally fixed on me, shiny like little black pebbles. "Yeah?"

The man with the glasses pulled out a camcorder, the type my parents used to bust out for birthday parties. He flipped it open and pressed power. Then he nodded at me, as if to say *action*.

I stared. I didn't say anything. I didn't know what to say. It took me a second to register his Italian accent—I'd become saturated with it, I almost didn't notice. But the accent sent up red flags. The accent said that this had something to do with the Vitellis.

"Hey, I just handed you your script." Pit bull man snapped his fingers in front of my face. "You don't have to be creative, just spit it out, then you can just shut up."

I made up my mind right then, that I wasn't going to say anything he wanted me to say. "Who are you?"

"It's doesn't matter—"

"Well, doesn't she deserve to know?" said the blond woman.

"No, she doesn't. We discussed this."

"I dunno Diego," said glasses man.

"Why am I here?" I asked. "Why am I tied up? I didn't do anything, I don't *know* anything, there's no reason. And my family has security cameras in my apartment, they'll know I went missing and they'll know who did it."

"That's the point," snapped the pit bull man. "Jesu—" The woman looked at him sharply. "—geez," he corrected. "And you don't have security."

I wasn't totally dense. Sure, it had taken way, way too long for me to realize something significant was wrong with my family. And sure, I'd only dug halfway into the wall of bullshit they'd built up around the ugly truth. But I was in deep enough that I was starting to detect trends. "Scarpaci."

They blinked at me.

"Are you *Lorel's dad?*"

The blond girl blinked. I saw the resemblance—a light sprinkle of freckles, the same heart-shaped face, even if she was much older and a bit more severe. "Lorel told you about us?" She sounded touched.

Diego Scarpaci shook his head. "Sara. *Porca miseria.* Shut up."

"Does Lorel know you kidnapped her roommate?"

"Cousin," said glasses man. He still had the camcorder rolling.

"What?"

"Angelo, *shut your damn mouth.* Both of you. *Jesus.*" Diego rubbed his neck, scowled at me. "Look, just say the damn lines, okay? It's simple. Valentino needs to know who you are, needs to know you're alive. We're not gonna kill you, we won't hurt you, we just need to get this thing moving, alright?"

My fear has turned into something else—this felt like a dream, like I was someone else entirely. It wasn't so much adrenaline as it was complete disbelief and irritation that flooded my body. "No," I said.

"No?"

"No."

"*No.*" Diego turned the word over in his mouth. Then he snatched the camcorder and stormed out of the room.

Glasses man blinked. He followed.

Sara flicked off the light switch. The closet was plunged into darkness. She stood silhouetted in the doorway for a moment—behind her, black-and-white photographs of the New York City skyline lined the corridor.

"Is Lorel doing alright?" she asked.

I didn't answer.

She left. The door locked behind her.

I would have liked to escape, but I didn't see how. Once my eyes readjusted to the dark, I clambered to my knees, and from there to my feet. I backed up against the door and tried the knob with my bound hands—I don't know what I was hoping for, maybe a loose bolt in the knob or something.

Then I stood there in the dark, with my duct-taped wrists and my pounding skull.

What did they *want*? For a fleeting, horrifying second, I wondered whether Lorel knew where I was after all—whether she was in on this whole thing, whether she'd only befriended me and gotten the apartment as set-up to this kidnapping. But she'd always said she didn't get along with her family. And she clearly hadn't spoken with her sister in quite a while.

Valentino. Why did it all come back to Valentino?

I paced the room for what felt like hours. Then I sat on the edge of a cardboard box and stared at the opposite wall of similar boxes. Everything was boxes and dust and dark.

What time was it? It must be early morning by now. I knew nothing about chloroform or anything like that, but I didn't think it should have put me out for more than a couple hours at the most. Which meant it might be hours before someone realized I was missing. Which meant Diego Scarpaci and his family had plenty of time to do whatever they were planning.

It sounded like a ransom. The camcorders, the rigid scripted lines. If they wanted money, they were out of luck: there was nothing valuable about me.

My brain was foggy and the air was thick with dust. Breathing was difficult and uncomfortable, with my arms pinned behind me. I dozed in the dark. I tried not to think.

The door kicked in.

I started upright.

A man charged into the room, slammed himself against the wall by the door, and swept the shadows with a handgun.

My heart hiccuped. I scrambled to my knees.

Shadowy figures were framed in the doorway, silhouetted against the harsh light. They crowded into the room, rushed towards me—I ducked, as if that would help, as if anything would help at this point—

Savino hit his knees. He grabbed my shoulders. "You okay?"

My voice scraped out of my throat, thick with dust and fear. "Yeah." The instant adrenaline began slipping away, and I almost vomited. Raul Salone slipped past and knelt behind me. I heard a *click*, something nicked my forearm, and then my hands were free. I peeled off the duct tape with trembling fingers.

Savino took my elbow. He pulled me to my feet. "Go. Go, now."

We dashed past Gio with his handgun, and Achille, who stood in the hallway with his hand on a holster. At the end of the hall, a cold breeze drifted through an open window.

I hit my head on the window frame and stumbled out onto the fire escape. I almost stepped on a body.

Savino clapped a hand over my mouth. "Shhh."

I wasn't going to scream. At the time, I didn't even register that the person half-covered in a discarded coat might have been dead. My mind said *he's unconscious* and moved on to the next thing. Anyway, his hands were cuffed to the edge of the stairs. They wouldn't cuff a dead body—that's what I told myself later, when I looked back on the scene.

I pulled Savino's hand away. "I'm fine," I breathed. I wasn't fine.

Somehow, I made it down the fire escape without my legs collapsing. I took deep breaths of night air—I thought about the sunrise, about the steadily purpling sky. There were skyscrapers in the distance, buildings I didn't recognize. I didn't even know where I was.

Ezio stood in the alley at the bottom of the stairs, a gun in one hand and a phone in the other. He hung up just as my feet hit concrete. "He's coming."

At the end of the alley, a green Mercedes peeled around the corner. It knocked over a garbage can and screeched to a halt by the fire escape—I stepped back. I didn't recognize it at first with the top on, but then Tonio flung open the passenger's door and sat back in the driver's seat. "Get in."

We piled into the car. There weren't enough seats. Savino sat up front, Gio and Ezio crammed into the back and left room enough for me on the bench. Raul crouched on the floor at his older brother's feet, gripped Tonio's headrest to steady himself.

We were off before the doors slammed shut. Tonio sped down the alley, screeched out onto a busy street, and took off into the gray morning. Traffic was light, but still he swung lane to lane, passing other vehicles with reckless abandon. Car horns barked in our wake.

Billboards and lights flashed by. Times Square. Forever and always, this would be my impression of one of the great New York City landmarks: a mellow gray-purple sky, dim headlights, the slow crawl to full-speed morning hustle. The car was silent. It smelled like sweat and bread, like the back of a bakery. I wondered if Savino had come from the *panificio*. I wondered how he'd found out, how he'd found me.

My hands were shaking.

The Rite of Spring played on the car stereo. I only recognized it because Lorel thought the story behind the piece was hilarious—a deeply-disturbed audience driven mad at the ballet's premiere, ensuing chaos in the theater.

"Turn that off," said Savino.

Tonio switched it off.

My uncle twisted around in his seat and spoke to Gio. "Take care of Nicole and the kids, Ezio and Achille will lock down the Vitelli house. Tonio, drop them off and find a place to hide the car for a while."

For once, Tonio had no snarky comebacks. He just nodded.

Savino tapped the dashboard. "Drop us off here."

He pulled up against the curb. Savino was out of the car in an instant—he opened the back door and gestured for me to get out. "Raul, come on."

Then Tonio was gone, speeding off in his absurd green car. Savino looked up and down the sidewalk as Raul adjusted his sports coat to conceal the holster at his hip. They both seemed unbelievably composed.

"Alright," said Savino. "This way."

117

ii.

It was cold out—chances were it would heat up throughout the day, but for now I shivered in my shirtsleeves. My wrist braces were gone and my wrists were still red and tender where the duct tape had stuck.

Savino and Raul had long strides, forcing me to keep up. The streets were unfamiliar, but they seemed to know where they were going.

They walked like they were going to kill a man. I didn't pursue that train of thought.

Savino stopped at a corner diner with advertisement-plastered windows. The bell rang as he held open the door for me. Raul stayed outside without being asked; he leaned against the storefront, arms crossed, casually cautious. A one-man security team.

The diner was nearly empty, just a couple construction workers sitting in the back corner. It was the sort of place that smelled perpetually of chemical cleaner and bad coffee. Savino pointed at a table. I pulled out a chair—metal screeched against the linoleum floors, too loud—and sat. Outside, through a collage of posters and ads, I could just see Raul's back as he scanned the street.

"Three coffees."

I stared down at my wrists. The hair had been ripped off. My body had been twisted at such weird angles, everything hurt, and I couldn't even sort out the tendonitis pain from everything else.

Savino ducked outside—the bell rang again—and handed Raul a coffee. Then he joined me at the table. He set down a steaming paper cup in front of me and settled back in his chair, hands wrapped around his own coffee. As always, he seemed relaxed—serious, but his body language said *I'm fine, I'm calm, it's under control.* "Are you hurt?"

"No." I held the coffee to warm my hands.

"Head hurt?"

"A little."

"What, chloroform?"

"Maybe."

He sipped his coffee. I didn't touch mine. My stomach churned. He set the cup down and sat forward. "You've never asked many questions about our family, Pia."

I almost laughed. "Not to *you*." For an instant, I could have hit him; I was furious. Somehow all of this was his fault, I was sure of it—somehow he'd made Lorel's father angry, and I'd been attacked as a result, and here he sat with all his typical stoicism, commending me on my ignorant, unwilling complicity.

"Massimo?" he asked, and I nodded. "How much did he tell you?"

It wasn't a threatening question; I didn't think Massimo would get in trouble. Savino just sounded curious. "Not much."

118

"Well, I'm gonna tell you everything else." Most people would look away, would glance out the window or focus on their coffee while they spoke. But Savino held my gaze, like he was waiting for a reaction—any reaction—to any given word. "Do you know anything about the family business?"

I shook my head.

"We traffic products from Italy. We work with your dad's family, with Valentino Marzano—he's over there in Sicily, we distribute the stuff over here."

I thought about the beginning of the summer, about Savino and Johnny and Raul in the back of the house. "What *stuff*?"

Drugs. That was the obvious answer. Cocaine or meth or something—wasn't there a history of drugs in the mafia? Because that's what this was: mafia business. I didn't want to say it aloud, but there was no other name for it.

Savino drank his coffee. "Olive oil."

"What?"

He raised his eyebrows. "We traffic. *Olive oil*."

I opened and closed my mouth a few times. All I came up with was "*How?*"

"Shipments. We have warehouses sprinkled throughout the city. Drop-off points on the Sound."

"No, I mean, how…how do you traffic *olive oil*?"

"You mean *why*." He thought about it. "Well. A few reasons. One, we can bypass customs and import fees, any inspections over in Sicily, which makes the whole process a lot cheaper. Which means, we can sell it cheaper over here, without Valentino sacrificing quality. You see"—he tapped the tabletop—"you can hardly get real olive oil in this country. Even in parts of Europe. By the time it gets to you, it's gone through three other processing companies and middlemen, so when it ends up in your home kitchen or restaurant or bakery, you can't guarantee it's the real thing."

"Why not? What do you mean?" An *olive oil racket?* I tried the coffee—it was bitter and it had gone lukewarm while I let it sit, but I barely registered the taste. I needed something to do with my hands.

"They'll adulterate it," said Savino. "They'll *dilute* it. They'll keep it in tankards till it's gone rancid, then deodorize it or cut it with rapeseed. Making real extra-virgin olive oil and getting it to Italian-Americans over here, it's hardly profitable between the harvest and the milling, the exporting fees—it's a crooked industry. It's got to be crooked, to make money off the product. Are you following? If the oil is cut and sold for a fraction of the price of real extra-virgin oil, everyone makes money off the deal. The consumer either doesn't know the difference because they've never had real oil, or they don't care, or they convince themselves that it's fine because it's cheap and it's passably extra-virgin. Every year, in Sicily, in Italy, you've got whole families falling apart because someone knew the business was exporting pomace oil, and they didn't take the safety precautions to protect their family." He sipped his coffee, glanced out the window at Raul. Then he turned back to me. "That's crooked. We've got a legitimate business with the Marzanos."

"So…it's legal?"

Savino swirled his cup, unconsciously. "The trade in Italy is. But good oil is easy enough to get your hands on over there, in the Mediterranean. Here, in America—that's where the real money is. Here's where you get people who can't afford the stuff coming through customs, because the companies have to tack on those fees to the price. And these people, they know good oil—they want the real extra-virgin product. You go through too many middlemen to get it over here, and who knows what happens to it on the way. You know from the bakery, how you can taste and even smell the difference between good oils. Some people know when they're buying quality oil gone rancid, or a diluted product with chlorophyll added, and they'll pay good money for the genuine stuff. Some people care. *We* care."

I chewed the coffee grounds in my molars. I stared at the stained tabletop. "So. What you're saying is. This olive oil is simply *too high-quality*."

"Yes."

"And so you're…sneaking it into the country?"

"You remember *Macbeth,* when we all went to the theater? We had a shipment coming in, and it was an important one—large quantity, coming in that night. We needed an alibi. When the Scarpacis did a number on Achille, we thought he may have let something slip, but he gave them the wrong time. So, while we were at the theater I had some guys take care of the shipment. And the next night we went down to the yard and took care of the guys Diego Scarpaci sent." He sat back and sipped his coffee, as if that explained everything perfectly.

I ground my knuckles into my eye sockets. A headache was kicking in. What did *take care of* mean?

"So," I said. "So, the bakery…"

"We launder the money through the *panificio*. We donate some of it to the Church, that's why Thomas Aquinas has got the baptismal font out front. If anyone asks—no one asks—but if anyone does, then we've got money from the Marzanos. Old money. Family money." He looked deadly serious. "It's why our family won't ever want for anything—we keep the money in our family, we keep each other safe. We've hit pitfalls before, but we'll always be able to take care of each other."

That explained the apartment in the Financial District. That explained the million-dollar homes, the fifteen-thousand BMWs, Massimo's Lexus and Tonio's Mercedes, the checks going to my home in Augusta.

I set down my cup. "Sabine."

Savino nodded.

It made sense now. "Does she know? She's a fashion journalist for a magazine. She's got to know that her salary—"

"Sabine doesn't have to know anything," said Savino, "if she doesn't want to." He crossed his arms. "She doesn't pay attention to the extra deposits in her account. Maybe she knows, somewhere in there"—he tapped his temple—"but she doesn't care enough to investigate. She'd rather live comfortably in denial than acknowledge the truth."

I reached down to tug on my wrist braces. Then I remembered they were missing. "What about the Scarpacis?"

Savino's face tightened. He took a long sip of coffee, set down his cup, and looked thoughtfully at the tabletop before answering. "That goes back to *Sicilia*. Me, your parents, we were all born over there, we came over when we were young. But it started with the Marzanos. You know anything about them?"

"*Oliveto Marzano*," I murmured.

He nodded. "They were a big deal, your family—big, affluent political family. Still are. But even back then they had a lot of clout, had these sprawling orchards and the oil mill. The Scarpacis were in the gambling scene, still are. We found you in their casino, Pia—they've got a casino in town, that's where they got Achille this summer. Back in Sicily, they were connected to the 'Ndrangheta, to Rogoli and those guys. The Cosa Nostra families. But Devota Maria, she didn't care, right? She saw people and she loved them, she didn't care about their family name."

"Who's Devota Maria?"

Savino rubbed his neck. "Your grandmother. Valentino's wife—a wonderful lady."

"Where is she?"

"Buried back in Sicily. Died of a cancer, ten years ago. Wonderful lady." He tossed back the rest of his coffee. "She didn't care that the Scarpacis were gamblers, or that the Vitellis—we did our best, but it wasn't always honest work. We did our best. But the Scarpacis have just got something out for our family. So." He leaned forward, rested his forearms on the table. "The Scarpacis knew we worked for the Marzanos, they thought they could get to us through Devota Maria and Valentino. So, they kidnapped their daughter."

I blinked. "Who?" I was seeing concerning parallels.

"Calpurnia Marzano." He waited, and when it didn't seem to click he went on. "Your dad's sister."

"I didn't know he had a sister."

"Well," Savino said, "no one talks about her, and here's why: the Scarpacis kidnapped her, they told the Marzanos they wanted vengeance on the Vitellis. They kept her on their pistachio orchards, up in the mountains. Devota Maria talked them down from it, said she wouldn't let anyone do anything to anyone else, and the Scarpacis eventually gave Cal Marzano back. And then"—he looked down into the dregs of his coffee cup—"and then Valentino turned around, and he had us burn down their orchards."

"He had—?" I didn't know how to react to that. "Who, the Vitellis? Burn down—?"

"Yes."

"How old were you?"

"Five. I've got hazy memories, but that's all. Cal Marzano, she was fifteen, and as soon as the fires had died out, she'd run away with Matteo Scarpaci's oldest son, Diego."

So. So, Diego Scarpaci was my uncle, and...that made Lorel my cousin. It was one of those moments that made me question how intimately God and fate and shit directed people's lives—because it had been an accident, meeting Lorel. It had been totally coincidental that either of us had been in that classroom at the beginning of the summer. It was as if some greater power was pushing us around like chess pieces, and I found that deeply uncomfortable. "So, where is she now?"

"Calpurnia's married to Diego—they left Sicily before the Vitellis did, settled in New York. We've kept tabs on them since we moved here, they like to make trouble for us. And Calpurnia...." He dragged a finger around the rim of his cup, frowned at the tabletop. "We still pray for her. But she's a Scarpaci now, no one talks to her." After a thoughtful pause, he added, "Our lot will always be with the Marzanos—they've never done us wrong."

"Is that why I'm here?" Was I a favor for my family in Sicily?

"You're here because you're family," said Savino. "And we take care of each other."

My eyes dropped to the table. I didn't know how to say this next part, though I felt like he already knew. "How did you find me? At the casino?"

"How do you think?" I could almost feel the disapproval in his voice.

"Lorel."

Savino sat back. "Diego's son Matteo called your roommate. She called Massimo Di Natale. Massimo called me."

My coffee had gone cold. I didn't think I could stomach it at this point. "Is everyone going to be okay?"

"I'll take care of it. We're at a standstill with the Scarpacis. They know about the business, so we can't report them to the authorities or else they'll start an investigation. And this makes two kidnappings now within the same family; if they try to hurt us, they'll just incriminate themselves." He crossed his arms. "You knew she was a Scarpaci, huh?"

"I didn't know what it meant. I didn't know Papa had a sister."

"Well."

That was all. *Well.* That was a Mamma face, the face that said *you know what you did,* which wasn't fair. I hadn't known I'd be kidnapped—I couldn't have known. No one had told me how deep this stuff went. And Lorel wasn't responsible for what her crazy family did. I needed to call her; I needed to make sure she was okay.

Outside, Raul was on the phone. Traffic had picked up while we'd been sitting there, and the sky had lightened to silver-gray.

Savino reached across the table and took my coffee. "You gonna drink this?"

I shook my head.

"You're an adult, Pia. We let the kids make their own choices, right? Tonio and Massimo, they call their own shots, they live where they want. Betta and Giovani make their own plans. I can't force you to move back in, but that's the smart thing to do, now that the Scarpacis know who you are."

I was Cal Marzano—the girl to kidnap, to lord over Valentino, to ransom for vengeance or orchards or something. I was a piece in this reenactment, and I didn't like it. "You think they'll try it again?"

Savino shrugged. He sipped my coffee, but he watched me over the top of the cup. "They're gamblers. I think they're used to trying their luck—it's in Diego's blood."

I tapped the table's surface. "So."

"So."

So, I started having a panic attack. It began as an uncomfortable flutter in my belly, then my hands were shaking—my fingers kept tapping the tabletop, they wouldn't stop or slow down—and my heart was beating fast and I was sweating. *Mafia?*

"We should go," said Savino.

I nodded. At this point—even if he was a mafia boss or whatever, even if he was technically a criminal—I wanted him to take me somewhere safe and leave me alone. I wanted to go somewhere I wouldn't have to worry about Diego Scarpaci. Deep down, I even wanted to know that someone like Ezio was standing outside the door, guaranteeing security.

Savino discarded the coffee cups and I followed him out front, where Raul was already hailing a taxi. We all piled into the back and took off for Brooklyn.

By now, I should have been helping open the bakery. In an hour the *Zeppole* would be booming. And then I'd set out for school, get my first day of Tuesday classes out of the way, maybe meet Lorel for lunch. But not like this—not with sweat soaking through my shirt, not with trembling hands pinned under my legs. I couldn't go to school. I couldn't go anywhere. I'd been kidnapped. There were guns. There was the family business and I was unwittingly, *unwillingly*, steeped in it.

Achille was waiting outside the Vitelli house. There was a whole fleet of cars parked out front. The taxi sidled up beside them and emptied us into the space between two BMWs. I was still shaking as we hurried up the walk, as Achille threw open the door to let us inside, as Raul bolted it behind us and Ida wrapped me in her arms. I didn't hug her back.

Ida extricated me from the men in the house—Johnny and Oscar and Alonzo Salone, and a flock of others I only vaguely recognized. She walked me upstairs, past Marc's and the twins 'rooms, and into the bedroom with the blue sparrow window. I think she asked me if I needed anything, probably said some consoling words, but when I didn't reply, she left the room quietly and shut the door behind her.

I sat on the edge of the bed. I stared at the window, at the little brown sparrow with its wings spread and its body haloed in aquamarine light, like it was struggling to break free of the fractured blue-stained glass. I'd liked the sparrow before, just as I'd liked the sparrow curtains in my apartment, and the embroidered bird on Papa's green polo. Now I wondered where the window had come from. Had the Vitellis had it shipped over from Italy, just like the oil? Had they thought about it before giving me the room, or had they enjoyed the irony of the thing—a Marzano from Georgia, sleeping in the room with the sparrow from Sicily?

I should call Sabine. I should call Cristine or Carlo, immerse myself in the life they were living back home. But I didn't want to talk to any of them, not really. I wanted to talk to Mamma—I wanted to ask why we hadn't moved farther from Brooklyn, farther than Augusta. I wanted to ask how long she'd stayed, knowing what was happening in her family, and how hard she'd really tried to disentangle herself from the business in New York. I wanted to ask Papa about burning orchards and revenge, about his mother who was a wonderful lady.

I went over to the window. Down in the square, someone in slacks and a long gray overcoat stood beneath the oak tree.

At some point, I made my way downstairs. Traffic had cleared in the front room. Down the hall, voices drifted out from Savino's office—loud voices, overlapping. I got the sense that, if they found me here, they'd assume it was time to talk and I'd get roped into some intricate Marzano-Vitelli business.

I slipped out the back door.

Tonio Salone leaned against the oak tree. He was smoking. He watched me walk over, that same amused smile twitching at his lips, as if my every movement was somehow immensely entertaining to him.

"Don't talk to me," I said. I sat back against the oak tree, planted my butt on a coil of knotted roots.

"Okay," he said. He continued to stare off at the house. The cigarette smoke played in gentle silver spirals through his fingers.

My hands were still numb. My heart rate had slowed, but I couldn't stop breathing—breathing—breathing. "Can I have one?"

Wordlessly, Tonio reached into his coat and passed me the pack of cigarettes. He followed that with a lighter.

For an instant I felt a stab of guilt, but it was chased by relief. By calm. My breaths evened. I looked up through the branches of the oak tree and pretended, for a moment, that I was back in Augusta. The smoke smelled like Papa. The soil smelled like fall.

Massimo was right, this family was an addiction. You were sick if you stayed, you were sick if you left. Here, I belonged to the Vitellis. With Lorel, I belonged to the Scarpacis. And every day I woke and breathed and worked, I was a Marzano.

"So." I exhaled smoke. I shut my eyes against the morning light filtering through the oak leaves. "So. Mafia."

Tonio was silent for a beat, basking in the hum of traffic, the rattling leaves, the gentle clamor of morning in Brooklyn. "*Mafia*," he echoed, and I heard the smile in his voice. "Welcome to the family business, *Marzano*."

VII

Mafioso

i.

Savino got me a handgun. I told him I didn't want it; he told me he didn't care.

"Don't I need a license or something?" I was from Georgia; I knew a little something about guns, mixed in there with my knowledge surrounding rednecks and living in the sticks. I was pretty sure you needed a permit to carry. And I was pretty sure I was too young for a permit.

"We don't care," Savino said, as if he were offering me a glass of wine at a family function.

"I think the state of New York probably cares."

In the end, I took it. Mostly because, against everyone's counsel, I was moving back in with Lorel. *Lorel*, who was actually Lorella Lucia Scarpaci, who was actually my first cousin. And also because, when Savino Vitelli tells you to do something and he's got that particular air about him--you simply can't say *no*.

I stayed at the Vitelli house for two days while Savino got everything ironed out— *taking precautions*, he called it, defending the family against any Scarpaci back-lash post-kidnapping. He made it very clear that I wouldn't be perfectly safe at my apartment, even if they went all-out with the security. He made it clear that I was willfully putting myself in a dangerous situation.

Massimo showed up the evening of my first day, wearing cheap sunglasses and flinching at loud sounds. He gave me his phone so I could call Lorel.

"Massimo! How is Pia? Where is she? Is she alright?"

I held the phone away from my ear. Several feet away, on the back step, Massimo winced. "This is Pia," I said.

"Oh my gosh, uh. Pia, I am so, so, so sorry. And I know that doesn't cut it, but I don't know what else to say. I should have been there, I should have known something was wrong—"

"It's fine, Lorel. I'm fine." I pressed my knuckles into my temple. "How much of this did you know?"

"I don't talk to my family," she said, in a way that reminded me too much of Sabine. "I knew there was something about the Vitellis, but that was about it. Matty explained it after he called me."

"Tell Matty thank you."

Massimo made a face, like I shouldn't be thanking *anyone*, least of all a Scarpaci. I made a face back, like he shouldn't judge, since he was basically *dating* a Scarpaci.

"I would," Lorel sighed, "I'd talk to him and let him know everything's okay, only the landline at home isn't secure. He moved back home this summer, there's no privacy, I haven't talked to him since he called. And no one knows he ratted out Dad—if Dad knew, we'd all be in hot water, me included."

I could easily imagine Diego Scarpaci blowing up on his children. "Your dad is...uh..."

"He's a piece of work, isn't he? And my brother Lucio, he's just like him. Matty accidentally let slip something about my roomie being a Marzano, and they blew up—he didn't know it would be like that, honest. And Mom didn't know till after it happened, they didn't tell her. I didn't know your last name was...you know." Nervous laugh. "Sensitive information, I guess."

"I didn't either."

"Matty didn't know. I didn't know. Mom doesn't talk about her family at all, we didn't know her maiden name, we didn't even know she had a brother. I'm sorry."

"It's not your fault. I'm moving back in."

"Oh, Pia, I don't think that's a very good idea. I mean, I've got a baseball bat, but I don't really want to give my dad a concussion, and you know what Tonio called this place? A dumpster fire. And I think that's what it is, it isn't secure at all. Uh...yeah, that's probably why it fit my budget."

No shit. "I'm coming back anyway."

"I would be scared out of my mind," she said. "Why are you so tough? You're New York tough, and you're from Georgia."

I didn't think I was tough. I just didn't want to be stepped on, and I wanted to put things back together—I needed to go back to normal. I wanted to work in the bakery and go to school and then watch *David Copperfield* with Lorel, I wanted to seamlessly slip back into the old pattern, forget this had ever happened, and forget everything I owed to the Vitellis. To Savino.

After I got off the phone, Massimo rose to his feet. "I'm sorry I wasn't there this morning."

"It's fine." Truth be told, I preferred him staying out of the rescue—Massimo was a calming presence, and I didn't want to associate him with the events of the past day.

"So Savino talked to you, huh? He told you about...?"

"Yeah."

He crossed his arms. I couldn't see his eyes through the sunglasses. "So. What do you think?"

I understood what Betta had meant, about the Vitellis living like kings—the hefty checks dispersed from the *panificio*, the enormous house and fancy cars—and even in my lingering horror and shock from the day, there was temptation to rest in the knowledge that *we were okay*. I didn't have to break my back trying to keep me and the kids afloat, I didn't have to lose sleep and make myself sick worried for their security, because Savino and the Marzanos and Marco Vitelli in New Orleans would take care of us.

I felt like I was hovering on the cusp of something too big to fully understand, something that would pick me up and sweep me away before I could think to slow down.

"I don't know," I said.

Massimo just nodded, as if he'd expected that answer. I wondered what *he* thought of it—him with his Lexus and late nights out with Savino and the guys, his enormous apartment. "How's the lab with Burnett?"

The question caught me by surprise. Had that been yesterday? It felt like a lifetime ago. "Good. We just went over lab safety, but she seems pretty great. Thanks for that."

He lifted his sunglasses and squinted at the sunset. "It's a cool lab."

I watched him watch the skyline. I had a heap of homework back at the apartment, syllabi to read and first-week assignments waiting for me. "Do you know anything about organic chemistry?"

Massimo blinked and lowered his sunglasses. "I know lots of things about organic chemistry."

ii.

By the time I moved back into the apartment—now outfitted with an alarm system and three extra locks on the fire escape—I'd missed two days of classes. So on top of trying to settle down emotionally, I had to contact my statistics and microbiology professors to explain that there'd been a break-in at my apartment, which was why I'd missed the first day of class, and could I please have my spot back please? And then, once they'd said yes, I had to actually catch up on the work.

Massimo came over a couple evenings that week to help me with organic chemistry and physics. His presence also doubled as protection, though Lorel and I never said anything about it, and maybe he wasn't even aware of the fact—the apartment just seemed a lot more safe with Massimo sitting in the living room, eating Lorel's old Chinese food and clicking away on the calculator.

Lorel had *Wicked* call-backs the next week, for Galinda. Once she got the part (no one ever really doubted that she would) she was missing most evenings from the apartment. She'd come back late at night, humming and grinning and wearing lots of pink—a character study, she called it, really immersing herself in this role, even if it was only rehearsal. I was happy for her. But I missed her presence.

At the bakery, Betta was fascinated by my ordeal. "Savino gave you a gun, right? Do you have it?"

"Not...with me," I responded, standing in my apron by the deep fryers, wishing she'd leave me alone so I could pretend to be a normal baker in a normal bakery.

She shrugged. "Everyone has guns, in this family."

I didn't think that was true, but she clearly enjoyed saying it—there was a glint in her eye. For all the confused revulsion this business caused me, Betta clearly thrived on it, and her personality was starting to make a lot more sense; her whole "the thug life chose me" attitude was still off-putting, but at least it had context.

No, I didn't take the gun everywhere with me. I didn't argue anymore when Savino had Oscar walk me to school—I was a lot more cautious, a lot more *checking around* corners and *keys between my* fingers—but I also wasn't packing every time I left the apartment. In fact, the gun didn't leave the apartment at all. It was loaded with the safety on, stashed under a notebook in my bedside drawer. I didn't intend to ever use it. But it was there.

I wasn't the best student, I wasn't inclined to studying and academic papers and my attention span didn't tolerate long bouts of menial mental tasks. But I wasn't dumb. I was tactical about my academics.

Lorel constantly asked if I needed help, she'd even drop hints throughout the week that we should study together and get ahead on homework—uncharacteristic for Lorel, who notoriously procrastinated. But, though I knew I was on the path to self-destruction and burn-out, I felt that I'd committed to this method and there was no coming back from it. I was trying to cope in small ways, and it wasn't my fault that those small coping mechanisms added up into terribly late nights, early mornings, and copious volumes of stress redirected into my school life.

What Lorel didn't know—and what I was unwilling to admit even to myself—was that I simply wasn't sleeping right since the Scarpaci kidnapping. Sure, I knew there were locks on the doors and windows and a probably-expensive alarm system ready to go off at the smallest sign of forced entry. But I'd still lay awake at night and my mind would race, and my heart rate would pick up as I imagined things in the dark.

A couple weeks after the incident, Dr. Burnett gave out an assignment for group projects. It was about calorimetry and energy values—preparing a single food product in a variety of ways and then using one of the many bomb calorimeters in her lab to determine the caloric value yielded by each. By the end of the semester, each group of three needed to have constructed a lab procedure, conducted several trials, and pulled together an extensive lab report on the findings.

It weighed heavily on me.

The baseball cap guy from the first day was in my group. His name was Kyle Litwiller, he was normally high, but he was also surprisingly lucid when it counted. Whenever we met outside class to work on the project, he'd sneak fresh fruit into the library to share, since he was convinced all college students suffered from scurvy. He also did all his thinking lying flat on his back on the gross library carpet, eating fruit and tossing out constructive ideas.

The other kid was a grad student named Samantha, who'd done a summer internship at Columbia and was now convinced that she was the bee's knees. This lab was beneath her, so she put in minimal effort and refused to eat Kyle's proffered citrus. She was probably ticked that she'd been lumped in with Kyle and me, an undergrad— so I understood her irritation to some extent. On the other hand, she was a total butthead. She forced the two of us to carry the entire project.

A sample conversation:

Kyle: "Our food sample should be fruit."

Samantha: "FRUIT is not a food sample, it's a food group."

Me: "Okay, what kind of fruit?"

Kyle: "Oranges."

Samantha: "You can't prepare oranges in different ways, it's just an orange."

Kyle: "Well, actually, you can do a lot of stuff with citrus. Like...hey Pia, Google orange recipes. Like, marmalade, orange juice, you can use the zest in like cake and stuff, and jam, and orange juice."

Me: "I don't think we should juice anything. We shouldn't separate the fiber from the rest, that just means more work."

Kyle: "Oh, yeah, definitely, it undermines the whole experiment. No, I'm just proving that fruit is super versatile. No one eats enough of it, though. We have chronic Vitamin C deficiency in this country, that's what caused the Western Disease."

Me: "We could steam some oranges."

Kyle: "Oh, dude, wait—I want to use a *blowtorch* on one."

Samantha: "Good Lord."

The tutoring lab was in the back of the library. Unfortunately, this meant the occasional run-in with Tonio Salone. He'd come sauntering in sometimes in the afternoon, a leather satchel like Lorel's slung over his shoulder, in his slacks and wrinkled button-down and long gray overcoat, sometimes with an unnecessary scarf, always with terrible slicked-back hair. Usually I was able to avoid him, ducking away to the bathroom or behind shelves. Sometimes, I wasn't.

Around mid-October, Kyle and I were in the back of the library, putting together the report on our first citrus trial—brûléed orange wedges. Samantha was tilted back in her chair at the rickety table, scowling at the ceiling, muttering every now and then about how she had better, more important things to be doing for more important classes full of very, very important people.

"Oh, hey, *Mar-saw-no*."

Without turning, I winced.

Kyle sat up on his elbows, from where he was sprawled on the floor. He pushed back his cap and stared at the person behind me.

"Hi," I said. I refused to look.

"Hey, I didn't realize you had more than one friend. *Brava, brava, bravissima*."

"Eat your heart out, Tonio."

He just laughed. Then he made himself comfortable in Kyle's empty chair, across from Samantha. The distinct scent of cigarette smoke clung to his gray overcoat, and he carried a thermos that I doubted held coffee—he didn't believe in American coffee, he only drank *caffe*. Whatever was in his thermos, it definitely wasn't steaming.

"I don't recall asking you to sit down," I muttered.

"Funny, I don't recall asking permission. Isn't that funny?"

He nodded smartly—and slightly condescendingly—at my lab partners. Kyle nodded back, ever-chill. Samantha seemed offended to be lumped in with the two of us, and grimaced.

"So, Marzano." He regarded me from far back in the chair. He *lounged*. "Have you spoken with my sister today?"

I guess he thought me and Ida chatted on a regular basis. I hadn't spoken to my aunt in weeks. "No." I gestured at the lab work spread across the tabletop. "And we're in the middle of something."

He ignored me. "You see Savino this morning?"

"At the bakery that he owns?"

Tonio's eyebrows slinked up.

Apparently he wasn't backing down, and he wasn't going away. I shrugged. "No. Betta and I opened."

"When was the last time he didn't show up?"

I narrowed my eyes. He was trying to make me feel dumb, or think, or maybe just get under my skin. But I was in the middle of work, we had a deadline coming up, and Tonio Salone was being stupid. I jabbed at my lab notebook with a pen. "I'm busy. See this? This is schoolwork, I'm trying to get a degree and get out of the school system so I can do something *useful* with my life."

132

I'd meant it to sting at the least. But a smile slunk across his face. "Just food for thought."

"HEY," said Kyle, from the floor, "*pun.*"

Tonio gave him a cursory, amused glance, then rose to his feet. He ambled off across the library, into the tutoring lab, and more than ever I couldn't imagine going to him for help. Did English students really crawl on their knees into the lab, hand him their essays, and invite his judgement upon their lives?

Samantha watched him go. "What the hell was that about?"

"Dude was cool," said Kyle. "He's got style."

"He's got his enormous head stuck up his ass."

Kyle laughed.

"Seriously, who *was* that?" Samantha asked.

"Uh." I thought about it. "Just...this guy. My...aunt's...brother."

"Hey, you work at a bakery?" Kyle took back his chair and leaned forward intently. "Hit me up if you guys need fruit, any kind of fruit, even off-season. I got this fruit guy—he's the real deal. Got all sorts of fruit. Heirloom varieties, too. I can hook you up."

"Good Lord," said Samantha.

Despite myself, I did think about what Tonio had said. I knew he *wanted* me to think about it—he was probably sitting there in his throne in the tutoring lab while English students groveled at his lordly feet, a smile on his smug skull-like face as he thought about how I was turning his words over in my head. Still. It was hard to keep my mind focused on the homework; it kept drifting back to Savino.

Last time he'd been absent from work, besides the week of the kidnapping, had been this summer. The day I'd taken Lorel to see Tonio at his apartment, the afternoon Massimo had been drinking sambuca from a coffee mug. He'd said he and Savino and some guys had been out the night before. And Savino hadn't been at the bakery that morning.

What did it mean? Had a shipment of oil come in last night? Or was it tonight? For a crazy moment, I almost followed Tonio into the lab, armed with follow-up questions for his vague hints—like he'd offer up any useful information, even under interrogation.

I didn't. I was a student; I had studying to do. This family business wasn't mine, and I refused to get involved.

iii.

Lorel had rehearsal that night, but I bumped into Betta around the time I was heading home, and I asked if she'd drop me at my apartment.

She said she would. Under one condition.

Actually, she didn't tell me about the condition until after she'd dropped me off. She insisted on walking up to the apartment with me, "in case the Scarpacis were back". Then she stood just inside the door, crossed her arms, and said, "You're going to a party with me."

I dropped my backpack on the sofa. "What? When?"

"Tonight."

It occurred to me, then, that she was wearing an awful lot of perfume. "Oh, no. Betta. No. Hey, it's Wednesday, you know that? We have work in the morning, and school—"

"Yeah, I know." She threw herself onto the sofa, picked up one of Lorel's art history textbooks and flipped through it—they were piled on either end of the couch, books everywhere. I walked into the kitchen; she shouted after me. "I don't want to go alone!"

"Bring Giovani." I needed coffee. It was going to be a long night of studying, to get my portion of this lab report done.

"Ew, I'm not gonna take my little brother to a college party. Would you do that?"

"Well, Carlo is thirteen. So, no. But Giovani's an adult."

"He won't go."

"He's smart, probably studying."

"No, he has some stupid D&D game scheduled with his friends. Hey, is this Massimo's?" She paged through my physics notes, stacked against the foot of the sofa. "This is his handwriting."

"He's been helping with physics homework. He's not *doing* it for me," I clarified, as if Betta would care. "But he helps."

"Does he come over often?"

I narrowed my eyes over the top of the coffee maker. This was an awful lot of questions coming from Betta, who tended to not concern herself with other people's affairs—they weren't nearly as interesting to her as her own. "Sometimes."

She smiled at me from the sofa—a slow, wide smile that reminded me uncomfortably of Tonio. "So come to the party," she said, "or else I'll tell Dad about Massimo and Lorel."

I froze. The coffee maker clicked to life. I tried to not let it show on my face, but Betta looked like she knew she'd got me cornered. "How do you know about that?"

"Someone like Massimo couldn't spend so much time with someone like Lorel without *that*." She laughed, like she found this whole thing and my reaction ridiculous. "Come on, Pia. It's one party, you don't even have to stay late. It's not like I think you're gonna be fun or anything, I just don't want to go alone. I have to work early, anyway."

134

Was this blackmail? Was she seriously using my cousins to blackmail me? "Would you really tell your parents?" Even for Betta, it was a bold move. And mean.

"I might let something slip to Mom. And she'd tell Dad, and he'd tell Savino. And Massimo would be in tons of trouble."

That seemed less like *my* problem than it did Massimo's. "That's really sick."

"You don't have to worry about it if you come to the party."

"I hate parties."

"You haven't been to any good parties. I've been to tons. Come on, it'll be fun."

I hated parties. I hated huge groups of people and loud noises, and whatever it was that people got from parties—a rush, communal frenzy, whatever they called it—it bounced off me like water off a duck's back. I was impervious to fun at parties.

But if Betta told on Massimo, Lorel might be in danger. And I couldn't control Betta.

Betta drove us across town in her BMW while I sweated and tried to calm my nerves. I hadn't even changed clothes. I didn't know what to wear to a party, and I didn't particularly want to fit in anyway. Truth be told, I didn't know what to expect. The last party I'd been to was my parents 'funeral reception—which probably didn't count as a party, but it was a nice ice-breaker to pull out if things got tough.

At some point, Betta looked over at me, sitting rigid in the passenger's seat. It was getting dark outside; we drove east, crawling through traffic. My fingers were numb and I stared straight ahead, convinced that if I didn't think about it, my nerves would simply disappear.

Betta laughed. "Have you ever been diagnosed?"

I blinked. "What?"

"Anxiety."

I scowled. "*No*. I don't have anxiety."

"I'm a psychologist, Pia, you can't lie to me."

"You're not a psychologist, you're *studying* psychology, just like half the student body. You don't know anything." That last bit was mean, but it didn't seem to hurt Betta.

She just smiled. "Yeah, keep telling yourself that."

I should have stayed at the apartment. I should have let Massimo and Lorel fight their own battles. But I had this weird idea that it was my responsibility to keep their relationship secret, since Lorel was my friend before she was Massimo's, since I'd encouraged the whole thing—which had possibly been a bad choice, looking back. I hadn't known about the Vitelli-Scarpaci thing before, but I'd suspected that something was going on with my family, and I'd still had the audacity to befriend someone and drag them into the mess.

135

I crossed my arms tight. "Where are we going?"

"There's a kid in the Bronx whose dad owns an empty plot at Hunts Point."

"It's outdoors?"

"Yeah, why?"

"It's really cold, Betta." I was wearing a sweater, but it wasn't enough for spending any amount of time outside.

She just smiled. A couple minutes later, we shot over the Harlem River. The sky was pitch-black by now, headlights drilling into the dark, traffic lights splashing red and green across the tarmac. Betta took a turn down a narrow alley between two buildings. Then the walls fell away behind us, and she parked the car in a cluster of other vehicles in the shadows.

There was a roaring bonfire. The sprawling lot was a patchwork of dirt plots and concrete slabs, sparse grass and random stretches of gravel. Behind the cars, close to the river, the pillar of flame rose up behind a flock of young people, shedding tendrils of orange light across the lot.

Figures were silhouetted against the dark. The car doors were still shut, but vibrations shook the car from a boombox.

"This is a *bad* idea," I said.

"Oh, it's fine, I do this all the time."

"That doesn't make it safe. It's a bad idea. We shouldn't be here, it isn't safe."

"Oh, don't be like Massimo. He's got a stick up his ass all the time, such a killjoy." She kicked open the car door and leapt out. Cold night air crept into the BMW, and I shivered. "Come on."

"One hour," I said.

She grinned. "Two."

"One."

"Fine, okay. One hour."

Bass shook the ground. I couldn't believe no one had called the cops on these idiots yet, with their giant fire and terrible hiphop remixes.

"Hey," I hissed in her ear, and she rolled her eyes, pushed me away. "Betta, listen"—I had to shout to be heard over the music—"if the cops show up, we'll get in trouble—our *family* could get in trouble. Savino wouldn't like this." I couldn't believe those words were coming out of my mouth.

"Killjoy," was her only response.

My temple pounded. I didn't recognize anyone—they were faceless, cloaked in shadow. Everything blurred and seemed to grow slower with every passing second, and the noise faded out until all I felt was the music, pounding through the pavement, hammering against my skull and inside my chest. I followed Betta through crowds of drunk students and clouds of acrid smoke, all the way to the bonfire. From the start, it was terrible. But the absolute worst part was that, in order to keep warm, you had to stay relatively close to the bonfire, which meant that *everyone* was right there.

"Betta."

But she was gone. I'd lost my cousin in the crowd. She'd disappeared, and there would be no finding her—I could barely see.

My spine crawled. The shadows grabbed at me. I was so far from Brooklyn, so far from Lorel, so far from Augusta. The fire would spread. The police would show up and I'd be stuck here. What would Savino say? What would Mamma and Papa say? I needed to get out. Maybe as the oldest, I should have gone off looking for her. But at the moment I was more concerned with self-preservation.

I couldn't hear anything for the music. I pushed through bodies—I'd never felt so short—until I got far enough from the bonfire to breath again. But the air was heavy, it was thick with smoke.

I felt sick. Someone slammed into me, laughed, and stumbled away. I backed up from the fire, shivered, and stepped on someone's toes. Stepped back. "Sorry."

"Oh, no, chill—hey." Kyle squinted at me through a haze of smoke. "Hey, Pia, hey, what's up?"

"Hey," I shouted, "did you drive here?"

"What?

"Did you *drive here?*"

"Yeah, sure."

"Are you sober?"

"Yeah, yeah, I only had a beer—you want one?"

Betta could go to hell. "Kyle, I swear, if you drive me home I will do your part of the lab report."

His eyes lit up. "Aw, for real?"

"Yeah, I'll do it."

"You won't tell Samantha?"

Never had I thought that Kyle with his fruit and backwards baseball cap might be my savior. "No, Samantha's the worst, I wouldn't tell her anything."

"Oh, *fire*, okay—I was just leaving actually." He put out his blunt, palmed his car keys, and headed off through the crowd. I followed on his heel. "Hey, how'd you get here? You know Jason?"

"My cousin brought me." I didn't have to scream over the bass anymore.

Kyle swung into the drivers seat of a battered blue Corolla. I got in the back—I didn't want to offend him, because I thought Kyle was an okay sort of guy, but I was already feeling pretty paranoid tonight. He didn't seem to notice or care. He started the car and peeled off into the night. "Hey, who's your cousin? Is it the Lord Byron guy from the library?"

If I hadn't been so rattled, I might have laughed. "No. Betta Di Natale, she's in psych."

"Di Natale, cool, cool." Eyes on the road, he felt around in the center console for a half-empty bottle of kombucha. "Okay so I've been meaning to ask, but I don't know if this is offensive or whatever, but are you *Spanish*? Or like...Portuguese or something?"

"I'm Italian."

"Oh, chill. Hey, I was sort of close, Mediterranean type area. They got some mad produce over there, you know? Artichokes, olives, these real wacky zucchini things that grow to like two feet long, grow in spirals and shit—hey, where am I taking you?"

I thought about it. For one insane second, I thought about going to the Vitelli house—I thought about Ida and the kids, getting ready for a night in that big safe house, and I missed my bedroom with the sparrow window. Savino guaranteed safety. But he also asked questions. And Lorel was still at rehearsal, she wouldn't be back at the apartment till ten o'clock at least. I didn't want to be there alone.

"Financial District," I said. I rattled off the address.

"Hey, you want some pomegranates? They're in the trunk, my buddy in Jersey sent some up last weekend, I forgot to tell you guys—good pomegranates, too, they're totally seasonal and shit."

"Yeah, thanks." I didn't plan on taking any pomegranates, even if they were seasonal. I rubbed my hands on my legs, like I could wipe off the smell of the fire, the smell of weed. But it was everywhere.

"Hey, so how do you feel about pizza?"

My sweater stank. "Pizza? What about it?"

"Do you have like strong feelings about Pizza Hut and shit?"

No, this was about me being Italian. "Not really."

"I always heard that Italians were like super sensitive about pizza. And Olive Garden. You know, you've got to admire a people who are so passionate about their cuisine—like, I'd totally just eat whatever, plus a ton of fruit, but it doesn't matter where the food comes from, you know? I could eat freezer burritos. But like, to have a culture with real cultural food is a totally *fire* idea, that's rad—"

I tuned him out, at some point.

I had missed calls. One was from Lorel, one was from Ida, and the other two were from a number I recognized as the bakery. Savino? I pocketed my phone. I'd have to call them all back at some point, but it wouldn't be right now, with Kyle swerving through late-night traffic and talking my ear off.

"—so like in Biosphere 2 they royally fucked up the system by not adhering to the rules they'd put on themselves, so that's just the scientific community out a billion dollars. Tax dollars, I dunno. But wouldn't it be better if they just slapped a dome—like that Disney dome, the Epcot ball and shit, you know? What if they just slapped one of those babies over an orchard or a permaculture farm or something? Now, *that* would be a *good* idea. Hey, is this it?"

I peered through the window. It took a second for my eyes to focus. "Yeah. This is it. Thanks, Kyle, I'll get the report done and I'll email it to you."

In a perfect world, he'd have driven me just because it was the right thing to do. But this was college, and ethics were shaky with the youth. As I clambered out of the car, he called back to me, "Cool, thanks Pia, you're cool. Hey, take a pomegranate."

And since I couldn't come up with any excuse in the moment, I took a pomegranate from the cardboard box in his trunk. I waved at him with it from the curb as he pulled away.

More work. By noon tomorrow, I needed to have both mine and Kyle's lab reports done, and I'd only just started on the rough draft. That was what tonight was supposed to be, before Betta had pulled me away. And then, if I still had energy by two in the morning, I might put a dent in that statistics homework.

Massimo's and Tonio's apartment building was quiet. I took the elevator because the stairwell felt too deserted—this night felt a lot like the beginning of the semester, with the Scarpacis. There was dread and foreboding in the air.

I knocked on the door, but no one answered. I had a key; Massimo had made them for us back in September after the incident. I hadn't use it yet, but apparently Tonio hadn't gone behind his back and changed the locks, because the door swung open.

I locked it behind me.

iv.

The candles were out, but there was a faint smokiness to the air that suggested they might have been lit recently. A corner lamp was on. Past the heaps of old furniture and tapestried walls, the scent of something cooking drifted from the kitchen. But the apartment was quiet.

"Massimo?" No answer. "Hey, Tonio, you here?" Still nothing, but as I went to stand in the entrance to the hallway, I thought I heard the shower running.

I sat at the foot of the couch. I wondered if Betta was still at the party—I wondered if she'd throw a fit at work tomorrow. Would she tell on Massimo? Probably not, now that I thought of it; Betta liked power, she liked holding all the information, and if she played that card it was one less secret she had to lord over me and Massimo and Lorel.

I checked my phone. I had voicemails, just two of them. One from Lorel, one from Ida—apparently Savino or whoever else was at the bakery couldn't bother leaving a message. Wasn't Lorel still at rehearsal? I checked Ida's first.

"Pia, Savino can't get hold of you, you need to answer—"

I deleted it.

I checked Lorel's voicemail next.

"Pia, it's Lorel, don't come back to the apartment. Okay? I just got back"—I checked the time, it was from twenty minutes ago—"but you need to stay clear. Maybe go to your uncle's house, I don't know, I don't know where you are. Matty called me—he's here now, just in case. Someone set fire to some of your family's property, and Matty says we didn't do it, but I think your uncle thinks we did—oh, Matty's taking the phone, tell her—"

Matty's voice came on, deep and gravelly. "Hi, Pia, it's Matty. There was a fire, we don't know who did it, but if you talk to your uncle tell him it wasn't us—it wasn't Dad and the guys, because the Vitellis sent over some guys who busted up the windows and trashed the casino, so they think it was us but it *wasn't*. Uh, we're just hunkering down here, but you shouldn't come back. Okay. Bye."

My heart raced. If I hadn't already been cross-legged on the floor, I'd have needed to sit down. I retrieved Ida's message, and this time I listened with bated breath.

"Pia, Savino can't get hold of you, you need to answer because you might be in trouble. Someone started a fire, Diego Scarpaci's guys are probably behind it. You need to stay away from your apartment and your roommate, you should come back here—call me or Savino, we'll send someone to get you—we'll send one of my brothers—it isn't safe—"

"Oh, hi, *Marzano*."

I dropped the phone from my ear. Tonio stood in the hall, in his flannel pajama pants and bathrobe and, confusingly, a green sweater-vest without a shirt underneath. The outfit clashed so terrifically, my eyes couldn't make sense of what they were seeing at first—like a horrific Picasso, deeply disturbing yet somehow artistic in its atrocity. His hair was wet, and for once it wasn't slicked back.

We stared at one another for a moment. I saw way too much of his chest hair.

Apparently over his initial surprise, Tonio shrugged and moved towards the kitchen. "Thought I heard someone come in."

"What's with the vest?"

"It's warm." He said it like that should be obvious.

I frowned down at the phone, still playing Ida's voicemail. It ran for two minutes. "So's a sweater."

"No sleeves equals *mobility*." Tonio flapped his arms in the bathrobe to demonstrate. He grinned thinly back over his shoulder and disappeared into the kitchen.

I dropped my phone on the carpet and followed. "Has Savino called you?"

"Oh, I don't know, I haven't used anything as trivial as a *phone* in quite a while. He's probably called me thousands of times." He paused over the stove, stirred a simmering pot with a ladle. "*Stracciatella*?"

"No thanks. Wait, you don't have a phone?" I leaned against the counter. "So you haven't gotten anything from Ida?"

He thought about it, absently stirred the soup. "Maybe she faxed me at work."

I couldn't tell if he was joking. "I've gotten calls from Ida *and* Savino *and* Lorel. There was a fire."

"Is that why you're here?"

What a strange response to me telling him there'd been a fire. "No. Betta dragged me out to a bad party, and I bailed, and Lorel wasn't at the apartment, and I didn't know where else to go. I *don't* know where else to go, because there's a *fire.*"

He tossed back a wicked grin. "And you thought of me. Marzano, really. How sweet."

I was fed-up. "Is Massimo here?"

"No, he isn't." Tonio shut off the stove and combed his hair back. "What sort of party?"

I scowled at his back. "That is the least important thing I've said."

"Well, I'm fascinated. Was it one of those functions with expensive drugs and foul cheeses from the Auvergne, or the type with chocolate fountains and cocaine in the middling-range of quality? Or junkies rolling in obscene quantities of Doritos and buffalo dip?"

"Uh—"

"Oh, who am I kidding." He grabbed a bowl from an upper cabinet and served himself a ladleful of soup. "It's Betta. It was probably the third type, right?" He selected a spoon and slammed the utensil drawer. Then he leaned back against the counter by the stove, bowl cradled in his hands, watching me with those terribly amused black eyes.

I ground my back teeth together. I wasn't sure how he kept pulling the conversation away from something as important as a fire, but I was too tired to deal with it. "You're telling me no one called you?"

"Would I know?"

"For someone wearing a sweater-vest with flannel pants, you act pretty superior."

"I'm not acting." He smiled, stirred his soup. "Want a drink?"

In the other room, the apartment door banged open. And it slammed shut again. My head shot around.

Massimo's voice rang through the apartment. "Tonio? I've got to hide this stuff. Is your balcony still unlocked?"

He sounded winded. And strangely wound-up, for Massimo. I looked at Tonio, who rolled his eyes up towards the ceiling and sighed deeply. "I'm in here," he called.

A second later, Massimo appeared in the doorway.

He wore black pants, ripped open at one knee, and Tonio's gray overcoat over the top. A dark baseball cap was pulled down over his hair. I saw the shock flash across his face when he saw me, saw his eyes widen in the shadow.

And me? I was just as surprised. The smell of smoke drifted into the kitchen after him, and in one white-knuckled fist he clenched a container of lighter fluid.

"Oh, hey, Massimo," said Tonio. "Want some soup?"

VIII

Renegade

i.

Tonio and I sat in silence at the kitchen island—him eating his soup in a slow, disturbingly undisturbed way, me gripping a glass of water like it was going to run away.

Across the apartment, the shower clicked off. The bathroom fan faded out, wet feet padded down the hallway, and a door thumped shut.

My hands were numb. I wasn't sure whether it was from the ice water or just...my body doing weird things. I couldn't feel the glass in my hand. I felt like I did at Vitelli family dinners: far away from my body, a disembodied spectator, watching the scene play out with a train-wreck can't-look-away mentality. It felt a bit like dreaming, a bit like a waking nightmare.

Tonio tapped his spoon against his bowl. The clinking was obnoxiously loud in the silence. "Needs salt," he announced.

He got up to retrieve salt.

By the time he sat down again, salt cellar in hand, Massimo was back in the kitchen. His hair was wet and he wore a faded Columbia t-shirt with his sweatpants. He didn't meet my eyes, just walked on past us to the corner cabinet, where he poured himself a drink.

Tonio made a production of sprinkling salt over his soup. "You didn't answer my question," he said—again, too loud. He cast a glance over his shoulder at Massimo. "*Stracciatella?*"

"No thanks." Massimo finally came over and set his glass on the counter—something amber and iced. He sat a stool down from Tonio, across from me. His face was tight. I'd never seen him like this—a tightly-wound spring, like the adrenaline was still pumping and he was fighting to keep it together. His hand had a tremor as he raised the glass to his lips. His eyes flicked at me for the briefest moment, wary, and maybe a little afraid. *Why?*

He set the glass down.

143

Tonio sprinkled on more salt.

Finally, I spoke. "Tell me this isn't...you didn't..." I couldn't even finish the sentence, I didn't know how to broach this. A nightmare. Neither of them was acting natural.

Tonio wasn't concerned with tactics. "Oh, it's exactly what it looks like."

I looked at Massimo. "*Why?*"

"Pia." He swirled his drink, refusing to meet my eyes. "It's...hard to explain. You'd have to understand this family."

"I think I'm starting to," I said. "Give it your best fucking shot."

Massimo glanced at Tonio.

Tonio grinned, stirred his soup, and tasted it. "Perfect."

"Okay, I, uh..."

"Can you look at me when you say it?" I sounded like Mamma. Inside, I was disappointed and confused, but on the outside it was all stone-cold disapproval.

But he looked at me. "You know how we talked about getting roped into this family?" His words came in a torrent. "I told you we basically sign our lives away, or they're signed away for us. It's a death warrant—you're in it till you die, like it or not."

Tonio smiled into his soup. I wished he'd leave. I focused back on Massimo, attempted to wrap my mind around what he was saying. "Okay."

"I'm done." Massimo squared his jaw. "Maybe it was watching you get sucked into it that flipped the switch—"

"I'm not sucked into it," I snapped.

"But you're here. You're in it. And you wish you weren't. Maybe it was watching that happen, or seeing Giovani and Betta get pulled deeper into the mess, and maybe it was...Lorel. But I'm done."

"Are you leaving?"

"Did that ever help anyone? You know, my mom was married before she met my dad. Norma, my older sister—she's from Mom's first marriage, with a guy named Mario Mansi."

"I didn't know that."

"Well, not many people do," said Massimo, "because he isn't around anymore. This was back when Marco Vitelli was running the business out of Queens, before he left for New Orleans. My mom married Mario, but he didn't like the Vitelli business, how our grandfather was running things, so he tried to take Norma and leave. He'd had enough and he wanted custody so he could take Norma and get out of New York and get away." Ice clinked against his teeth. "Mario's gone now."

"Gone where?"

"I don't know."

144

"Are you saying—?"

"*I don't know*," he repeated.

"Oh, we all know where he went," said Tonio, helpfully.

Massimo shot him a look. "We don't *know*. I'm just saying, he's gone. He isn't the only one it's happened to, the Marzanos have got too many ties to the Sicilian mafia, the Vitellis have always done their dirty work. That's the only way you make it out of this family without any strings trailing after you. Look at Zia Sabine—Savino still has influence in her life, and she's done everything she can to distance herself. Look at your parents, they did everything they could, and here *you* are."

I wiped my freezing hands on my jeans. "Getting arrested for arson isn't going to get you out of New York."

"Oh, that isn't his plan." Tonio finished his soup and dropped his spoon in the bowl. He planted his elbows on the counter and rested his sharp chin on his fists. "It's more ambitious than that, isn't it, *capo*?"

Massimo scowled. "It makes sense." He tossed back the rest of his drink and looked at me. "We're stuck in an infinite loop. The family business will keep replacing worker bees and paying off the authorities, and no one can touch Valentino, and he's funding it all from his olive fortress in Sicily."

"*Olive fortress*." Tonio shook his head and got up to get more soup.

I stared at Massimo. "So call the cops."

"Savino will just pay them off. People have tried before, but Valentino and Marco Vitelli, they've set up a bullet-proof shield around this family, starting a long time ago—Savino's got guys who make the rounds, pay off the right people, pay visits to their families. It's what my dad does. Him, Joey, Little Tony, Stefano—they just pay off the guys, there's no way law enforcement's intervening in the business. The only way this operation is going down is if it crumbles from the inside."

"So you're burning buildings?"

"Here's the deal," said Tonio over his shoulder, from where he stood at the stove. "My brothers take care of the shipments. Raul and Savino's cousin Stefano are in charge of keeping contact with Valentino, settling the times for the drop-offs. Johnny Moriondo works directly below them." He set his bowl on the counter and took back his seat. He waved the spoon for emphasis. "The Vitellis have warehouses, four of them. They're spread out throughout the city under different names, but they belong to the Vitellis, and that's where the oil's kept when the shipments come in. Johnny coordinates storage. Then, he and some of the other guys take it out of the city in trucks to the drop-off points."

"I only got one," said Massimo. He stared into his empty glass, like it might magically refill itself.

145

"Yes, I was going to ask you about that."

"I only got one, but I meant to hit at least three, if not all of them."

I rubbed my temple. "You were going to burn down *three warehouses?* Tonight?"

Massimo shrugged. "That was the plan. If not all."

"You realize that makes you an arsonist, right? Even if it is family property—and that arguably makes it even worse—you could be arrested." Looking back, there had always been something subtly ominous about Massimo's serene exterior; I'd chalked it up to composure, to masterful self-control, but I wasn't so sure anymore. My personal version of Massimo slipped through my fingers; he wasn't okay, he was running around New York City burning buildings. And if Massimo wasn't okay, what did that say about *me?*

"That's why I didn't hit the others." He ran a hand through his wet hair, pushed it back from his forehead. "Someone called the fire department, it must have gotten back to Savino real fast. I don't know how."

"How was that supposed to help? Anything?"

"There's a shipment coming in tomorrow," said Tonio.

Massimo nodded. "If I could have hit the others, they wouldn't have a place for the oil, they'd have to turn the shipment around. But it's too late for that now. They'll be watching like hawks." He got up to grab another drink. "I want to get between Valentino and Savino. If there's trouble with the business over here, Valentino won't like the way the Vitellis are running things, they might cut us off. I didn't mean to get the Scarpacis in trouble."

I stared at him. "They are. Lorel called me."

He froze with his back to me, a bottle and glass stopper in either hand. "Where is she?"

"At the apartment. Matty's with her."

"Her brother?"

"Yeah. She left a voicemail. Savino knows where she is, Massimo."

He set the bottle down and came back to the counter with his drink. He rubbed the back of his neck, suddenly agitated. "Can I hear it? The message?"

"My phone's in the living room."

He went to get it. He came back with my cell phone and Kyle's pomegranate. "Where did this come from?"

"Someone gave it to me."

"Oh, you go to the *crazy* parties, Marzano." Tonio laughed.

I grimaced. "Here." I took my phone and played the message—the guys stayed silent the whole time, intent. A muscle in Massimo's jaw twitched. When Matty hung up, I went ahead and played Ida's message too.

Massimo was quiet for a long moment. He rubbed his neck and finished his second drink. Then he tapped the phone where it sat on the counter between us. "Can you call Savino back?"

"Why?"

"Because if you don't, he'll probably send someone to your apartment."

"Oh. Sure." I didn't want Savino to find Matty and Lorel. Still, it took me a moment to put in the number and hit *call*, and sit in silence waiting for my uncle to pick up.

Now that I thought about it, Massimo did talk about fire a lot. I wondered if this was his first fire. I wondered how long he'd been planning this. Since Lorel? Since my arrival this summer?

The ringer clicked off. "Pia, where are you?"

That was Savino. His voice was low and even, but there was shouting in the background. "I'm at Massimo's apartment. We're studying physics."

"Did you get Ida?"

"I got her message. Is everyone okay?"

"Is Massimo there?"

I licked my lips. I looked across the counter—the guys watched me—and I wondered if they could hear my uncle on the line. "He's here, why?"

"He hasn't answered his phone."

"It died." I was surprised how easily the lie slipped out. "Do you want to talk to him?"

"No. They're both with you?"

"Yeah."

"Then stay there."

At that moment, I could have said something about Lorel. Something like *don't go to my apartment*, or *she didn't have anything to do with this*. But if Savino was fixated on Diego Scarpaci, I didn't want to remind him of my roommate.

"Are you there?" It sounded like loads of traffic in the background, but it was too late at night for that. Or was it? This was New York, the city that never slept. I wondered where he was. Somewhere with sirens.

"I'm here."

"Don't leave their apartment. Someone will get you in the morning. Don't go anywhere alone."

My jaw was tight. And my mouth had gone dry. "Alright."

"Tell Massimo to fix his phone. Be careful."

"Okay. Bye." I hung up and set the phone back down. Then I downed the entire cup of water while Tonio and Massimo watched. I looked at my cousin. "He said he's been trying to call you."

"I left my phone here."

"I told him it was dead. Just so you know."

"Thanks."

I stared at the tabletop. "He doesn't want me going anywhere."

Tonio slapped Massimo on the back. "This family and its cryptic threats, am I right? If you step out of this apartment or dare set a toe outside New York, Valentino Marzano will hurl a bolt of lightning and eviscerate you. Don't you know?"

"I told you," said Massimo, his voice low. "You don't like this family any more than I do."

"I don't want anyone to get hurt!"

"People always get hurt," said Tonio. He looked at Massimo. "Have you told her?"

"No."

"Told me what?"

"You sure you don't want a drink, Marzano? Even a small one?" Tonio got up. "I want a drink. You?"

"No." I leaned across the island. I did want a drink, but—no. "Massimo, what?"

He rubbed his jaw, dark eyes drilling into the counter. "Pia, I don't...we don't have proof. It probably isn't worth saying." He cast a glance over at Tonio, who stood in the corner and mixed a drink with the dexterity of a practiced bartender, while humming some classical piece under his breath. "Make me one, huh?" He faced me. "I've been thinking about this for a while, me and Tonio both. You coming up here, living with the Vitellis, working for Savino, it's all great timing for the business. You, a Marzano. You're Valentino and Devota Maria's oldest grandchild, that means something."

"What?"

He shrugged and took the glass Tonio handed him. "It means...you're a Marzano."

I swallowed. I was still trying to digest everything—the fire, Massimo's renegade plans, and I didn't see why my being in New York affected that. "Is it about the Scarpacis?"

Tonio waved a hand. "Oh, no. Valentino hasn't got any contact with Cal Marzano, she's dead to him and the whole clan. No, this is about Marco Vitelli."

"Savino's dad," I said.

"Carla's dad," Tonio emphasized.

Massimo followed the silver veins of granite with his fingertip. "The family business belonged to our grandfather, before Savino took over. It was between Marco Vitelli and Valentino Marzano. Then Marco moved down to Louisiana, expanded the business to Italians in the New Orleans area, and he left Savino and my mom in charge."

"Nicole?" I couldn't imagine her in charge of the business.

"Yeah, but she doesn't care. She and my dad, they'd rather both let Savino rule the world than call the shots." There was a lot of bitterness in his voice. He sipped his drink. "Your mom, marrying Leo Marzano—in the Vitellis 'books, that was the best thing that ever happened to this family. It meant a permanent agreement between the Marzanos and Vitellis, it meant the whole fiasco with Cal marrying a Scarpaci was behind us. Then they left."

Tonio raised his glass. "The end of an era."

"Yep." Massimo tossed back the rest of his drink. "They left. No more Marzanos in Brooklyn." He pointed at me across the counter. "You'd just been born. The Marzano-Vitelli covenant, in flesh. They left in the night, didn't tell anyone, and didn't turn up for another eighteen years or so—we didn't know where you were—until Sabine called us with the news. From Georgia."

Something squirmed in my gut. Maybe I did need a drink; I didn't like where this story was going. Tonio and I both watched Massimo, waiting, hanging on the silence as he traced the countertop and took deep, calm breaths.

"I mean, isn't it perfect?" he said, without looking up. "After all these years, you're back and working for Savino. You're back, and now he's got a Marzano to hold up and show Valentino."

"A reminder," said Tonio.

Massimo nodded. "A reminder of the contract. A Marzano of his own."

"You make it sound like I don't have a choice," I said.

Massimo barked a laugh. "Do you, Pia? Do any of us?"

"You make it sound like my parents failed." My voice had a hard edge.

"Not failure, *per se*," said Tonio. He placed both hands flat on the kitchen island, either side of his glass. "More an underestimation of the extent to which this family will go to preserve itself."

"Savino will do whatever he needs to keep this family afloat," said Massimo. "Marco Vitelli's the same way."

How many people had told me Savino kept this family safe? How many times had Savino himself said, in that same borderline-sinister way, that he took care of his family? Did that include orchestrating my move to New York?

I swallowed. "Sabine said she arranged me moving up here. But you think Savino gave her the idea?"

Massimo looked at Tonio. Tonio's eyebrows shot up—he finished his drink and slammed it on the counter. The ice clanked around inside. "Tell her, then, you opened this *pithos*."

Massimo met my eyes. "I think Marco Vitelli had Carla and Leo…taken care of."

A chill crawled up my spine. "What?"

"We're speculating, Marzano. But it makes sense and honestly it's perfectly in character for the Vitellis, with their history. All those years working with the mafia in Sicily, they'd already done some dark shit before and it's pretty on par with their track record."

I shook my head. *Taken care of* didn't mean sending me and the kids checks from New Orleans, it meant something else entirely, and I couldn't go there just yet. "They were in a car accident."

"Those can be staged," said Massimo. "It was at night, right? You distract the driver, you throw something in the road at just the right moment—fuck, you could even put a *person* in the road. People think it was a deer or something."

"That's a stretch." My chest felt tight. It's what the cops had said, *they swerved for a deer.* Even though I knew Papa would never swerve for any animal. "That's a big stretch." And the implications shook me—the idea that my grandfather might have had Mamma and Papa killed, just so Savino could drag me up here so he'd have a Marzano puppet. It was ridiculously far-fetched, and there were a thousand other explanations, but Tonio was right—there was an underlying vein of *Vitelli* running through that story, the desperate need to keep the family secure at any cost. Did that cost include killing one's own family members? Did Savino know?

It's speculation. There's no proof. What a relief, that there was no proof.

"If that were the case," I said, evenly, "you wouldn't have to burn down warehouses to ruin the business. You'd just tell Valentino that Marco Vitelli had my parents killed."

"Oh, yes, he'd definitely believe that," Tonio scoffed. "Especially with the business doing so well. Yeah, he'd bite."

"I thought about it," said Massimo. "But we don't have proof. Even if we did, I don't think we could get the message to him—I wasn't exaggerating about his *oliveto* fortress, he's got enemies both here and back in Sicily. You've got to get through too many people to even talk to one of Valentino's guys, let alone Valentino himself. Chances are, someone here would hear about it first. And we'd…" He glanced at Tonio. "You know."

Tonio smiled thinly. He drew a line across his narrow throat. "We'd get *Mario Mansi-d.*"

I didn't believe that. I didn't *want* to believe that. "When did you decide this?"

"That it might have been orchestrated?" Massimo rubbed his neck. "Sometime towards the end of the summer. But after the Scarpacis kidnapped you, I started thinking about it again—they wanted to use you against Valentino probably, so what would keep Savino from doing the same thing?"

Even if it wasn't what Tonio and Massimo believed it to be, I acknowledged that Savino had probably manipulated Sabine into sending me up here. It sounded like something he'd do, and my aunt was the perfect measure of both gullible and oblivious to fall for the trick.

She should have known. She knew what her family was like, and I hadn't, but she'd sent me up here anyway. I needed to call her, I needed to talk to Cristine and the kids, but it was almost midnight and I didn't trust myself to stay composed over the phone.

"Someone should track down Betta," was all I said.

"Why?" said Massimo. "Where is she?"

"She dragged me out to a party in the Bronx and I bailed on her. She's probably still there."

Massimo sighed. "She needs to stop doing that. Does she have a car? I'll let Mom know where she is."

That reminded me. "Oh. She knows about you and Lorel." Another blow, because this night hadn't been shitty enough.

Fear flashed across Massimo's face. "How?"

"Figured it out, I guess. That's how she got me to the party, she threatened to tell your parents and Savino about it."

Massimo put his head in his hands. "I need to call her."

"Betta?"

"Lorel."

"Are you gonna tell her?"

He laughed—a crazed laugh, a sleep-deprived laugh, the laugh of a man who'd just burnt down a family warehouse and fled through the streets of New York City. "Tell her what? Which part? The part where I started the fire and set the Vitellis on her family? The part where Betta is gonna tell our dad and we're both gonna end up at the bottom of the Sound?"

"I'll come to your funeral," Tonio offered. "*Momento mori,* and all that. It's a very Italian-Catholic way to go, very gothic."

"*Drown us in the river.*" Massimo rested his head on his arms. "The fire won't even work. It was too small, Savino can bounce back from that. He's got the other warehouses—it went to hell."

Tonio clinked his glass against his bowl. His hair had dried in waves, almost curly. "Well," he said. "I have work in the morning."

151

"It is morning," I said.

Tonio set his dishes in the sink and nodded at me. "*Marzano*." He gave Massimo a pointed look. "Don't stay up too late, yeah?"

"Hmm."

He and his bathrobe exited the scene.

"Massimo?"

"Yeah."

I pressed my knuckles into my eye sockets. "I feel sick." My lungs couldn't get a good breath of air, and my stomach turned over every few seconds. Nausea hit me in waves. I wanted to smoke, I wanted a drink, I wanted anything but to sit here in this agonizing in-between moment of *not knowing*.

He finished his drink. "Me too."

Moonlight played through the kitchen windows, casting the room in a silver sheen. My cousin looked like a black-and-white photo of a soldier come home from war, like an old man who had seen too much of the world and hated it.

And I felt like a ghost. I was a ghost.

Massimo made up a bed for me on the sofa. He lit a couple candles, checked the door and window locks, then said goodnight and disappeared down the hallway.

I lay there on the cigar-smelling sofa, under layered quilts, staring at the candle flames. I lay there and I felt like I was trapped in a nightmare. It was one of the dreams were you couldn't run fast enough, only it was like that with everything—anything I did, someone else was one step ahead. Any choice I made had been made for me years before. This was what Massimo had meant: our very existences had been signed away to the family business, long before we had any say in the matter.

And what about Savino? I wanted to trust him—I understood why everyone else did. But trusting him to take care of the family and trusting him to do the right thing weren't the same. I believed him when he said he'd do anything to keep us safe.

So what if Massimo and Tonio were right? What if Marco Vitelli had gotten Mamma and Papa killed? I let myself dwell on that thought for a moment. The Vitellis were capable of lots of things, I had no doubt, but *murder*? Forgetting Ezio's spat in Naples, ignoring the Mario Mansi story...*murder*?

Even if that part wasn't true—and like they'd said, there was no proof—I firmly believed by this point that Savino had manipulated my aunt, and that in itself scared me. That scared me because it meant he was comfortable using people as pieces in this game, playing the role of puppet master without his puppets even realizing.

After the funeral, all I'd wanted was security. I'd only needed something safe and stable—I'd thought Ida and Savino a soft place to land. But I was a puppet. I was a chess piece. There was nothing safe about that.

I blew out the candles, watched the smoke drift up through the darkness, and I cried myself to sleep.

ii.

I didn't hear Tonio get up and leave. Next thing I knew, Massimo was clanking around in the kitchen at half-past six.

"I called Lorel," he said, once I'd pulled on my marijuana-smelling sweater and joined him in the kitchen. He was tamping down espresso. He didn't look like he'd slept. "Coffee?"

"Yeah." I rubbed the sleep from my eyes, combed my fingers through my hair—it had knotted around the hair clips. "Is she alright?"

"She and Matty stayed up in the living room. He had a gun. She had her baseball bat, the one with the butterflies." His brow furrowed. "But they didn't get any trouble. Though…Diego tried calling them. A few times."

"You think Savino will leave them alone?"

"You know what I think, Pia?" He sounded exhausted. He pulled the espresso and handed me the ceramic cup. "Here. You know what I think? I think if we wanted our uncle to leave Lorel alone, you could make him."

I blinked. "Seriously?"

"As far as he knows, you don't know anything about him moving you up here or the Marzano-Vitelli deal." He sounded like he'd thought about this a lot, possibly during a time that was meant for sleeping. "Savino doesn't know you have any suspicions about the other stuff. You could make it perfectly clear that if something happens to Lorel, you'd consider moving back to Georgia—you could even just insinuate it. In fact"—he tamped down a second shot—"in fact, I think you might be the only person who has that sort of influence."

Manipulate Savino without him knowing he's being manipulated? I almost laughed. "He'd know."

"You know how people say you're like him?"

"Yeah." For a while I'd liked the idea that people saw Savino in me, even if I didn't understand it—he was collected and charismatic, confident, unnaturally invulnerable—and who didn't want to be like that? Who wouldn't want to be compared to someone as untouchably god-like as Savino Vitelli? Anyone. Me. A girl floundering without parents or leadership or plans for the future. Until the dawning realization that gods lost connection with humanity, drowned in their immortality, gradually grew more comfortable with puppet-mastery and sloughed off the ethical shackles imposed upon mere mortals. People like this really existed, and my uncle was one of them.

"They're right." Massimo leaned back against the counter. "And it's not just because you look like him. You lost everything—"

"Thank you," I said, "for reminding me."

"No, I mean, you lost everything, and you'd do anything to keep what you have. Right?"

"I'm not Savino."

"No," he said. "You're Pia Marzano. And the Vitellis need you so much that it makes you dangerous."

I set down my cup. "Massimo." He watched me. His eyes were molten. "I'm not a part of this."

He didn't say anything.

"I don't *want* to be a part of this. I'm going to finish the year," I said. "I'm gonna get through school. Then I'm leaving." Even as I said it—and I knew it was the right thing, I couldn't get the kids caught up in this family drama, in a business where people went missing and people burned down buildings and paid off the cops—but even as I heard myself say the words, I wondered if it would be so terrible to stay. It was a fleeting thought: what would it be like to stay in Brooklyn, to let Savino take care of us, to be confident in my siblings 'continued security?

I ground the heel of my hand against my temple. *No.* "I can't do that to the kids. This—I can't drag them into it."

Massimo worked his jaw and frowned into his espresso. "Leaving…it doesn't work like that, Pia, you know that. They find you after a while, it catches up. As long as the business stands—"

"I'm not getting pulled into this," I said. "I have people to take care of, I have to at least *try*."

"Okay."

And that was the end of it. No *but you could help, you're a valuable piece in the puzzle, you can manipulate our uncle.* No begging, no deals. For all of Massimo's faults, he respected people—he understood the value of free will.

We finished our coffee, then we ate toast at the breakfast table while morning crept into New York skyline. Massimo cut into Kyle's pomegranate and picked at the ruby seeds.

"I have two lab reports to get done before noon," I said, absently. School felt like a dream. I was supposed to be at the bakery right now.

"Why two?"

"I'm doing Kyle's. Because he gave me a ride last night."

"I can help."

"I don't have my computer."

"You can use mine."

He retrieved a laptop from his room and brought it back to the table. I logged into my school email account and dug around for the spreadsheets my lab group had emailed each other—Kyle's was a mess, but it had all the necessary information. He was chaotic, but he wasn't stupid.

Massimo stared at the data for a moment in silence. Then he scratched his head. "Why are you...blowtorching fruit?"

"I don't know, Massimo, it's college."

"You need sources for this? How many studies do you think have been done on..." A smile twitched at the corner of his mouth. "Brûléed oranges?"

"I'm leaning on the Maillard reaction with fructose thing. It wasn't my idea."

"This isn't Maillard. This is caramelization. But that's good, it might be easier to find."

A couple hours later, we'd finished my portion of the report and were almost through with Kyle's. For a while, sitting there at the breakfast table over empty dishes and scratch paper, while golden light crept slowly across the room and up the opposite wall, I could pretend I was just another student, cramming assignments at the last minute. This was normal stress. This was the only stressor I was supposed to have in my life, at this point—even if Mamma and Papa had still been alive, school anxiety would have existed. *Normal.*

Massimo had a nice computer. It had all the high-tech software, the spreadsheets I could only get on school computers in the back of the science library. It was probably because he'd done chemistry at Columbia, but it got me thinking. I leaned back in my chair while my email downloaded Kyle's finished assignment. The loading bar inched forward. "What do you do?" I asked. "Really? You work for your dad, right?"

"Right."

"What's that mean?"

"It means I work for Savino. It means I've got my concealed-carry permit, I've got a fast car, and I keep a handgun in the glovebox."

"I knew it." The document finished loading and I pressed *send.*

Massimo shrugged. He tossed back the rest of his cold espresso. "Everyone in this family has a gun. I'm surprised you don't, yet."

I still had Savino's handgun in my bedside drawer, but I didn't want to admit that even to Massimo. I didn't like the idea of being another armed soldier in my uncle's legions. "So is the Lexus yours?"

"It's under my name. Sometimes if there's a big oil shipment coming in, Savino will have me and some other guys drive to the drop-off point—supervise, make sure it gets to the warehouses."

"What's *capo* mean?" Tonio had called him that, last night. I shut the laptop and crossed my arms, faced my cousin.

"Nothing," he said. "It's nothing. He was being stupid."

iii.

I didn't get another call from Savino or Ida. I did call Lorel—she relayed the events of the night, how she and Matty had built a pillow fort in the living room and sat up all night—how her brother had fallen asleep at one point, and she'd heard something at the door, but when she'd bravely emerged from the fort with her baseball bat and checked the peephole, it had just been some kid leaving catalogs on doorsteps.

"I'm going to school," she told me, around noon. "Do you think it's safe?"

"Is Matty still there?"

"He's asleep on the couch."

"It's probably safe. Probably safer than being at the apartment, anyway—only Betta and Tonio know you at school. They don't care. Oh, Betta might be mad, if she's even there." Now that I thought about it, I doubted the Di Natales would be allowed at Fortuna today. I doubted Savino would allow them.

"How come?"

"Stupid reasons."

"She's your cousin."

"Yeah," I said, "it's an unfortunate fact, I'm coming to grips with it slowly. Please humor me."

She sighed. "You sound like Tonio. Okay, well, Matty will be here for a while. I'm going to get ready for school, but it should be safe if you want to come around at some point."

"Once I'm freed from house arrest," I muttered.

House arrest was lifted that afternoon. Again, Savino didn't contact me—he called Massimo and passed on the details from the night. "All the details he thought pertinent, anyway," said Massimo. He rummaged through his coat pocket for car keys. "He's reopening the bakery tomorrow, he says you can be there, but he thinks the Scarpacis might try something. So be careful."

I got my few belongings together, and we drove to my dumpster-fire apartment. Massimo parked his Lexus on the curb and walked me upstairs. I felt weird announcing my presence to my own apartment, but I also didn't want Matty Scarpaci shooting me in the head.

"It's Pia," I said, as I wrestled open the squealing door.

"Hi, Pia," said a voice from the kitchen.

The living room was empty, but there was an impressive pillow fort constructed from sheets and couch cushions, filling half the room. It was clearly the result of rigorous childhood practice. Lorel's baseball bat was propped against the coffee table

I glanced up at Massimo. "Want to sweep the apartment?"

"You joke," he said. He wandered off down the hallway, hands in his pockets, peering around corners.

I dropped my stuff by the door and stepped into the kitchen. "Nice fort."

Matty sat at the rickety blue table in the corner, in a muscle shirt and sweats. He had a book in his lap and a mug in one hand. "Thanks." He was steeping tea. It was funny, watching a man with biceps the size of my face dip a tea bag in Lorel's *Pride & Prejudice* coffee mug.

He didn't look like Papa. He looked only vaguely like Lorel—I found it hard to believe that we were related. I set my keys by the sink and leaned against the counter. "Did you know we were cousins?"

He shook his head. "Mom doesn't talk about her family, we didn't even know her surname till recently. She told us after...you know, after Dad kidnapped you. Didn't know she was a Marzano." He made a face. "That was stupid, him and Pietro—that's our brother, he and my dad and our uncles, they're insane, they'll do stuff behind Mom's back and they pay for it after. Not one of them thinks before making a move. And no one bothers to tell us, tell the kids, because having everyone together in New York is dangerous enough without everyone knowing about it. That's what they say, at least. But I don't believe that. I think not knowing is worse." He set his mug down. His pale, freckled face was tired—bloodshot eyes, dark circles, and his curly hair, though cropped short, was flat and matted on one side. "Sorry about your dad," he said. "And your mom."

"She was a Vitelli." His family was supposed to hate Vitellis, for reasons I still didn't quite understand.

Matty shrugged. "What was his name?"

"Leo. Leonardo."

"You have siblings?"

"Three."

"Huh." He sipped his tea, winced. "Cool. More cousins. Do you think they'd like us?"

I hadn't really thought about it, the relation between the New York family and the Augusta one. They were separate worlds. "Cristine doesn't like a lot of people," I said. "I think Lorel would annoy her just by...being Lorel, I guess. But Carlo and Vince would like you."

He nodded. "Cool."

"Hi." Massimo had come into the kitchen behind me. He stood in the doorway and watched Matty with a sort of guarded curiosity.

Matty set down his tea. He matched Massimo's expression perfectly. "Hi."

I felt like I was standing in the middle of a collision, so I stepped to the side. Didn't want to obstruct their battle of skeptical eye contact. "Matty. This is my cousin Massimo."

Matty rubbed his neck. "I know." He put up his chin, looked Massimo up and down. "I know. Lorella told me."

For an instant, Massimo looked vaguely uncomfortable. Then he put back his shoulders and stood straight, the picture-perfect Nice Italian Boy. "Matteo," he said.

"Oh, please," said Matty cooly, "I go by Matteo the Third."

Lorel got back from rehearsal around half-past nine, and Matty left after a late dinner of scavenged leftovers.

"Are you alright?" I asked her, once we were alone. She sat cross-legged on the living room floor, gripping a cup of tea in one hand and painting her toenails with the other.

She thought about it. "Yeah, I think I am. This isn't the first time something like this has happened, you know, and I doubt it'll be the last. These things are just cropping up a lot more often since you've come to town."

"Sorry."

"It's not your fault."

I inspected her nail polish collection—a jumble of bottles and polish remover and foam toe separators in a tattered Dillards shoebox. She had mostly clear coats, but there were a couple small, colorful bottles mixed in there, with tiny brushes for designs. "You talked to Massimo."

"Yeah, I did. Actually, he called me last night." She paused, looked up at me. "Did you know?"

I shook my head. "I didn't know he was planning anything." Although there had been warning signs. Not necessarily for arson, but certainly for some form of a breaking point. "Are you okay with that?"

Lorel shrugged. She kicked her skirt around to get to her other foot. "Who hasn't been moved with passion so that they nearly burn down family property?"

"Who *has*?"

"Massimo, apparently. Our families are insane, Pia." Lorel set down her mug. She switched nail polish, gave the clear-coating bottle a good shake, scrunched up her face as she struggled to open it. "Can you—?"

Probably not, but I took the bottle anyway. The second I gripped the top between thumb and forefinger, and squeezed, a flash of pain shot up through my wrist, into my elbow. *Shit.* I shook out my hand and handed it back. "Sorry."

"No worries." She tossed it back into the box and picked a different one.

The tendonitis was back, and I didn't even have my braces anymore. "Are you going to help him?"

She managed to open a second bottle, wiped the excess off the brush. "I don't know. No, I don't think so." She paused. "I don't like getting involved in family stuff, that's why I moved out into my aunt's house last year, that's why I don't talk to Mom and Dad, they're so dramatic and immature. This is just getting involved in that stuff all over again, except with a different family."

I almost made a joke about it being her family soon, except it probably wouldn't help, and also it probably wasn't a joke.

"Anyway," she said, "I need to graduate. I need a job, then I can worry about family stuff, *maybe*. And I need to finish this show."

"When is it?"

"The weekends before and after finals—hey, I've got posters, I'll give you a couple for the bakery."

We both sat in silence after that, thinking about it. She'd paused in her nail-painting. I rubbed my wrists and tried to imagine going into *Il Panificio Zeppole* tomorrow, then I tried to imagine going into the *panificio* laden with posters advertising Lorel Scarpaci's performance.

"Maybe not," I said.

Lorel nodded, her brows knit. "Yeah. Maybe not."

iv.

For what felt like the millionth time, I had to email teachers about my absences from class. It wasn't excused this time—the "break-in" at the beginning of the semester had been passed over, but by this point I had several late assignments and I'd missed a dangerously high number of lectures. My poor attendance alone was enough to fail me.

I could't afford to fail. I didn't have the funds to retake a semester.

The funny thing was, if I'd mentioned this to Savino or even to Sabine, they would have helped without a moment's hesitation. They wouldn't have even thought much about it. Savino would have been quick about sorting out any miscommunication with my teachers; he'd take care if it. And what was a few thousand dollars for the semester, to someone like Savino Vitelli?

When Betta picked me up for work the next morning, she acted perfectly normal. I was uncomfortable throughout the drive, waiting for her to rip into me about the party, about my deserting her, but the lecture never came. She complained about some teacher who was giving her shit, then she complained about the traffic, then when Giovani finally told her to shut up from the backseat—he was trying to sleep—she cranked up some aggressively-bad pop music and stopped complaining.

When we'd parked out back of the bakery, Giovani muttered his usual tirade about hating being late, and stormed on in. But Betta hung back—she grabbed my arm to make sure I held back, too.

Here it comes, I thought.

"Sorry," she said.

"For what?"

"You know what. The party. I'm sorry."

I was fully aware that it was something she needed to apologize for; I just hadn't thought she'd actually do it, or even acknowledge her own fault. I nodded. "I appreciate you saying that."

"Do you forgive me? Pia? Do you forgive me though?"

"Yeah, I forgive you, just don't do it again." I didn't trust Betta, not with my safety nor hers nor anyone else's. She had poor judgement and even poorer taste in company.

That seemed to console her, though. She tossed back her braids and marched ahead of me into the bakery.

The fry oil was already hissing, and the walk-in cooler hummed beside me as I stood in the back and tied on an apron. Giovani was reading the list of orders for the day off the cork-board, and Betta had disappeared into the pantry, leaving me alone with barrels of focaccia dough and cannoli shells to be rolled out. If I closed my eyes, the smell of bread and cleaner and the faintest tinge of caramelized sugar hovered in the air, and the sounds of machinery and soft footfalls and very distant music punctured the silence. It reminded me of home, of the bakery back in Augusta.

This felt more real, somehow. Graduating and going home, this was what I'd miss. I wouldn't miss the fact that it was a laundering front, but I understood why the family was built up around this place. It made me wonder what it was like over in Sicily, at the orchard and the mills.

"Pia." I looked over. Savino tied on his apron, nodded at me, inscrutable as always. "Ida wants you over for dinner tonight."

He overturned one of the buckets on the butcher-block counter. Silken, bubbled dough spilled out across the floured surface. He took a bench-scraper in hand and started portioning it out.

I watched him. Everything Massimo and Tonio had said the day before flashed through my mind, and I had to force myself to respond. "I don't think I can. I'm really behind on homework. I need to catch up tonight."

Savino nodded in a distracted sort of way, as if he'd expected this. "Then let's talk in my office before you leave." He put his hands in the oil and gently shuffled the dough off to the side—green-gold streaks gleamed on the countertop.

"Alright."

"You're back at your apartment?"

I nodded. He couldn't see me. "Yeah, I am. Hey, my roommate—Lorel—she didn't know, she doesn't have contact with her family. She says they're crazy, she hasn't lived with them in years. She didn't know anything about it." I held my breath.

But Savino didn't answer. He finished weighing the first batch of dough, stepped down the bench and heaved a second bucket onto the counter; he made it look easy, but that would have killed my wrists. He reached under the counter and set a pile of trays down by the portioned dough. Only then did he look back at me, eyebrows raised, and tap the space beside him.

I stepped in. I dipped my hands in the bowl of oil. I guess I hadn't noticed before, hadn't been paying attention, but it smelled thick and peppery, almost burned my nostrils—and something sweet, like fruit and fructose. Vegetal and mineral and sacred. It was chrism oil, it was the smell of Vince's head at Baptism, Cristine at Confirmation.

I forgot about Lorel. I stared down at the bowl, at my hands slick with the oil, and my throat closed up.

Savino had stopped. He was watching me.

I picked up a piece of dough and slapped it into a pan.

I didn't know, then. I didn't know that obsession runs through a bloodline like ancestral sin. I was just making focaccia and trying to ignore the pungent scent, the way the oil clung thick to my skin—brow furrowed, trying hard to forget it, because it was stirring things up, as if my mind was struggling to uncover a distant memory. It shook me, but I couldn't explain why. Not at the time

Passion and obsession aren't the same thing. You can be passionate about tradition and culture and cuisine, but when you narrow your focus to a single item, everything else slips out of proportion, and it can grow to obsession. Looking back, perhaps that was the best word used to describe my uncle: *obsessed*. Obsessed with the process. Obsessed with olive oil.

So was I. I just didn't know it yet.

Savino knew.

My uncle left after a while, to work in the office. Giovani stood frowning at the fryers and Betta clanked around at the sink, and I finished the focaccia and put it up to proof. I washed my hands, but the oil somehow stayed. Lorel would have made some joke about my smelling like a breadstick, but I couldn't shake the scent for the rest of the day, long after it should have washed away, like it was engrained in my senses.

"Pia," Dora called. She ducked out of the pastry case where she'd been rearranging some trays. "*Look*." She held up her hand, elegant fingers splayed. There was a chunk of diamond on her ring finger.

"There's a rock stuck to your hand," I said.

She sighed.

That probably wasn't the right response to someone getting engaged. "Congratulations, Dora. Who is it? It it, uh...? The guy from...?" I couldn't remember his name, the guy from Ida's dinner party.

Dora nodded. "Francesco."

"That's exciting."

It wasn't. Well, sure, it was exciting for Dora probably. It was just startling to see someone as young as Dora Di Natale—all of nineteen-years-old, *my age*—get engaged to a guy she'd only been with for a maximum of three months. The worst part was that now I'd have to go to a wedding. I hated weddings. Weddings were for crying people and bridesmaids in expensive horrible dresses and old people sneaking up behind you and gripping your arm and pointing gnarled fingers to say *You're next, kid.* I didn't want to be next.

I distracted myself for the next few hours by filling countless cannoli—we had an order, whole boxes of the pistachio-crusted ones to run down the street. The motions were soothing in their repetition, the monotony, even if I did start getting those familiar pains in my elbows, the strain in my forearms.

When it was time to head out for school, I dropped off my apron and went to find Savino. He was still in the office.

"I'm heading out."

He looked up from the desk—the huge, out-of-place desk that looked like it belonged in a professor's office—and set down the manilla folder he'd been flipping through. There was a light dusting of flour in one of his eyebrows. He pointed at a folding chair set up nearby, and I took it. "Are you alright?"

What a broad question. I wanted to be mad about it. "I'm fine." Was that what he'd wanted to talk about, or was this the intro to a lecture?

He tilted his head. "You seem fine. But by all rights you shouldn't be. Sometimes we convince ourselves we're alright so we don't have something else to fix. So. Are you really alright?" He had his hands on his knees, and sat forward in his chair. His eyes were Mamma's eyes.

"Actually," I said," I'm pretty stressed out."

"Why?"

School was the quick answer, but it was more than that. I thought about it. The words came out slowly—they shouldn't of come at all, I shouldn't have said anything to him, but there was something about Savino sitting there so still and attentive, something about the idea that someone cared deeply about what was going on in my soul that made me want to turn my heart inside out and dump it at his feet. "Every time I get into a routine and I start to figure things out, something throws off the rhythm. And I have to figure everything out all over again. And it's been like that, over and over again, since Mamma and Papa died…like it's never going to be the same, I'll never settle, I keep getting tripped up."

"That's life."

"Is there a way to control it?"

He inspected my face; I could almost see the thoughts turning over in his head. "Control *everything*." Savino shrugged. "No, you just adjust. You roll with the punches, one day at a time."

"It doesn't get easier?"

"It gets easier when you're dead."

"I don't know how to deal with it. I don't know what I'm doing." Mamma and Papa, they'd done their best, but they couldn't have prepared me for this. "And if I fail," I said, "I'm not just ruining my life, I'm failing the kids."

"Then don't fail." He was serious. "You've got people depending on you, you do what you need to do to take care of them. That means pushing through. Your life becomes less about you and more about taking care of the other guy, that's why you keep going. Yes?"

I wanted some secret trick, some perfect algorithm to get me out of this rut. I didn't want to hear that I'd have to walk through life dragging this weight behind me, I wanted to hear that it was going to get better, and I wanted him to hand me the tools to *make* it better. "Okay," I said.

"You're not alone, Pia. We're gonna take care of you, we're not just gonna cut Carla's kids loose to fend for themselves."

That was tempting. It really was. I almost forgot about Massimo and Tonio last night, about the deal with Marco Vitelli, and Savino manipulating my aunt into sending me to Brooklyn—I *wanted* to forget. And I couldn't get the smell of the olive oil out of my nostrils.

"How are your wrists?"

"They're alright."

"You're not wearing the braces anymore."

"I lost them." I held his gaze. "At…the Scarpaci place."

He rubbed the heel of his hand. "You're having trouble with your thumbs." I *was*, but I hadn't told him that—I hadn't told anyone. "Your grip is different, because you can't grasp, so you're compensating by holding things differently. How are door knobs?"

"I manage. It's not too bad." It was bad.

"Because if you come up with different ways of accomplishing repetitive motion, you're only going to end up hurting something else. Shoulders, elbows, your back."

"I know," I said. "I know, but there's nothing to do about it. I can't stop, I can't take off working for a year to let something heal, that isn't realistic. It's something I just…"

"Need to get used to?"

"Yes."

"Adjust." Savino crossed his arms and sat back. Here was a man who didn't have to work his whole life; he didn't need to slave away in this bakery every day, he could sit back in his fancy house and let the olive oil shipments roll in. Unlike me, if he ever wanted to heal his arms, he could take off not one, not two, but every year of his future from manual labor, and he could live comfortably without pain. Savino Vitelli could afford to rest, but he *chose* to lead this life. He chose to stay in pain.

"What are you doing after school, Pia?" he asked.

I really didn't want to talk about this. "I haven't even thought through all of school yet," I said, truthfully.

"What was your plan?"

I thought back to that evening in Augusta—the smell of cigarette smoke, my aunt sitting beside me, her calling Vince onto the back porch to ask him: *"What does Pia want to do?"* As if everyone else knew better than I did, what I was supposed to do with my life. Maybe they did. "Sabine's idea was that I get my degree in food science. I get a job back home. Then we work on putting Cristine through school."

"What was *your* plan?"

I stared at him. "I don't know. It doesn't really matter anymore."

Savino thought about that. "And how old is Cristine?"

"She just turned fifteen." Last week, actually, and I'd missed it. I'd never missed a birthday before. I'd called her, but I should have been there.

"So." He paused, narrowed his eyes at the ceiling. "What if her school was paid for?"

I shook my head. "It isn't. Mamma and Papa only got as far as me, with the college funds." Those were nearly run out by now, though I was only pulling from them when my scholarships didn't cover a course or a textbook. That dwindling fund, combined with my apartment expenses, combined with the small amount I was sending back to the kids every month" Cristine's smart and she might get some scholarships, but then I have to start on Carlo next, and then Vince, and then…" And then, I thought, there went ten years of my life, tripping and stumbling and trying to stay afloat. And maybe that was why I never made plans, because I'd accepted long ago that what my parents wanted and the needs of my siblings would always come before anything else. No one had ever told me this. I'd just learned it.

"What if their school was paid for?" Savino repeated.

"It isn't."

It occurred to me what he was saying. He held my gaze and I refused to look away.

"I think I need to do this myself," I said.

"But you don't have to."

"I think I do," I said.

He clasped his hands between his knees and nodded, his eyes still locked on mine. "Is anything else bothering you?" he asked.

If it had been anyone other than Savino, I would have laughed. Everything was bothering me, from the kidnapping, to our discussion months ago in the diner, to Betta and the fire and Massimo downing three drinks straight while he poured out every family conspiracy theory he and Tonio had concocted over the course of the year. Who was manipulating and who was being manipulated? Who had the power?

Savino did. He had all the power. And for all of his quiet calm, for the flour on his forehead and the way he sweated shoulder-to-shoulder with the rest of us—he knew.

"I don't think so," I said. "But I have to get to school."

He nodded, rubbed his neck. "Thank you for talking to me, Pia."

"Tell Ida I said hi."

I wasn't sure how he did it. But Savino Vitelli made every conversation feel like a battle of wills.

School was a blur. I went from class to class in a sort of haze, struggling to fit the information into categories with the other homework I'd crammed over the past few days.

Around noon, I waited for Lorel outside the liberal arts building. I sat on a bed of rust-colored leaves, under the dogwood branches. It was cold, but somehow it was less overstimulating to sit outside than it was to be locked up in a stuffy classroom. More air to breathe.

Lorel had come from Classics and she seemed just as dazed as I felt. "You know what, Pia," she said, as she lay flat in the grass and pulled her peacoat over her head, "I don't want to talk about the two bricks in my school bag."

"What...what bricks?" I asked, suddenly concerned.

"The ones with Leo Tolstoy's and Victor Hugo's names on them."

I laid back and tucked my arms behind my head. A group of students hurried by, laughing. What would it be like, to set my textbook-loaded backpack aside and forget the family business and my siblings, and to just be a kid? Or even a young adult? What had I done to be denied this small window of time between childhood and adult responsibility? And why did it feel so terribly far outside my grasp, even if I actively tried to gain it back? I must have done something wrong. I must have messed up, somewhere along the way. Because even Lorel, for all her family issues, had fully embraced the freedom of her youth—moving out, joining clubs and theater groups, falling in love with academia and my cousin—she'd painted a stunning life for herself. She was surrounded by an oil and acrylic landscape. But when I stepped back and looking at my own life, I couldn't imagine a clear backdrop—it was shifting and chaotic, a tornado, a Category 5 hurricane throwing fatal debris.

Lorel peeked out at me from beneath her coat. "Are you okay?"

"Yeah," I said, instinctively. "I'm fine."

"Are you though? You don't look okay."

I blinked up through the branches. "I don't know." She stayed silent, waiting for me to go on, but I didn't have much to add—I *didn't* know, I didn't *feel* alright, but my brain couldn't pinpoint what was wrong or how to fix it. "I don't think I've been okay for a while. Maybe I'm scared and confused and probably angry, but...I can't do much about any of it. I don't have time to do anything. I don't have time to *not* be okay."

"Then you're not really okay. You know the thing about helping yourself on the plane first, with the oxygen masks? You have to help yourself so you can help your little brothers and your sister." Lorel folded down the peacoat onto her stomach, rested her head on her arm. She looked like an oil painting—sunlight shading half her face, her intense blue eyes fixed on me. "Matty and I left home after Sara got married. Two years ago. Because the guy she married—his name's Edward, he's nice, I didn't hate him...he learned stuff about our family that he didn't like. I think Dad's brothers talked to him about some of the stuff they used to do back in Sicily. It spooked him. And some friends of Dad's were worried that he might rat on them. And...I didn't want to be around to watch what happened, neither did Matty."

This reminded me uncomfortably of the Mario Mansi theory. I must have made a face, because she waved a hand and shook her head.

"No, no, he's fine, they didn't kill him or anything, he's fine. But we didn't know what might happen and we were honestly just so tired of not knowing what was going on and having to tiptoe around Dad's old friends. And he has problems with anger. Dad. We just wanted to get out. So the second I turned eighteen, we moved in with my uncle's ex-wife in Hoboken—it sounds weird, but she's really nice, Matteo's an asshole for breaking it off, but he's actually an asshole any given day. Anyway. We were staying with Holly this summer until I moved out with you and Matty moved back home. My point is: our family life is trash, and from the outside it probably looks like my whole life is falling apart. But I've decided that I'm not my family, I'm not a...culmination of all my parents 'bad choices. Matty and I both made that choice, we talked about it, we took care of ourselves physically *and* mentally, and when one of us couldn't do it, the other person propped them up while they found their feet."

I didn't have anyone to prop me up, not really. I didn't want to say it aloud for fear of excluding Lorel from the list of potential *props,* but maybe I was too aware of everyone else's wavering balance to trust leaning on any one of them.

Everyone was swaying in place. Except Savino.

"You've got to take care of yourself," she said, "if you're going to take care of other people."

Sabine called me that evening. I was eating oatmeal, because I didn't have time to make a real dinner between studying and sheets of homework problems and periodically typing a couple sentences into a microbiology essay due the following night.

"Hi," I said, "is everything alright?"

"Oh, yeah, *cara*, we're fine, Vince just went to bed but he said to tell you he loves you. Hey, how's your school, huh? They're teaching you things?"

I blinked at the sea of homework spread across the table. "Lots of things. Not all of it useful."

"Oh, good, good. Hey, I went by the bakery the other day, the place by the gym. They said they missed you, they asked about you, I said 'Oh, she's up in Manhattan, she's impressing everyone up there, Savino only has good things to say', and honestly *cara*, I think these guys were only holding you back. Because you've got some good family recipes now, right?"

That was the farthest thing from my mind. "I guess, I don't know. I like the bakery back home, but the *panificio* is nice too, it's just different."

"Well, I don't know, I think you're better off with Savino—he's a good baker, he knows what he's doing, I'm sure he's teaching you lots of stuff. Hey, Pia, maybe we should think about moving the kids."

I froze. "Moving their *what*?"

"Moving them, the kids, Cristine and Carlo and Vince—they miss you, Pia, and I don't think this house is good for them. They need to move on, you know? This house is full of Carla and Leo, and they need to start moving on, but they can't while they're here."

My hands were cold. I dropped my spoon and pushed my oatmeal away, across rustling paper. "I...what?"

"Just think about it, okay? We can talk when you come home for Christmas—we can talk to Cristine too, she's old enough to be a part of this, you know? My brother knows some real estate guys in Brooklyn, there are some nice places that don't totally break the bank, you know? Anyway, just think—"

I blinked. "Savino? When did you talk to Savino?"

"I talk to him all the time, Pia, he's my brother, why? What's wrong?"

"Did he bring this up?"

"No, this was my idea. Hey, what's happened, *cara*? Are you okay?"

167

Would she even know if he'd planted the thought? My heart raced. "It's...I'm fine. I've just got a lot homework to do, can I call you back tomorrow?"

"Yeah, okay, you go study."

I didn't study. I grabbed my things and went downstairs and stepped out onto the curb, where I hailed a cab—something I'd only seen done in movies and from a distance, but was surprisingly easy. I paid the driver and hurried into the apartment building. I dashed up the stairs and banged on the door to Massimo's and Tonio's apartment.

No one answered.

I fished for the key. My fingers trembled. I finally fit it into the lock, but before I could unlock the door it swung open and Tonio stared down his nose at me.

"Oh. Marzano. *Buonasera.*" Then his magma eyes narrowed and his wry smile slipped away. He called back over his shoulder. "Uh, Massimo, your cousin is here and she's *crying.*" He widened the door and stepped back, as if he wanted to keep his distance, as if the emotions might scald him.

"I'm not crying," I hissed. I stormed into the apartment. "Where's Massimo?"

"Oh, God, what did he do?" Tonio drawled.

"Where is he?"

"I'm here." Massimo appeared in the hallway. He froze when he saw my face, and his eyes widened. "What's wrong? Where's Lorel? Are you hurt?"

I held up a finger to emphasize something. I was ready to launch into a tirade. But the words didn't come. My throat had closed up, a bear trap had snapped shut over my chest, and my body did not feel like my own.

"Pia?"

I took a deep breath, steadied myself. My hands shook—I pressed them against my legs. And the words came in spurts. "Savino. Is trying to move my siblings up here. Cristine, Carlo. Vince."

Massimo's brow furrowed. He had that look of tired despair, just like the other night—like he'd seen this tragedy play out before, and he was wearied by it. "He told you that?"

I swiped away the angry tears blurring my vision. "Sabine. She called me, she talked to Savino." It was all about preserving the business. Why was he like this? Two sides of a coin, one person—one moment he was Savino who sat with me in his office and told me he'd take care of everything—and then he turned around and became the thing that everyone said he was. "He's just doing this to control the people in Sicily, isn't he? Control the Marzanos."

Massimo didn't answer. He just watched me.

"Or," said Tonio, seating himself on the couch amongst a pile of cushions, "perhaps you're the one he's trying to control."

That was the wrong thing to say. Or maybe it was perfectly calculated, maybe it was the first right thing to be said that night, because something in me *snapped*—like a rubber band pulled tight across my chest, like the first spark in a bonfire.

A line had been crossed, a line I hadn't even known existed before today.

"I'm in," I said. "If you have a plan to take down the business, I want to be a part of it."

People always said I was like Savino. And maybe this was why: I'd do anything to take care of my family.

Anything.

PART 2

"An angry cloud, precursor of the storm,
Behind the mountains rose, and still increased,
Till moon or star no longer could be seen."

- "Fragments", Giacomo Leopardi

IX

Luca

i.

A few weeks before the end of the semester, Lorel, Tonio, Betta, Giovani and I were out at the park kicking the soccer ball around. Betta and I were on one team, Tonio and Lorel and Giovani were on the other. Tonio was actually quite good, which was both incredibly infuriating and also lucky, I guess, since Lorel was awful and Giovani was in a mood and refused to put in even minimal effort. My team also had a distinct advantage: Betta was fired up.

"I dumped Damien's ass," she spat, in a way that so clearly said *Damien dumped my ass*.

I stared blankly. I laced my cleats and narrowed my eyes at her from where she stood against the sun, fists on her hips, tight braid trailing down her shoulder. "Who's Damien?"

"You know, Damien. Guy with the cool car." She caught herself. "Not cool, really. It was kinda trash, you know? But he was *so* proud of it."

"Wasn't that Alec?"

"Who's Alec?" She turned away. "Let's beat Tonio's ass."

Lorel tried, I'll give her that. What she lacked for in practice, she made up for in enthusiasm.

"PIA!" she shouted, as she megged Tonio and sent the ball hurtling my way.

I stopped it, passed to Betta. She made a goal.

I shouted across the field to Lorel. "I'm not on your team!" But it was fun watching Tonio lose so miserably—watching his wry smile waver with every goal against, with every confusing maneuver on Lorel's part—so I stopped reminding her and just went with it.

About an hour in, Massimo showed up. He changed in his Lexus and headed across the green towards us.

"Aww, *il mammone*," drawled Tonio. He sent the ball spinning towards Massimo, who stopped it neatly and dribbled towards us. "Still making mozzarella with your mama?"

"Nicole makes mozzarella?" I raised my eyebrows, impressed. "You *help* Nicole make mozzarella?"

"Sometimes." Massimo stopped to tie his shoes. Lorel stole the ball away and made a production of scoring on Giovani, complete with throwing victorious fists in the air.

Giovani hadn't been playing. He scowled and wandered off to retrieve the ball. He didn't like Lorel, primarily because she didn't take most things seriously, but also because she was a Scarpaci and he considered scrimmaging with a Scarpaci to be borderline traitorous.

"Actually," said Massimo, straightening again. He propped his sunglasses in his hair. "Actually, I was with my dad. We were picking someone up from the airport."

Betta wrinkled her nose, as if running any sort of errand disgusted her. "Who?"

"The Catenacci guy."

"Oh," said Tonio, with his same expression of bored amusement.

"Catenacci?" Lorel squinted. "I know that name." Her short hair was pinned back in a bandana, and she wore athletic shorts I hadn't even known she owned—they might have been pajama pants, actually.

"Your folks might know them," said Massimo. "They're a Sicily family, work with the Marzanos."

"Oh, that's why."

I looked at Tonio, who stood closest. "They work for Valentino?"

"Hmm," he said, unhelpfully, "maybe."

"Well, why are they here?" I didn't like that Betta was standing right there, but this seemed important.

"Just the one," said Massimo. "Family business, probably. Savino wanted me to drop him off at the Vitelli house. That's all." The look he shot me, though, said something like *More on that later*. "Who's winning?"

"I am," said Betta.

"*We are*," I corrected.

"Yeah," said Lorel, "but we've got *Tonio!*" She said it like it meant something.

"It's true," said Tonio. It was weird to see him out of his slacks and button-down, and especially without his bathrobe, because those were the only two outfits I ever really saw him in. This was some expensive athletic get-up, all-black, with clean lines and brand names. I hated it.

"Right," said Massimo. "I'll play with the losing team."

"That's us!" Lorel cheered.

"*God*," said Giovani.

ii.

Here was the deal: I was failing school. Between the frequent interruptions in my education (kidnappings, fires, etcetera) and my generally-high level of stress and exhaustion, it was a miracle I was even passing one class.

I dropped statistics and microbiology too late in the semester; I'd have to pay the scholarship money back to the school. I didn't know how I was going to do that just yet. Thanks to Massimo, however, I was passing both physics and organic chemistry. Dr. Burnett's class didn't give me many other options than to simply be a good student. The amount of time even the most basic coursework required drove me late into the night, pouring over lab reports and meta-analyses and consuming far too much caffeine.

Few people noticed my predicament. Even I didn't notice until it was too late—the semester seemed to fly by, and the late-drop period ended, and here I was failing two courses, hardly sleeping, and working far too many hours in order to pay rent for my dumpster-fire of an apartment.

Lorel was possibly the first to notice. She'd watched it happen earlier on, but she saw that it was getting worse and she sat me down to talk about it.

"Do you need to talk to someone," she asked, "besides me?"

"What do you mean? A tutor?"

"I don't know, Pia, I'm worried. You're not eating—not real food, anyway, just coffee and oatmeal and focaccia—and you never sleep, and you won't slow down. Can I help? And if not me, can I help you find someone who *can* help?"

"You mean like a therapist." If it were anyone else, I might have gotten angry—like Betta asking if I'd been diagnosed with anxiety, unhelpful and rude. But Lorel was genuinely concerned. "I'm okay," I said, even as I was drowning. "Thank you. But I'm okay."

Massimo noticed. Granted, he was dealing with his own issues, but as the homework stacked up and I started smoking more often, he asked me over coffee whether I'd thought about taking sleep meds. "I have them," he admitted. "Sometimes."

"Why?"

"To help me sleep, so I don't crash my car and die."

It was a stupid question, anyway. Massimo, like me, had dozens of reasons to not sleep. I wondered if that was why he drank so heavily in the evening.

I didn't take the pills. The whole point was that I didn't have enough hours in the day, that I needed that time normally allotted for sleep to get my work done. Not being able to get to sleep once I'd paused my studying was another issue entirely.

Savino probably noticed me running myself into the ground way earlier than anyone else, only he didn't say anything about it until I came into the bakery one day after pulling an all-nighter and chain-smoking my way through an organic chemistry study guide for the final.

I wandered into the back after Betta and Giovani, unzipped my coat with shaking fingers, and left my things on the hooks by the door. I didn't know where the others had gone off to, but the next thing I knew, Savino was standing right in front of me—I hadn't even noticed him come into the back. He stood there and handed me a light cotton blanket of blue and green gingham, which I accepted without thinking. It was warm.

He took my arm and propelled me into the office.

"Wha—?"

"I want you to stay in here," he said, his expression deadly serious, "and sleep for a solid five hours." He set me down in the padded desk chair.

I opened my mouth to protest. I couldn't sleep—I didn't know if I could *get* to sleep, for one, and for another: I needed to work. I needed to pay back my scholarship for these failed courses, I needed to save up for rent. But Savino held up a hand to stop me.

"You can't work if you don't sleep," he said.

Well, that was absolute bullshit. I'd been doing *just that* for the past two months. But all I said was: "I can't."

He seemed to understand, as he always did, the bastard. He nodded. "Pills are in the top drawer."

Then he left. He shut the office door behind him, and in the bakery beyond, pans clattered as Betta and Giovani got to work with opening.

I sat there for a moment, unsure; I wanted to go after him and explain that I was too busy for basic human needs. Then some primal drive to sleep kicked in, and I slid open the top drawer of the enormous mahogany desk. There was a first-aid kit, a couple tubes of antibacterial ointment, a few prescription pill bottles—I found the sleep ones after a bit of investigative work, inspecting the labels. They were all made out to Marco Biasi, which didn't necessarily surprise me; any one person in this family could keep a pharmacy in business.

There was also a flask in the drawer, metal with a worn leather grip. It seemed like a Massimo sort of thing to have. But I hadn't taken Savino as a day-drinker. Maybe Marco again? On a whim, I unscrewed the top and sniffed.

It wasn't alcohol. That was abundantly clear, right away. It took a second for my mind to digest this, and then to actually place the smell. It was rich, warm, almost *spicy* tang—reminded me of home, of the few times Mamma had geared herself up to make an award-winning dinner. And of focaccia—it reminded me of standing over the gallons and gallons of dough, dipping my hands, pouring the brine.

It was olive oil. And it certainly wasn't the stuff we used in the bakery.

I did sleep. I took the pills and I was dead to the world for several hours. When I woke—bleary and disoriented and strangely wracked with guilt for my need to rest—I sought out my uncle, who had relieved Dora up front. He was taking a phone order. I waited by the cannoli bench.

When he'd hung up, he turned to me and tapped his pen against the counter. "You need to cut back."

"Cut back what?"

"Hours, Pia. Something has to give, and you work more days than Marco." He held up four fingers. "Four days—Monday, Wednesday, Friday, Saturday. You can come in early if you want—Oscar can pick you up—but no more than four days, yeah?"

"I can do it," I said. "I can handle it, I just need to get through—"

"I know you can do it," Savino cut in. "But you don't have to."

There he was, even with everything else going on—manipulating me and my aunt and my siblings—even now: he was taking care of me. I had mixed feelings about it.

"Okay," I said, because you don't say no to Savino Vitelli when he looks at you like that, like he's laid down the law. Maybe it was a plot to make me fall behind on rent and have to move back in to the Vitelli house, or maybe he was genuinely concerned for my health and sanity—it didn't matter.

That was the end of it.

iii.

Massimo had driven Lorel to dress rehearsal, so I sat on the living room floor in his apartment and waited for him to get back. Tonio watched me from a high-backed armchair by the window, candle flame flickering off the glass in his hand. He had a book open in his lap, but apparently staring while I sweated over astrophysics calculations proved immensely more entertaining.

"Enjoying the view?" I asked, finally, tired of his eyes drilling into the side of my head.

"Enjoying isn't the right word," he returned, swirling his amaretto. "It's more a morbid fascination with your spiral into self-destruction."

"Says the man who wears a sweater-vest as a shirt. Please shut up."

"Why are you here again?" he droned.

I wanted a cigarette, more than anything, but the room was already smoky from a dozen candles, and somehow I figured smoking in front of Tonio was a bit like flaunting a terrible weakness.

"I have an idea," I said. "About the business."

"How droll. Are your equations going to save the day?"

I slammed my notebook shut—probably the exact reaction he'd been looking for, but I was tired. "You don't have to project your disdain for science on me. You could just keep it to yourself. It isn't your thing, that doesn't make it stupid by default."

Tonio's skull face split into a grin, just as the front doorknob rattled. "Speaking of self-destruction." He finished his drink. The door opened and Massimo stepped inside, coat hung over his arm. "Your cousin has ideas."

"Hi, Pia." Massimo pocketed his keys and dropped into a chair. "How's orgo?"

"Final is next Wednesday."

"She has ideas," Tonio said again, echoing himself. He rose to his feet. "And I think I need another drink."

When he came back, I set my physics work aside and leaned against the couch. "The next shipment is coming in next week, right?" This question was addressed to Tonio.

Tonio nodded. "I did say that, didn't I? Yes, Stefano confirmed it with Valentino's guys, and Raul and Johnny confirmed it with the folks out of state. It gets in and out, Marzano—they drop it off, store it for a day or two tops, and get it out of state. And of course Achille can't keep his mouth shut, so I know all the details in between." He frowned and sipped his drink. "Have we ever considered the possibility of my brother being a liability? Has anyone ever vocalized a concern to Savino perhaps?"

I ignored that last bit. "So we know where it's getting dropped off?"

"Certainly."

"So here's my idea," I said, aware that I could very well end up saying something unwittingly ridiculous, and Tonio would jump me immediately. But Massimo was still, leaning forward with his elbows on his knees; he listened intently, so I went on. "We have to take down the family business from the inside, right? The problem is, if we keep burning down warehouses, the Vitellis will just think it's the Scarpacis giving us hell, and things will get worse. One way or another, we're going to have to draw Lorel's family into this."

Massimo's brow furrowed, but he didn't speak.

Tonio set his glass aside. "Right. And we wouldn't want to do that, because Diego Scarpaci is...an absolute sweetheart, yes?"

"We don't want to do it because it isn't their fault," I stressed. "They busted up the casino last time something like this happened—the Vitellis did. We can't just blame our bad decisions on someone else. Even Lorel and Matty—they're pretty much separated from their family, and they'll still get flack for anything that happens. So: we go ahead and set them up. We make sure the Scarpacis and the Vitellis are both doing something they shouldn't, then they get caught in the act. By police, or something—"

"That's no different from Massimo's manic escapades," Tonio cut in, "since the Scarpacis will get in trouble all the same. His little girlfriend"—he retrieved his glass and waved it in Massimo's direction—"will still be in trouble, yes?"

"No," I growled, "Savino will know Diego isn't involved, since the Scarpacis get penalized as well. It wouldn't make sense for them to call the cops on themselves, he'll just figure the cops got wind of a fight or something. The authorities break it up, investigate. The business goes down, the Scarpacis get off easy since they weren't really involved anyway."

"Savino pays off the law enforcement," Tonio reminded me.

"But as far as we know, Diego doesn't. So if we report the Scarpacis, chances are no one will think to give them and the Vitellis space, or turn a blind eye or anything—they'll just break up whatever we report. That's why we couldn't just phone the cops about the drop-off, it's why we have to involve the Scarpacis, if only a little bit."

Massimo rubbed the back of his neck. "That is…"

I waited. He didn't finished the sentence—the words just hung there, disappointing. I hadn't really expected enthusiasm, but something would have been nice. I gave him a moment to digest.

But Tonio was already overflowing with choice words. "Ambitious," he supplied. "Wildly optimistic. Chock-full of holes, gaps big enough to drop a bus through."

My jaw tightened. I wanted a cigarette between my teeth. "Shut up, Tonio, I wasn't asking you."

Tonio grinned; the ice clinked against his teeth. He set his glass aside again and twisted in his armchair to face Massimo. "Why don't you tell her *your* plan, then? Go on."

My eyebrows shot up. "You already have a plan? Why didn't you say something?"

Massimo ran a hand through his hair. He frowned at the floor between his feet. "I…"

"Oh, he always has a plan," Tonio drawled. "He's had this one for a while probably—I've seen it blossoming, but he's only just now vocalized the thing. Wildly ambitious takes on a whole new meaning with Massimo Di Natale."

Massimo ignored him. "It's a good plan, Pia, with some work. I like the bit about the Scarpacis, if we can only make sure it doesn't backfire on Lorel. I mean, even if the cops decided to investigate the Scarpaci family and they found out about the kidnappings and stuff, it wouldn't really get traced back to her and Matty, I guess."

I sat back on my heels, feeling stupid and belittled. "But…you already have a plan."

"I didn't *not tell you*, it's just…I only just now decided that it's a viable option."

"*Viable.*" Tonio smirked.

Massimo would look anywhere but at me. "I'm a chemist," he said, slowly, "and at Columbia, I specialized in chemical engineering. I did internships. Particularly in...explosives."

"No," I said.

Tonio laughed.

Massimo shrugged. "We plant explosives at each of the Vitelli warehouses. Time bombs. We wouldn't even be there when they detonated, we could have alibis. If Valentino Marzano sees how the business is literally burning to the ground, he'll cut out the Vitellis, at the least. No more business, no more mafia."

"Except..." We both looked at Tonio, who rubbed his sharp jaw with one hand and pointed at me with the other. "Except, *her*."

"What *about* me?"

"Well, come on, put the pieces together. Savino's got a Marzano to hold over Valentino. If Massimo goes all Unabomber on Savino, there's always promise—or threat, depending on how you look at it—of a Marzano in New York, working at *Il Panificio Zeppole*."

Massimo frowned. "Explain."

Tonio leapt to his feet. He started pacing—long strides, aggressive strides, while he gesticulated wildly. "Look, it's like this—say your plan goes through, Valentino gets news that the system is busted up over here. Then Savino has two options. Either he leans into the whole familial relationship, pulls Marzano here into the discussion and holds her up like a little Sicilian trophy—'Hey, Val, remember when this happened? Leo and Carla?'—that sort of thing. And because this family has got a significant hang-up on the fact that we're *family*, that just might be enough for Savino to get away with it. The business survives."

I didn't like being compared to a little Italian trophy. But Tonio was—dare I say it—making an interesting point. "Or?"

"Or"—Tonio paced, he ran a hand over his slicked-back hair and untucked his button-down from his slacks—"or, he uses you as a threat. Not a ransom piece *per se*, but it's essentially the same. Here"—he waved a hand at me—"Savino's got Valentino's granddaughter, right here—and he didn't really like Cal, did he? From what I've heard, Calpurnia Marzano-Scarpaci is totally estranged, I hadn't heard that name in years until that escapade at the beginning of the fall. All that to say, Leo Marzano was the favorite child, everyone was ecstatic when Leo and Carla tied the knot, Valentino won't want the eldest grandchild from that marriage in a dangerous situation."

"Savino won't put her in a dangerous situation." Massimo said it instinctively, like there was no doubt in his mind, like he didn't even have to think about it.

180

He was right. Savino wouldn't. It wasn't just the underlying feeling that my uncle was keeping me safe for *something*—there was also the fact that he was family, that he was protecting me and trying to take care of me in the same way he protected the Di Natales and the Salones. I doubted the Scarpacis would have another chance to get at me, or even dare to try,

"He wouldn't harm Pia," said Massimo. "Savino won't hurt family."

Tonio snapped his fingers softly. He did it in an unconscious way—he wasn't emphasizing anything, just snapping out of excitable habit. "You know who else was family? Mario Mansi. Remember him? Norma's dear papa? At the bottom of an estuary, no doubt. No, Savino won't harm *the family business*. There's a crucial distinction there, between the family and the business. Most times, if you protect one, you're protecting the other. They go hand-in-hand. Until"—Tonio stopped pacing, raised one eyebrow at me—"until they don't."

I hated it, I really did, but he was making a lot of sense.

Massimo sat back in his chair, crossed his arms. "What are you saying?"

"I'm saying, as much as I know you'd love to blast the whole East Coast with TNT and nitrogen gas, there are better options."

"Wait." They both looked at me. I narrowed me eyes at Tonio, standing above me, the candlelight casting weird shadows on his weird, skull-chiseled face, orange flickers reflecting off his hair. "Are you agreeing with me?"

"I'm as surprised as you are," he deadpanned.

"You're taking *my* side?"

"Oh, there are no sides." Tonio waved a hand, as if to say, *so-so*. "It's me pointing out that, between two bad plans, one is slightly less horrific than the other. It needs work, but we might be able to swing it."

"Massimo?"

My cousin finally looked at me. From his kind face and calm eyes, it was hard to imagine he was the trigger-happy *capo* ready to blow the family property sky-high. "There's a lot that could go wrong," he said evenly.

"We'll minimize the risk," I said. "We have a week, right? Less than a week."

"That's right," said Tonio.

Massimo rubbed his jaw. "If I could get into a lab for a few hours—"

"What'll happen to Lorel, then? And Matty?" For as much as I loved Lorel, I understood Massimo's quandary—this would all be so much easier if I'd never met her. But if I hadn't befriended her and we hadn't moved out, where would I be? Pinned under Savino's thumb, living upstairs in the Vitelli house, getting his mafia guys to drive me to school. If I didn't have Lorel, I'd be a lot deeper in this mess than I currently was. Yet I recognized that hint of regret in Massimo's face.

"Okay," he said. He stood, stuck his hands in the pockets of his khakis. He nodded. "Alright. Let's do it, then."

And just like that, he disappeared into the kitchen.

Tonio watched him go, then stood there facing the kitchen doorway. I sat in silence for a moment, the corner of the couch digging into my lower back. Behind me, a candle spluttered. The clink of a bottle echoed from the back of the kitchen, the sound of liquid sloshing into a glass.

I looked at Tonio's own glass, empty but for the ice cubes, sitting on the side table. "Are you drunk?"

He blinked, turned away from the kitchen. "Of course not," he scoffed. "Italians don't get drunk."

"Massimo does," I said.

Tonio smiled. He loosened the collar of his shirt. "I don't know if you've noticed, Marzano, but Massimo is terribly depressed."

This was the first I'd heard of it. "How depressed?" Clinically? Chronically?

"Terribly," said Tonio. He checked his watch. "Do you need a ride home?"

I stared down at my physics work. I wouldn't be getting any studying done tonight, I realized. My mind was far from school matters, and I doubted Massimo was in the right mood. I'd seen him work complex equations while absolutely tanked, but he sort of forgot I was there and ended up doing my homework for me. "I can get a cab."

He shrugged. "I can drive you."

I stood, gathered my notes and textbooks. "I'll get a cab."

"Have you got a gun, Marzano?"

I flinched a little and didn't answer right away. But he waited, hands in his pockets and eyebrows raised, unrelenting. "Yeah," I admitted.

"With you?"

"In a drawer."

"Can't do you much good sitting in a drawer, can it?"

"I can take care of myself, Tonio." He, of all people, had absolutely no right to make me feel bad about the way I lived my life. *Sweater-vest.*

"Yes, well." He shrugged again. "That's what the gun is for, yes?"

I threw my stuff in my backpack and slung it over one shoulder. "Bye."

iv.

I got to work early the next day. Since Savino had cut down on my workdays, I'd picked up a few extra hours, so I got to the *panificio* around the same time as my uncle. Betta and Giovani didn't normally pick me up for another hour, so I'd started taking the bus—it was a couple blocks down from the apartment, and I had to stand at the bus stop in the dark for a good fifteen minutes around four in the morning. That part was a bit stressful, but the bus was mostly occupied by other early-morning workers, and I kept my cell phone on hand the whole time.

It dropped me off outside the Little Italy district. I walked down near-deserted streets, past windows where faint lights glowed in back rooms and employees shuffled their way through a morning routine. *Take down the chairs, sweep the floors, wipe the counter.* I didn't like the back alley at this time of day, so I used the front entrance. The bell clanged and I locked the door behind me.

Savino was already in the back, mixing the next day's focaccia while today's dough came to room temp on the counter. "You sleep?"

"A bit."

"Good. Focaccia?"

I nodded, went off in hunt of an apron, and then started oiling the focaccia pans. This olive oil we used in the kitchen was good stuff, high quality like he'd said, but I knew just from the smell that it wasn't the Marzano oil. It didn't match the scent from the flask in the office. Which made sense, since Savino wouldn't want anything incriminating on the bakery premises. I wondered what sorts of restaurants bought illegal olive oil; I wondered if I'd ever tasted it. Whether or not the oil at home was *real* wasn't a question I'd really entertained till recently, but I wasn't sure that I'd ever experienced actual extra-virgin olive oil except for here.

Marco came in a bit later, said good morning, and disappeared into the office. Savino set aside one of the proofing focaccia breads and turned it into *sfincione*— Sicilian pizza, topped with roasted breadcrumbs and *caciocavallo* cheese and whatever extra produce we had laying around. He chopped it up and the three of us ate it for breakfast amidst morning tasks.

Betta and Giovani came in around 6:30. Giovani was in more of a mood than usual, and Betta was terse with him, so they must have fought on the way over. They went to work without saying hello, and virtually ignored me the rest of the morning, caught up in their own worlds.

Dora Di Natale was still high off her engagement. She refused to take off the enormous ring, even when she had to pull on gloves to remove pastries from the case, so she ended up splitting a lot of gloves. I liked Dora, but I was glad to work in the back, because for the amount she talked Marco's ear off about the wedding and Francesco and florists, I could only imagine how much worse it would be if she had another girl at which to direct these topics.

Around opening time, I was helping Giovani fill *cornetti* in the back—lemon curd and orange cream, mascarpone and Nutella. Savino came to get me.

"Pia." He beckoned me up front.

I set down the *cornetto* I'd been working on. "I'll be right back." Giovani grunted. I followed my uncle out of the kitchen.

The first customers were trickling in. They were probably regulars, at this hour—Dora seemed to know them. Oscar was reading Consumer Reports at the window table, apparently gripped by the new microwave content.

And there was someone new, standing behind the counter. I was so used to only seeing Marco and Savino and the Di Natales, it really threw me to have this extra presence beside the cannoli bench: a young guy, not much older than me and not a lot taller. Compact build, clean-cut and comfortable in khakis and a navy sweater. He had hair like Giovani, black and curly, only a bit longer and combed neatly to the side.

Savino put a hand on his shoulder. "Pia. This is Luca Catenacci."

This was the guy Massimo had picked up from the airport. I waited, and Luca Catenacci smiled, and I figured I should say something. "Hi."

"*Ciao.* Hello."

Ah, a man after Savino's own heart. Only this wasn't Italian under a thick layer of Brooklyn accent, this was pure Sicilian, like Mamma and Papa when they lapsed into their first language.

He had a nice face—handsome, I guess, with its classic features, the Roman nose, long black lashes and warm-toned skin. Only *nice* was somehow different than good-looking. He had that Nice Italian Boy quality that Lorel sometimes talked about when referring to Massimo—remarking on how Massimo was, first and foremost, a total knock-out, and then that he had that cleaned-up characteristic that adults seemed to like, that made people want to trust him. Luca Catenacci, I could already tell, had that same quality.

"Luca's gonna start working in the back," Savino said, "with you and Giovani. Betta, she already knows, I'm gonna start her working up front more."

Weird. Warning sirens were going off in my head; Betta was the last person who should be working the counter, interacting with customers, and Savino had to know that. But it was his bakery, so I just nodded.

"You're gonna train him."

"Oh." Train him? Train *anyone*? I'd only started this past summer, I seemed like the least qualified member of the staff to do that.

"His English isn't that good," said Savino, "he just got here, but he's working on it. So take it slow. Find him an apron and a hat, huh? Pia Marzano," he said to Luca, nodding in my direction.

Luca's eyebrows shot up. "*Marzano?*"

"Pia," I said, determined to keep the number of people calling me by my last name to a minimum.

Savino said something to Luca in Italian—I only caught a few words, *Leonardo, daughter, dead.* Luca's eyes widened.

I couldn't take much more of this. Finals were coming up, I was tired, and my tolerance for any sort of familial weirdness was at an all-time low today. "I'll get a hat," I said, and I slipped back into the kitchen.

Here was the thing: Luca Catenacci was a perfectly nice guy. From the little I was able to converse with him—I didn't try particularly hard, to be honest, I just wanted to concentrate on getting stuff done—he seemed polite and respectful and like a hard worker. He listened intently when I explained how to portion the focaccia dough and spread it into its pans, and repeated my instructions back to me to make sure he'd gotten them right.

As I understood it, he had no previous baking experience. His parents ran a restaurant—*un ristorante di pesce*—in Sicily, so at least he knew his way around a kitchen, and about safe food handling.

The language barrier wasn't really a problem. His accent was thick, but I'd grown up around thick accents, and I could handle it. When he occasionally forgot a word in English, I'd hunt through my spotty Italian vocabulary and try to help him out. I think, for the most part, he understood a lot more than he could say.

"The uh, the Marzano family." His brow furrowed, he used his hands a lot and leaned forward when he spoke, as if closing the distance would make it easier to understand. "My family, the Catenaccis, we know the Marzanos. My father is good friend with *Signor Marzano*."

"Really." I piled up the pans by the sink, almost tripped on Luca when I stepped back. "I've never met him."

"No, I have not—me too, never met him—Valentino Marzano is a big man, yes? Super, uh, *important*."

My annoyance had little to do with Luca, and more to do with my uncle. I was sure he'd singled me out over the Di Natales to train the new guy, and not just because I was arguably the most even-tempered out of the three bakers—Giovani would have ignored Luca, and Betta would have tried intimidating him or something. No, this had more to do with the fact that that Savino had a history of treating me differently than everyone else—protecting me, like Tonio had said—and I had the feeling he was trying to slow me down by sticking a ball and chain to my ankle; training Luca meant I spent more time standing at his shoulder and overseeing than I did running around. It was somehow more tiring, yet not so physically exhausting.

Savino knew what he was doing. I just needed to figure out what it was.

I'd have talked to Lorel about it, only *Wicked* was opening the next night and she'd been spending virtually all of her time either in the library studying for finals or in the Fortuna auditorium running through dress rehearsals. So most nights I ended up at the apartment in the Financial District, and I complained to Massimo and Tonio instead.

"Well, what did you think, when you picked him up from the airport? You went with Gio, right, to get him when he flew in?"

"Right." Massimo sat back on the sofa with his drink in one hand and a graphing calculator in the other. "He seemed alright. The upstanding sort this family likes." He said it distastefully.

I decided to not mention that Massimo was also the upstanding sort. "It's just weird," I said, "how in the middle of all this, I get thrown a curveball. You don't think he knows?"

"Savino?" Massimo shook his head. "No."

Tonio wandered into the room in his bathrobe. "Oh, Savino would never suspect you of conspiring, Marzano—the golden child, the great prized Sicilian piece in his collection. And me and Massimo? No way. We owe too much to the Vitellis."

"I didn't actually ask you," I mumbled. I ducked back to my physics study guide. I was tired, my brain was exhausted, and the fact that I was nestled into the most comfortable armchair in existence was making it difficult to stay awake.

"Yet"—Tonio threw himself onto the sofa, bumping Massimo, who steadied his drink before it could spill—"yet, here I am, brimming with things to say. Say, how's Mo's daughter?"

"Who? Dora?"

"Yeah, that's the one."

Massimo frowned at him. "She's fine."

"Hey." Tonio patted my cousin's shoulder. "I asked Marzano, let the woman speak. Hmm? So how is she? Happy? Does she have that sparkle of nauseating romance in her eyes, like she's been swept off her feet, head in the clouds, slightly useless because she can't focus for all thoughts of Prince Charming?"

"Could you go away, please?"

"She asked nicely," Massimo murmured.

"Uncharacteristic, isn't it?" Tonio laughed, but he pulled himself up off the sofa and wandered back across the apartment.

"I don't know, Pia." Massimo shifted on the couch, scratched his eyebrow. He was frustratingly picturesque, my cousin, sitting there in his dress shirt and spotless slacks, terribly perfect hair. Like a tragic hero in the candlelight. It was easy to see how Lorel blotted out the less savory aspects of Massimo's character; the better qualities, the pleasant parts—they were considerably more apparent than his flaws. It was tempting to see him like that. Except, like it or not, he was budding mafioso, and he was an arsonist, and he was twenty-three and had put away three drinks within the hour.

"I don't know," he said again. "I do think it's weird how the timing worked out with the Catenacci guy. His family did work for Valentino in the past—they were in on the orchard thing, burning down the Scarpaci place. I don't think he's a problem though." He set down his glass. "Physics tomorrow?"

186

"At noon."

"You'll be fine. You're in a good spot."

"You know." I rubbed my temple, which suddenly ached. "You know, I don't know what I'm going to do next semester. I dropped too many classes. And I can't even get Savino to talk to the school people, I haven't even told him about it. I don't want to. What would he say to them? What would he *do?* You know"—a wave of despair hit me, and I almost asked Massimo for a drink, or for one of Tonio's cigarettes, anything to distract from the sudden panic—"you know, I've lost my scholarship. Not officially yet. But I'm going to have to pay off those classes I dropped, pay the scholarship money back to the school, and even if I ace my finals, I'm barely passing and there's no way my GPA has held up. It's—no, I know it's dropped too low, I'm not self-deprecating or anything, it's just a fact."

Massimo watched me spiral. "What are you going to do about it?"

I ran my hands through my hair. "I...don't know. You know, I was trying to send my salary back home to the kids and Sabine, but I can't even afford to do that now, between the shitty apartment and next semester's tuition and paying off this semester and the textbooks. Savino pays me too much for what I do, but not enough for all that." I dropped my pencil, physics work forgotten. "I wanted to finish up, next semester. I wanted to get out of here."

"Did you?"

"Yeah, I did. You know that. Maybe I can't totally extricate myself, but I can try, I can move back home and put some distance between me and the Vitellis, I can reason with Sabine and we can keep the kids far away from Brooklyn."

Massimo ran a finger around the rim of his glass. "You could ask Savino for the money," he said—and before I could respond, he nodded—"but you don't want to do that, I wouldn't either. But if you tell him, he'll offer it, so you should be ready for that."

"Maybe I won't tell him. Does he have to know?"

"It's the apartment, Pia. Hey, you shouldn't be thinking about this stuff right now, just focus on tomorrow. Finals. Worry about it later."

I sat forward. "No, what do you mean, *it's the apartment?*"

"I mean, he'll find out. If you have to give up something, it'll be the apartment with Lorel. And you'll end up back in with the Vitellis."

I sat back in my chair. "No."

Tonio poked his head out of the kitchen, an unlit cigarette between his fingers. "Or," he said, "you could move in with us."

I blinked. One, it was a crazy idea. Two, it was even crazier that it had come from Tonio Salone of all people. "I can't do that."

187

Massimo looked just as surprised as I was. He chewed a piece of ice and glanced at me. "You could, you know."

"I can't leave Lorel." And I *couldn't* move in with Tonio. Massimo, maybe, but *never* Tonio.

Massimo sat forward. "Well. Look, talk to Lorel about it, the apartment and the rent. She'll understand, she's talked about—I mean, she's been here through everything, she's seen it happen, she understands." Meaning, they'd been talking about me behind my back. "She mentioned that Matty wants to move out, she said maybe she'd get a bunk or another trundle, put him up on the couch or something. He'd split the rent a third way."

That was an option. Not my favorite, but a possibility.

Tonio had disappeared again into the kitchen—I heard him banging around some dishes. He had this habit of making a huge dish once or twice a week, then freezing it and eating the same thing for every meal until it was gone. Except for breakfasts, which were usually composed of a cappuccino and heaping spoonfuls of Nutella on saltine crackers. As someone who had a lot of feelings about food, I found it a fairly scandalizing arrangement, but I figured it would be just as upsetting if witnessed by the average person.

"I don't want to think about it," I declared. "Finals. I'm getting through finals, then we're calling the cops on our family. Yeah?"

"Yeah," said Massimo. Then he got up to refill his drink.

v.

My physics final was a blur, and I left the classroom in a confused haze. I'd normally have lunch with Lorel, but I hadn't seen her for two days; she got in late from rehearsal, then she was dead to the world when I left in the morning. And she had her first performance tonight, which meant a flurry of glittery makeup and nerves this afternoon when I got back to the apartment.

Instead of lunch, I hunted down Kyle in the science library. He was in the back, high as a kite and peeling limes.

"I am interrupting something?" I dropped my backpack to the floor and took the seat across from him.

He had a paring knife, which definitely wasn't allowed on the school premises. He carefully peeled the small mountain of limes stacked beside his computer, as one might peel an apple—leaving curled green strands on the coffee-stained tabletop.

"Hi, Pia," he said, barely looking up. Apparently it took all his concentration. His brow was as furrowed as it ever got. He sliced open the peeled lime—slowly, methodically—laid the two halves on a napkin, and sprinkled flakey sea salt on top. He had a whole salt canister beside his laptop, next to his kombucha bottle.

I watched, transfixed, as he placed one half of a lime in his mouth. He closed his eyes and savored it.

My face hurt. "…Whatcha doing?"

He swallowed. "It's lime season," he said, as if it was obvious and this was a totally natural thing to be doing in the back of the library. "Citrus season, actually. Good stuff from this guy I know in Florida, he's in the Keys, they're key limes. Want one?"

"No thanks. That's kind of weird, Kyle."

"I call it *a disassembled margarita*." He seemed proud of himself.

"That's great, Kyle. Finals?"

"I'm done." He ate the other half of his lime. "Sure you don't want some?"

"I'm fine, thanks. What do you mean, *you're done*, we've got the report on Monday."

"Well, nearly done." Kyle dusted salt off his hands, fixed his baseball cap, and leaned back in his chair. "What's up?"

"What are you doing after school?"

"Indian. Or pizza."

"No." I rubbed the back of my neck. "No, I mean, after college. Do you have plans?"

"Oh." He picked up his paring knife and carefully started on the next lime. "Oh, actually, yeah, I do. So last year at the internship fair—you know, they have it in the auditorium, mid-spring I think, before midterms. I met some guys there, they had this international farming program. Mostly focused on botany and chemistry and shit, but they had this branch in food science where they collected heirlooms and did this cool rotational farming thing—you know, like collecting soil samples and determining pH and shit, optimal rotations for nutrient content, that sort of thing. I sort of kept in contact, and they asked if I'd come out after winter break—they're down in Georgia right now, but they've got places everywhere. They've got like a traveling lab, goes to their different farms and stuff, sends back data. Well, I've been talking to these guys, and they say they've got a spot open, and if Burnett can write me a rec letter, they'd consider me for the job."

"That's great." But there was a sinking feeling in my stomach; I hadn't gone to any internship fairs, or job fairs, or anything like that. Even Kyle of all people, with his weed and parties and limes, had planned for graduation and a career thereafter.

"What about you?" he asked. "Hey, want some kombucha?"

"No, thanks. Uh, I don't know, actually."

"You work for your uncle, right?"

I wished he hadn't said it like that. "Yes."

"What are you doing again? You're doing food science, right? You could work in a test kitchen or something, come up with bread recipes or whatever. I know a guy who does gluten experiments at Columbia, you want his number?"

In an alternate reality, maybe I would have taken him up on that—in a world where my parents were still around and I had the luxury of messing around in a lab. "I've got to do something that will help me support my siblings."

"Oh." He rubbed his nose, fixed me with his wide golden-brown eyes. "Right. Samantha said, Burnett told her about your parents."

"Yeah."

"Sucks."

"Yeah. So, I don't know what to do. I just want to bake, that's the only thing I can think of, and I can't support them and put them through college with that."

"Well, what else? What do you do? You've got to have hobbies. Like—I was always in the kitchen when I was a kid, I fermented these huge crocks of kimchi and stuff, and sometimes it went bad, but sometimes it was really good."

I could easily imagine that. "I mean"—I rubbed my temple—"I mean, I had hobbies. I played some soccer, I read a bit. I could always be a teacher, I guess—I'm good with kids, I know how to deal with them—but that's depending on whether I could get a teacher's certificate or whatever." Those weren't hobbies, not current ones anyway. I had less direction in my life than Kyle Litwiller.

He looked at me with perfect sincerity. "If you can get through Burnett's class, you can get a teaching certification." He shrugged, halved his lime, and sprinkled the salt. "Hey, my big sister's a ditz, and she did it—she teaches little kids in Jersey, has like a mountain of art supplies and coloring pages and like, *kazoos and shit*."

I smiled at that. "I don't know that I want to do that. I'm not very musical."

"Hey, you don't gotta be musical for the kazoo. It sounds like a shrieking cat, whoever does it." He thought about it. "Like a violin."

I didn't want to get into his beef with violinists. Every now and then Kyle went on a rant about how some instruments still exist only because people feel like punishing their ears periodically, something about keeping their "ear nerves" strong, but how those same people also grow up to be become psychopaths. I think his sister played violin.

Here was the thing: lots of kids had the opportunity to explore what they wanted, in high school and early in college. I'd been too busy baking and taking care of the kids, and I'd missed my window, and now I was floundering. Looking back, what I needed more than anything was some sort of parental guidance.

I desperately wanted to trust Savino—only I couldn't. I had the sense that my uncle always possessed some ulterior motive. He'd make these inscrutable moves that left me pondering his intentions.

Case in point: Besides moving Betta up front at the bakery—where she bickered endlessly with Dora and drove Marco Biasi to the end of his rope—Savino stopped sending Oscar with me to school. Instead, he pushed Luca's company on me. After a full morning of struggling to train the new guy, Savino had him walk me a few blocks to Fortuna, which was stupid for several reasons: Luca wasn't all that bigger than me, so it wasn't like he'd offer much protection; he didn't know how to navigate New York City any better than I did; and this left Savino and Giovani alone in the back of the bakery, which seemed like an inefficient setup. I actually missed the walks with Oscar, when the lanky computer scientist would update me on the new stuff he was learning, the family apple orchard he'd visited over Thanksgiving break, the Cuban girl with the penguin tattoo who'd let him take her to coffee last week.

Luca liked to walk me to my classroom building. He didn't talk much, and when he did it was mostly questions, which meant I had to respond in a shoddy patchwork of Italian and English. And when I finally managed to get him to shove off back to the bakery, he wandered away in a distressingly confused, lost manner that haunted me for a while after, lingered in the back of my mind where I could easily imagine Luca accidentally wandering in the wrong direction and ending up in Pennsylvania or something.

I figured Savino was trying to keep tabs on me. The bit that didn't make sense was that Oscar was in a much better position to work intel, and with Luca I felt more closed-off than with anyone else. So whatever my uncle was planning, either it was failing miserably, or I hadn't figured it out yet.

vi.

My last final was scheduled for Wednesday. The oil shipment was coming in Friday night. I spent the weekend hanging out with Massimo, going to Lorel's performance at Fortuna and ironing out our plans over the kitchen island.

"Tonio said the drop-off point is…" I traced my finger down a map of long island, stopping at a spot marked with red pen. "Here."

"We haven't used that one in a while." Massimo tapped another red-marked point. "We did this one last time. But that's Montauk, I've been there. They've got a private dock, Stefano usually gets Valentino's guys to come around this curve here in a motor boat. To be discrete. But at night it's pretty deserted out there."

"So we tip off the Scarpacis to the drop-off, they show up. Then we tip off the cops and hell breaks loose. Will Diego go all the way out there, you think?"

Massimo shrugged. "If he's angry enough."

I shuffled the papers, searching for a piece of scratch paper. "You don't think he's angry enough? After Savino stormed the casino—"

"Well, Achille busted out some windows, but that might not be enough."

191

"We've got till Friday." It was Monday, I had my organic chemistry final on Wednesday, and doomsday was coming up too fast. "What can we do to make Diego Scarpaci even more angry, *and* tip him off to get to Montauk, and—God, Massimo, next week we could be—"

"It could be over," he said.

This was my plan, and it was a stupid plan, and I was insane for ever attempting it. "It could," I said, "but there's so much that could go wrong, we haven't thought this through enough, how are we going to control—?"

"We're not," said Massimo. "That's the point. They'll destroy each other, we'll sit back and watch, then we're out of here."

"And Lorel? Have you told her?"

He didn't respond. That was answer enough.

"Look." He pointed out the timetable. "Drop-off near nine, that's what Tonio said. We need an alibi. That's it—an alibi, then we're done."

I put my head in my hands. An alibi, just like *Macbeth*, just like Savino messing with everyone's heads. And here we were, doing the same thing to Lorel. Me and Massimo and Tonio, we were skirting the edge of the mob, circling the maelstrom, blending in and adopting our family's way of thinking without getting sucked in. Though I could never say it aloud, I knew it well enough: we were dancing the border between calculated preservation and self-destruction. I sensed that I was losing.

"Okay." I ran my fingers through my hair and clasped my hands in front of me. "An alibi." A way to convince my uncle and Massimo's parents and Tonio's brothers that we were otherwise occupied on the night of the showdown." Lorel has a performance Friday night."

Massimo nodded. He didn't seem depressed or worn-out when we sat planning like this—he was fast, pages snapped like flames when he flipped through them and tapped a word, a number, a pinprick on the map. It was like with physics or chemistry—he was ears-deep in the task, fully engaged. "Right," he said. "Seven-thirty show."

Which meant Lorel would be on stage while the drop-off went down. The Vitellis couldn't reach her there.

"So." My fingers steepled, I leaned over the island and examined the time table. "So—Friday night. How do you like theater?"

vii.

The only reason I caught the call Tuesday morning was because I was texting Lorel when the box popped up on the screen—incoming call, Vitelli house. I almost didn't answer. I didn't want to talk to Savino.

It was Ida. "Hi, Pia—oh, I didn't think you'd pick up. Nicole and I, we're going Christmas shopping, we want you to come with us? We'll be at your apartment in…thirty minutes?"

I blinked. "Oh." Yes, it was December. And December meant Christmas, which I was never terribly excited about, because my birthday was Christmas Eve and I was always a little bitter.

"Are you at school?" A car door slammed on her side, another voice murmured in the background. Ida's voice faded out for a second—"Yeah, yeah, Fortuna"—and then she was back. "We can pick you up at the school, alright?"

"No," I said, "I'm at the apartment. That's fine." I couldn't come up with an excuse fast enough to get out of this.

"Okay, we'll be there in thirty minutes."

I was in pajamas, it was ten o'clock, there was a burnt-out cigarette butt floating in the toilet bowl. I'd woken in a daze about an hour before, a headache drilling into my temple, my thoughts wrapped around sleep-fogged images of fires and car crashes, dashes of Lorel's glitter makeup mixed with a shimmering sea of green-tinged oil. Massimo's sleeping pills had hit me like a truck. I'd stumbled like a blind drunk down the hallway and into the bathroom, where I'd realized we were out of toothpaste, so I'd gone back to the bedroom and searched around for my phone—went back to the bathroom and sat on the edge of the tub to text Lorel, asked her to pick some up on her way back from her British Lit final. It was right about then that reality and the dream-world had finally come into equilibrium. I was awake, and my life was a nightmare, and the world was a terrible place with dead parents and psychotic relatives and lies upon lies. So I'd sat there on the edge of the tub and smoked and stared at the floor and smoked for a long time with the cigarette burning my fingers, dull shock spreading though my body.

Then the phone buzzed.

I dragged myself back to the bedroom and chewed a stick of gum while I got ready. My clothes were in piles on the floor—pajamas and socks, dirty stuff that hadn't quite made it to my laundry basket, a mountain of half-folded clean clothes stacked against my closet door. I scrounged together a halfway-decent outfit, chugged a scalding mug of burnt coffee, then went out front to wait for Ida.

When the black BMW pulled up on the curb and Ida waved from the driver's seat, I discovered that it wasn't just her and Nicole on this excursion. As I slid into the back seat, face burning from the wind, I bumped up against Dora—on her other side, her mom Serafina smiled in a polite, detached way. I didn't know Serafina well, but she and Dora had the same slender build and gorgeous caramel hair.

Ida gave my apartment building a nice long inspection before she pulled out onto the street. "Pia, this neighborhood is not nice—not a good street. You're careful, right?"

"I'm careful."

"Savino," she told Nicole, "he put in alarms, extra locks. His friend Joey does security for one of those big companies, he does our systems, we trust him."

"Pia," said Nicole, turning in her seat—a flash of Mamma in her eyes, that motherly severity—"you look thin, why are you thin? She looks thin, *si*?" She said this to the other women in the car, who all seemed to disapprove of my apparent thinness.

"I think you look lovely," said Dora, always polite.

"Thank you," I returned, although I was sure I didn't.

Nicole patted my cheek—I flinched, but she'd already faced front again. "She needs food, get some food in her, yeah?" She said this to Ida, as if Ida had any control over when or what I ate. "Pia, you've got to eat good food, if you don't eat good food you'll disappear and get sick, you won't be pretty anymore, you can't survive off this *college diet*—the kids told me, people just eat the Pizza Hut and those caffeine energy drinks and the—uh"—she mimed smoking, through her thumb and forefinger—"you know what it is, the thing."

"The cigarettes," Serafina supplied.

"No, the other one—"

"Vape?" said Dora, in a small, inquisitive voice, as if she knew nothing about it.

"Yes, the vape. You need real food, these are *children*, and they're not eating and they're drinking and doing parties and the vaping." Nicole glanced back at me—I supposed she didn't know much of what Betta was getting into. "You don't vape, Pia, alright?"

"I don't." I wasn't sure if it was a question or a command. "I won't."

She clicked her tongue, patted my face again. "Oh. Poor baby." She addressed Ida again, as if I wasn't even there. "She looks like Savino—more like Savino than Carla."

The city had gotten snow a few days before, but it had melted to ugly gray sludge in the gutters. Ida found parking near the Brookfield mall. We walked through the wind while Nicole explained that Ida had a day off from the dentist office where she worked, and Serafina had taken the day off weeks ago to go shopping with Dora, and I gleaned from this that Nicole was probably a stay-at-home mom. Being a Vitelli and all, she probably didn't *need* to work.

And then there was Dora.

I found out soon enough that this shopping trip was just as much Christmas shopping as it was a planning meeting for the big Dora-Francesco wedding—and, before that, the equally extravagant engagement party (I hadn't even known people *had* engagement parties). If I'd known before, I definitely would have fought to keep from coming along on this nightmare parade through jewelry stores and aisles stocked with white-and-silver heels and wedding registries. Throughout the morning, my aunts and Serafina switched constantly between fawning ladies-in-waiting and severe wedding dictators—frog-marching us between stores and telling Dora exactly how it was going to be, then just as quickly squealing and clapping when the bride-to-be tried on that perfect pair of strappy heels.

I felt sick.

"Pia—these earrings, no? Serafina says yes, but I think they're too big, they don't suit her face, huh?"

"You like hats? Does Cristine wear hats? She should, and you should too, you don't want old skin, you want to get this hat for your sister?"

And Dora, pulling me aside to show me the ring for the thousandth time: "He brought it over from Italy, it's been in the Battaglini family for centuries—"

I kept thinking about how much Sabine would hate this, how she'd have a few choice words for my other aunts and Dora. She'd have a few colorful stories about Nic Tabone from the Bronx and her skipping town like she was ducking out of a court date.

The only good part of the outing, as far as I was concerned, was lunch. I hadn't eaten good food in a while, and Ida got us a spot at this seafood restaurant in the mall, where we ate fish in lemon sauce and prawns and scallops swimming in butter. Ida, Nicole and Serafina ordered wine, and as soon as the server turned his back they contributed liberal splashes of their drinks to mine and Dora's empty water glasses. They didn't really bother with discretion; like my parents, they expressed complete disregard for US drinking laws.

"We don't care," Nicole shrugged.

I wondered if she knew her son was an alcoholic.

"Francesco wants a summer wedding," Dora was saying, flashing her diamond around as she gesticulated. "His family can make it over then—"

"Five sisters," said Serafina, holding up five fingers for emphasis. "And two brothers. Lovely family, he is the third oldest. Anna and Gianluca own a restaurant. I've talked to them, very nice, Anna Battaglini is a *sommelier*."

Ida and Nicole nodded their approval. I watched with bated breath, simultaneously horrified and hypnotized by the proceedings. Dora, with her illegal glass of wine and her perfectly legal engagement ring on her very young hand.

"His parents," Dora went on, "they want to meet me, they might come over from Sicily a bit earlier, we'll vacation with them at the house up north—what is it, Maine?"

"Yeah," said Nicole, "Gio's parents, they've got a house up there?"

"Hey," said Ida, and suddenly the conversation was focused on me. "Hey, how's Luca, Pia? Luca, at the bakery, huh?"

Ah yes, Luca Catenacci, who was probably a source of great frustration to Savino right now—whatever my uncle was hoping Luca might pick up from me, whatever information, I wasn't telling the guy anything. It wasn't especially difficult, either. Luca was pretty transparent. "He's doing alright," I said, "I think Marco's giving him more hours after Christmas."

"Is he nice?"

My hands were sweaty despite the cold. I wrapped them around my glass. "Yeah, I uh. Uh." They were all staring at me. I hated it. I wished we'd go back to discussing Dora and Francesco and the greatest romance of the modern day. "I guess. Isn't he staying with you all?"

"Oh, yes." Ida sipped her wine, moved some scallops around on her plate. "Yes, he's upstairs in your old room, the one in the back, you know?"

I nodded. It wasn't really jealousy, but it was weird knowing that Luca Catenacci was in the room with the blue sparrow window. Had I left any cigarettes under the mattress? Did he open the window to let in fresh air? Did he ever see the smoking man in the square below, or was that specter reserved for me?

"I think he's nice," said Dora, her huge engagement rock flashing on her slim hand, sparkling in the dim lights, "and handsome, right?"

"Oh, yes," said Ida, a knowing twinkle in her eye, "very handsome, like all the Catenaccis, they're good people. Beautiful dark eyes, dresses well."

They all seemed a lot closer, suddenly—the table was small, the chairs were pressed in tight together, every pair of eyes drilled into me.

Nicole reached across the table, grabbed my wrist. Her hand was hot. "You like him, Pia? Nice boy, speaks good Italian—beautiful Italian, Sicilian, it's the best, like poetry."

"Poetry," Serafina agreed.

I still tasted the cigarette smoke—did they? Could they smell it on me, the exhaustion, the multiple glasses of wine I'd had late last night at Massimo's, how I chain-smoked on the balcony until the sleeping pills kicked in and I stumbled off across the apartment, leaving the door wide open behind me, and collapsed fully-clothed on my bed?

"He's good, very smart—Catholic, and Savino likes him—"

Dora's ring clinking against her glass, the shopping bags of wedding things rustling beside the floor vent.

"Oh, so does Gio, he's very respectful, good manners—"

"The girls love him, the twins—oh, and Marc, he can't wait till Luca gets home every day, Luca's great with the kids, he's going to be a *good* father—"

I carefully pulled my hand away, tossed back my wine. "I need the restroom."

They were still talking when I slipped away, still singing Luca's praises in a conspiratorial tone of voice. I got turned around in the maze of tables, I had to have a waiter point the way to the ladies 'room. When the door swung shut behind me, I breathed in the sharp scent of lemon cleaner, the fake perfumed flowers by the sink. The rest of the restaurant pressed into my back, chased me into a stall.

I was alone. Classical music drifted down from hidden speakers. I fumbled for my phone, every breath weighing heavily in my chest.

My fingers were numb. They punched in the number. "Massimo?"

"Hi, Pia." After a beat, when I didn't follow up with anything: "Are you alright?"

"Where are you?"

"I'm in my car, I just dropped my dad and Achille off to talk to some guys in the Bronx, I'm just driving round the block till I pick them up. Are you okay? Where are *you*? Where's Lorel?"

"Look, I'm at the mall, I'm—Ida and your mom, they took me out, with Serafina and Dora, they're doing wedding shopping but they told me it was Christmas shopping, and I didn't know how to say no. And Dora's here, they're planning the wedding and the engagement party—I didn't even know there was an engagement party—and they're doing registries, they're all talking about weddings and how great Francesco is—"

"Good Lord," Massimo sighed.

"Yeah, but I just realized, you know what? You know Luca Catenacci? I thought Savino wanted him around to keep an eye on me, you know?"

"He'd never suspect you," Massimo said, quickly. "Savino isn't suspicious—"

"No," I said, "exactly. I know, we talked about this with Tonio. But I don't think that's it. I don't think he's here to spy on me or even just follow me around the bakery, Savino didn't just hire him to get some extra help. I think they're pulling a Dora—"

"They're *what*?"

"Look, it's like Sabine, you get it?" I couldn't even say it, the words were caught in my chest.

The turn signal clicked on—car horns honked in the distance. It took Massimo a moment, and he sounded tired when he spoke. "Oh. Oh, uh, Savino, he wants...he wants you to stay."

Stay. Stay forever. "You get it? They're jumping all over me, Nicole and Ida, they're shoving it under my nose, *down my throat*. Luca's my Nic Tabone."

"Your what?"

I was pacing, I was angry, I felt panic clutching at my throat. "He wants Cristine and Vince and Carlo in Brooklyn, he wants me to stay so he can control Valentino, but that's not enough, Massimo, he's got me my own Francesco—he shipped this guy over

197

from Sicily—because if I settle down with a NICE ITALIAN BOY, I won't leave—I'll end up with a bunch of babies and I'll get stuck here, you get it?"

"I get it, I'm sorry, I didn't know—but he can't make you—"

"He can!"

"He *can't*," Massimo pressed. "Savino can't force you to marry the Catenacci guy."

God, when he said it like that. I was nineteen, going on twenty, dead parents, three siblings to take care of, my whole bleak train-wreck of a life ahead of me—plenty of bleak empty canvas to paint with more tragedy and bad decisions. I couldn't *marry*.

"Does he think I'm *stupid?*" I'd rather the original idea be true—rather Savino use Luca to ply me for information, at least *that* suggested I posed something of a threat. "Does he think I don't *see it?* Dora's waving around her ring and your mom is out there telling me Luca's Italian sounds like fucking poetry, and I'm gonna be sick, Massimo, I'm serious—I'm gonna vomit—"

"No, do you want me to come get you? He can't force you, Pia, it feels like that, I know it does—"

"He's *forcing my hand*," I seethed.

Savino was trying to turn me into another Sabine, another Dora, trying to frame my future—*Pia doesn't have any plans, let me make some for her—let me pin her like a moth to this frame, pin her down as the prize Marzano child, pin her down for the sake of us all. For the business.*

"You know—you know, he's given me no choice, now I'm angry." I was beyond angry; I was unhinged, I was furious. "We've got to do this. We've got to make it work. We've got to bring the business down in flames."

"In flames," he echoed.

Even in the midst of this nightmare, I recognized the reverence in his voice. In that moment, Massimo and I spoke the exact same language. Fury. Fire. And utter, helpless desperation.

X

Present History

i.

No one told me the story in whole. I don't even think most people in the family had all the pieces—they were either content with what they knew, or else they were too scared to dig much deeper.

I had to drag the family history out of one person at a time. Betta knew next to nothing, mostly because she didn't care. Lorel was ignorant by choice, but also because Calpurnia Marzano had hidden her past from her children. Massimo knew more, but it was Tonio of all people who'd done the research and found our family history intensely entertaining. Perhaps he enjoyed the discomfort it elicited from people, garnering cruel amusement from old family troubles, impersonal enough to him that he might find them compelling for their storytelling potential alone. Apparently he'd grilled Ida for the juicy details long ago, and had constructed an approximation of the events leading to the Vitelli-Scarpaci rivalry and the Marzano connection.

It went something like this:

On St. Joseph's Day about thirty years ago, the Marzanos, Scarpacis, and Vitellis all lived in a village in the province of Enna, surrounded by rocky rolling hills and sprawling *oliveti*. Even then, the Scarpacis were gambling people—maybe they were crooked, no one could necessarily catch them at it, but the general consensus was that the only family shadier than the Scarpacis was the Vitelli clan. The Vitellis didn't bother hiding their criminal activity; they wore their mafia ties with brazen pride. They might not have staged magnificent coups, but they owned the streets and they wanted everyone to know it. There was some vague attachment to the Cosa Nostra, a few Vitellis disappearing into those ranks, but their names were lost to memory.

And the Marzanos—dear Devota Maria and Valentino Marzano, the most affluent of families—came from money way back, and they'd been smart enough to keep their hands on it. They lived in a huge stone house on a hill surrounded by acres of olive trees, with their two children. And everyone loved them, because fortune seemed to follow Valentino; his business was good, he was cunning, but he was generous. Devota

Maria was professed a living saint by the common people. It was just like Savino said: she was a great woman, and she loved everyone, and everyone knew it.

And this was where it just got ridiculous.

Every year, Devota Maria Marzano would host the biggest *Festa di San Giuseppe* celebration in the whole province. It commemorated the end of a devastating drought in the Middle Ages, when the people prayed to St. Joseph and rain finally broke through the heavens. In typical St. Joseph's Day fashion, everyone would gather round the table and celebrate the feast day with food and festivity. The women from nearby villages would come up days ahead of time to the estate on the *oliveto*, and they'd prepare an altar heaping with cakes and sesame-seeded breads and biscotti, candied almonds and *sfingi*, meatless soups and pastas and plenty of olives. And most notably, *zeppole*. People would bring out their old family recipes and Devota Maria's favorite would achieve lofty status at the St. Joseph's Table, bearing the mark of honor until the following year.

This next bit was still foggy, even Tonio couldn't quite puzzle it out. But one year, the Vitellis decided that they wouldn't bring their own family recipe. Instead, Marco Vitelli and his brothers thought it would be fantastic (for some unknown reason) if they filched a treasured Scarpaci recipe instead. So they pulled off a simple heist and ran home with old Lucia Scarpaci's secret recipe for *zeppole*.

It didn't escape the Scarpacis that the dish Norma Vitelli plopped down on the altar the next day was the same secret recipe they'd guarded for so long. Matteo Scarpaci and his wife Lucia complained to Devota Maria, they told her what had happened, but my grandmother liked to keep the peace, and she didn't take the issue too seriously—in fact, she proclaimed the Vitelli *zeppole* entry the winner for that year.

It was a bad move.

Matteo Scarpaci and his children did not have a sense of humor, could not back down from this travesty, and decided to have the Vitellis arrested. Granted, Marco Vitelli and his gang had raised enough hell over the years that they probably should have landed in prison decades before. The only reason they'd dodged prison (or anything harsher) had a lot to do with the fact that Valentino Marzano was fond of the Vitellis. He was political, he was crooked, and so Marco and the boys got off easy on a regular basis. In return, they occasionally did a job for old Valentino. Vitellis got shit done.

Devota Maria wouldn't stand for this sort of vengeful behavior from the Scarpacis. So the Marzanos got the Vitellis out of prison.

Like any balanced family in a feud, the Scarpacis retaliated by kidnapping Devota Maria's and Valentino's daughter. This was Calpurnia Marzano, just fifteen at the time; they put her up in their pistachio orchards outside Nicosia, and they told the Marzanos they could have their daughter back when they punished the Vitellis for their thievery and rescinded the St. Joseph's Day win.

200

The Marzanos were pissed with Matteo and Lucia and the whole Scarpaci clan. In response to their ransom note, Valentino sent the Vitellis to burn down the pistachio orchards, which they did, promptly and efficiently, because Vitellis got shit done. Valentino wouldn't let anyone help put out the ravaging fires until the Scarpacis gave back his daughter.

But by the time Calpurnia Marzano got back home, safe in the family *oliveto*, she'd fallen in love with the oldest Scarpaci boy, Diego. Seeing how the families were in a petty and highly destructive feud, this was problematic. Shortly after her return, therefore, she disappeared once more, only this time she'd left of her own accord— gallivanting off into the sunset with Diego Scarpaci, far away from Valentino and Devota Maria and their one remaining child: Leonardo Marzano.

From there, it was easy to piece the story together. The Vitellis stayed by the Marzanos 'side when the family business picked up, and when Valentino decided to expand to New York, he trusted Marco Vitelli and his children with the task. So Marco and Norma, their daughters and Savino and their aunts and uncles and cousins, they traipsed across the ocean and set up shop in Brooklyn. They opened the bakery to launder Valentino's money, and they named it *Il Panificio Zeppole* as a dark reference to the St. Joseph's Day scandal.

While Calpurnia and Diego married and followed their own Scarpaci relatives to Harlem, where they eventually started their casino—Leo Marzano visited his father's business in Brooklyn. He fell in love with Carla Vitelli, and the family was thrilled.

The rest was history. Only it still felt terribly present.

ii.

There would always be a *before* and *after*. Everything before that night in April, everything that fell into place in the years following the accident.

Mamma and Papa had gone out for the evening. It was their anniversary, and while we simply didn't have the sort of money for a fancy getaway vacation, I'd done all my homework earlier in the day so that I could take care of the kids while they went into town for dinner.

Mamma wore her blue dress with the small gray flowers, her medals clinking on the chain as she whisked out of the house, and Papa followed in his sports coat with the patchy elbows. Looking back on that moment, I could only remember the backs of their heads, the curve of Mamma's neck below her silky black ponytail, Papa's dark, callused hand pulling the door shut behind them. The *click* of the lock is audible in my memory.

I helped the kids with their homework—Cristine bitching about her civics class, rolling her eyes at the ceiling when I pointed out a mathematical error. Carlo wanted to be left alone, deep in his head while he poured over worksheets, but Vince needed me to look over his fractions. I spent the evening flitting between my siblings and periodically ducking into the kitchen to deal with whatever I had on the stove—I can't

201

remember now, it seems trivial, I couldn't even recall if we'd eaten dinner before I got a phone call from the sheriff.

They hadn't even made it to their dinner reservation.

The car had gone off the road before the old bridge outside town. They'd narrowly missed the river.

The car was crushed like a can, the front accordioned against an ancient oak with heavy roots. They found deer tracks in the area—they said Papa had swerved, the car had flipped, it had lodged itself against the tree. They'd seen this sort of thing happen countless times before, nothing special about the incident.

It was an old car. No airbags. There wasn't even power steering, that had gone years ago, but we couldn't afford to fix the damn thing and Papa never had the time to get around to it.

Later, after some of Mamma's coworkers came by the house to stay with us, after I'd told the kids, someone told me Papa had died quickly. Immediate, they said, like that was supposed to console me. Not a moment of pain—he hadn't even known what had hit him. They were trying to comfort us, I knew that, but I didn't want to believe Leo Marzano's life could be snuffed out that quickly. They made it sound fragile, like breaking a wing off an insect—here one second, *snap*, gone the next.

Mamma held on. Someone found the car and called the cops. The ambulance came. And they said she fought to stay with them, they all did their best.

She was dead before they reached the hospital.

Sabine came into town. The next few weeks were a blur of forgetting and then remembering again, holding myself up and keeping it together so I didn't splinter into pieces—holding myself up to I could keep the kids together.

I imagined the old car smashed up against the tree, nestled among its gnarled roots, tipping towards the river, with a smoking engine and the radio still playing. Probably Ella Fitzgerald—Mamma had an album that lived perpetually in the CD player, it would come on every time we turned on the car. And I imagined the night being so still around them—Papa slumped in his seat, Mamma still from the shock, the cicadas and river and the music from the radio playing a soundtrack that hummed in her ears.

It was quick, they said. It was painless.

I wondered what Mamma had thought about, those last few moments. Had she known Papa was dead? Because maybe, once she'd realized that—maybe that had been the moment she'd let go.

Leo and Carla Marzano had made it to their twenty-first wedding anniversary. I wondered if Marco Vitelli had known the date, when he'd sent his guys to do the job— *if* he'd sent them at all, if any of it was true. Because maybe, after all, it had been a deer. Maybe Papa had swerved, despite years of telling us not to do just that, despite living outside Augusta for twenty years and knowing better than anyone the limitations of his vehicle.

There would always be a *before* and *after*, but maybe that was life. Maybe my whole story would be a series of *befores* and *afters*, in such rapid succession I wouldn't even know one thing had ended and something else had begun. Maybe I was constantly turning pages—chapters opening and closing, losing things I wouldn't even realize were lost until years down the road.

XI

Wicked

i.

I didn't sleep much on Thursday, the night before the show. I was worried about taking Massimo's sleeping pills because I didn't want to *not* wake up, I didn't want to sleep through my alarms. As a result, I tossed and turned, woke up to drink from the bathroom faucet once, got up to smoke another time, and by the time my alarm went off for work, I felt like I'd been hit by a truck. I felt physically ill as I dragged on my work clothes, grabbed my things, and tiptoed past Lorel's room.

The oil shipment was coming in tonight, and nothing would be the same after that.

I thought about writing Lorel a note—good luck!—but I'd probably see her before the show. This was her last performance, this Friday night showdown, and the nerves flickering through my body assured me that *I* was the one with the big performance to put on—no room for error, no slip-ups, forget a line and someone dies.

No one's dying, I reminded myself for the thousandth time, as I tugged on my sneakers by the front door.

Then Sunday, I was flying home, back to Augusta for Christmas. On one hand, I couldn't wait; I missed the old house with its familiar smells and creaky floorboards, I missed the spotty gravel drive and Sabine's fancy car parked under a dogwood. I wanted to hug Vince tight—sweet Vince, innocent baby—and wrestle Carlo into a headlock and sit in silence with Cristine, appreciate her calculated quiet.

And at the same time, I was terrified. I felt like I was ducking out of the nightmare for this short time, coming up for air, and when I went back under I'd find it more terrifying than I remembered. If I looked away for even a few weeks, everything might be doubly bad when I got back.

I hadn't been to work since the mall fiasco. Which meant today I'd have to go into the bakery and look my uncle in the eye and pretend like nothing was wrong, like I wasn't desperately furious with the corner I'd been backed into, like I wasn't hurt by how condescendingly obvious his Luca plot really was. And I'd have to be around Luca too, which was a separate, exhausting task in itself.

I'd told Lorel about the Luca plot, and she'd found it fantastically funny. Her eyes had lit up and she'd leaned forward like we were sharing a thrilling bit of gossip. "What? Well, is he cute?"

"That isn't the point."

"Well, is he?"

I tried to not get annoyed; she didn't understand how horrifying and embarrassing it really was. "I guess. Maybe. He's not really my type. But that's not the point, he's trying to tie me down and he doesn't think I'm smart enough to notice what he's doing. It's insulting. And manipulative."

"Well, what's your type then?"

"What?"

"If *cute* isn't your type, what is?"

"Lorel—I don't have one. I can't think about that sort of thing right now. But especially not Luca—no one, but especially not him. I don't even know him, and Savino thinks I'm going to fall head-over-heels just because he has a Sicilian accent and a...a weirdly symmetrical face."

She didn't understand my aversion, and I didn't understand the attraction of getting pinned down with a relationship, signing her life away, even if Massimo was a good person. Romance, I thought, was a poor replacement for freedom.

I wasn't paranoid. But did paranoid people know when it became an obsessive thing? Sometimes I thought I saw things around town—at school, in my apartment, at the bakery.

Every now and then, I recalled the image of that man out in the square behind the Vitelli house: the lone figure under the oak tree, standing beside the park bench, smoking and staring up at the sparrow window. I didn't think it was one of Savino's guys, I figured it was some Scarpaci attempt at spying, and the idea that I was being *spied on* sounded ridiculous, except that I'd also been kidnapped and I wouldn't put anything past these people at this point. So maybe it wasn't paranoia—maybe it was reasonable caution, the type Savino and Massimo talked about when they said *be careful* in an ominous tone.

There was someone living on the floor below me and Lorel. Sometimes they stood out front of the apartment, reading on the front step or walking the sidewalk on their phone. But other times this heavyset man with his weatherbeaten face and buzzed hair would be downstairs checking his mail when I got back from school, or he'd stand out in the hallway texting someone while I walked down the hall, and his eyes, pale behind

206

the dark frames of his glasses, seemed to follow me. I never saw him smoking, but he always called to mind the figure below the sparrow window.

I mentioned him to Lorel a couple times. She didn't seem too worried. "It's New York, there are lots of weirdos—it's a city of weirdos and famous people and famous weirdos. There was a guy who used to live out back of the casino and he called himself the Rat King, but I think his name was James. He told Dad he could control the rats and if Dad didn't give him a job, he'd send a rat infestation to destroy the business. And Dad didn't give him a job because the guy was certifiably insane and catcalled Sara a few times, and we didn't get invaded by giant rats, which means he was either a liar, or else this is a story about mercy and forgiveness."

I didn't know whether to be relieved that she didn't recognize the guy. Sure, he definitely wasn't some Scarpaci spy her dad had sent over. But I'd almost prefer sharing the building with Lorel's extended family than with the typical sort of creep. A kidnapping attempt by my dad's side of the family was comparatively less horrible than trafficking or rape.

I didn't bring this up to Massimo; I figured he didn't need one more reason to be terrified for Lorel's safety. And I definitely didn't tell Tonio, who was already convinced that my apartment was located in some circle of hell, sandwiched between a Wal-Mart and an Apple store. But I did tell Matty. He was over often enough that he'd probably seen the guy, and since he'd talked about moving in, I thought he should know.

"Have you got a taser?" he'd asked, when I first brought it up.

"Is that legal?"

He'd shrugged. "Lorel's got one. Maybe you should get one too. Have you got a gun?"

"Does *Lorel* have a gun?" I found that hard to imagine.

"She hates guns. But someone should have one, you seem like you could handle it."

That day, as I climbed aboard the bus and slid into a window seat near the front, I watched my apartment disappear behind me. Whatever happened today, there would always be a before and after. Next time I went back to the apartment, the next time I slept or showered, it would all be different.

I resisted the urge to ring up Massimo. He had the burner phone.

We'd gone over the plan once more the day before, and while it was as solid as we could make it under short notice, the frustration was palpable; once we set it into motion, there was nothing any of us could do about the consequences of our actions. We just had to sit back and wait it out.

"I'll call the Scarpacis on the burner," Massimo had said. "Give them an anonymous tip about the drop-off. Then I'll call NYPD and tell them the same thing. So the cops show up, take care of the Scarpacis since Diego doesn't pay off the law enforcement, as far as we know. And they'll find Savino's guys out at Montauk as well."

"I can make the calls," I volunteered, more because I wanted to *do something* than out of an actual desire to call the cops on Lorel's family.

"Bad idea," said Tonio.

I'd grimaced at him. "Why?"

"Your voice is too distinctive."

We'd stood on the balcony, Tonio and I smoking, Massimo with a drink in one hand and the burner phone in the other. It was late, but the city was loud, and it somehow diffused the nervous tension by peeling it away at the edges, blending our own chaos into that of the the streets below.

"What's that supposed to mean?"

"Yes, Marzano. Take offense before you even understand my suggestion. How terribly like this family." He shook his head, tapped out the ash, and glanced at me out of the corner of his eye as if to gauge my reaction.

Massimo sighed. "Tonio."

"Well, am I wrong?"

"He's not wrong," said Massimo. "You did meet the Scarpacis before, so they could recognize your voice. You have a distinctive accent—a little Italian, little southern, little Brooklyn. We can't risk anyone recognizing that."

"And I don't touch phones," said Tonio.

"You say that like it makes you superior," I said, and put out my cigarette. "But it's kind of stupid."

"It's very stupid," said Massimo.

"No offense," said Tonio, in a way that suggested he hoped we took full offense, "but you two are the last people I'd accept lifestyle advice from."

I wasn't happy about it, but Massimo was probably the right choice to make the calls. He dealt with people well—he stayed calm, he spoke evenly. Funny, how the same reason I'd been drawn to him in the beginning—all that placidity and resolute detachment, a glass of wine in the back of the room, something constant and unshakeable in his character—it was ironic that this same virtue was what would drive us into the home stretch of our self-destructive journey.

I didn't call him. I sat on the bus and tucked my chin to my chest, curled and uncurled my gloved fingers into fists. I had work, I had to pack, so I tried to ignore this rising tide of disaster lapping and growing above my ankles.

If there was a balance to this madness, I hadn't found it.

The front of the bakery was dark. Usually Savino at least put on the case lights when he got in, but those were out too. I went in anyway and locked the door behind me—the bell clattered, echoed around the empty shopfront.

"Hello?"

"Hm? Pia?" Footsteps. Marco Biasi with his distracted eyes, squinting at me through the darkness.

"Why are the lights out?"

"I just got in." He disappeared into the back.

I followed. "Well, where's Savino?" The kitchen was empty, the oven was cold, the fryers were quiet. I dropped my coat and bag on a stool and ducked into the office. "Marco?"

He was back at the desk, sipping his coffee, pounding away at his laptop. "I'm doing the books," he said without looking up, "what is it?"

I crossed my arms. "Where's Savino?"

"He's out."

I blinked. "For how long?"

"All day, probably. Look"—he finally dragged his eyes away from the screen to look at me—"there's a thing going on tonight, he's gonna be busy all day, he's not here. So?"

"So, what? It's just me?"

"Luca, Dora, and Betta will be in later," he said, all monotone, like I should know this shit by now. He clicked through his spreadsheets. "Look, I've known for weeks, I don't know about the other kids"—it irked me, being called a kid—"but this happens time to time, you know it, and you guys deal with it in the back. We pull our weight up front, everyone does their best, but we can always close early and it isn't the most important thing anyway."

"He didn't tell me," I said. Some people in this family were more concerned with the whole laundering scheme than they were keeping the bakery functioning like a normal business. I had little patience for that.

"Well, that's the point, is not telling everyone this stuff." He glanced at me sideways, like he was surprised I was still there. "Do you need something?"

"I need help."

"They'll be here soon."

"It'll be an hour, what about Giovani? Just Betta, not him?"

"Giovani's with Savino."

"Uh." I stepped out of the doorway, pressed the heel of my hand to my temple. "Uh. Okay."

I opened the bakery by myself, cursing Savino and Marco with every breath. For the next few hours, I buckled down and shut out everything else. I barely noticed Dora and Betta come in, only half-registered Marco's suggestion that he lend me Betta for a while, at least until opening. I ended up tripping over Luca a lot, pinning menial tasks on him so I could focus on getting stuff done. I'd be elbows deep in dough, though, and I'd turn around and he was right there on top of me, asking what I needed with those big dark puppy eyes in his disgustingly personable face.

It was nearly ten o'clock when I finally caught a break. I escaped onto the back step with a cup of tea and a corner piece of focaccia for breakfast, leaving Luca preoccupied with filling cannoli.

I checked my phone. There was a missed call from Massimo, and a voicemail from around six in the morning. I listened to the recording.

"Pia. Problem. I'm at the Vitelli house"—he was whispering—"Achille picked me up early, Savino has me and the guys working with him all day out at Montauk. He just called me first thing and I was out of the apartment before I had time to think—hell, Tonio's already gone to work. Look, I don't have the burner, I—" His voice dropped even lower, shouting in the background—maybe Gio, maybe someone else. "I don't have it, I can't slip away to do it either—do the thing we talked about, you know. But Tonio can do it—don't try, don't try to do it yourself, bad idea, like we talked about. We're heading out in a few minutes, we'll be out there all day, I can't do it. So get Tonio. I left it in the dining room somewhere, you need to do it soon. I...uh...I've got to go. I'll see you tonight, maybe, at the show, but maybe not. Be careful."

I dropped the phone into my lap. The focaccia was stale in my mouth.

Fuck.

My stomach turned over. I scrambled to my feet and slipped into the back of the kitchen.

"Your rest," said Luca, suddenly at my shoulder, "you are done?" His apron was stupidly pristine, his voice gentle and attentive.

"Wait," I said. I brushed him off and escaped up front, where Betta was arguing with a customer and Dora was handling two phones at once and Marco manned the register. The customers at their tables shouted to be heard over the foot-traffic—it was the holidays probably, that drew such a crowd at this time of day.

I still had the phone clamped in my fist. The second Dora was between calls, I tapped her shoulder. "I've got to go."

Her eyes were distracted. "What?"

"I have to go. The ovens are off, everything's taken care of, but Luca's in the back."

"Oh." Dora waved a hand—her bulbous earrings swayed, her ring finger flashed in the light. "Take him with you, go somewhere, take a break."

210

"No!" A headache hammered at my skull. "No, I've got to go right now, but you all can handle closing, right?"

"What?" Betta ducked away from her conversation, interest piqued by my tone. Her hair was wrenched back in two tight braids. She wore a sweater under her overalls. "Where are you going?"

"Out," I said. "Yes?"

Dora nodded. "Fine, sure, uh…Luca can go home with Betta."

"Oh, gosh." Betta took my arm and led me away to the kitchen door. She had a purposeful way to her walk, and I didn't like it.

I stuffed my phone in my pocket, shrugged her off. "What?" I hissed.

"Look." She leaned in, cut her eyes over at Marco. "Look, I'm going tonight."

I didn't know what to say to that. It seemed preposterous that anyone had told Betta anything about the drop-off, and even more ludicrous that she'd be involved in any way. Savino wasn't stupid. "Going where?" I said, carefully.

"You know. Jason's thing."

I breathed. "Jason's the—"

"The fire guy, yeah, from the Bronx—you remember. Well, I want you to come. I won't force you," she added, hurriedly. "It's just you're leaving and this is the last party before break. We don't have to stay long—look, I'll even give you the keys, you can drive us, we can leave whenever you want. It's the same place, you know the spot—"

"I can't," I said. "Lorel has a show."

"You can't get out of it?"

I disliked the suggestion that there was something to get out of. "Betta, I've got to go." I clapped her on the arm. "If I don't see you before break, have a good Christmas."

"C'mon Pia—"

"Bye." I skimmed past her into the back, where Luca was waiting, concern in his eyes.

"Pia," he said, "you are good? I can help?"

"You can help." I wiggled into my coat and buttoned it to my chin. I swung my backpack over my shoulder and pointed out the small mountain of dishes piled beside the sink. "You can do those. You can help Dora and Marco with closing. I've got to go."

"But—"

"*Basta.*" I shook my head—everyone was clinging to me, I felt like everything in the universe was conspiring to pin me down here, and more than ever I desperately needed to break free. *Get Tonio.* "*Buon Natale*, if I don't see you again."

"*Buon Natale.*" He seemed confused—stunningly, politely confused.

Out behind the bakery, Betta's BMW, Marco's red sports car and Dora's modest Kia were parked bumper-to-bumper on the curb. I slipped between the BMW and a cluster of garage bins, out onto Mulberry Street. Little Italy bustled with holiday activity, tourist crowds, sightseers—neon and Christmas lights gave me a headache, the wind was wet and chilled me to the bone—I might as well have not worn a coat at all, it didn't do much good. How many times had Ida offered to buy me a new one? Augusta winters just hadn't prepared me for cold like this.

I didn't have a car, I didn't have time to try and catch a cab, and it was only a thirty-minute walk to the Financial District from the bakery. And stupid Tonio didn't have a phone—I couldn't call him, the absolute *idiot*.

I stopped halfway to his apartment, near Foley Square, and I reassessed the situation. Where was I going? He wouldn't be at the apartment. I didn't know where he worked on Fridays—was he at Fortuna? Or his literary agency place uptown? I didn't know. I couldn't call anyone to find out. So I prayed he was in the tutoring lab today, and I switched directions and headed toward Fortuna.

My hands were numb by the time I got close—they were cracked and bleeding, every time I moved my fingers they bled a little more—but I couldn't operate the map on my phone with my gloves on. My teeth were chattering, body shaking uncontrollably.

Where was Massimo now? Montauk? And with Giovani...I bet he hated that. I should have caught on when Marco said Savino had taken Giovani with him, that should have told me Massimo was gone as well. I wished his message had been longer, I wished I could text him or something, but I didn't want anyone to see—I didn't know where his phone was, who he was with.

The school parking lot was mostly deserted. Every now and then a student would wander out of the cluster of buildings, looking dazed and tragic, mill their way over to a vehicle and just sit there in the driver's seat for a long time, staring out the windshield at the school like they couldn't believe what had just hit them. I cut through the quickest route to the library, which was nearly empty by this point; only a few desperate students cramming last-minute for finals populated the wobbling tables in the back, past a maze of dusty bookshelves.

I burst into the tutoring lab. I scanned the room—tables with computers and stools lined the walls, big round tables with padded seats dotted the blue-carpeted floor. A coffee machine spluttered somewhere. There were a couple dozen people scattered around. At a nearby table, three students gathered around a grad student I recognized from Burnett's lab—Dylan, maybe, or Ryan or something like that; one was tearfully working out the steps of a problem, while the other two leaned close to Dylan and explained, emphatically, in hushed voices flooded with desperation that *they hadn't been taught this shit, how should* they *know?*

I skirted by the table—"Oh, hey, Pia"—"Hi"—and I don't think I'd ever been happier to see Tonio's stupid slicked-back hair, glinting black in the fluorescent lights. He sat with his back to the room, beside a girl who seemed on the verge of weeping, and stabbed a stack of papers repeatedly with an expensive-looking pen.

"I get your reasoning, I'm sure it makes sense to *you* but the fact of the matter is that it simply won't hold up as a valid argument. What a stretch—I mean"—he leaned forward, flipped through a couple pages—"you really staked the entirety of this behemoth on *that* thesis? What percentage of your grade is this thing?"

"Uh…uh, seventy, I think, oh god, is it that bad? God, I don't have time for this, it's due in an hour—"

"Look." Tonio stretched, crossed his arms behind his head—he was wearing his big gray overcoat, his emerald scarf was draped on the back of the chair. "Look, Jules Verne wasn't writing an allegory for global warming. That's all I'm saying. I know Chester, and she won't go for it, so I'm not saying you should write this thing over from scratch with an actual decent thesis, I'm just saying it needs a significant bit of work within the next hour. And by *significant amount of work*, I really mean you should scrap the whole thing, chuck it in the bin, because I wouldn't even use this mess as a fire-starter."

"Fuck." The student covered her face with both hands.

"Questions?"

"Tonio," I hissed. I slid into the chair beside him, across from the crying girl.

His expression of condescending superiority dissolved into a condescending grin, and his eyebrows shot up. *"Mar-saw-no.* What a delightful surprise." He dropped his arms. "To what do I owe—"

"Did Massimo call you?"

Stupid question, and he made sure I knew it. "Oh, well." He refolded the stapled essay and passed it back to the English student, who didn't look up from her silent despair. I wondered if she was crying. "Well, as you know, I don't burden myself with the tribulations of modern technology. You know, I've told him he can simply fax me, but he's never so much as attempted it."

I scowled. "Well, he called *me.*"

"La," he said blandly. "What news from dear Massimo, then?"

I nodded at the crying girl.

Tonio looked up like he'd forgotten she was there. "Oh." He tapped her shoulder. "Look, I think we're done here. Come back when you've got a workable thesis—I'll be here for the next half hour. And don't procrastinate next time. Kids these days," he said, shaking his head in disappointment as the girl rose and stumbled off across the lab.

"Massimo's gone." I leaned forward and spoke in a hushed voice. "Savino's got him and Giovani out at Montauk, it was last-minute, he didn't have time and now he can't make the call because he's with the Vitelli guys and he hasn't got the burner." Oh, right, and that was why I'd been heading to their apartment—the burner phone was back in the Financial District—in the kitchen maybe? *Stupid.* "You need to make the call."

"Who, me?"

"Yeah."

He leaned back and rubbed his jaw, assessing me with quiet amusement. "*Moi? Usa il telefono?*"

"Yeah, you, *vaffanculo.*"

"Whoa, look who's using their Italian. Very nice."

"Can't you take this seriously?" I rubbed my temple. I hadn't stopped shivering, and my patience was nearing its end. "I need help, I can't call them myself, I can't get Lorel to call—"

"Yes," he agreed, "that would be weird. Well, I don't have a phone."

"Let's get the burner, then."

"I don't think we have time for that. I get off work in thirty, and you said they're already at Montauk?" He rubbed his neck, looked thoughtfully up at the ceiling. "*Fanculo. Vaffanculo.* Where'd you hear that, was that Achille? Okay, look, we can't use a phone here, it could get traced back—I've seen them do it before. A bit frightening. Might make you rethink your usage of technology. And if we used anyone else's phones here, we'd be inviting the Scarpacis or the cops into their lives, and I'm not sadistic enough to do something like that to one of these pitiful, boring students."

I was still pissed, but at least he was being helpful now. "There's a payphone," I said, "on the corner with the bodega."

"How close?"

"Far enough that it might not be associated with Fortuna, but probably a five-minute walk."

He rose to his feet and grabbed his scarf. "Fine. Let's do it, then." I raced after him between the tables—he looped on his scarf as he walked, clasped a man on the shoulder—"I'm gone, James, take care of Kelly if she comes back?"

He paused outside the library, put up the collar of his coat. "Which way?"

"Here." I set off at a brisk pace, which he matched.

It had started drizzling a bit, which didn't help my shivering. Dogwood branches creaked overhead as we wound our way across the campus, raining down the last of their brittle leaves. I crossed my arms tight and kept my head down.

"That's a terrible coat," said Tonio.

"Well, thanks."

He sighed and stuck his hands in his pockets. "Ahh, *Marzano*." He tilted his head to the pale silver sky, Roman nose and sharp skeletal lines—his eyes were so dark and set back, I could easily imagine empty eye sockets staring out of that skull. "You think I don't care, right?"

"You certainly act like you don't."

"Well, I do. I just make light because I strongly believe that in a given situation, there should be at least one party devoted to emotionally disengaging—helps with getting things done, right? I know you think I'm disinterested. Most people do. So it really helps that I don't give a damn, right? Because"—he tossed back his scarf over his shoulder—"because I've lived with Massimo Di Natale long enough, I know what needs to be done, I know the man's limits. He's fairly predictable, is he not? You've known him less than a year, and even you can see that."

"What are you saying?"

"Remember when he showed up after the fire? Or all those times he gets dead drunk and disappears into his room? Massimo plays the hero, the knight in shining armor, and that's what your little Scarpaci roommate likes about him, right? But you get close and the facade fades quickly. Massimo is terribly depressed, he's an alcoholic. He acts like the sort of person you can count on in disaster—the sort to step up and take charge and turn everything around—but the truth is, before we get to that point, he'll be crumpled down too. He'll burn in his own flames."

I shoved my gloved fists deep in my pockets, but my fingers were still numb. My nose burned in the cold. "I know he's not perfect," I muttered. "I'm not saying he is. I *know* he isn't, I've seen it all happen, but he's also deep in this and he's weirdly experienced with it."

"Yes, family sabotage. He excels, certainly."

"He's the best person for the job, I guess."

Tonio laughed at that—head back, too loud for public. Passersby stared. I cut my eyes at him.

"What? Stop. Stop, I'm not kidding, he *is*."

"Massimo Di Natale is *not* the best person for *the job*," he said. "Do you know how long he's been doing this stuff? I can track his attempts at destroying our family back at least five years, and he's only just now getting close—*we're* only getting close—since this summer when you showed up."

"Why?"

"Because—picture this—we've got a chess board set up, we've got the pieces arranged at the beginning of the round—" He paused, hands spread in the air, framing the scene. "Do you play chess?"

"A little."

"Well, it's like the opponents know each other too well—they know the old tricks, they know where you'll move the rook when your bishop goes *there*, they know you like to take out this piece early in the game, so they can protect that straightaway—do you get where I'm going with this? No, I guess not. We're at a standstill, the two sides of the chessboard, everyone's backed into a corner. Boring. Every game ends the same, we use the same moves and the same players in an endless cycle of *lose and reset the board*, until—another piece gets introduced." He dropped his hands, tucked them into his pockets, apparently satisfied with the image he'd painted. "Throws off the equilibrium. Suddenly, the game's interesting again, the odds are stacked differently—we don't know *how* differently, maybe, but it's different all the same, and I'd say that's an improvement over an indefinite standstill, wouldn't you?"

"So." I'd spotted the payphone in the distance, hiding under a clear plastic cover plastered with stickers and posters and scrawled over with graffiti. "You're saying I'm a wild card."

He sighed—his breath dissipated as mist. "I mean, sure. I think my analogy was a bit more eloquent than that, but okay."

"Well. That's real nice, Tonio, I'm glad I'm a useful tool in your game."

"Our game," he corrected lightly, "it's *our* game, until we die, or until we put a stop to it. And Massimo won't be the one to do that, it's on you."

"Not you?"

"I'm a Salone, *Marzano*. I've got many valuable attributes, but being able to manipulate people just by the fact that I exist isn't one of them." He tapped his temple, looked sideways down at me. "You've got to sober up, though."

I scowled. "Oh, that's *rich*." Like he was one to talk—every time I saw him, it seemed he had a scotch glass in one hand and a cigarette in the other. I had lots of bad habits, but drinking wasn't one of them. I stopped under the plastic cover, dug my wallet out of my backpack, and hunted around for quarters. Tonio eyed the payphone with open disgust.

"That's not what I meant," he said. "You know, you really put *words* in my mouth, Marzano. *I* don't get staggering drunk—you should see Massimo on some nights, it used to be worse before you showed up. After a shipment came in, after a night out with Savino, he'd drink till he got sick and blacked out and he couldn't remember the rest of the evening, and he did it on purpose. I handle my alcohol well. Do I smoke?

Sure. Tis a vice. I've had bad examples, I daresay you have too. But"—he tilted a hand, off-balance—"you're wavering on the edge of a pit."

I paused with a palm full of quarters, hand on the phone. I looked at him with equal disgust as he'd expressed towards the payphone. "I've had a shit year, Tonio. I *know* I'm struggling, I'm not in denial, and I definitely don't need *you* pointing out all my...."

"Damage?" he supplied. "Because here's what I see happening: you're leaning too heavily on Massimo, you're putting heaps of faith in him, and it's only because you refuse to acknowledge what a mess he is—because if you admit he's in a bad place, you've got to acknowledge that *you 're* going off the deep end? Am I right? I'm not wrong."

My jaw was tight. I glowered, shifted the quarters to my other hand, wished I had any other option than to stand here right now and get help from stupid Tonio Salone of all people. "You're wrong," I said, and left it at that—I didn't have to explain myself. I handed him the phone and inserted quarters. "Just do your thing."

"*My thing*," he repeated. But his smile slipped away as the phone rang, loud enough I could hear it standing beside him—he looked unnatural holding the phone, seemed supremely uncomfortable, as if he'd broken some solemn vow and he might be caught in the act. He glanced over his shoulder and huddled closer to the phone-box.

Idiot. He thought he was so superior and untouchable, but I'd seen him in a sweater-vest and bathrobe. I crossed my arms and shivered, stared at my shoes—shut my eyes—it was cold, I was tired, a headache pounded my skull—

"Hello."

I looked up. I almost didn't recognize Tonio's voice

"Hey, am I speakin to a, uh, a Scarpaci? I need ta speak to a Scarpaci, are they around?"

Tonio waited—his eyes met mine. *Chicago?* I mouthed. He shrugged, but he seemed smug. At the same time, his knuckles were white on the phone.

"Okay," he said, after a pause. "Okay, well, I want you ta give Diego a message, alright? No—name doesn't matter. Tell him it's going down at Montauk tonight, and I wouldn't be mad if some guys busted it up, you know what I'm sayin? Yeah? Well, I've got de address—" He waved a hand at me, I fished for my phone and pulled up the address Massimo had sent a few days before. "You writin this down? Right."

He rattled off the address—repeated it, just to be sure. "Yeah. And just tell him—no, you tell Diego, we've got more information he might like, about the Marzanos, and, yeah, we'll be in touch. Yeah? No, no name."

Tonio abruptly slammed the phone back into its cradle. He sniffed and adjusted his coat.

I swallowed. "Well?"

He shook out his hand, like he'd touched something gross. "I hate phones."

"Right." I couldn't care less. "Whose voice was that?"

"Oh, I don't know, some midwest actor."

"And?"

"And, that was your aunt on the phone."

The wind had picked up—I blinked the hair out of my eyes. "It—what?"

Tonio shrugged. "At least, I'm pretty sure it was." He looked thoughtful. "Cal Marzano, Leo's sister? What's that number Massimo gave you?"

"It's the casino."

"Well, maybe it was. Huh. Bet I'm the first person to speak to her in so many years. Huh." He cast me a cursory glance, noticed me shivering, and sighed. "Alright, who's next? Police?"

"Yeah. Hey—" I threw in some more quarters, handed him back the phone—he took it gingerly, grimacing—"did Massimo tell you what he meant about Diego being angry?"

"Sorry, what?"

"I mean. He seemed pretty confident that Diego Scarpaci would be angry enough that he'd take the guys over to Montauk, at short notice, just to screw up the Vitelli business. If I were him I'd be suspicious, but Massimo's sure he'll show up."

"The Vitellis did a number on the casino, the night of the fire. Savino and the guys busted it up pretty bad. I heard Achille threw a Molotov cocktail through a window— yeah, that's what he told *me*, anyway"—in response to my incredulous expression—"so I figure the Scarpacis are probably angry enough to do just about anything right now."

Maybe he was right. But I had an unsettling feeling scratching at the back of my skull, like something was breathing down my neck a second before it attacked—a foreboding sense of anticipation, waiting for the boom, waiting for the lights to come on and everything to make sense.

Because if anyone was the wild card, it wasn't me: it was Massimo.

ii.

Tonio dropped me back at my apartment in his green Mercedes. He blared staticky Italian opera the whole time and didn't say much, but I didn't think I could speak anyway—I was shivering badly and I couldn't stop, I was simultaneously terrified and furious—and, oh my God, we were doing this and there was no turning back.

"Did Massimo say if he'd be back tonight?" Tonio looked at me over his sunglasses.

I stood on the curb, peered down into the open window. I stared at him for a moment. I didn't register what he'd said. And then it clicked: we'd planned to go to Lorel's final show, as an alibi. It had been my idea, after all. "No," I managed, "he didn't. I don't know." My throat felt thick.

"Right, well, he's always so helpful." Tonio cranked up the music. An aggressive cello solo drifted out onto the sidewalk, and it rattled my eardrums when the percussion kicked in. "Catch you later, *Mar-saw-no*."

He peeled off the curb.

I rubbed my nose—it was numb. Once he'd disappeared out of sight, I turned and entered the building, sick to my stomach. I climbed the stairs slowly, taking my time, muscles tight and sore from the cold. The buzz-cut man with the glasses was in the hallway. He was on the phone, but he looked up and met my eyes as I continued up the stairs. I stared right back. *I see you.* He looked away an instant before I climbed out of view.

I'd have to remind Matty about him, before I left on Sunday. Although I'd given it some thought, and I didn't have a clue what might go down after break. I had some foggy idea about coming back and working at the bakery and finishing school, but what if there *was* no bakery after tonight? If the family business died, I wouldn't have a job, and I wouldn't have the money for an apartment *or* for out-of-state tuition.

I might not be coming back. That gave me a pause.

I leaned against the doorjamb, keys in hand, but I didn't unlock the door. I stared back down the stairwell.

I was on the edge of a precipice. I'd never made plans before, and maybe this was why: because if you didn't have plans, they couldn't *not* work out. Suddenly I was staking a lot on a single event—a few phone calls, a drop-off, the perfect reactions at the opportune moments—and the chance of failure was staggering, and the aftermath was pandemonium.

Lorel was eating a stale scone over the kitchen sink. I walked in and she jumped a little, then gave me a long, guilty look and said, with one hand over her mouth, "I am a goblin, I apologize."

I sat at the table in the corner. "I've seen you at your worst, and this isn't it. Your worst includes sitting on the kitchen floor at two PM—"

"Oh *no*, we don't need to revisit that," she choked.

"—and eating shredded skim-milk mozzarella out of the bag. You could have at least eaten real mozzarella, and that's probably the worst part. This," I waved a hand, "this is nothing."

She'd just showered—her hair fell in damp ringlets and she was in her pajamas, even though she'd be getting ready to head out again soon enough. She finished her scone and dusted off her hands over the sink. "I thought you'd still be at work."

"No, I...got off early."

"Hmm." She got down a mug and her tea kettle from a cabinet above the sink. "Do you need help? Packing?"

"There's not much to pack," I said. I only had two suitcases and my backpack—some clothes, a few knickknacks, toiletries. I'd returned all my textbook rentals yesterday. "Do you need help? Getting ready?"

"I've got this down to a science, Pia. I shower, eat a bunch of carbs, crash on the couch and nap for an hour or two, then I do my vocal warmups and rock out to Queen on the drive over to hype myself up."

"Wow."

"Yeah," she said, and put the kettle on. "Science."

I'd finally stopped shivering, but I didn't take my coat off. I played with my gloves and inspected the chipped tabletop instead.

"Hey," she said. "I'm sorry for teasing you about Luca. It's stressing you out and...I'm sorry for pushing it."

"It's alright."

She leaned back against the counter. "Is he really that bad?"

I shook my head. "No. He's not. He'll make some nice girl really happy someday, but it will be someone who's ready to settle down and have a dozen babies at the ripe age of twenty."

"Are you going to talk to your uncle about it?"

Lorel hadn't met Savino. She didn't really get it, and I didn't think any number of stories could do justice to Savino Vitelli. You had to see him in person, you had to hear his voice and sense how his eyes missed nothing, they constantly scanned a room and could pick out the faintest change in expression on a face.

"I don't know," I said. "If I let him know that *I* know he's trying to manipulate me, he'll be more discrete, and it'll be harder to pick out. And he might sense something is wrong. I don't want to draw any more attention to myself and the kids than I have to, so I'm...I don't know."

I realized she was watching me with a concerned expression. "Your uncle sounds scary."

"I guess. Not really. I mean, he's actually really nice." Why did I feel like I had to defend Savino? I scuffed my shoes over the linoleum. "Have you talked to Massimo today?"

"Hmm? No, why? Is everything okay?"

"Yeah." I responded too quickly, probably. "I just don't know if he'll make it tonight, my uncle has him driving around."

Here I was, lying again, hiding things from her—because Massimo and I, neither of us had told her about the plans. She didn't know we were trying to get her family arrested, and I didn't have the guts to tell her, even if they *would* theoretically get released while the Vitellis were held up.

"Oh." Lorel paused in her tea-making preparations. "Are you sure? He told you he can't make it? We're all getting drinks after, the whole cast. I wanted him to come with me. You can come too, if you want, I just figured you don't like hanging out with a lot of people and it's going to be *loud*—like, lots of musical theater nerds pumped with adrenaline loud."

I picked at the tabletop, the flaking paint. "I'm pretty tired, actually. But thanks."

"Or we could just come back here, we can watch a movie?"

She knew something was wrong, she was trying to make it better, but that only made me feel worse. "No, don't worry about it. I've got a lot of packing to do—"

"Do you want help?"

"No, it's...not a lot." We'd gone round in a circle. I crossed my arms and stared at my shoes.

Lorel plopped herself down in the chair across from me. She knitted her fingers together on the tabletop and pursed her lips. "Pia."

"Hmm?"

"What's wrong?"

I didn't trust myself to speak. Tonio was right—we were in a dangerous place. I didn't want to go home, I didn't want to stay.

I tilted back my face to the ceiling, my eyes following the water damage along its discolored gray spiderweb. "Here, everything I do—every breath, every *first* thing I do—first day of class, first day working, little victories, holidays—it's like they're just out of reach and I can't really grasp them. Mamma, and Papa. It always hurts. I think I should tell them something, I get excited for a second because I think about how they'll react when they hear about it. And it hits me over and over again that.... And when I go back to Augusta, it's like they're standing right there, they *are* the house, it smells like them, the stairs sound like my dad leaving early for work. And the kids...."

Lorel just listened. There was pity in her eyes, but Lorel was the only person I'd accept pity from. "You don't want to go back," she said.

"I don't know what I want," I whispered. "I don't know how to take care of the kids and myself at the same time."

"What do you need?"

221

I need to not cry right now, I thought. But my body was still too numb for tears—every bone ached with exhaustion. "I need...to sleep. And you need to get ready for your show."

She smiled a bit.

"I'm sorry about Massimo."

She shrugged, like it didn't matter, but I could see she cared a lot. "He'll make it if he can. Do you want tea?"

I shook my head. She had her final performance tonight, and here I was close to tears, unloading my burdens on her. Looking into her eyes and knowing that, after tonight, nothing would be the same, but I couldn't bring myself to tell her. She'd done so much for me, but I couldn't even tell her the truth.

I got up without speaking. She hugged me—quick and tight—and I left her alone in the kitchen with her whistling kettle. I wandered down the hall to my bedroom, didn't even bother to shower the bakery and streets off me. I shut the door gently, kicked off my shoes, and shuffled over to the nightstand. Loose cigarettes and matches, mechanical pencils and chapstick and little containers of prescription pills rattled in the drawer. For some reason, *that* made me cry. I didn't sob, I didn't lose myself in the fetal position on the floor, but my eyes just unloaded buckets of tears while I stood there, and my nose ran, and cold shock gripped me.

I took two sleeping tablets. I collapsed on the bed and wished I could sleep through the whole night. I wanted to sleep without thinking about Montauk and Massimo, about Cal Marzano on the phone with Tonio, about what Lorel's face would look like in the morning when she found out what we'd done. Where was Matty? Was he safe? Were Massimo and Giovani both going to be caught in the ambush? We hadn't planned for that.

Everything was too big, I thought, as my eyelids got heavy. And the ceiling faded to black.

iii.

I didn't dream when I took the pills. I just suffocated under a blanket of exhaustion until the darkness finally lifted and I emerged like a drowning man.

The bedroom was painted orange, sunset filtering through my sparrow curtains. Everything ached. I rolled over and checked the time. Half-past six: Lorel had probably been gone for a while, but I hadn't even heard her leave, and Lorel was *loud*. Which meant I'd been out cold. Which meant I probably wouldn't sleep tonight, not that I'd sleep anyway with everything going on.

Eight. The drop-off was at eight, the show was at seven—

My stomach clenched. I forced myself to my feet.

Jeans. A couple sweaters and my coat. I brushed out my hair and grabbed my phone and wallet, where I had my ticket stashed. I stood shivering beside the bus stop for a good fifteen minutes before it finally showed up, and I sat in a window seat next to folks heading home from work, dread in my gut, sleep in my eyes.

Massimo was out at Montauk. If I shut my eyes and tried to imagine it—the motorboat pulling up on some sort of dock, emptying crates of olive oil, darkness concealing Savino's guys as they loaded up the trucks—and then the Scarpacis would show up. And then, in the distance, sirens—flashing lights—

Massimo, what have we done?

The bus dropped me off outside Fortuna, and I hustled to the auditorium. It was five minutes from starting when I flashed my ticket at the staff by the door and slipped inside. The pit orchestra was warming up, the Munchkinland set was up on stage—big wooden cutouts of houses and mountains, a backdrop with the Yellow Brick Road fading into the distance. For a community college production, it wasn't bad, and the turnout wasn't terrible for a student performance being held a few blocks down from Broadway.

It was like *Macbeth* all over again, I thought, as I hunted out my row. *Back and center.* Tonio sat on the edge of the row, legs crossed at the knee, flicking through a program with a bored and faintly amused expression.

"Scoot over," I said, nudging his leg.

He did. The seat beside him was still empty. "Nothing from Massimo?"

"No." I ground my back teeth together, tried to ignore the growing tide of anxiety. "You?"

"Oh, actually, he faxed me earlier."

"What, really?"

"No, he did not." Tonio sighed, flipped to the back of the program. "Lorella Lucia Scarpaci, plays Galinda. Lorella grew up in East Harlem, she is a Junior at Fortuna Community College studying English Literature. Previous Fortuna roles include Little Red Ridinghood in *Into the Woods* and Lady Macbeth in...*Macbeth!* Lorella would like to thank the Fortuna Theater team, her brother, blah blah blah, her wonderful roommate and her *boyfriend* for all their love and support." He snapped the playbill shut. "La. Isn't that sweet? She didn't even mention me, by the way, but she *did* manage to slip in that cleverly discrete line about our dear Massimo, did you notice?"

I scowled. "Yeah, I noticed, I helped her write it."

"Well, it's just..." He waved a hand at the empty seat, raised his eyebrows.

"Tonio, I can't deal with this right now."

"Oh." He watched the stage and fanned himself with the program, sending obnoxious drifts of cold air in my direction. "Are you *nervous*?"

"Can't deal with this."

"Well, I was only asking."

The lights flickered, and the chatter spiraled down into hushed whispers. The pit orchestra tuned, then the automated announcement came on, booming overhead—no

223

flash photography, no crying children, please stop throwing things at the stage, thanks! And the orchestra began the overture.

"You know," Tonio whispered, "there's nothing we can do about it now. What's done is done, it has a mind of its own and it'll blow wherever the wind sends it. You know."

"Yeah, I know."

"So," he said, "you look like you're trying to swallow a brick."

Lorel on stage, clad in pink and splendor. It never got old, watching her like this— I'd never get used to seeing her put on another person's character, take up their mannerisms, perfectly in her element with every dramatic gesture. Her Fiyero was a guy named Dave, who was tall and blond and gay. He and Lorel had very little chemistry, but she threw herself into the role regardless, which had made it slightly uncomfortable sitting beside Massimo the first time we'd come out to see the show. He'd been kind of rigid and disturbed the whole time, sitting very straight and fixating on Lorel with the sort of focus that told me he was trying awfully hard to blot out Dave's existence.

What if the Di Natales ended up in prison too? Massimo had to know that was a possibility, but what could he do about it? Even if he'd wanted us to call the thing off— even if he changed his mind at some point—he couldn't tell us so.

I was sweating. I fanned myself with my program until Tonio leaned over and muttered, "Are you dying, Marzano?" Then I stopped and sweated in silence.

Until the last number before intermission, when someone dropped into the seat beside me.

For a half second, I thought it was Massimo. Then my eyes adjusted to the dark and I realized it was just Matty.

"What are you doing here?" He hadn't said anything about coming to the show tonight, although I guess I'd mentioned we were going—that was the whole idea of an alibi.

Matty's fingers locked on my arm. He looked wired, all nervous energy and wandering eyes. "Is he an *idiot*?" he growled.

I blinked. "Who?"

"Massimo, you know, is he *stupid*? Does he *know* what he's done, does he not *care*? God, *I* was stupid, I shouldn't have let this happen." He tore his eyes away for a moment to watch his sister on stage, then they returned to me. His grip tightened on my bicep. "Why? Did *you* know?"

"Ow, Matty—"

There were people looking. The old lady in front of Matty craned her neck around and fixed me with a disapproving glare, to which I responded with a scowl, which made her nudge the man beside her and mutter something into his ear. The old man took his turn grimacing over his shoulder at us.

"*The fuck* is wrong with you?" I hissed. I grabbed his wrist. "Cut it out." He reminded me of Diego Scarpaci in that moment, of all the stories Lorel had told me with her Dad losing his temper, going on a rampage—there was an awful lot of Diego in Matty's eyes, and I didn't like it.

"Hey, mate, careful there." Tonio's arm snaked around, his hand carefully pried Matty's death-grip from my arm. "The lady's got tendonitis."

I swatted away Tonio's hand and fixated on my cousin, who glared at Tonio, as people often did. "What are you talking about? What happened?" My chest tightened, made it hard to breathe." Where's Massimo?"

"I don't know," Matty said, still staring over my head. "I don't know, but I'd like to, I'd like to know how Mom found out about—hey, who *is* this guy?"

Tonio watched the proceedings with bored interest, as invested as a spectator without stakes in the game, merely here for the thrills, the cheap entertainment. He smiled in response to my scowl.

"This is Tonio," I said. "Ignore him. He's my aunt's brother—we aren't even related." I didn't want anyone thinking I had any sort of responsibility for Tonio Salone's actions. "What did Massimo do? What's happened?"

"I don't know," said Matty, "my phone's blowing up, Sara was saying something about my dad doing something tonight with his guys, but the important part is—my mom called. I don't really talk to her much, so it was weird anyway. But she said she knows about Lorel and Massimo."

Everything froze for a fraction of a second. My ears buzzed, the music faded to a distant hum, and I gripped the armrests tight. "What? How?"

"Someone told her, she heard about it somewhere, *I don't know*, but I think Massimo screwed up and now *Lorel's* in trouble."

"Sounds like *he's* in trouble," Tonio supplied, helpfully.

Betta, I thought, but then something Massimo had said caught up to me, and the implications fell into place. "Shit," I hissed. I sat back hard in my seat. "Shit. Massimo said he was gonna make Diego angry—"

"Why the hell would he do that?" Matty looked like the vein in his temple was gonna pop. He was intimidating on a normal day, all barely-suppressed rage and pure muscle mass, but right now he looked downright murderous. "He doesn't know my dad, he doesn't know my dad *angry*. Why would he do something so *fucking* stupid—?"

"Because," I whispered, "because *I* came up with a stupid plan and he was trying to make it work."

Massimo...he took risks, he went full steam ahead with a narrow focus. Which meant *this* happened. Which meant Diego Scarpaci was psycho and all the Di Natales were in danger and Lorel was in heaps of trouble. She didn't know it yet; she'd just exited the stage, "Defying Gravity" was in full force, she was probably doing a costume change, thinking about getting drinks with Massimo later. And I'd never meant to involve her, none of us had.

Giovani. Why was I thinking about Giovani? Massimo had known the trap he was setting, but his brother hadn't. And Savino had grabbed up the two of them like toy soldiers, thrown them into the scheme out at Montauk.

"What plan?" Matty hissed. "What stupid plan? What else haven't you told me? Or *her?*"

I was sweating, sweating bad. I looked at Tonio—he looked back at me, expression curiously blank and guarded—and I grabbed Matty's arm. "Has it happened yet?"

"Has what happened?"

"The drop-off." He didn't know, and I didn't want to tell him—I didn't want him to hate me—but if I didn't, I was pretty sure he'd get Massimo killed. "Look, your dad—"

"SHHHH." The lady in front of us had had enough.

I shoved Matty. "Go, lobby, I'll tell you." I felt sick. My stomach churned as I trailed him to the auditorium doors, slipped out during the climax of the musical number. Tonio followed me and shut the door gently behind us.

The lobby was mostly empty. A couple staff members sat in folding chairs by the donor's table, and across the lobby a dad walked his sleeping child up and down the hallway. Matty looked like he'd run out of the gym at a moment's notice, sweatpants and a hoodie, hat clenched tight in one fist, and he towered over me.

"It wasn't supposed to go like this," I said in a hushed voice. "It was always a bad plan, I admit that, but it got screwed up and it got even worse—Massimo was supposed to be here, Giovani was supposed to be at home—"

Matty interrupted me. "What did you *do?*"

"We're trying to take down the family business."

He stared at me with Lorel's eyes, but somehow colder and a lot less merciful. "What does that have to do with Lorel? Why would that—why'd he tell Dad about them? That was the stupidest—"

"I know." It was clear that Lorel hadn't told him about Massimo and the fire, and I figured it would only make matters worse if I brought it up now. "Look, we thought we'd bust up the drop-off my uncle's getting tonight, we'd tip off your family and get the cops to show up too—"

"Seriously? Cops, Pia, seriously? God, I can't believe—"

226

"You guys weren't even supposed to get in trouble. The only way we'd get law enforcement to show up was if we involved your family too, because my uncle pays off the cops. I'm sorry, you know I'd never get Lorel in trouble on purpose—"

"I'm honestly more angry with Massimo." He looked livid. "Ever since he's shown up, he's putting Lorel in danger, he's getting her in trouble, and he does it over and over again—"

"It's my fault, Matty!" I yelled that bit, surprising myself.

The theater staff looked over at us.

Matty glanced at them, crossed his arms. "I don't care whose fault it is," he said. "I'm gonna break Massimo's fucking face."

"But Lorel—"

"He needs to stay away from her."

"Lorel isn't yours to control," I hissed. "She's her own person, she's an adult. She can choose to tell him to stay away from her if she wants—"

"She doesn't have any choices because you guys are making them for her." Matty ran a hand over his hair. He looked like he wanted to punch something. I took a step back.

"Listen, Matteo." That was Tonio, smoothing his lapel, totally detached in the raging beam of Matty's fury. "Massimo's a mess, but he's a good guy. We all messed up a little—"

The doors crashed open. I jumped back as a line of people pressed out of the auditorium, a stampeding herd to the bathroom line. Shouts and laughter echoed out into the lobby, deafening joy, the piercing shrill of tuning instruments while intermission ticked down to Act Two.

"I'm gonna talk to him," Matty muttered under his breath, watching the stream of audience members fly past us.

"Who? Massimo?"

"Dad. I'm gonna talk to Dad."

"But—" Diego? Who was out at Montauk? Who might be in prison right now because of *me*?

"I'm gonna talk to him," Matty said again, resolute, "before he does something stupid."

I caught his sleeve as he stepped away. "It wasn't supposed to be like this."

"It shouldn't have happened at all," he snapped. He didn't meet my eyes. He pulled his arm away and disappeared into the crush of bodies, leaving me gutted and numb, like everything was dropping away around me.

I liked Matty. I liked that he was pleasant and easy, polite and protective, how he watched Dickens dramas with us and made sure leftovers never got chucked out before they went bad. And I loved Lorel, and everything Matty had just said told me plainly that what I'd done—what *we 'd* done—was unforgivable.

For what felt like several minutes I stood there frozen, his words ringing in my ears. Then a voice cut through the moment.

"Well, what a prick." A finger prodded my shoulder. "Hey. *Marzano.*"

I swatted him away. "Why did he do that?"

"Well, probably a combination of testosterone, machismo and bravado, that's usually—"

"No. Massimo. Why did he tell Diego about him and Lorel? If we needed to make him angry, we could have tried something else, he should have just *told me* what he was planning and we would have worked something out. He should have asked. Why would he just...do that?"

"Because he sees what needs to be done and he does it, because he's got a limited range of vision and he doesn't foresee the aftermath of his choices."

I hadn't expected a real answer. I looked at Tonio. "What do I tell—? And why am I asking you?"

"Wisdom and maturity," he suggested.

But he was the only one here. Matty was gone, Massimo was part of the problem, and no one stood between me and telling Lorel the truth. Nothing.

"We have to go back inside," I said. I stuck my hands in my pockets and watched the crowd around us grow thin, watched the audience empty back into the auditorium as the pit orchestra tuned and, in the distance, the lights flickered dim. "We have to finish this."

Tonio rubbed the back of his neck. "I suppose so."

"It's a mess."

"We knew it would be."

Somehow, that was comforting. There was repose in knowing you'd hit rock-bottom, knowing there was no reason to keep clawing for a handhold when you were already falling hard. At the same time, I understood how entirely insane that was, and what a terrible philosophy I'd latched onto. But it made sense in the moment; it was enough to propel me back into the auditorium and into my seat for the duration of the musical, until the lights came on once more and the audience rose to their feet in applause and the cast took their final bows.

Tonio and I waited outside for Lorel. I checked my phone; I had two missed calls from Massimo, and one from a number I didn't recognize.

"He called me."

Tonio leaned against the side of the building, hands in his overcoat pockets. Above him, old posters from shows past were tacked onto the brick. They fluttered in the breeze. "That could mean a lot of things."

228

I didn't want to think about that. I stepped into the shadows at the edge of the sidewalk and returned the call.

The phone rang for an extraordinarily long time. When he finally picked up, his voice was low. "Hi, Pia."

"What happened?"

He sighed.

My fingers were numb. "Where are you?"

"I'm at the Vitelli house. Out back. Savino says he's been trying to call you—"

"I saw, I don't want to talk to him—"

"Pia, it was bad. The cops didn't even show up. There was no one to stop anyone else, I thought someone was gonna die."

I looked up at Tonio, aghast. His eyebrows shot up, but I didn't have time to stop and explain. "Why didn't the cops come? We called them, I swear—they said they'd look into it—"

"Savino paid them off." Massimo's voice was gruff. I could visualize him out back of the house, pacing the sidewalk, one hand in his pocket and the other gripping his phone with a white-knuckled fist—glaring into the dark, into the distant city lights. "He always pays off these guys, and I guess having the Scarpacis involved wasn't enough to get them out there—"

"Massimo, you told Diego? About you and Lorel?" *Silence.* "Matty found us—me and Tonio, we're at Lorel's show—and he showed up and tore into me, he's gonna *kill you*—"

"I can deal with Matteo."

"Can Lorel deal with her dad? She didn't ask for this." I felt the anger rising, I checked myself. "You should have told me."

"I'm sorry."

"Why didn't you tell me?"

"I thought the less people who knew, the better. And it was last-minute, Pia, I wasn't even sure I was going to do it until this morning—Achille was out front with the car, I was running out of the apartment and I realized I wouldn't have time to use the burner and follow the plan perfectly. So I called the casino and left a message. I didn't plan it."

No, it was because he wanted to be a hero. He was *okay* with being a tragic martyr. I swallowed, clenched my jaw as I stared out into the dark parking lot. "What happened?"

"We got out there—Savino had us out there all day—and Valentino's guys showed up early. It wasn't even dark yet. While we were unloading, Diego and his guys pulled up and just started going to town with it—I think he really wanted to kill us, Pia. Kill *me.* They had clubs and guns and shit, and...Giovani broke his arm, Achille got hit in the leg and they've got him upstairs now, they don't want to bring him to the ER because they don't want questions, so Ida's up there with her dental tools pulling a bullet out of her brother's leg." He sounded a little crazy, like *can you believe this? Our family? Wild.*" My mom and Norma and Marco took Giovani to the Urgent Care, they just left. And I don't know how bad we got the Scarpacis, but Savino really gave it to them—do you know how many guns you can fit in a glove compartment? Or in the trunk of a car, under the floorboard? A lot. And ammo stored under the seats. Diego took his guys and they pulled out pretty quick, but the people Valentino sent with the shipment freaked and skipped town, they took their stuff and left when the Scarpacis first showed up."

"They're gone?" Did that mean the shipment hadn't been delivered?

"Yeah, they're gone. Valentino's gonna be pissed with Savino, maybe he'll kick the Vitellis out of the family business—I don't know. I don't know, Pia, I have to think."

I wanted to be furious. I wanted to scream at him for going rogue behind my back, behind Lorel's back, but this was Massimo I was talking to—Massimo, who'd die for any one of us. "Are you alright?" I said.

"I'm okay. Where's Lorel? Is she okay?"

"She's finishing up inside."

"Maybe I should come by tonight."

"Maybe you shouldn't."

"Why not?"

"Massimo, you just told her parents that she's been secretly dating a Di Natale behind their backs. Diego might want you dead now—Matty might too—but Lorel's also in trouble and you being around will only make that worse. I mean, you made him angry, right? That was your goal, to make him angry? It worked. Great. Good job."

"Pia. I need to be there in case something happens."

"No, you don't. Listen." He couldn't go near Lorel, not right now, not after what had just happened. "Listen, everyone knows where Lorel and I live, we're not safe from Scarpacis or Savino's guys busting in at any given time. If anyone sees you guys together...."

"I need to tell her."

"Not tonight."

In the distance, on his end of the line, a door slammed and someone shouted incoherently. Massimo sighed. "Pia, I have to go. Tell her I'll call her, okay? And lock up the apartment. You got Tonio?"

"He's here."

"Well, maybe he should stay with you guys, I don't know when I'll be able to slip away."

"Massimo, *lay low*. I'm not kidding, I know what I'm talking about—I just talked to Matty, he's furious."

A door slammed. "We messed up," he said.

"I know." *You messed up*. But it was my fault he'd even gone to those measures to begin with. It was my fault that Achille had been shot and Giovani had a broken arm and someone could have died.

"We can fix this."

I wanted to believe that, I wanted to trust him, I wanted to entertain the thought that we could bounce back from this and it would all be okay again. But from the bottom of this pit, it was hard to see any light breaking through. "I don't know, Massimo."

"We'll be okay. Be careful, Pia."

Tonio had leaned his head back against the building. He watched in a tired, resigned sort of way as I wandered up to him, spent and hopeless. "I suppose it went fantastically, yes?"

"No. It didn't."

"Well, we already knew that. Who's hurt?"

I sat down hard on the curb, banging my tailbone. I put my face in my hands and exhaled. "Giovani broke his arm, and Achille got shot in the leg."

"My brother Achille?"

"No, the other Achille."

"Of course it had to be him, that man is a magnet for bodily injury. Anyone else? No? Well. We should probably get out of here before Matteo shows up again, yeah?"

iv.

Lorel didn't go out drinking with the cast. She exited the auditorium a while later with her friends, laughing and singing with her arms thrown around Dave and some other girl, a gym bag slung across her back. She caught sight of Tonio and I and peeled away from the rest of the group, grinning, pink and glitter still flecked across her cheeks. But her smile faded as she looked back and forth between the two of us: Tonio, dark and mild and strangely subdued; me, perched on the curb with my elbows on my knees and my chin on my fists.

"Massimo couldn't make it?"

I shook my head.

"Is he okay?"

"He's fine." I glanced at Tonio, who raised one eyebrow and shrugged at me. "I need to talk to you."

231

She licked her lips, tightened her grip on her bag strap. "Okay, what's wrong?" Her cast-mates had stopped and were waiting for her by the parking lot, but she waved them on.

"Not here," I said.

Tonio pushed off the wall. "Do you need a ride?" I shook my head. "Then I'll away. Don't do anything dumb, Marzano, alright? I mean, if Massimo's left any of the dumb around for you to pick up—don't. Just leave it where it's sitting, I'm sure he'll retrieve it." He tipped an imaginary hat at Lorel. "Damsel. Admirable performance. *Buonanotte.*"

"Thanks for coming, Tonio," she said, and she sounded like she meant it, which was kind of funny.

We watched him disappear into the parking lot. Then Lorel turned to me, and it really was just her and me, no walls between us, nothing to hide the truth. That scared me. So I put it off till after the car ride, till we'd parked and gone up to the apartment and I'd locked the door behind us and done a quick walk around to make sure no Scarpacis were lurking in the shadows.

Lorel followed me on my rounds, openly concerned. "What's going on, Pia? You're scaring me. Where's Massimo?"

Where *was* Massimo? Probably still at the Vitelli house, trying to patch up all our problems. Or drinking—maybe he was on the back step with a bottle of wine.

God, I was mad. I was furious with myself, with him, with Tonio for his stupid Chicago accent on the phone and encouraging us and with Matty for making it even worse. I wanted Lorel with her poetry and music and Massimo with his steady hands and sensible eyes, I even wanted stupid Tonio in his bathrobe doing nothing but going over student papers with a massive red pen. I wanted to go back and wipe out the past few months, go back to this summer when I'd been oblivious enough to not have to look these things in the face and try to do something about them, try to fix my family, try to protect the kids *from* my family.

I wanted to erase all the lies. I didn't want to know that Lorel was a doormat and I was abusing that, or that Massimo was an alcoholic and I abetted his habit, or that Tonio's cigarettes and my cousin's sleeping pills and the increasingly frequent drinks were becoming crutches for something inside me that was screaming to feel something—tarps tossed over a body, because I couldn't face looking at it, I wasn't strong enough to look my trauma in the face without breaking into a million pieces. So I did what weak people did and I bottled it up, or maybe that was the strong thing to do, and either way I looked at it, I was a coward and a liar.

"Pia?"

I froze in the hallway. I'd pulled her into this pit with me. Whatever Savino did to her—whatever happened because of her parents or Matty or Massimo or anyone else—was my fault now. She hadn't asked for this.

"I have to go." My voice stretched down the hallway in a whisper. I couldn't speak any louder, it felt like there were weights on my lungs.

Lorel's brow furrowed. "Where?"

"I'm going home. I have to leave. Tonight."

"But your flight isn't till Sunday, what's wrong? What happened?"

"Lorel, I have to go, we can't stay here. You have to come with me."

"Pia, are you crying? Hey, what happened? Look, I can't go, I—why? What *happened*?"

"Please. Please, just come with me. It isn't safe to be here, not right now. I made a mistake, Lorel. I tried, it didn't work. And now..." I made my way to the floor, gently, carefully settling myself on the carpet against the wall. My hands shook. "I messed up."

Lorel crawled down onto the carpet beside me. "It's going to be okay."

She didn't get it. She thought this was a mental breakdown, that I was overreacting. "Lorel." I rubbed my eyes, I couldn't look at her. "Your dad knows about Massimo."

She froze, her hand stiff on my arm.

"And it's worse than that," I whispered. "And we need to go, now. Please. Please come home with me. We need to get out of this place."

"They know?"

I nodded. "They know."

"How?" Her voice echoed such sadness, such disappointment, that I almost wished I could take it back—patch it up with more lies. But I couldn't do that anymore.

"I'll tell you," I whispered. "I'll tell you everything."

XII

Buon Natale

i.

We drove through the night.

Hastily-packed duffel bags and suitcases filled the trunk and back seat of Lorel's car. We drove past flashing lights and construction zones, crawled through late-night traffic jams, the old car humming around us. We ate leftovers from the fridge at out apartment—old fried rice and good New York apples, packaged tortillas close to their expiration date and a knob of asiago.

Lorel didn't want her family contacting her. I didn't want calls from Massimo or Savino, from Ida or Nicole or anyone else. I wanted to feel like I was leaving it behind for the last time, like I'd finally turned my back on my family.

I texted Sabine. Then we turned off our phones and we just drove.

I wondered if this was how Mamma and Papa had felt, leaving New York in the dead of night with me as a baby. I imagined how that must have been: cutting off the Marzano and the Vitellis. The immense freedom—a breath of fresh air, the first good breath in a long time. And the crushing terror of *it's just us now, us against the world.* Had they thought about going back, at any point along the way?

We switched out drivers near Baltimore, and again outside Charlotte. Exhausted, but neither of us could sleep. We crossed the Georgia border around eight the next morning.

I told her about how I'd found out about Massimo that night at their apartment— how he and Tonio had been scheming long before either of us knew anything about it. I told her the theory about Marco Vitelli having my parents killed. I told her how my plan had spiraled into catastrophe, how Massimo had splintered off and made it, somehow, even more chaotic. We'd put her in danger, we'd put both our families in the way of physical harm, and we'd done it all behind her back.

Lorel was quiet for a long time, once I'd finished. We were only a few hours into the drive and she hadn't asked any questions, but she'd listened intently and handed me tissues from the passenger's seat when I started crying.

"Does your uncle know?" she said at last.

"Which part?"

"Any of it."

"I don't know. Massimo thinks Marco Vitelli might have gone behind everyone's back, to get me sent up to Brooklyn, to keep the family business going. Savino couldn't know about Mamma and Papa—I don't think so. Can you imagine knowing your dad had your sister killed, and being alright with it? I'm not sure how much he knows about that—or if it's even true—but he's definitely trying to use the kids to control me."

"Does he know about me and Massimo?"

"I don't know. That's why we had to leave."

Massimo sometimes talked about ending up at the bottom of the Sound, him and Lorel both, but Massimo tended towards extremes. Savino Vitelli was our uncle. He went to church on Sunday, he donated focaccia to the local soup kitchen. He wasn't a mafia boss.

"Pia, it's a mess," said Lorel.

"You can be angry with me. And Massimo. And Tonio. But mostly me, because it was my plan and I should have told you."

"I can't believe I didn't notice." She stared out the passenger's side window, at passing fields of scraggly pines in red dirt soil. "I guess…I decided I didn't want to."

The neighborhood was decked out for Christmas, cheap inflatables and plastic nativity sets on the front lawn. Carlo always decorated the front of our house with Christmas lights; he made a production of it every year, brought everyone out front for the big reveal one evening in December, and carefully took everything down after the Epiphany.

The sun was rising gold on the horizon when we pulled into the cracked pavement driveway. Vince was waiting under the drooping strings of Christmas lights, nestled under a pile of blankets in a wicker chair.

His face lit up when when appeared; he leapt off the porch and down the front step. Bare feet slapped the drive. "PIA!"

I scrambled out of the car and threw my arms around him. He hugged me tight, all skin and bones. His hair had knots and he shivered—he smelled like gardenia and morning soil, he smelled like home.

And I got scared. Really, really scared. Because images of Giovani flooded my mind at that moment, and kids getting pulled into the mess, and trips to the Urgent Care after nights out at Montauk. And I couldn't let that happen to Vince, or Carlo, or Cristine.

I didn't want to, but I let him go. "I brought Lorel."

"Who's Lorel?"

"She's our cousin."

Lorel climbed out through the driver's side door. In the morning light, she still had traces of glitter around her tired eyes. Vince looked at her reproachfully, unsure.

"She likes *David Copperfield*," I said, my attempt to put him at ease.

"Sabine told us last night you were coming home early, but we were planning a surprise party tomorrow for when you got here. So pretend to be surprised."

"I forget it's my birthday," I said, taking his hand, "every single year. I'm constantly surprised."

I waved at Lorel to follow, and she did, hands clasped behind her back, glancing curiously at our front yard with its overgrown shrubs and patchy brown lawn, the collection of rakes and shovels propped against the garage door, which was broken and hadn't been opened for several years.

"Is she Massimo's sister?" Vince whispered, as we mounted the creaking porch steps.

"No, she's dad's niece." I glanced at Lorel and explained, "They know about Massimo because he drives a Lexus and Carlo thinks that's terribly important."

"Oh, it is," she said.

Vince ran inside to wake Sabine. I turned to Lorel, one hand on the screen door. "I'm sorry."

"I forgive you."

"You don't have to. I'm—"

"Pia, I'm confused and I'm tired, but I don't think most of this is your fault." She tucked back her hair and took a deep breath. She paused, eyes on the doorstep. "Can I hug you?"

"Sure."

"I smell coffee," she mumbled into my shoulder.

"It's really bad coffee. My aunt makes it like motor oil."

Lorel released me and squeezed my hand. "I don't care, I want it." She put back her shoulders, stretched her neck. "We're okay?"

"Okay," I said. Something was squeezing my lungs, and I felt like a piece of trash flattened in a gutter. But I smiled and squeezed her hand back. "We're okay."

Sabine was in a pink bathrobe, platinum-blond hair frizzing in every direction, and she hugged me so tight I could hardly breathe.

"*Cara*, you're thin, what's wrong, you been sick? Hey, what's wrong, I thought you were flying down Sunday, what happened, huh?" She held my face between her hands and stared into my eyes. "You need sleep," she announced, and moved on to Lorel before I could even try to answer her questions. "And this is *Lorel*, right? Is that right?"

Lorel nodded, caught up in my aunt's embrace, and squeaked, "That's me."

I met Cristine's eyes. We had a sort of mental score where we kept track of who could handle our aunt and who totally lost their cool.

"Who do you belong to?" Sabine held Lorel out at arms length, looked her up and down. "Oh, you're beautiful, very skinny, beautiful hair." She patted Lorel on the head. "You're Nicole's?"

"Lorel's from Papa's side," I said. "She's his...sister's daughter."

"I didn't know Leo had a sister."

I couldn't count the number of things my aunt didn't know.

Sabine finally released Lorel, who looked like she was trying to suppress a laugh, or maybe she was on the verge of tears—it was hard to tell, neither of us had slept in twenty-four hours, I felt distinctly unstable.

Sabine had moved in to our parents 'bedroom, leaving my room upstairs unoccupied in case Carlo decided he wanted it. She gave Lorel her bed for the day and sent me upstairs with strict instructions to not come back down until I looked like I could walk in a straight line. Lorel disappeared into a shower.

Cristine followed me upstairs while Carlo and Vince went to get our luggage. "Is it bad up there?" she asked.

I looked at my little sister, perched on the edge of my bed. She ran her hand down the pink and green bedspread; it was something Mamma had made in a quilting class at the local library, when she was pregnant with Vince. I'd wanted to bring it with me to New York, but hadn't had space. I thought about curling up under it again. Tears sprang to my eyes.

"Please don't cry," said Cristine.

"No. I'm not." I took my suitcases from Carlo, shut the bedroom door. "It isn't bad," I said.

Cristine stared at me. She'd grown this year, without my noticing. Longer, more maturity in her face. Her hair was twisted back in a bun and it made her look older. "Where are your braces?"

"My—" I hadn't seen the kids since the kidnapping, the Scarpacis, that whole ordeal. I rubbed my wrists and suddenly missed the comforting pressure—something to fiddle with, something familiar. "I lost them."

"You look like shit."

"Don't say shit," I said, instinctively. "Not around Vince."

"So, what's wrong?"

I couldn't tell her. She was fifteen, she had to take care of Vince and Carlo—she didn't need one more thing to deal with.

"You know." I unfolded my pajamas, tucked them under one arm. "You know, it's just...family drama."

The kids didn't know how to deal with Lorel. Vince, always wary of strangers, kept his distance. Carlo largely ignored her. And Cristine just seemed uncomfortable. Confused.

I slept through most of the day, and woke in time for dinner. Sabine had made something she called pesto lasagna—her personal spin on *lasagne alla Portofino*—which sounded alright in theory, only she used a watery jarred pesto sauce between the layers of soggy pasta. We ate it anyway.

Lorel was clean and glitter-free. She took me aside before dinner, pulled me into the hall out of earshot of the kids.

"I talked to Massimo."

"What did he say?"

"We talked for a long time. He told me everything you said before. He said he'd talk to Matty, but I told him to wait, I should call first. Was he bad?"

"Matty?"

"Yeah. He's got a temper, Pia—he's really good, really, you know that—but, I mean, our dad...." She trailed off, crossed her arms. "I'll talk to him. I think Massimo wouldn't have tried that if he'd actually known Dad. Oh"—she caught my arm, like she wanted to tell me before she forgot—"he says your uncle is trying to contact you. He says to be careful."

Lorel went to bed early, but I stayed up with Sabine. The house grew dark and quiet, Christmas lights twinkling outside the front blinds.

I slumped on the couch with my aunt. "How have they been?"

Sabine had a wine glass balanced on the edge of the coffee table while she painted her toenails—red, not festive, but glaring. "They're okay. It's been rough, you know, but...I think they're okay. Cristine is talking to a counselor at school, the boys keep busy. Sometimes on Sundays we'll drive to the graveyard and the kids put flowers out, I don't think it's good for them to be surrounded by all those gravestones, just surrounded by death and all—but they insist, so I do it. What do I know about losing parents?"

I watched her paint her nails with practiced perfection, an old throw pillow on my lap and a store-bought pizzella cookie on a napkin set on the arm of the couch. "What happened to Norma Vitelli? Your mom?"

My aunt raised her eyebrows without looking up. "Nothing. Why?"

239

"She's alive?"

"Well, yeah, I'm not *ancient*, my parents aren't *ancient*."

I just didn't think it was safe to assume people in this family died predominantly of natural causes. "No one talks about her. Is she in New Orleans too?"

"I haven't talked to my family in years, I don't know, maybe." She paused and eyed me steadily. "Well, what about you? The kids are okay, we're doing alright down here, but what about you, Pia? You look a mess, *cara*."

I played with the tassel on the pillow. "Thanks."

"Well, you do, you know? You look tired, you aren't eating well, you say you're coming home Sunday, then you drive all through the night and come home early like you couldn't wait one more day. And with Leo's niece, what's with that, huh?" She dipped the nail brush and looked at me. "So, what's wrong? Savino's not treating you good?"

I stared at her. She stared back, wide brown eyes and bleached-blond hair, garish red talons, so genuine yet superficially so; I wondered if all the makeup and dye and crazy trendy clothes were armor against a past she was running from, walls built up against someone she'd once been. I couldn't fathom the constant turmoil that must be going on in her head, day after day, fighting back the rising tide of undeniable truth. How was it that Sabine had lived in this family for so many years—she was so much older, even older than Mamma—and she had no idea what was going on? How could she pretend for this long?

"Savino's in the mob," I said.

Her eyebrows shot up again, and stayed there. She looked at me through her curtain of hair, legs pretzeled around to get the right painting angle. She held the pose. "He what?"

I hugged the pillow tighter. "Valentino Marzano, Papa's dad—he's running an illegal olive oil trade from Sicily, the whole family's in on it. The bakery's a money laundering front. They're all living in these huge houses and driving fifteen cars, everyone's got a gun, it's like the fucking *Godfather* up there."

Sabine thought about this. I held my breath. Her pink-glossed lips twisted into a variety of shapes as she inspected her toenails. I waited for a moment of clarity or outrage or something, but it never came.

"So," I said, "that's what's wrong."

Sabine fixed a nail, dipped the brush, did another sweeping coat. She didn't look at me. "Well, they're not hurting anyone, right? They're still going to church?"

I narrowed my eyes.

"Pia, look, I've always known *something* was going on, but you don't ask these questions—it's a family thing, alright? I don't keep up with what my little brother does. It's just how our family works, it's like how the Rondolfos down the street do palm-reading stuff in town by the dry-cleaner's, you know the Rondolfos? Every family has stuff like that, that's how it is, just go with it because they aren't hurting anyone. Hey, it isn't drugs—it *could* be drugs, but it isn't."

I could hardly believe it. "Sabine, you can't send the kids up to the Brooklyn."

"What?"

"You said a while back Savino offered to take the kids—"

"No, hey, I had the idea that maybe we should move up north, it would be good for them, Pia—"

"I know you *think* it was your idea, but that's how Savino works, he plants stuff like this. He wants me to stay in New York, and he thinks bringing the kids up there would keep me in Brooklyn." I could make her understand. "Look, he got me a Nic Tabone."

She froze.

"They shipped some guy over from Sicily. For me. So I'd settle down in New York and make Italian babies. He doesn't even speak English, they're not even being sneaky about it." It sounded crazy, and it was.

She shook her head. "Oh, Pia, you can't get married."

"I *know I can 't*," I hissed, "I don't want to, my point is that Savino's trying to control us and we can't let him."

She finished her nails, put the brush back in the bottle, and set it aside. She tossed back the last of her wine and combed her fingers through her hair. Sabine, who was obsessed with uncomfortable volumes of eye contact, wouldn't meet my gaze.

"What about the money?" she said.

"What money?"

"I know where the money comes from, Pia, it isn't all your salary, there's a lot more than that." Her nails clinked against the wine glass. "I know it comes from my family."

"I can take care of the kids," I said. I leaned forward, tossed the pillow aside. "I'm gonna move back this summer, I just need to get through the spring, get a degree—"

"Pia, I'm not trying to drag you back down here. Hey, look." She waved a hand to get my attention, and met my eyes finally. "I'm not leaving, *cara*, I'm not abandoning you and the kids. I love you guys, I'm not going anywhere. You do what you need to do, okay? I'm just saying—do you want to keep taking the money, or not?"

I sat back hard against the sofa. "Not."

"I can't keep Carlo in gymnastics, then."

Were we really that tight? I rubbed my temple; a headache was building. "Then...I don't know. I need to think."

"You need to sleep," said Sabine.

I tried. I said goodnight and went upstairs, head pounding, confusion clouding my judgement. I wanted to wake up Cristine and tell her everything—I wanted Lorel or Cristine or even Massimo to review the scene I'd just been a part of and confirm for me that it was insane—that something was wrong with Sabine, that I wasn't overreacting. I paused outside my bedroom and was about to go in when a door opened behind me.

"Pia." It was Carlo, in his pajamas, hair tousled. He stood in the crack of his and Vince's bedroom door; the room was dark behind him, fan blades clicking, the gentle hum of a white noise machine.

"Hey," I said.

"When you left this summer," he whispered, "I helped Sabine move her stuff into Mamma and Papa's room."

"Yeah?"

"Yeah." He squinted at me through the dark. "There was a loose baseboard in the back of the closet. I was gonna nail it down, you know, with the nail gun. But I pulled it off and here was a space back there, like a hole in the wall."

"Yeah?"

"Yeah," he said, "and Papa had a lot of guns back there."

I stared at him. He stared back.

"Good night, Carlo," I said.

"Good night."

ii.

I didn't sleep much that night. When I finally rolled over and checked my phone, it was 6:00 AM. The world was still dark outside, the house was quiet, and Lorel was dead asleep on the spare mattress at the foot of my bed.

I had five missed calls. Some of them were Ida, some were the bakery, some were from numbers I didn't recognize. I could almost imagine Savino trying everyone's phones, hoping I'd pick up at some point. I couldn't believe he hadn't tried Massimo's yet, because I'd probably fall for that.

It was my birthday. I was twenty years old.

My parents were dead, and with every year that passed, I'd get further away from the person they'd known me to be.

It was also Christmas Eve. *Buon Natale.*

The kids wanted to make a birthday cake, so I took Lorel and Vince with me to the grocery store mid-morning. Sabine was sorting out the fake Christmas tree pieces, putting the dusty thing together in the corner of the living room like the world's largest, scratchiest jigsaw puzzle. Cristine and Carlo were hard at work in the kitchen, and they were out of vanilla, and also I got the feeling they just wanted me out of the house.

242

We wandered the aisles of the IGA for a good half hour, just killing time before checking out with our singular bottle of vanilla extract and heading back to the house. The cracked and sun-bleached parking lot was crowded with last-minute Christmas shoppers, people I vaguely recognized, vehicles I'd seen around town hundreds of times. Two stores down was the dry-cleaner's, and right beside that was the sketchy palm-reading shop run by the Rondolfos from down the street—a light-up neon hand in the window, candle smoke and incense drifting out into the parking lot from the propped-open door.

There was a black SUV parked a few spots down from Sabine's car, its windows tinted dark. Shiny car, good condition—out of place in the lot crammed with old pickup trucks and vehicles destined for the scrapyard in the near future. It was running, and as I climbed into the driver's seat of Sabine's car I thought I caught sight of someone through the tinted windows—just sitting there, staring out at the parking lot. Watching us.

Maybe I'd become paranoid, living in that dumpster fire apartment, but I started the car quickly and pulled out of the space.

As I drove out of the cracked parking lot and bumped out onto the street, I glanced in the rearview mirror. The SUV pulled out and drove away.

My phone kept buzzing all throughout the day, and I continued to ignore it. Until Sabine came and found me on the back step, smoking and watching the sun set.

"Hey, *cara*, it's the phone, it's for you." She held out her cellphone, disapproving eyes on my cigarette.

I took the phone before I could think. "Who is it?"

"It's my brother, it's Savino, he says he's been tryin 'to call you and you haven't picked up. Is your phone broken? You need a charger?"

I stubbed out my cigarette on the step. "No," I mumbled. "It isn't."

The screen door slammed behind her as she went back inside. I balanced the cellphone on my knee for a moment, watched the play-set swings sway in the breeze. I heard Sabine clanging around in the kitchen, and it was a familiar sound—like waking up in the morning to a parent making breakfast, or sitting on the back step just like this with Papa, smoking and listening to Cristine and Carlo argue through the back door.

"Pia."

Sabine always had her volume cranked way up. I finally brought the phone up to my ear. "Hi."

"When did you leave town?"

"Friday night." I was in Augusta, I reminded myself, as I dug my feet into the cold dry soil. I was in Georgia and he couldn't reach me here.

"We've been trying to call you. Nicole finally got Massimo, he said you'd left in the night. We didn't know where you were. I sent some guys to check out your apartment and it was empty, anything could have happened. And you didn't answer your phone."

"My phone's been kind of…spotty."

"You left, so why didn't you tell me? You had a flight this morning."

"It was a last-minute thing."

He was silent for a long moment. Did he know the effect he had, how everything he said sounded just a little bit threatening?

"Are you okay?" he said at last.

"Yes."

He didn't believe me. "Did someone hurt you?"

Something twisted in my gut. It was almost like he wanted me to say yes, like he wanted a reason to beat down the Scarpacis or anyone else who dared mess with our family. "I'm fine. I just…got homesick." He didn't speak up, so I went on. "Massimo said Giovani got hurt the other night. Did something happen?"

"Just business. He'll be fine, I dealt with it."

Silence lingered again. He wasn't going to explain further, and I didn't want to let anything slip. "I've got to go," I said," we're decorating the Christmas tree." That wasn't true—we'd finished decorating that morning.

"Call me before you come back, alright?"

"Next week," I said.

"Well, talk to me first, because we might have to make some changes."

"What do you mean?"

"Don't worry about it."

I clenched my jaw. "*What* changes?"

I could almost hear him narrow his eyes. "Pia. We're in a delicate situation, I wouldn't put it past Diego Scarpaci to try and pull something again. So we're gonna need to sit down and talk about this, about you living where you're living with the Scarpaci girl, alright?"

He wasn't my dad. He didn't get to tell me where to live, who to live with. I even had a moment of insanity where I thought I might ask him about the black SUV, about feeling like someone was always watching. Did he have people in Augusta, watching the kids? He had no right. *But*, cautioned some frequently-suppressed voice in the back of my mind, *but he is also a mobster, and that's a pretty good reason to not push his buttons.*

"Right," I said. My toes curled into the dirt. "Okay."

"You take care, Pia. *Buon Natale.* And, uh—happy birthday."

I didn't bother asking how he knew my birthday; he was Savino Vitelli, he knew everything. "Thanks."

I hung up. And I decided to never take the phone from Sabine again.

244

iii.

I moved in with Massimo and Tonio.

Matty had moved back in with his and Lorel's aunt and was trying to avoid their parents as much as possible. Lorel talked her brother down from shunning me permanently—"I SAID I WAS SORRY," I shouted over her shoulder—"Pia says she's sorry, Matty, get your panties out of a twist"—and instead he agreed to split rent with Lorel and take my room. None of us were happy about it, but it made sense: Savino wouldn't look too hard at Lorel anymore since I wasn't around, and Diego wouldn't know where I was.

I did call Savino before Lorel and I drove back to New York. I told him I'd talked to Massimo, that I'd move in with the guys until the summer, then I'd figure out the rest from there. He seemed relieved. I didn't mention that I'd be coming home after that, that I wasn't planning to stick around. I figured any indication that I wasn't planning to put down roots in Brooklyn might cause him to panic and encourage Luca Catenacci to propose or something.

The spring semester started in a week. I'd scrounged together enough money to take twelve credit hours composed of statistics and microbiology (my two failed courses from the fall), and a public speaking class to count as a communication credit. The *panificio* was open for limited hours over the winter break, since most of the staff were on vacation, so only Savino and Marco were going in until school started back. That meant I had time to get settled, gather my school things, and pretend to be merely a student for one whole week.

Matty wasn't at the apartment when we got there, but my things were boxed up. Lorel dropped her luggage inside the door and helped me carry my stuff downstairs. We somehow maneuvered two whole cardboard boxes into the back of her car before hitting the road again.

"I think he's embarrassed," she said, "with the way he reacted."

"It's fine."

"No, it's not. I'll talk to him. Pia, hey"—she turned to me at the next red light—"it's not your fault. Matty's normally pretty good about it, but we didn't have the best childhood, and he's got a lot of the anger issues from Dad. It isn't always rational."

I put up the collar of my coat—Lorel's car heater was on the fritz, and New York had held on to its frigid winter like it wasn't letting go. "It's fine."

She tapped the wheel, swung around a corner. "It isn't fine. He once punched out a window."

"*Matty?*"

245

"Yeah, before we moved out. He was fighting with Dad and I guess he was trying to emphasize a point, and so he punched a hole through the dining room window. Dad made him pay for it and he got stitches in his hand. That's one of the reasons I moved out with him. I needed to get him out of there and I didn't want him on his own— Matty's sensitive, he looks big and tough, but we were best friends growing up, really close, and I can tell when he's teetering on the edge. Which is a lot of the time, these days."

"Is he seeing anyone?"

"Not currently, I don't think so. He was dating our neighbor Bree for a while—"

"No. You know, I mean a therapist or something."

"Oh. No, he isn't, although we both probably should. My whole family should."

I watched her silhouette against the driver's side window—flashing neon against her profile, the car growing darker as night crept into the streets—her short curls pinned back from her face, her small upturned nose. My Scarpaci cousin belonged in that world of glitter and lights, the applause and costumes and painted faces. And somehow she'd ended up down in this pit with me and Massimo and Tonio.

"Do you ever wonder," she murmured, "what would have happened if we'd never met?"

I swallowed. "Sometimes." Mostly, I thought about how much better her life would have been without me in it.

"How did we even find each other? We're cousins, I still can't wrap my mind around that, but we found each other in the basement of the liberal arts building. What are the chances?"

I'd wondered about that before, and I didn't have a real explanation. "Bad sense of direction runs in the family?"

"Ha! No. I don't think so. I think fate's a poet. Because if I hadn't met you, I'd probably still live with my aunt. I definitely wouldn't have Massimo. And—I think I've grown up a lot, Pia. I've seen enough that I have more an idea of what I want out of life, if that makes sense."

"What do you want?" Surely not this.

"Peace," she said, immediately. "Something simple. And pure. That doesn't mean *boring*, but I want to travel and experience things and I want to do it for the right reasons—not because I'm running away from somewhere, or from my family, but simply because I want to and I can. You know the Chesterton quote, about the angels?"

"'Angels can fly because they can take themselves lightly'?"

"That one." Lorel smiled. "I want to take myself lightly."

Tonio was alone in the apartment when we busted in, laden with cumbersome cardboard boxes and my squeaking suitcase. To be more specific, he was blasting

Andrea Bocelli from the kitchen. And when Lorel and I deposited our burdens on the living room carpet and wandered in to see what the racket was about, we found Tonio with a whirring buzzer in hand, leaning over the sink, trimming the hair around his ears.

"Oh, hey Marzano," he said, a grin gracing his face as we entered. He straightened and clicked off the buzzer, but he still had to shout to be heard over the music. "Hey, Marzano's friend."

"Hi, Tonio," Lorel shouted. She looked at me with crazy-eyes, the sort of expression that meant *can you believe this? What a great character study.* She hadn't spent nearly enough time around Tonio to have exhausted his novelty.

"Buon Natale." Tonio set the buzzer on the counter. He dusted off his shoulders into the sink, shook out his dress shirt, which he was wearing with a classy pair of striped blue-and-white flannel pajama pants and plaid wool socks.

"What's this?" I asked. Just when I thought Tonio couldn't get any weirder, he really pulled out all the stops to prove me wrong.

"Con Te Partirò," said Tonio. "Nineteen-ninety-five. Bocelli. Even you should know that, it's a pretty well-known piece—"

"I knew that," said Lorel. "Why are you cutting your own hair?"

"Why the hell not," said Tonio. He finally turned down the stereo by the coffee maker. He ran a hand through his hair, leaned forward and tilted his head to check his work in the backsplash's reflection. "Savino lost his mind after you left, by the way. He sent Massimo and Ezio to your apartment, had us driving all over the city, really exhausting stuff, until he figured out where you'd went. A fine waste of time when he could have just faxed you. I would have told him that too, but Massimo seemed to think your uncle wouldn't appreciate the suggestion."

I shrugged off my coat, folded it over my arm. "I don't think I can possibly communicate how little I care."

Tonio laughed—it broke out of his chest, and his eyebrows shot up like he was surprised to hear himself laugh. "Oh, God. Alright." He dusted a hand through his hair again and straightened. He yanked the buzzer plug out of the wall.

"But really," said Lorel, "why *are* you in the kitchen?"

"Better lighting," he said, like it was obvious. He stuck his hands in his pajama pockets—his laugh had settled into a narrow smile. "Right. I rearranged my books for you, Marzano, don't ever forget that."

He led us down the hall to the third bedroom, which had been converted into a library/office sort of setup: cheap shelves lined the walls, laden with books and binders and stacks of encyclopedias interspersed with ornate bookends and statuettes; an obscene number of candles, as thick around as my forearm and artistically laced with dripping wax. There was an antique desk pushed up against the window, a jumble of old furniture that had clearly been stacked out of the way to make room for a fold-out loveseat. An assortment of throw pillows was piled beside the mattress.

"Wow," said Lorel. "This is cozy."

"You're most welcome," said Tonio.

iv.

Massimo got back a few hours later from running errands with his dad. Tonio was in the kitchen making his dinners for the rest of the week, and I'd slipped out onto the balcony despite the cold. I stood against the railing and looked out at the city—lights as far as the eye could see, caterpillar lines of cars snaking through the streets, the distant wail of music and car alarms and the staccato echo of horns. Bursts of flashing neon painted the sidewalks below.

There weren't any stars; on a clear night like this, in Augusta, I could tilt back my head and see the whole sky full of constellations, I could even name a few, and the kids and I would run out into the yard and stare up into the night and feel like specks of dust in the infinite hugeness of the raging universe. Here, the sky loomed like a gray-black dome, like a ceiling. The surrounding buildings and skyscrapers were walls, trapping me down here in the mortal realm. No indication that there was something bigger than this moment, bigger and more important than whatever spectacle was playing out under the snow-globe shell of New York City in December.

I shut my eyes and let the cold freeze my face numb. I needed to get the kids out. The Vitellis had too much influence, even down in Augusta my siblings weren't safe, and Sabine wasn't willing to do anything about that.

What would Mamma do? What would Papa do?

Behind me, the door slid open.

"Hi, Pia." Massimo leaned against the rail beside me. In the night light, he almost looked normal—serene and steady, pulled-together in his dress shirt and slacks, the picture-perfect good Italian son—I bet his parents were proud, I bet it would take a miracle for them to see past his practiced facade. I wondered if he even knew about the facade. Maybe this was just pure Massimo Di Natale: a storm trapped in a human vessel, chaos concealed within walls of composure.

"Thanks for letting me move in," I said.

"Don't worry about it. You're pretty low-maintenance." He rubbed a hand through his hair. "And it will be nice to have someone else around who can roll their eyes at Tonio."

"What were you doing for Savino?"

"My dad and Raul had to meet some guys at Long Island, some meeting Stefano set up for Savino, with the Marzano guys. I don't know what it was about, though. Hey." He patted his pockets, retrieved a crinkled envelope and held it out to me. "Mom sent this for you."

"What is it? It's—" I paused, looked at him sideways, suddenly suspicious. "It had better not be money."

"It isn't. Worse than that."

I ripped the envelope open. A single sheet of thick paper slipped out—decorative lacy border, huge curling lines of cursive. "*Join us for an engagement banquet celebrating Salvadora Batilda-Annamaria Di Natale and Francesco Gianluca Battaglini.* Ugh."

Massimo snorted.

"December thirty-first." I looked up. "That's Sunday night." It was Friday. I hadn't even thought about New Year's. In Augusta, we laid awake at night while the entire town set off illegal fireworks from South Carolina—you had to cross the border to get them, but everyone did it, and they cracked through the night till dawn for two days straight.

I folded the invitation and stuck it back in its envelope. "Are you going?"

"Oh, Pia. *Everyone's* going."

My stomach flipped over. "Oh. Sounds like hell."

"It will be. Have you talked to Savino?"

I shrugged. "Little bit. I thought I could put it off till work started back, but I'll probably see him Sunday, won't I?"

"You might see him sooner than that." Massimo leaned his elbows against the balcony, stared down at the neon-splashed street. "He wants to see you tomorrow. Asked me to drop you off at the Vitelli house."

"He didn't tell me that. Why?" I wasn't something that could just be carted around town, and Savino hadn't even tried calling me.

"I don't know. He doesn't tell me that stuff."

"Great." What if he brought up the Montauk incident? He seemed like he could just look at a person's face and tell they were lying, or guilty, or scared out of their wits; the only thing he gave no indication of detecting was anger. Or maybe he just chose not to respond to it.

"Pia?"

I shoved my hair back—the wind was blowing it in my face, and I didn't have any hair clips on hand. I leaned against the railing beside my cousin and glared across the skyline. "Yeah."

Massimo's voice was low, almost lost on the wind. "I got a ring."

I narrowed my eyes, picked out the sliver of moon peeking out between silver clouds. I didn't know what he was talking about. "A—what? A ring for—"

Then it clicked. *For Lorel.*

249

He swallowed, bit his lip. "I got it...you know, before. Before Montauk, before we'd even planned it." He knitted his fingers together and stared at his hands.

"Oh." That was all I could say. I'd sort of stopped thinking. A car screeched by below, blaring rap—the glass door shook on its track. A moment later, sirens wailed in the distance. Panic surged in my chest. *They're so young, they're not Dora and Francesco—Lorel is too young, we can't drag her deeper into this—* "Massimo—"

"I know," he said. "I know I don't deserve her, I never could. If I'm being honest Pia"—he looked at me, eyes wide, his face bathed in shadow—"really honest, maybe the reason I told the Scarpacis wasn't just...you know, getting Diego out to Montauk, making him angry enough to do something. Maybe I just wanted someone to know. I've been hiding everything for so long, not just Lorel—I've hid everything from my parents, and they don't even care enough to look a little harder, and I just want the truth. Do you remember the last time you weren't lying about everything? Because I don't." He ran a hand down his face. "I'm selfish. I know that's wrong. And that's why I don't deserve Lorel."

"None of us do," I murmured.

"But I got a ring." Massimo laughed a little—his shoulders shook. "I got a ring, Pia. I carry it around like I've got a hope in the world that she might say yes."

This wasn't Dora and Francesco. This was something tragic and chaotic, bearing witness to a train wreck, the slow spiral of a hurricane creeping close—its outer bands tested us, and we proved weak mortals unfit to weather its storm.

I figured this was the moment I should hug him or something, but I hated hugs. I put my feelings about Lorel aside for a moment. I patted his shoulder. "It's gonna be okay."

Massimo looked at me. The corners of his lips twitched. "You really suck at comforting."

"I know."

"You just...patted me on the back."

"I—yes. I did. I don't know, Massimo, I—"

"*It's gonna be okay.*" He shook his head at the street below.

I laughed. I was exhausted, I was absolutely *freaked out* by everything happening right now, and it was such a stupid thing to say—stupid to *think*, let along say out loud. *It's gonna be okay.* As if either of us believed that for an instant.

"What cause for hilarity?" Tonio stuck his head out onto the balcony.

I hadn't seen Massimo smile in quite a while—I'd forgotten what a relief it was. "Hey," he said, "Pia says everything's going to be okay."

Tonio leaned against the doorjamb and grinned thinly. "Oh, thank God."

XIII

Odysseus

i.

I woke early, feeling restless and tired. Tonio was already awake.

"Guess who didn't drink himself to sleep for once," he said, sitting at the kitchen island, spooning Nutella onto saltines. He didn't look up, but he jerked his thumb over his shoulder in the general direction of Massimo's room. "That guy."

I shuffled up to the island and sat down across from him. "Hooray." My voice was hoarse from sleep.

Tonio concentrated on his saltines—he had some method behind this madness, a very specific portion of hazelnut spread per cracker, and he held it level to his eyes as he carefully covered the surface, as if checking for the perfect Nutella-to-saltine ratio. His lips twitched. "Do you have something to say, Marzano?"

I rubbed the sleep from my eyes, put my face in my hands. My body desperately wanted to go back to sleep. I straightened. "Nope."

"Really? Nothing at all? Because…you look like you have something to say."

He had the sleeves rolled up on his bathrobe, and it was a fairly jarring, chaotic picture he painted, yet somehow he made it seem lazily elegant. Like a sculptor shaping a lump of clay with muddy hands, like feeling along the edges of rolled-out pastry dough to check its thickness, or scoring a flour-dusted *bâtard*—something weirdly bold and confident about it. The seductive art of Nutella, as taught by one Tonio Salone. Unnerving.

He clearly wanted me to point out the abomination that was his breakfast habit, but I absolutely refused to do so. "Have you made coffee?"

He set the spoon aside, chewed thoughtfully on a cracker. "*Coffee.*" He narrowed his eyes at me for a long moment, then got up and started pulling things down from a cabinet, clanking around with no regard for Masismo's sleep. "*Coffee* is an…unsavory attempt to achieve a caffeine high—you want shaking hands, Marzano? Gastrointestinal distress?"

"Do they come with a huge cup of coffee?"

Tonio fixed a look back over his shoulder, equal parts disapproval and condescension. He pointedly clacked an espresso cup down on the counter and started tamping down grounds.

"Hey," I said, watching him work. "Did Achille get in trouble?"

"Oh, he's always in trouble. Why? Is he in jail again?"

That really didn't surprise me—the guy had his name tattooed on his hands, it was basically inevitable that he lived half his life in prison. "I mean, after the drop-off. This summer, when he was drunk and wandered into the Scarpaci casino, he gave Diego's guys the wrong date for the shipment, but he did tell them the place, right? Everyone was pissed."

While his back was turned, I leaned over the counter and stole a finger-full of Nutella—I wasn't hungry, but it was more the idea that I'd taken it from Tonio that made me happy.

"Oh," he said. He snapped the espresso machine together and switched it on. He turned halfway and leaned against the counter, arms crossed, face stretched into a yawn. "Oh, no, that didn't happen this time. He got off easy, maybe because he caught a bullet in the leg—not his first, he didn't have to be so terribly dramatic about it, you'd think he'd lost the leg or something. No, I guess you didn't hear? Massimo didn't tell you?"

Uneasiness settled in my stomach. It was too early for this. "Tell me *what*?"

Tonio shrugged. "Savino decided it was probably Betta."

"What? Why?"

"Everyone knows about these parties she goes to—I mean, even her parents know she goes *out*, they don't really know where, but Betta *loves* Achille. She's the perfect scapegoat. She tells him everything, so maybe he just decided to point out that she was in a better position to have let something spill, to save his own ass." Tonio pulled the espresso. He came back to the kitchen island, settled on his stool across from me, and slid the glass cup across the counter. "*Caffè.*"

It was a nice shot—perfect crema, good color. "Uh. Thanks."

"Or maybe he didn't say anything at all. Probably wouldn't need to. If you think about it for any length of time, Betta leaking sensitive information about a drop-off is the natural conclusion."

"But she doesn't know anything. No one would tell her anything, right? Betta's the sort of person you don't tell things to if you don't want them getting around, and everyone knows that. So it doesn't make sense that she'd leak anything."

"Look, Marzano, logic has little place in any of this. Betta Di Natale goes to sketchy parties, maybe she bumped into a Scarpaci or one of Diego's guys—and she's in this family, maybe she heard something. Again, she spends too much time with

Achille. Betta," he said, tapping his Nutella spoon handle against the countertop, "she has potential—she's enthusiastic and aggressive and mindlessly loyal, and if she were a boy she'd be endlessly useful to Savino—a bit like Achille, probably—don't look at me like that, I don't make up the rules, do you see many active females in this family? Do you see my sister or Nicole or Dora Di Natale *packing*? The damsels that *aren't* just avoiding the dirty work are too smart to get involved, anyway."

There was something distinctly insulting about everything he'd just said, only I wasn't sure whether he was being directly sexist, or if I was just generally offended by this family's dumb traditions. It certainly wasn't often that Tonio *wasn't* the main source of offense.

He'd forgone his crackers entirely and was just eating spoonfuls of Nutella now. It was horrible and transfixing. "Is *damsel* offensive?" he muttered, more to himself than to me.

"What, are you developing a conscience now?"

Tonio smirked—narrow slash of a smile on his haunted skeleton face. "God, I hope not."

ii.

Massimo dropped me off outside the Vitelli house around noon. The looming narrow house front with its brick and crawling ivy felt more ominous than I remembered. After Massimo pulled off the curb and his charcoal Lexus disappeared down the street, I stood on the sidewalk and stared up at the door, its brass knocker hanging like an invitation. Two black BMWs and a red Tesla were parked outside the house. I'd never seen the Tesla before. I wondered who else was here.

I would have stood longer, but the wind swept down the street and my coat was too thin for this weather and my fingers were already numb, so the cold drove me inside; I mounted the steps and rapped on the knocker.

Raul answered the door. He looked most like Ida, I thought, out of all her brothers—narrow face and sharp, perceptive eyes behind thin wire frames. He loomed over me for a moment in silence, then adjusted his sports coat, straightened the cuffs, and opened the door a bit wider. "He's waiting."

I wondered if he knew just how ominous that sounded. "How are you?" I asked, pointedly.

"Fine."

The house was quiet—no sign of Ida or the kids. Maybe Luca was around though, probably doing something responsible like laundry, but possibly lurking in a corner waiting to jump me. I checked around the back of the door as I stepped inside.

Raul went ahead through the front room, gestured down the corridor—"In here"—and followed me into the dark hallway. Savino's office door hung open, lit dimly from within.

The office was a cavern of mahogany and antique armchairs that reminded me faintly of an ancient tavern with a tinge of hushed, sacred library. Factor in the heavy-draped windows with their thick warped glass, and it felt like a chapel—everything too still and quiet, too large and out of proportion, as if to remind the worshipper of their own smallness. I'd only seen the room before in brief glances, snapshots stolen from the hallway. Four chairs were arranged around a side-table in the center of the room. One of them held a man with remarkably thick eyebrows, and meaty hands clasped around the armrests; his thick frame was squeezed into a black athletic jacket, though the room was warm and flames flickered low in the gas fireplace.

Savino sat behind his desk, which was almost identical to the behemoth lurking in the *panificio* office. He was leaned back in his chair, a fist to his lips, staring at the fire on the opposite wall—but his eyes flicked to me when I entered before Raul. "Pia."

"Hi." I paused inside the doorway. The atmosphere was tense, full of anticipation, foreboding. On one hand I registered the cracking fire and faint after-odor of cigar smoke, and I knew these were calming things, and I should be calm. But on the other hand...this whole thing reeked of mafia business.

Raul shut the door behind me. Savino nodded at the armchairs. "Take a seat."

I did—uncomfortably, carefully, with my hands deep in my coat pockets and my back rigid against the velvety cushion. The side-table was empty but for a single silver tray. The man in the athletic jacket didn't say anything, but he stared at me with small eyes and a wide, unsmiling mouth.

Raul sat across from him. I didn't really know Raul, but he brimmed with quick, nervous energy—like he knew what to expect, he knew how things were done, and he anticipated them falling into place. He nodded a little—almost as if mentally checking off a box—when Savino stood and opened a drawer in his desk.

"How was your break?" Glass against glass—a chill crept up my spine. I glanced over my shoulder and watched my uncle round the desk.

"Fine."

"How's Sabine?" He stepped between mine and Raul's chairs, set four tulip-shaped glasses on the silver tray. I thought about the beginning of the summer, when I'd come back into the house and I'd heard him in the middle of some activity—something with glass and a few of his guys. And I thought about how ridiculous it was, how family worked, that we were supposed to trust each other based purely on a shared bloodline, even if we didn't really know the other person at all.

"She's okay," I said. "She's still blond."

That gave him pause, halfway to the fireplace. He looked at me sharply, and for an instant Savino Vitelli was nearly human. "Since when?"

"A few years."

His eyebrows shot up, and he shook his head. "I'd...like to see that, actually."

"Her eyebrows are a different color every time I see her." *Damn.* Did he know what he was doing? I bet he did—he knew how he put people at ease, he knew I *wanted* to talk to him. And he was the only person I could talk to about Sabine. I bet he knew that, too. *Damn.*

Raul was looking at me. I met his eyes, and he glanced away quickly.

Savino retrieved something from the mantel. He settled down in the armchair across from me, his back to the fire, and set a corked black bottle on the tray with the glasses. "Johnny."

The man in the athletic jacket heaved a backpack onto his lap from the floor, dug around inside for a moment before retrieving two bubble-wrapped bottles—a little smaller than wine bottles, a little darker, and the tulip glasses suddenly gained significance. I knew what this was.

"Pia, this is Johnny Moriondo."

"Hi."

Johnny grunted. He worked his jaw, openly staring at me.

With the door shut, the smell of smoke was a lot thicker in the air. I sat in rigid silence with these dark-haired men in their black and sports coats and faintly flour-dusted sleeves. My uncle picked one bottle, unwrapped it, and pulled the cork.

"That's *Moresca*," said Johnny.

"*Sicilia*," said Savino. And he poured a green-gold stream into each tulip glass. "Pia, this is your family's oil. This is the new shipment we're getting, Stefano brings in the samples from Valentino's guys, Johnny works with Stefano. You remember what I told you about the oil industry? The real thing, unadulterated, better than the bakery stuff. This is it." He picked up a glass, placed it in the palm of his hand, and wrapped his fingers around it. He covered the top with his other hand and swirled the oil gently. Johnny and Raul did the same. "Have you ever tasted oil?"

I took the fourth glass—Savino nodded—and I followed suit. "No. I haven't."

"There's a method," said Raul, brow furrowed, fixated on the swirling oil.

"This"—Savino tapped his glass—"this is real extra-virgin, yeah? You don't get this stuff in stores. They adulterate it with *lampante*—that's oil for lamps—or pomace oil. Seed oils. And this stuff comes straight here from Sicily, but we make sure it's genuine once it gets here. And the only way to do that is to taste it."

"The chemical tests—" Raul paused his swirling to adjust his glasses, but fell silent when Savino cut in.

"The chemical tests tell you nothing," said my uncle, his voice low, watching the oil slosh against the glass—his eyes followed the movement, as if entranced. "They tell you polyphenols, oleic acid—you can add those things later, they can add back the color, they can deodorize *lampante* and pass it off as extra-virgin. But the flavor, the aroma, that's how you know it's the good stuff."

Sitting there and watching Savino watch the oil, I felt like I'd been caught up in some corrupt ritual. I felt like I was doing something wrong. Like police might kick in the door, catch us swirling glasses of oil, and arrest us on the spot. Like Mamma was standing disapprovingly over my shoulder. But I held my breath as I swirled the oil—I watched the green waves slide up against the glass, leave a trail of gold—the faintly opaque liquid, the source of so much strife and tradition—I caught myself holding my breath, both vaguely repulsed and morbidly fascinated. It was sacred and sensual. Profane.

They uncovered their glasses. I inhaled something earthy and sharp and vaguely bitter.

Savino tossed back the contents of his glass. Raul and Johnny did the same.

It was warm, and lukewarm oil might not sound appealing, but the flavors that hit me—flavors, or smells?—set off a series of rapid images in my mind. Something light and sharp, cutting—acidity like an unripe tomato, the earthy taste of fresh-cut grass in the air. Round, biting fruitiness. It coated the inside of my mouth. I expected it to be greasy, but once I'd swallowed, the oily feeling disappeared; I was left with a faint aftertaste and a burning pepperiness in the back of my throat.

I coughed.

Savino and Raul coughed as a well, but Johnny only cleared his throat; he was already peeling the bubble wrap off the next bottle, moving on. "This is the...uh...the *Tonda Iblei*, you know. You know this one." He was talking to Savino, who nodded.

The oil was more golden than green this time. The aroma was sweet, like ripe fruit, yet bore undertones of pepperiness.

"Why is the color different?" I asked.

"It doesn't have to be green. Color isn't an indicator of quality, it changes based on the cultivar, the olives, the time of harvest. It tends to be green early in the harvest, more golden as the season progresses. But it isn't necessarily an indicator of quality."

"The professionals," said Raul, eyes downward cast, "use tinted glasses."

"Use what?"

He held up his tulip-glass of oil. "Blue-tinted, hides the color. Unbiased assessment."

This one was bitter. It singed my throat going down, and there was something animalistic about it, sweetly smoky, but not in a bad way. Somehow I felt terribly insignificant all of the sudden, lost in this shadow of this oil.

"It's ancient," I'd explain to Tonio, later, when pressed. "It makes you feel small and...young. Like—don't laugh—it's this ancient, sacred thing, like standing in front of ruins and knowing someone built that, and it was important to them, and they're dead now, but it's still standing."

"It's Homeric," he summarized.

"What?"

"Odysseus washes up on the island of Scheria—it's in the *Odyssey*, that's Homer—"

"I know who wrote the *Odyssey*."

"—and the women there give him olive oil to wash with. And apparently a naked man on the beach covered in oil really did it for them, because Nausicca fell in love with Odysseus. It made him godlike."

And while the story was entirely unnecessary, Tonio admittedly made a good point. There was something godlike about this oil—real oil—not just the stuff we used at work, or at home. It was emotional. It was humbling.

I sensed Savino's eyes on me. He smiled a little as he poured from the third and final bottle—smiled, because he knew. He knew it was setting off synapses in my brain, that things were clicking into place. That chilled me. Yet it was also horribly thrilling—everyone sitting here in this room, they understood, they'd dipped their toes in something completely ancient. A hedonistic experience. It was like a stolen artifact, unveiled for our eyes only—raw in the naked firelight, depraved and uncensored on the senses.

"This one's for Pia," said Savino. He handed me the tulip glass and took one for himself.

The aromas were different—bitter and clouded, something faintly unpleasant that reminded me of cat piss. It was greasy going down. No tomato or grass this time, no delightful pepperiness in the back of my throat. I grimaced. "What *is* that?"

"Reference." Savino blinked away the taste. He set his glass on the tray and picked up the third bottle. "That was labeled as cold-pressed extra-virgin, from the supermarket shelves. Most bottles don't have a production date on the label. This one did. This one"—he tapped a stamped line, below the company's contact information—"is from three years ago. That's the closest date I could find." He sat back in his armchair. "Reference."

We all sat in silence for a moment. The fire popped and crackled. I stared at the three black bottles and tulip glasses with their green-gold residue coating the sides. My family had made this, out of their own olives, lording over their *oliveti* from within a fortress in Sicily. This was decades and probably centuries of labor and politics, covert trade, power and money and sacred tradition. My family. Not the Vitellis—not Savino's family—but *mine*.

Finally, Savino spoke again. He cut his eyes at Johnny and rubbed his jaw. "Tell the guys we're on schedule. We'll have the delivery to them by Monday—first shipment of the new year."

Johnny sniffed. "They might need more compensation. After the last time."

"Huh."

"But," said Johnny, "they aren't the ones breaking their backs hauling that shit all over the city, dragging it in and out of warehouses, throwing it on and off the truck. They don't even have to worry much about getting caught. They're just gonna use any excuse to increase their rate."

"Use Achille instead," said Raul. "He doesn't ask questions."

"I think Achille might need a vacation," said Savino. "He needs to take some time off."

"It was just a bullet," Raul deadpanned. "He can drive a truck." He said it like everyone was overreacting, like Achille was just being dramatic about getting shot in the leg. Which was sort of how Tonio had reacted too.

Savino rubbed his eyes. "Maybe. Johnny, tell them, yeah? And if they cause problems for you or Tony, asking for *more compensation,* you direct them back to me. I'll sort them out."

"Yeah." Johnny stood. He motioned at the bottles. "Leave these?"

"Nah, get them out of here."

He rewrapped the bottles and set them down in his backpack. Then he slung the bag over his shoulder and nodded at the door. "I'll tell 'em. They got spooked, they were jumpy the other night, I had to twist some arms to get guys to show up, they aren't jumping for it. I don't think they care about the distinction—how one drop-off is different from another. They don't care about how some of us are shouldering the risk more than they are. So they'll bitch about it."

"Hm." Savino leaned against the armrest. He was like an oil painting, my uncle: a dark figure nestled into a dark armchair, black eyes like fluid embers, dim orange flames lighting the back wall. Like Lorel, he was a figure from one of Tonio's books— the charismatic lord, the god trapped in mortal flesh, the most relatable mafioso and untouchable human wrapped in a paradox of understanding and dismissal, care and cruelty. Unreal. "They issue any threats, they get cold feet, they make this transaction any harder than it has to be, you direct them to me. I'll take care of it. We'll do what we need to do."

Johnny left with the oil. A moment later, Raul stood—he straightened the lapels of his sports coat. "What time do you want the truck?" The firelight flickered off his round spectacles, giving him an unnerving, slightly demonic look.

Savino stared at the table where the bottles had been. "Midnight."

"I'll let Ezio know. I'll see you and Ida on Sunday, at Mass."

"Tell your mother to take it easy."

"We tell her every day," said Raul. "Does she listen? No. She won't let the maid in the house, locks her out and hides the damn key. She makes sure everything is done the way she likes it because she *does* it—we can't make her slow down, she doesn't know *how* to take it easy, but she's always been that way, huh? Like the rest of us, got to do it ourselves. Ask Ida, she's always been like that. What a woman."

Raul saluted. Then he left, and it was just me and Savino sitting across from each other. The silence was thick with smoke and shell-shock, as if a bomb had just gone off, like he'd delivered some gutting news.

"You understand," said Savino.

I'd crossed my arms, eyes fixed on the side-table. "I don't know." I met his gaze—he was focused, gauging my reaction. If I hadn't known better, I might have thought he was waiting for my seal of approval. "It's illegal."

He tilted his head. "But is it wrong?"

"It's dangerous."

"But. Is it wrong?" He crossed his arms, mirroring me, and tilted his chin up. In that moment he looked terribly like Mamma—the cold, knowing gleam in her eye when she'd made her point, won the argument, done and dusted the situation.

I hated the family business because it put the kids in danger. I didn't care that the Marzanos in Sicily had an oil mill, that they were sending the stuff over here for select customers—I cared that it happened to be illegal, that the bakery was a front, that the family was built on a delicate foundation of lies and blind trust. But besides the illegality, was there anything terribly immoral about this?

I didn't answer him. I didn't know how. "Is Luca here?"

"He is. Do you want to see him?" It wasn't amusement in his eyes, it was calculation, it was sizing me up and testing my boundaries and seeing if I'd notice.

I noticed. "I know what you're doing." He didn't say anything, so I went on. "Luca and me. I see what you're doing, but it isn't gonna happen."

"Does Luca know that?" Was that a hint of a smile?

I straightened. Did he think this was funny? "I don't think so. I think someone's encouraging him. You should tell him."

"Why don't you tell him, Pia?"

I flexed my jaw. The oil had gone to my head like wine—or maybe it was the smoke, the faint sweet aroma of tobacco, the fire and the dim light. "I don't have to tell him anything, he's not my responsibility, he isn't gonna be my Nic Tabone."

Savino's eyebrows shot up.

"The guy Sabine was supposed to settle down with. The reason she left."

"I know who Nic Tabone is." He settled back in his seat, and something about the quirk of his eyebrow told me he was laughing on the inside.

He really did think this was funny—not me in the specific, but the situation, and perhaps my reaction to it. *Infuriating.* But the instant Savino thought something was amusing, it broke the tension and suddenly that thing *was* quite funny. For a second, it all seemed impossibly ridiculous, like I'd been trapped in the middle of an action-comedy movie, I'd stumbled onto the set and couldn't find my way to the exit. It was a good story. But I hadn't asked to be a part of it. And stories are always more enjoyable when you're reading about the characters going through hell. They are suddenly a lot *less* entertaining when you're suffering right alongside the lot of them.

"Is he so bad, Pia? Has he done something to you?"

I sniffed. Rubbed my wrists, but the braces were gone. "No. He's nice, he's fine, but I don't even like him enough to be friends, let alone—and I'm too busy, I'm too young."

"You're two months older than Dora. She's engaged, if you haven't noticed."

"Dora's really young too." My jaw was tight. "I'm not getting married, and Luca isn't gonna keep me in Brooklyn."

The moment I said it, I would have liked to take the words back. That was what I'd been skirting around for these last few months—the thing I wasn't going to tell my uncle. That New York City was temporary, that whatever plans he concocted were delicate, that I could disappear and never come back, and nothing could tie me down to this place.

My heart hammered in my chest. The room suddenly felt a lot colder. I held my breath.

I watched him, waited for an explosion, but Savino just pursed his lips and looked thoughtfully over the top of my head. "You never met Valentino Marzano."

"No."

"You know what happened, the last shipment?"

"Yes."

"We don't get the oil, the drop-off is interrupted, we can't sell it. We had to send back an entire shipment. That increases the risk of Valentino being investigated, of inspectors and customs—the oil business is all about politics, it's all about people being compensated to look away at the right moment—but there's always a risk there. We don't unload the oil, we double that risk when the shipment goes back to Sicily. And we don't get paid."

I didn't know why he was telling me this. "Are you...worried it'll happen again?"

Savino shook his head. "It got dropped off yesterday. It's in storage now, the trucks are coming in Sunday night. And that's a good thing, Pia, you know why? Because Valentino's got a short temper." He rubbed a hand down his face. "We'll be in trouble, if it happens again. The fire, now this—we're only lucky *Diego Scarpaci* didn't get a ransom tape to the Marzanos. Valentino would've reacted."

"What—"

"He'd cancel shipments, send his guys over to supervise the business—who knows." He teetered his hand, side-to-side. "We're balancing on the edge of a blade, Pia. The business has taken a lot of hits this year. You know why we're still standing?" I didn't. "You."

I blinked. "Why? What did I do?"

"Nothing. You're a Marzano, that's enough. You are testament to a union made decades ago, between Vitellis in Brooklyn and Marzanos in Sicily. For over twenty years, we've done what we could to keep that tie strong. We've made sacrifices." The fire popped behind him, but he didn't flinch. "What would you do for your family, Pia?"

Was my family the Salones, the Di Natales, Oscar and the Biasis, Dora and her sisters? Or the Marzanos and the Vitellis? Or was it just Cristine and Carlo and Vince, tucked away in Augusta with Sabine, temporarily safe from whatever I'd unwittingly invited into our lives?

"Because"—I hadn't realized he wasn't finished, but Savino raised his eyebrows and went on—"because you've already decided to give away your life to your siblings, to your brothers and sister. But you haven't sacrificed your future to them. Just the life you would have led. There's a difference." He always spoke deliberately, but his words came slow just now; careful and calculated, as if searching for the perfect phrase to get his point across. "When you choose family over and over again, giving everything away, it doesn't leave you empty-handed. It gives you a role. Respect. Purpose."

"I don't have anything to give away." It sounded self-pitying, but it was the fact of the matter: I was empty-handed from the start.

"I've given away every life I might have led to this family. I've poured everything into it, and I'm not the only one. By doing that I've built a future for myself and the people I care for. Life is about dying to the people we love—you understand that." He tilted his head, deadly serious. "If the family business is ever in trouble, you have the power—the influence—to keep it afloat. In other words"—he nodded at the side-table, at the empty tulip glasses streaked with oil—"blood and oil, it's on both our hands. If a hole ever opened up in leading this family, you'd be the natural fit."

My throat went dry, and my chest was tight. I stared at the glasses. I thought about blood on my hands and I pictured dipping my fingers into a bowl of oil, pressing them into focaccia, my skin glistening gold in the bakery lights.

It was sweet poison. I was power-drunk and terrified.

"How are your wrists?"

That caught me off-guard. "Oh. Fine."

"You swirl with your elbow," he said, "instead of your wrist."

He was talking about the oil tasting. I tensed. "I'm fine."

I wasn't fine. I'd lost the braces and I'd stopped taking care of myself and around the same time I'd been running myself into the ground and not sleeping, my forearms had gotten stiff and wrist movements sent shooting pain up to my elbows. I was careful that no one noticed it and pitied me. The only way Savino recognized this was because he'd experienced the same thing, and he'd been watching for it, and it hurt terribly—like a stab to the gut—that someone cared enough to notice when I was falling apart, and that it was the one person I could never trust completely.

We sat in silence—me in a sort of numb, rattled stupor. And Savino leaned back in his armchair, regarding the tulip glasses thoughtfully, brow furrowed. Until he nodded, as if something had been decided, and rose to his feet.

"I've got pain-killers, Pia," he said, "whenever you want them. Think about it."

I did think about it. I was quiet on the car ride home, quiet with Massimo and Tonio, and I stayed in the bedroom on my pullout loveseat bed, thinking till I made myself sick with racing thoughts and crippling anxiety.

I thought about olive oil, about the sacred depravity. I thought about how oil meant power, and how Savino Vitelli was testament to that—he was untouchable, ancient, godlike, and olive oil had made him that way, much as it had made Odysseus something more than a mere mortal. It elevated.

And I wondered, if I let it, if olive oil would do the same for me.

iii.

I woke up a while later, without even realizing I'd fallen asleep. Evening light filtered through the drapes, beams of golden-orange hitting the opposite wall, lighting up dancing dust motes in the middle. I stared at the ceiling.

I knew what my uncle was doing, and I wanted to trust him, I wanted him to guide me and lead me and provide some semblance of the parental care I'd lost. It was intoxicating, the pictures he painted—power and respect, stability. How must it feel, to have an army of people supporting you?

I wasn't in that army. And they'd never support me—they'd support Savino, and Valentino, and the fucking family business.

That army had killed my parents. It could kill me. It could kill Cristine, or Carlo, or Vince—and if Sabine took my side and helped me keep the kids down in Augusta, they could make her disappear, too. They could kill Lorel and Massimo and even Tonio, and just like Mario Mansi, they would eventually forget about their fallen brethren—the cursed traitors to the hive-mind cause would fade away, till no one spoke their names, and we all bled oil.

I showered. I changed into clean clothes—sweatpants and a sweater, the warmest socks I could scavenge from my piles of clean and semi-clean laundry. Then I went to find Massimo.

The living room and kitchen were empty; Tonio didn't occupy his usual reading chair by the window. The apartment was quiet. I wandered back down the hallway and knocked on my cousin's bedroom door.

"Yeah," came his voice.

I'd never been in Massimo's room. It looked like the sort of place you wouldn't live full-time, but only as a guest: sparse and orderly, impersonal. There was a sepia canvas of the Manhattan skyline above his bed, the sort you'd find in a hotel room. A heaping pile of laundry stood at the foot of his dresser, and an ironing board was set up by the window.

Massimo was cross-legged on his bed, back to the headboard. He looked up from his computer when I entered. "Hey. Is everything alright?"

I rubbed a hand down my face. "Huh. Maybe. No." He raised his eyebrows. I stood in the doorway, wet hair dripping on my shoulders, and blinked across at the window. "Savino is...."

"...a piece of work?"

"Is he human?"

"I don't know," said Massimo. "I saw him sneeze, once."

"Wow."

"Yeah."

"He's obsessed," I said. "But...it isn't repulsive, like when you know someone who's deep in something they probably shouldn't be. Like Betta"—he nodded—"she shouldn't be doing half the stuff she's doing, running around the city like that, and everyone knows it, and we're worried about her. But with Savino, it's infectious. You *want* it, whatever he has. It almost makes sense."

"He's charismatic."

"How does he do it?"

"He doesn't have a conscience."

I didn't think that was true. Savino was human and he had a conscience, but he had something else too—something none of us possessed, something I was positive he'd gained from olive oil. I wanted it. I was repulsed by it, and I wanted it. Perhaps it was that same unattainability that pushed me over the edge.

"We need to talk. Where's Tonio?"

"He had a meeting or something." Massimo closed his laptop and set it aside, crossed his arms. "What's wrong?"

"I have an idea." I leaned against the doorframe. "Savino told me the new shipment came in already. Johnny and Raul and the guys are picking it up from the warehouses Sunday night."

Massimo's eyes narrowed. He worked his jaw. "Okay. During Dora's engagement party?"

"Midnight." I paused, collected myself. "Valentino's fed-up with Savino, he's on the verge of cutting off the Vitellis. And it's like you said, right? We've got to take this down from the inside."

"Sure," said Massimo. "So what's your plan?"

"It's *your* plan," I said. "We've got about twenty-four hours. How quickly can you make explosives?"

XIV

Grenade

i.

Fortuna's campus was nearly deserted. If there were teachers and faculty planning for the start of semester next week, they were locked up tight in their offices, far from the thickening night and dropping temperatures. We only saw a couple students as Massimo and I navigated our way across campus.

"If anyone asks," he said, "I'm Burnett's TA, you're a Learning Assistant, we're testing labs for the semester."

"Can I ask you something?" My coat was zipped to my chin, hands deep in my pockets. "I have lab access because of you. Because you got me into the class. Did you know?"

"What?"

"Before Christmas, you wanted to get into a lab and blow up the warehouses. Were you already planning this, when you gave me Burnett's business card? Last summer?"

Massimo shrugged. "Loosely. But"—he glanced at me—"I did think you'd enjoy it. It wasn't just about...."

"Okay." I didn't want to know, I didn't want to be disappointed.

The lab building came into view, dark with spiderwebbed windows, hunkering low to the ground like a pouncing animal.

"What are we gonna tell Lorel?" he said.

"We aren't."

"Pia." He stopped outside the door—I fumbled in my bag for the keycard. "If we do this, Savino and Valentino will think it's the Scarpacis. Lorel, and Matty, they'll get in trouble. They could be arrested if the Vitellis don't get to them first."

"They won't be," I said. I slid my card—the keypad blinked green, and the big metal door clicked. I dragged it open. "They've got alibis," I lied.

"What alibis?"

"It'll be New Years Eve, they'll all be gone." Maybe I was lying outright to Massimo, but did it count as lying to Lorel if I simply didn't tell her?

I had to act fast. Or else I'd think too hard about it—I'd change my mind. And this would continue for years to come, until I turned into Massimo with his halfhearted attempts at arson and espionage, milking my hurt and trauma, drawing out the drama until it made me sick.

The basic structure of a pipe bomb is something like this—a tube of specific strength, a method of increasing inner pressure proportional to and eventually exceeding that of the pipe's walls, and a timer. It was simple. But Massimo had been thinking about this for a long time, and he had other ideas.

"Calcium oxide," he said. "Quicklime." He rummaged around on the laboratory shelves until he found what he was looking for—a jar of chalky white chunks. "It's sometimes used as a food preservative, I figured she'd have it."

"Isn't quicklime—?"

"Supposedly used to ignite Greek Fire. Yeah. You add water, it's an exothermic reaction—you know military MREs, they've got portable heating sources, it's sometimes used for stuff like that. But an increase in pressure and temperature is what we're aiming at." He spilled the contents of his backpack on the lab bench—dented pipes with caps on either end, matches, an assortment of tools and wires. He slipped his computer out of its case and plugged it into an outlet.

"We're making Greek Fire. I thought this was..." I picked up a tube. "Pipe bombs. Time bombs."

"We're not making Greek Fire, but we're using the quicklime to ignite the pipe bomb. Look." He held up a pipette. "At a certain level of hydration, calcium oxide can reach a temperature above five-hundred Fahrenheit. We need to get to something like four-hundred. Olive oil generally hits its flash point above four-thirty—"

"But this isn't refined," I said. I thought about the cloudy, opaque liquid. "It'll hit its smoke point a lot quicker. At a lower temp."

Massimo pointed at me like a proud teacher. "Exactly. We just need to add enough water, over a period of time, so that the quicklime builds up enough pressure that it'll burst the pipe, and also expel enough heat that the olive oil nearby will hit its flash point. That'll set off a chain reaction."

"Wouldn't it be easier to just start a normal fire?"

"We couldn't control the timing. Not at all three spots—Savino's got three warehouses, the fires need to start all at the same time, if it doesn't they'll sound the alarm after the first explosion and they might rescue the oil too soon at the other points. I'll label the bombs, time them twenty minutes apart, and we'll plant them in that order;

they'll all go off around the same time. And if we do it like this, Savino can't hide the fact that he stored oil there. That'll start an investigation."

"He could just pay off the guys."

"Not if Valentino stops working with him. The Vitellis can't come back from this."

It was captivating to watch him work. Massimo gave me busy jobs—fill these with DI water, turn on that vent, hold this while I seal the top—but I spent hours slumped on a stool at the end of the lab bench as night crept into morning and Massimo keep his head down. It was like when he drank too much and got too deep into my homework problems, how he became emotionally invested in calculating the electric potential of a circuit. He jotted calculations on a notepad, looked up equations, and his fingers moved over the materials with familiarity, almost as if he'd done this before, or he'd thought about it so often that the movements seemed rehearsed.

"It's like you know what you're doing," I said at one point, watching him expand a formula across a second sheet of scratch paper, then swivel and type it in to a spreadsheet on his computer.

"Well." He looked up, shrugged. "I am a chemist."

"Nah, you just went to a good school."

"Who said that? Was that Betta?"

"Last summer, yeah." It felt like so long ago. It felt like years had passed since I'd come to New York, but only days since Mamma and Papa had died. "Why *do* you hate Columbia?"

He set down his pen and blinked up at me, eyes tired. "I don't hate it," he said. "I hate…that I went there. I didn't want to go."

"You didn't want to go to college?"

"I didn't want to go to college *there*. I wanted to go out-of-state, there was a small private school out west, they offered me a full ride. Not for academics, for soccer—they were desperate, I think. I wasn't that good. But my parents wanted to keep me in New York." He frowned. "Savino too, probably. Half the shit my parents pull, it's because Savino told them to do it, or he suggested it and they decided it was their idea to start with. Like your aunt, you know?"

"Yeah." Boy, did I know.

"Anyway." Massimo put his head back down, picked up the pen and added a few marks. "I was seventeen, I wasn't an adult, I couldn't just leave without their consent. So they sent me to Columbia."

"Would you have left, if you could? If you'd been a year older?"

His pen paused on the paper. "I like to think that I would," he said, brow furrowed. "But I don't know."

I thought Massimo was bulletproof until he had something to lose, and until he was on the brink of losing it. Then I realized that the stolid demeanor was a facade built up to hide an interior like dragonfly wings—beautiful yet delicate, easily crushed. He knew he was tight-rope walking his way through life, living in the shadowy regions between our family and the world beyond.

But he was alive when he was moving. When I saw him acting, lighting fires and connecting wires, my cousin was a different person. I think it was this: the overwhelming yet fleeting idea that he could flip the switch and make everything right. He was drunk on it. And that was when Massimo was most powerful, was when he was gripped with this drunken sense of control. It was sporadic and toxic and effective.

He finished around four in the morning, with six pipe bombs laid out side-by-side on the lab bench. Two for each warehouse; they were labeled with tape and marker. Massimo wandered off to find a cardboard box while I inspected his work—the sealed metal caps on either end of the tubes, the wire pins that, when removed, would start the water release until finally the pressure built up to an explosion.

Massimo came back with the box. We used wads of paper towel to cradle the pipe bombs, then he packed up his equipment and we cleaned the lab top to bottom. Quicklime dust went down the drain (probably not correct lab protocol, but who was watching?); I wiped the lab benches and returned the chemicals to approximately the same positions they'd been in before.

Campus was dark and truly deserted this early in the day. And cold. We tried to walk as inconspicuously as possible, with our hefty backpacks and cardboard box full of bombs.

Massimo stashed the box in the back of his Lexus and cranked up the heater. We sat in his car in the empty parking lot, slowly thawing. I was shellshocked and a bit numb, yet at the same time a thrill hummed through my body—I was doing something, and it was insane, and I never planned any of the shit that happened to me, but just this once I'd taken the reins and I refused to think about it. Or the consequences. Some things, I thought, just had to be done—and maybe that was a bad philosophy, maybe that was what had gotten Massimo into trouble so many times, but I sensed that this was different. Something had changed. We weren't holding back.

"I marked his warehouses on the map," said Massimo. He switched on the headlights and put the car in drive. "The places they store the oil, I marked them on the map where we were looking at the drop-off point in Montauk. It's back at the apartment."

"Alright." We were doing this. It was happening. *Tonight.*

"And we can't take my car."

"Why not?"

He pulled out onto the road, took off like a shot into the dark. "It's too recognizable. We can't take the box on public transit, that's suspicious even for New York, but we can take Tonio's car."

I narrowed my eyes. "He's got a green convertible. That's pretty recognizable."

"Oh, no. His other car."

"He has *two*?"

"Yeah. The Mercedes is the one he uses most often, but he's got a second car stashed away in a garage."

"Why on earth does *Tonio* need *two cars*?"

"Because sometimes, Savino has him put the Mercedes away for a while, if we need to lay low. That's the idea, is to have a pretty recognizable vehicle—people give a description to the cops, they're looking out for that vehicle, meanwhile Tonio's using the Porsche—"

"Of course it's a Porsche." That was something I'd never get used to: rich people and their stupid fancy cars. "Where is it?"

"We've got a rented spot in the garage around back of the apartment."

Tonio was asleep when we kicked in his bedroom door. He was facedown and shirtless under a pile of blankets, completely dead to the world until the door slammed against the wall and his head jerked up.

"GAWD Massimo." He rolled over and squinted against the hallway light. "And Marzano. To what do I owe this..." He trailed off—shook his head, sat up on his elbows and glared at us. "*God.*"

"Hi, Tonio, good morning," said Massimo. He flicked on the light switch, cruelly.

"No," said Tonio. "What time is it?"

"It's almost five," I said.

"Almost five, fantastic. So the insomniacs have returned." He combed his fingers through his hair, but without its usual load of gel, it sprang back in sleep-crimped waves. He grimaced. "What have you maniacs been up to?"

"Uh," said Massimo.

"We made bombs," I said.

Tonio stared at the two of us, framed in the doorway. I couldn't tell whether he wasn't processing, or if he was genuinely distraught and had no words to articulate his disappointment. It was a surprisingly satisfying reaction; I hadn't expected to find it so thrilling. He popped his jaw and sat up against the headboard. Then he fixed Massimo with an approving nod. "That's...creative. Like cathartic arts-and-crafts, I guess. You know, Marzano, when other people can't sleep, they normally just take drugs or hit the town or...read a fucking book."

"We need your car," said Massimo.

"What, did you wreck yours again?"

269

I glanced at Massimo, who shrugged. "That was one time, years ago. No, I didn't wreck it, I just need your keys."

Tonio scratched his jaw. "May I ask why?"

"We're gonna go plant pipe bombs in our uncle's warehouses," I said. "Blow up his olive oil. Then we're gonna get coffee."

"A lot of coffee," said Massimo, who was brain-dead after a night of bomb-building and math.

Tonio stared at me. I stared back. There was something wary and guarded in his eyes, but maybe he was tired, and I was tired, and I was misinterpreting whatever he was thinking. "Alright," he said at last. "I could go for an espresso. Get out so I can get dressed."

"You don't have to come," said Massimo, hands in his pockets. "We'll just take the keys—"

"Oh, I'm not missing this."

Tonio and I stood out front of the apartment in the dark while Massimo pulled the car around. I didn't know how he'd found the time to iron his slacks, but here they were, perfectly pressed at the crease. He flipped up the collar of his overcoat as a gust of wind crept down the street.

"Was this your idea?" he asked.

I set my jaw and prepared to defend myself. "Yeah."

"So, what about the Scarpacis? You don't think your little roommate will get in trouble for this? I assume you've thought about that."

"Yeah. I have. I told Massimo they'll be out of town."

Tonio looked down at me. "But?"

I didn't know why I was telling him this. "You know Massimo. He likes to be the hero, knight in shining armor, a martyr. He doesn't want other people taking risks, he'd rather suffer for all the mistakes in the world."

Tonio nodded acknowledgment. "That's accurate. And?"

"It doesn't matter what we tell him, I think Savino will know. The truth." I crossed my arms against the cold. The sky was gray; it was never completely black in the city, and I never saw the stars. I missed that. I missed the night sky in place of this featureless charcoal dome.

"Let me get this straight." Tonio cleared his throat. "You're gonna let the Vitellis know that it was you who blew up their warehouses, not Massimo, not the Scarpacis. You're going to confess to Savino?" He watched my face, waited, but I didn't speak—I didn't have to, he'd said it all. "Do you have a death wish, Marzano?"

"Why do you care?"

ABIGAIL C. EDWARDS

"Again, morbid fascination with your spiral into self-destruction. I'm just…perplexed. Almost to silence. But not quite. I think there are better alternatives, surely." His eyes followed a flattened paper bag as it flipped down the street. "What's the point?"

"When Massimo does this sort of thing, he goes halfway. He doesn't really have anything on the line. But I've got to take care of the kids, and I can't do that while the family business is alive—Savino's got guys in Augusta, I'm sure. Marco Vitelli might have people too. I've got to get them out of it."

"So…you're putting a target on your own back. You destroy the family business, you still have to reckon with the Vitellis and my brothers."

"That was always going to be the case."

"Not before. Before, they wouldn't have known you were directly responsible for their downfall. Can you imagine standing in the full force of Savino's rage? Are you prepared for that?"

I ground my back teeth together. I didn't really want to think about the technicalities, I just wanted to do it and think about it afterwards, like Massimo burning down a warehouse, like pulling a pin and throwing the grenade. "There's no good way to do it. Someone has to be the scapegoat. And I'm not putting that on the Scarpacis, or Massimo, or Lorel."

Tonio nodded. I didn't know that he understood, but at least he wasn't arguing. "When are you leaving?"

"I don't know. Maybe tonight. Maybe tomorrow. But not before the bombs go off, because I need to see this through."

"*How* are you leaving?"

"I don't know. Maybe the bus." I didn't know the bus system that well, but I assumed there was a Greyhound station nearby, and that should be able to get me out of New York at least. Could Savino track a bus? Could he get to Augusta before I did?

"How about a car?"

I looked at him. "I don't…"

"How about a Mercedes convertible furnished with all seven movements of Holst's *Planets*?"

I narrowed my eyes. "Are you trying to give me your car?"

He narrowed his eyes right back at me. "Don't flatter yourself, it's an extended loan, I'll get it back at some point. Not like it's actually mine, anyway—in my name, sure, but it's all your uncle's money, dirty mafia money. It's funny, it's almost as if Savino married the entire Salone family when he got with Ida. My brothers grovel at his feet, Achille's like a dog, he got a couple fancy cars to appease the youngest child." He scratched his jaw. "It's disgusting, isn't it?"

"Yep." I scuffed my shoes on the curb. The exhaustion was creeping up to me now, but I still had hours to go before sleep. "Do you ever look at your life and just…"

"Yes."

I dragged a hand down my face as if I could wipe the sleep away, wake up my senses. "My parents wouldn't know who they were looking at."

Tonio didn't say anything. He watched in the distance as headlights pulled around the side of the building, crawling towards us—a low navy-blue car, sleek and soundless.

"Sorry. I'm tired."

Tonio shook his head. "We're cynical because we know the world. If we were optimists, we'd also be idiots."

I thought about that. I pictured Lorel. "Innocence and idiocy aren't the same thing. Sometimes it's brave. Sometimes it's just how a person is."

"So, 'We are all in the gutter, but some of us are looking at the stars'?" I raised an eyebrow; he elaborated. "Oscar Wilde."

I liked that. "It's not wrong to look at the stars." But it also wasn't some failing of will or fall from grace that kept my eyes fixed to the ground. I'd just been down here in the gutter long enough to know to watch my step.

I sat in the back of the car, rattled around as we wove through dark and neon-streaked streets. I kept one hand on the box beside me, which felt a lot like flirting with death—instinct said to stay far away, to slide to the opposite side of the car.

From the driver's seat, Tonio pulled a left. "Isn't it funny," he said. His face was lit on the side by green neon—skull-like, haunted—then we took another turn and he was cast into shadow. "Isn't it odd, where a night will take you?"

Massimo sighed. But I sat in silence and absorbed the tension. Looking back, it felt like a fever dream; none of us were thinking straight, and the atmosphere hung heavy, invigorating and terrifying. It smelled like quicklime the faintly of cigarette smoke. It smelled like the leather interior of a terribly expensive car and Massimo's alcohol-breath and the near-imperceptible aroma lingering on my hands—olive oil, fresh-cut-grass, bitter notes in the back of my throat.

It smelled like desperation.

Not so odd, then, that we'd painted this chaotic scene. When you've lost so much, I think you come to a point in life where you'll do anything—anything at all—to preserve what you have left.

The warehouses were all out in the Bronx area. The doors were padlocked, but apparently we didn't have to worry about cameras or alarms. "You build up an old warehouse like Fort Knox," Tonio explained, "people start asking questions, that's what Raul says."

We parked around back, in front of the roll-up door. Massimo jimmied it open with some tools he'd brought in his backpack.

Tonio waited in the car while Massimo and I each took a bomb from the cardboard box and slipped in through the gaping doorway. The warehouse was dark, temperature-controlled for the wood-slatted crates stacked against one wall.

"Here." He flipped the bomb over and ran his hand down the pipe till he found the trip wire. He held it up to the headlights. "One at each end of the warehouse, that way if one of them malfunctions, we have backup. Hide yours behind the crates. Then pull out the wire, like a grenade pin."

He disappeared into the dark.

I stood near the crates. It smelled like wood and straw, dust and cool night air. And the faintest tinge of something sweet and bitter, a little fruity and a little medicinal. I crouched and slipped the pipe bomb behind the stack. My face was close to the crates, and I thought about the oil in Savino's office. I thought about the fruit of ancient tradition, oil like blood, and suddenly I realized that if olive oil was sacred, then this was sacrilegious.

I pulled the pin. I backed up and out of the warehouse, into the dimmed orange headlights of the Porsche, and a cloud of exhaust, thick in the frozen air. Against the glare, Tonio watched me from behind the wheel.

Massimo stepped out of the warehouse. In the light, his face was hollowed and intense, and so tired he looked sick. I wondered if I looked the same way.

He handed me his tools and turned to pull down the door.

"Two more," I said.

"Yeah." He blinked at the sky.

"You alright?"

"Yeah." Massimo looked at me, eyes unfocused. "You?"

"Oh." I stuck my hands in my pockets. The nerves had gone, and now I just felt terrifically numb and fatigued. "I'm fantastic."

He started back to the car. I followed. "You know, Pia"—he opened the back door for me, swung into the passenger's seat—"Savino thinks he's got you figured out."

"Oh, has he got her number?" said Tonio. He threw the car into reverse and sped out of there and grinned at me in the rearview mirror. Like we shared some joke—like my uncle couldn't possibly unravel these secrets and brittle facades.

"He thinks he does," said Massimo. "Which means he won't see it coming, he wouldn't think she'd do something like this."

I wasn't so sure. It seemed to me that Savino knew more than he let on—and he knew when people were holding out on him, too. It seemed that nothing was a mystery to our uncle, at least not for long.

273

ii.

Two hours later, the morning rush found us at a cafe on the edge of Washington Heights. Massimo and I had plowed through a pile of breakfast food, Tonio had watched us while sipping what he proclaimed to be the city's worst espresso, and now Massimo was nursing a cup of coffee, and Tonio and I were smoking; he'd offered me a smoke, and I'd figured—what the hell, I was about to blow up my family's business and throw my life into deeper chaos, why the hell *not* have a cigarette with breakfast. Smoke climbed up from the porch, from our little metal table slick with condensation, and into the frigid morning air.

Tonio tapped out his ash. "What are you telling Lorel?" he asked Massimo.

Massimo cast him a quick, almost irritated glance. "I don't know. Nothing. If it works, it works, and we'll get out of here."

"Oh, just like that? Is she planning on leaving?"

"She wants to finish school," I said.

Massimo frowned at the sidewalk. "I don't know what she'll do."

"So you'll tell her nothing," Tonio summarized. He turned to me. "What about you, Marzano? You gonna sort out anything with the Scarpacis? Blow their casino sky-high?"

"Screw you, Tonio." I shut my eyes and exhaled—the light hurt, I was too tired for a morning like this. It had felt wrong when dawn broke over the city, wrong that the world should cast light on our transgressions. Everything this year had happened at night, under cover of darkness. "*Fanculo.*"

"Yes, where'd you learn that word, anyway? Achille?"

"My aunt. Sabine." She'd said it under her breath—that, and other less savory things, words I only knew were bad words because of the furtive glances she'd given me after uttering them. *Don't tell your Mamma, Pia—hey,* cara, *don't say that, don't repeat it in front of Vinny, yeah?* She was the only one who called Vince that.

"Is your Italian really that bad?" Tonio took a long drag on his cigarette.

"Yep." I picked at a crust of toast on my tray.

"Say something."

Massimo rubbed a hand down his face. "Leave it, Tonio."

"What? I only want to be judgmental of her language skills." Tonio shook his head. "This man, always depriving me of wholesome entertainment."

I checked my phone. No missed calls, but there was an alert reminding me about Mass in a couple hours. "How long?" I asked Massimo.

He checked his watch; he'd set it on a timer for the pipe bombs. "Fourteen hours, forty minutes, unless something goes wrong."

274

Lots of things could go wrong, and it would be ten o'clock tonight when the bombs went off. I didn't know if I could wait that long. It had made sense, seeing how the whole family would be at Dora's engagement party and far away from the warehouses, at least until midnight when Savino had his guys picking up the oil. But now we had to sit through the whole day, try to sleep, try to act like doomsday wasn't on the horizon.

Back at the apartment, we showered and dressed. Then we piled into the Mercedes—Massimo was too tired to drive—to meet the family at church.

St. Thomas Aquinas was packed for New Year's Eve. Tonio parked down the street and we walked to the building, passing a cluster of outrageously expensive cars I vaguely recognized, sauntering in right before the processional hymn. Holy water, sign of the cross. We hurried down the center aisle as the choir started, right up to the front like pretentious tasteless bastards. As if donating one baptismal font meant our family perpetually owned the front pews.

I saw the backs of Savino's and Ida's heads, seated up front. Luca sat at the end of the pew, his hair a shiny gelled helmet, staring fixedly ahead at the altar. Beside them, Ella and Anna wriggled around, sandwiched between their parents and the Di Natales. Massimo split off to sit with his parents at the opposite end of the pew from Savino. I saw him lean over, kiss his mother. Gio looped his arm around Nicole to slap his son's shoulder.

Tonio threw himself down in the pew beside Achille, who leaned over and started whispering. Tonio swatted him away and dropped onto the kneeler. And because I didn't want to sit with Savino or Luca, or—God forbid—Dora, who was shoulder-to-shoulder with Francesco the next pew up from the Salones and trying to catch my eye—I took the spot beside Tonio, and elected to ignore Achille with his knuckle tattoos and open stare.

Up front, Massimo yawned.

Savino looked back over his shoulder. He spotted me, nodded.

I nodded back. *I'm going to blow up your warehouses.*

Throughout the first half of Mass, my mind refused to focus. I didn't pay attention to the readings, the responses were all automatic, and my attention kept slipping away to sleep, to time bombs, to the thick smell of dense, peppery olive oil. That thing about sweating like a sinner in church—I'd always thought it was a stupid phrase, but maybe some of us were more sinner than others. And maybe I'd reached that point, because my mind refused to capture anything the priest was saying, and even though the church was cold, I felt feverish.

Everyone knew. Everyone. This family, the priest and deacons, God and his angels and all the saints depicted on the walls in stained glass permanence. All the saints I carried on this chain around my neck. Was it really wrong, what we were doing? We were saving some people by destroying others, and there was argument there for justification. Yet I heard Savino's voice in my head as I followed that train of thought—*Is it wrong? Well, it's illegal—but is it wrong?* And Sabine: *Well, they're still going to church, right? And they aren't hurting anyone?*

There's always room for justification. But when you start to heap wrong atop wrong atop injustice, the lines blur and fade, and a space of moral gray clouds the playing field.

Communion. Luca got up, a few of the Di Natale kids—Betta, and Giovani in an arm-sling and cast—Dora and Francesco.

Massimo stayed.

And when it got back to our pew—as the other end of the aisle was emptying into the Communion line—I didn't budge.

And Tonio glanced at me under my mantilla. It wasn't an eyebrow-raised query, or even a vaguely judgmental stare. He already knew.

I was cold inside. I felt numb. I could feel myself falling, slipping further away with every passing moment from the person Mamma and Papa had known, and knowing they were watching me in this moment as I spiraled into a fall from grace, was the most distressing part of all.

Tonio held out his hand.

Before I could think, I took it. It was perhaps one of the dumber things I'd done up to this point.

"Your fingers are sweaty," he whispered.

"Asshole," I whispered back.

I slipped out at the end of Mass. I'd noticed Betta trying to get my attention, but I didn't want to stay and talk; I booked it after the recessional hymn and I waited out by the car for Massimo and Tonio. When they eventually made it out of the church, we got the hell out of there and made for the apartment, where Massimo and I promptly collapsed and slept for the first time in over twenty-four hours. I didn't even bother changing out of my church clothes—something I regretted later when I finally woke and realized I'd have to iron my dress before the party.

I stumbled out of my room at four in the afternoon. Massimo's bedroom door was still shut, but I found Tonio reading on the couch.

"What time's the party?" I croaked.

He looked up from his book, stared at me for a long moment. His lips twitched. "I know it's considered rude to comment on people's appearances, but—"

"Then don't." I turned and headed back down the hallway.

"We're leaving at six," he called after me.

I showered. I stood under the torrent of unnecessarily scalding water until I couldn't feel my face. Everyone always wants thick hair until they realize it comes with the burden of excessive volumes of shampoo and conditioner—it took me until the room was full of steam before I'd shaved and sufficiently washed the grime of the city off me.

Then I stepped out of the shower and switched on the fan. My dress was crumpled on the floor. I leaned my elbows on the sink and stared into the mirror as it cleared.

A blur of a face looked back at me, a mop of wet black hair—and tired eyes emerged, and hollows and shadows I barely recognized, only they reminded me of Savino. I rubbed a hand over my face, as if I could erase them.

Massimo was using his iron. I checked my phone while I waited, and was unsurprised to find a missed call. I didn't recognize the number. They'd left a lengthy voicemail.

"Oh hey, Pia, it's Kyle from Burnett's lab, what's up. So listen, I don't know if you're back in town or whatever—I forget, if you're a senior? Okay, anyway. If you remember I told you about those guys I'm working with next year, the guys with like all the organic farm connections and shit, I was talking to them over break, I actually ordered a bunch of seeds off them—like those pomegranates my buddy in New Jersey deals with, and like some really great radicchio varieties and shit. Well I was talking to them and they said—they were telling me about these real traditional olive orchards they've got out in Cali. Small producers, but they've got this real quality stuff—they sort of do equal parts olive production and agriculture analysis. Anyway, they're way understaffed, and I was like *whoa*, I know this Italian chick who's into food. Like, you. So, I don't know, they said they've got these rolling applications for positions out there, some temporary harvesting stuff, some long-term production jobs. I don't know if you're into olives or anything, but you're Italian, so like, I figure you probably grew up with the real deal. Uh, anyway. Sorry if that's a stereotype. I dunno. I can email you their contact info, or you can call me back—whatevs. Maybe I'll see you around campus. Uh, happy New Year. 'Kay, *ciao*. Oh damn is that another stereotype—" The message ended.

If it hadn't been Kyle, I might have thought he knew more about me than he was letting on. But he was obsessed with agriculture and the Italian thing, so it made sense.

I shouted down the hall. "Massimo, you done?"

"Almost. Uh, actually, Tonio's doing his shirt, sorry."

"You can fight me for it, Marzano, but I'll win."

I ignored him. I shut my bedroom door, sat in one of Tonio's big expensive armchairs, and called Lorel.

"Hi Pia! How are you doing?"

"Um. Fine." I pulled my knees up to my chest. "We're doing something tonight."

"There's a party, right? Massimo mentioned that. Like, your cousin or someone...? Is getting married?" I didn't respond. After a second, she seemed to catch on. "Oh. You mean, something else is happening. You're *doing* something. God, Pia." I could imagine her on the other line, face buried in her hands, cringing at the though of my next great idea. "Don't do anything stupid, please. Or rash."

"I don't really do rash things. You know that."

"Actually, you do. You're very careful and calculated until you have a burst of insanity, and it doesn't happen often, but I've seen you do it. So please tell me you aren't feeling insane."

"It's a little insane," I admitted.

"Oh, God. What are you doing? Are you safe?"

No, I thought. "Look, we're just...uh. I made some bombs—"

That definitely hadn't been the right things to say. "You WHAT? You made—"

"Well, Massimo and I, we made bombs." I was speaking quickly now. "Time bombs, pipe bombs, we put them in our family's warehouses with the oil, they'll go off tonight and no one will get hurt, but I thought you should know. I wanted you to know that your family won't get in trouble, either—I've got that under control, you're safe."

There was a pause. "Uh. Pia. I think...you should know that Matty's sitting right next to me, he just heard all that."

Matty's voice erupted in the background. "HE MADE *BOMBS*? The fu—"

"No one will get hurt," I repeated. "Tell him that. It was my idea, not Massimo's, but we've got to end this, Lorel—the kids are gonna get in trouble, I can't let anything happen to them. You know Vince, he can't live this life."

"I know. I know, Pia—I just...*bombs?*"

"I convinced him to do it, and—you know, he's really smart, Lorel, he stayed up all night doing it, he had calculations and everything, it was very impressive."

"Yeah, I know he's a genius. Ugh. He probably did it really elegantly too, didn't he?"

"All the elegance in the world."

"Shit. Okay. Well, I'm gonna hang up so I can call my stupid beautiful arsonist boyfriend and make sure he isn't planning something extra stupid."

"Bye, Lorel." And, louder: "BYE MATTY."

"He isn't talking to you. Okay, *bye.*"

A moment later, Massimo's phone rang from across the apartment.

Tonio stuck his head into the room. "The ironing board is now available."

I squinted at him, craned my neck to see around the door. "Is that a tux?"

He'd forgone his usual sports coat for an actual tuxedo and black tie. "Yes, it's a tux. Good eye."

"You're wearing *that*?" I had to see what Massimo was wearing, but I was pretty sure I'd underestimated the formality of this thing. By a long shot.

"Yes, I am. Why, are you wearing *that*?" He nodded at the crumpled dress balled up on my bed so that it barely resembled a dress at all. He knew well enough what it was, though; I'd only brought one to New York, and I wore the same black, quarter-sleeved dress every Sunday to church, with varying degrees of layers added over the top.

"Yeah."

"Well, it's good to know Achille won't be the most underdressed person at a party, for once."

I scowled. "Do I look like I'm made of money?"

He held up a finger, raised his eyebrows in a way that told me there was a lecture on the horizon. "That is an opportunity for me to say something very rude and potentially hurtful, so I hope you appreciate this moment. Of me refraining. And this thing is a formal, Marzano—have you even *been* to an engagement party?"

"Have *you*?"

"Pretty much every year, yeah. Last spring it was someone named Loreta"—he ticked it off on his fingers—"I think she's a Di Natale, she married this chump from Jersey, but he had a lot of money, so I guess that counts for something, apparently. And, let's see, before that it was my brother Raul, and Cassie, and Norma and Marco Biasi, and who knows who's next. You'd be surprised, how quick people in this family are with engagement rings and frankly very *forward* proposals. Or maybe you *would* know."

"Tonio, I swear—"

"I'm leaving." He disappeared back into the hallway.

iii.

For some reason I'd assumed the party would be at the Vitelli house. That was where all the family dinners had been, that was the only place I'd seen everyone gathered. But Mo and Serafina Di Natale had rented out a ballroom and banquet hall in Brooklyn; we passed the Vitelli house to get there, but the sidewalk usually lined with BMWs was empty, and the windows were dark.

I'd mentally prepared myself for the whole family being there, but I hadn't really considered that Dora and her parents would have their friends and coworkers, and for some reason a bunch of Savino's guys might show up, and other people who seemed terribly important yet not related to the Di Natales or the Vitellis: men with shady eyes and dark suits, women with loads of jewelry and heavy accents.

There was a band composed of a keyboardist and an old man on accordion. Tables lined the back wall, heaped with food brought in from a local Italian restaurant—I'd heard Nicole talking about it during the mall excursion, "The nice family from Lucca, beautiful family, they make everything from scratch"—the heaping *antipasto* and trays of roasted vegetables, a whole table just for *apéritifs*. An orderly line of candlesticks marched down the tables, between platters of *affettati* and pastas, but the candlelight was unnecessary: chandeliers glared overhead, much too bright in my opinion. I felt hungover, and the insane clamor instantly froze me in my tracks on the threshold.

A sea of evening dresses and expensive-cut suits, lazy strains of accordion mingling with loud conversation—voices trying to be heard over voices, a rising cascade of shouting—piercing laughs, meaningful eye contact. A hoard of bodies stood between the door and the food. But I wasn't hungry anymore, I just felt sick.

I was in my black dress (freshly, if badly, ironed) with leggings and heeled boots. I'd pulled back my hair into something that looked like I'd put in a bit of effort. I'd even worn earrings. But, looking back, the fact that I didn't look like I belonged in this terrific crush of opulence was probably the weakest factor contributing to my discomfort.

"What a delightful turnout," said Tonio, who managed to look mildly inconvenienced and terribly judgmental at the same time. "I find it difficult to believe that *all* these people showed up because they love Norma."

Massimo turned to him slowly. "This isn't about Norma. She married Marco two years ago."

"Huh," said Tonio.

"Do you even know who the party's for?" I asked.

"Someone or other's getting the ball and chain, is that right?"

Massimo shook his head in disbelief. "It's Dora. My cousin Dora. Tonio, we talked about this—"

"Well. God bless her soul."

"Massimo!" Nicole waded towards us through the crowd, marching with surprising stability in a pair of very tall, very narrow heels. She dragged Giovani and Betta behind her. "You're late!" She shouted to be heard over the music. She fussed over Massimo's coat and tie, licked her thumb and rubbed some invisible smudge off his face—he flinched. "Hey, I want a picture with you and Giovani and Betta, and Norma—she's here, she's been here for hours, come on, I want a picture for the hallway—"

Betta snuck up beside me, barely tucked into a tight red dress. "Hey, Pia—"

Tonio had disappeared. I hadn't seen him leave.

I was cornered, I felt an argument breaking out between Nicole and Massimo—"Hey, why are you late? You knew what time the party started, and Dora's your cousin, don't you care about her? You care about her feelings?"—and Betta was breathing down my neck.

"I have to go to the bathroom." I brushed her off.

"Hey, don't—"

She seemed upset, maybe even angry, but I couldn't deal with that right now. I dove into the crowd with no idea where to find the restroom, not even needing to use it, simply propelled by the desire to put as much distance between me and Betta and Nicole as possible.

I didn't know these people. I navigated around them, excusing myself though no one seemed to care. Some blurred faces seemed vaguely recognizable—that was Johnny Moriondo, that might have been one of Dora's sisters—but everyone else seemed painted into the scene. I almost slammed into Ezio Salone, with his brooding murder gaze, but I stepped around him at the last moment. Brushing past coated elbows and elegant swishing skirts, I had something like a flashback to Betta's bad college party: a freezing night, huge bonfire, loads of smoke and the ground shaking beneath my feet. A splitting headache emerged.

I ended up beside the dessert table, across the room from the band. I hadn't found the restroom, but this was easily the least-inhabited area of the room.

The problem with standing alone was that, sooner or later, someone would spot me and make their way over. Where had Tonio gone? I wished I could disappear that easily. I reached to tug at my wrist braces. Realized they weren't there. My forearms ached.

Dora was easy enough to spot in the crowd—everywhere she went, Francesco on her arm, people parted and exclaimed at the lovely couple. She was beaming and radiant in a glittering green cocktail dress with a lacy flower arrangement clipping back her sleek caramel hair. Francesco wore a matching green tie—like a prom couple—and his plastered smile made up for the fact that he could hardly communicate with the people around him.

They were so young. It felt like a tragedy playing out, and I felt sick.

"Hi, Pia, what are you doing back here?"

Oh God, I thought, but when I turned to face the person breaking into my isolation bubble, it was only Oscar.

He grinned and waved from the other side of the dessert table. He'd cleaned up, even slicked back his wild hair into a neat bun. Although, considering that he normally dressed like a homeless student, any normal attire would have been considered a step up.

"I didn't know they made suits that long," I said.

"Yeah." He kicked out a leg to show me the pants hem, which ended an inch too high. "There's this Swedish company that makes tall-people clothes, but I still had to get 'em altered. What're ya doing back here? Gonna blow some stuff up?"

My breath caught in my throat. I looked at Oscar—he smiled—and every muscle in my body tightened.

He bent his long frame and lifted the edge of the tablecloth, revealing a cardboard box stashed beneath the dessert table. Lifted it a bit higher, and a variety of colorful shapes appeared—large primary-colored tubes with fuses and lighters. "New Year's

281

fireworks. We picked them up yesterday, we're gonna set them up in the courtyard later."

"Are those legal?"

He just shrugged, straightened. "I dunno, but I'm setting them off. If I get back in time. Your uncle's got me and Mr. Moriondo working tonight."

I pricked up my ears. "What?"

"Savino's got us working," he said, louder.

"On New Year's Eve?" Tonight? That felt significant.

"Yeah, we just, uh, gotta pick up the truck, do the rounds, get the next shipment down to the guys at the depot." He shrugged again. "You know."

I did know, probably more than he thought. So would it be Oscar who arrived at the warehouses, only to find them in flames? Would he get in trouble?

"Oh," he said, "and Betta's looking for you."

"Yeah, I know."

"Yeah, she seems kinda bent out of shape. Hey, you seen your uncle around?"

"No, sorry." And thank goodness I hadn't. I held a hand to my stomach, suddenly nauseous—the floor bucked. "Hey, Oscar, where's the restroom?"

"It's behind the music, are you okay?"

"I'm fine—"

"Are you sick?"

"I'm alright, I'll see you later."

I left Oscar and the fireworks behind, skirting the edge of the room along the wall until I spotted the hallway behind the stage. I edged behind the musicians and slipped down the hallway.

The ladies 'room smelled like fake vanilla. It was empty. I locked myself in a stall and sat on the edge of the toilet and stayed there as waves of nausea wracked my body.

My arms hurt. My chest hurt. I was thinking too much and suppressing too many thoughts, trying to function while I knew there were pipe tombs ticking down in those warehouses, nestled up against crates of green-gold oil. And I'd gone into this unprepared—I'd worked for so long to stay stable, to create some semblance of security around me and my siblings, and Lorel was right—I'd experienced a moment of insanity and I'd thrown it all away.

I couldn't take it back now. It was out of my hands. Somehow, I'd thought it would be better to have it said and done, but it was worse this way. I couldn't do anything about it, only make sure everyone knew I was responsible for whatever happened, because if I didn't then Lorel and the Scarpacis would get hurt. If we brought down the business, who knew what Savino would do? He might burn the Scarpaci casino to the ground, he might take out hits on Lorel's family. *My* family.

ABIGAIL C. EDWARDS

They were all insane.

And somehow, I had to do it all without Massimo finding out I was doing it. Because if he realized I was planning to incriminate myself—to save Lorel, no less—he'd do something even more insane, he'd get himself killed—Savino *would* drown him in the Sound, I had little doubt about that.

And somehow, I had to do it all and then skip town. And protect the kids. I thought about the black SUV in the IGA parking lot. I thought about my parents' car, crushed like a can, bent around an ancient oak tree. What made me think they couldn't get to the kids before I did? What made me think I had any sort of power here, any hope that this might end remotely well?

I couldn't do anything about it anymore.

It was done. I'd done something insane, I couldn't take it back, and whatever happened tonight, nothing would be the same.

iv.

Later, once I'd calmed down a bit, I returned to the party.

Tonio was standing near the stage, drinking something out of a fancy crystal glass. "Thought you might be in there." He barely looked at me, just raised his eyebrows over the top of his glass.

"What's that supposed to mean?"

"You clearly love parties."

I ignored that. I crossed my arms. "Where were you?" A man nearby bellowed an obnoxious laugh and drowned out my words.

Tonio leaned closer. "Hmm?"

I raised my voice. "Where did you go? You disappeared."

"I had to run an errand."

"You *left*?"

"And then I came back. Obviously." He shrugged. "No harm, no foul—I didn't even know this was Dora's birthday party, remember? Where's our dear Massimo? Drunk again?"

"I don't know. Oh, God—" I turned my back to the room and faced him. Dread settled in the pit of my stomach, awful mounting anticipation like a scene in a horror movie. "Look at me. Look like we're having a serious conversation."

"A serious conversation...with you?"

"Tonio—"

"Metaphysical, or existential? Alright. I think fate is bullshit and providence was invented as a false sense of security."

I narrowed my eyes at him, determined to seem engaged. "Lorel says fate is a poet."

283

"That is *also* bullshit. *We* are the poets and the art we produce is abhorrent. Is that serious enough for you?" Then Tonio's eyes flicked over the top of my head, and the corners of his thin mouth tugged up in a barely-suppressed grin. *Screw him.* "Good Lord, Marzano, do you hear that?" He cupped a hand to his ear, and I wanted to kill him. "Hear that? Wedding bells?"

"Pia!"

Shit. I jumped. Luca Catenacci stood at my shoulder, perfectly groomed to a sickening extent—hair combed and parted with an ass-ton of product, teeth so white they seemed fake. His beautiful face was graced with an earnest smile, and I figured—correctly—that Savino had *not* talked Luca down from his main purpose in life.

"Oh, hi, Luca." I crossed my arms tighter. "Hi."

"Pia, I have not seen you since…Christmas," he said, in faltering English—*Pia* was one of his few words, and about half his communication revolved around my name, anyway. "*Buon Natale.* Uh, you look, uh—"

"Luca, this is Tonio," I said. I had to be truly desperate at that point, to willingly involve Tonio in a conversation, but *desperation* was pretty much the theme of today. "Tonio, say something intriguing."

Tonio switched his glass around and held out a hand to Luca, a self-important smile plastered on his skeleton face. "Tonio Salone, CEO of Nutella. Pleasure."

"Oh my God."

Luca shook his hand, but he'd apparently missed half of what Tonio said. He immediately turned back to me. "Pia, you look, uh, *bellissima*."

It was strange, because under normal circumstances—I had no idea what those might be—I might be completely taken by Luca Catenacci and his beautiful face and charming accent. The problem was that I looked at him and all I could see was my uncle's hand pushing pieces around on a chessboard.

"Thanks," I said. "Uh…you too."

Luca laughed. It was a perfect, charming laugh, and I wanted to punch his stupid perfect teeth out of his face. He looked at me like we'd just shared a good joke, with an actual *twinkle* in his eye. I was having trouble controlling my face at this point. He addressed Tonio again, like I wasn't even standing there. "Pia is, uh, she's *very* nice."

Tonio coughed on his drink. "Ha! Uh." He recovered quickly, casting me a wildly amused glance, addressing Luca with false sincerity. "Yes, very nice. Marzano is the epitome of goodness. Finishing School took her and said—'what are we supposed to do with this? Nothing to work with but perfection, send her away'—"

I stomped on his foot. He shut up.

Luca looked at Tonio, at me, his confusion evident. "Uh, yes." And he drifted away in the crowd.

I turned on Tonio. "Bitch."

"Yet, he's gone. He thinks you're *bellissima,* Marzano. Is your Italian really that bad, or should I translate?" He raised his glass to Luca's retreating back. "That boy is inexplicably besotted with you, for reasons far beyond my comprehension. He looks at you like you're his sun and his moon."

"Tonio, I'm gonna vomit."

He swirled his drink and stared off into the crowd, terribly satisfied. "Have you ever seen a face so weirdly symmetrical? Put our man Luca Catenacci on a poster for...Sicilian cologne. Those genes? With the whole Vitelli-Marzano thing you've got going?" He issued a low whistle. "Unstoppable."

It felt like he was both insulting and complimenting me in the same breath. Neither was good, not right now. "I told Savino to stop with the Luca thing."

Tonio's eyebrows shot up. "You said that to your uncle's face?"

"Yeah, I did."

"Hmm." He sipped his drink. "And how did he take *that?"*

"He said I should talk to Luca about it, I told him it isn't my job to do that—I didn't start this." I shifted on my feet. With every passing moment the partygoers seemed to grow in number, spreading closer towards the walls from the center of the room. Like a multiplying colony on a petri dish.

"Well, I'd hazard a guess you're the only person Savino Vitelli would let talk to him like that." This statement did nothing to reassure me. "Betta's heading this way."

"Great."

Tonio leaned forward and pointed her out to me, wading through the crowd in her tight dress, wobbling a bit in too-high heels—leave it to Betta Di Natale to wear the most outrageously tasteless outfit. Her hair flowed free almost to her waist and kept getting caught up on other people as she pushed her way towards us.

We made eye contact. I turned away. "Where's Massimo?"

"Why, you think he can protect you from his little sister?"

"We need to make sure he isn't doing anything stupid."

"You know, I feel like you really understand your cousin." Tonio pointed with his glass. "Him and Achille are over by the dessert table."

A recipe for disaster. I darted away, hoping I'd lose Betta in the crowd.

I hadn't seen Achille since he'd taken a bullet in the leg, and he looked rough. It seemed like every other time I saw him, he was recovering from some wild injury. He leaned heavily on a crutch, although all evidence of bandages (and maybe a cast?) was hidden beneath his pants leg. His face was a bit puffy, his tattooed fingers were locked in a death-grip around his beer, and he seemed more on edge than usual. Twitching eyelid, twitching jaw. He gesticulated with his bottle and swayed against his crutch.

Massimo leaned against the dessert table, wine glass in hand, and he looked like he was barely tolerating whatever Achille was talking about. He was silhouetted against the candelabra light, idly watching the party-goers, eyes distracted. He didn't seem to notice the growing clump of young women who also occupied the space: vaguely Mediterranean-looking girls with shiny dresses and shiny hair who couldn't hold a candle to Lorel. Half were holding on to Achille's every word—one even laughed dumbly—and the others kept looking at Massimo, as if waiting for him to speak or glance their way. I couldn't tell whether he was purposefully ignoring them, or just oblivious.

I slipped out of the crowd and edged between two of the girls. "Massimo."

He looked up. His eyes were still there, still focused, so I guessed this was at least only his second glass of wine. "What's wrong?"

"Hey, Pia Marzano," Achille interjected. He pointed his beer bottle at me, brow furrowed. "Hey, she can attest to this, she was here when it happened. You remember, right?"

I blinked—glanced at Massimo, who stared blankly back—and shrugged at Achille. "What?"

He shook his head, like I should know this. "I beat up those Scarpaci bastards, in Chinatown, I got this"—he touched a silver scar on his chin—"and they came back for me, didn't they? I recognized that guy who hit me, he was looking for me, but you know what?" Achille nodded to the girl on his left, who seemed faintly unsure, and he tapped his temple. "I remember him too, I've got his face filed away up here. We'll see who gets the bullet next time. That's just how I live—you're a guy like me, you've got people after your head, it comes with the territory, but I get shit done."

Apparently he'd forgotten about me. I poked Massimo's arm, kept my voice low. "Hey, have you talked to Oscar?"

He leaned down to hear me. "Who?"

"Oscar Hely?"

"Who is that? Is he here?"

"He works for Savino, he hangs out at the bakery—he used to walk me to school so I didn't die or something. I was talking to him, he said he's working tonight—"

"Tonight?"

"Yeah, him and Johnny, you know what Johnny does?"

Massimo's fingers tightened on his wineglass. "They've got the trucks."

"Yeah." I was struggling to be heard over the music and thundering voices, while at the same time keep this conversation just between the two of us, not the lingering girls eyeing up Massimo, or—God forbid—Achille. "He said—he's gonna be back by midnight, he's got to set off the fireworks—"

"What, he said that?"

"Yeah, he said that."

"Where's Tonio?"

"Over by the stage."

"Does he know?"

"Hey—hey, Massimo," said Achille. He waved his beer at my cousin. "Hey, Massimo! Hey, you live with my brother, who'd you say has more sway in this family? You know, you see Tonio with his stupid candles and that stupid effing thing he does with his hair—"

Massimo set down his glass. "Achille, I'm not doin 'this—"

"Hey!"

Fingers closed over my arm, yanked. I stumbled, almost twisted my ankle, and slammed into one of Massimo's admirers before regaining my balance and taking back my arm. And taking a step back because Betta was right up in my face. She looked down at me from her great height in her great monstrous heels.

And she was livid. She stuck her finger up in my face. "Hey. You told Savino about the parties, right?"

I stared at her, trying to process what was happening. I smacked her finger down like I might do with Cristine. "What? What do you want?"

"Someone told Savino and the grownups about the parties I went to, they think the shit at Montauk was my fault, like I told someone at a party, and that's why the whole raid thing happened, but I didn't even know about it!" Her finger came back up, almost poking me in the chest. "You told them, huh? Pia? You knew about the parties, no one else knew that—"

"Literally everyone knew about the parties, Betta, and *stop doing that*." I pushed her hand away.

"Don't touch me!" she yelped.

"Oh my God," I said, "what do you *want*?"

"They all think it was me! I'm in trouble now! My dad—my parents *grounded* me, because Savino told them I was responsible, because someone told *him* I was apparently doing *sketchy shit*, which is *not* true—"

I couldn't deal with this. The shouting, the shrill accordion music puncturing the back of my skull, the faintly vibrating floor and the prickle of sweat slipping down my back. And Betta in her tight red dress and bloody lipstick and fake eyelashes, acting like *I* was the reason there were repercussions for her poor choices.

"I don't know what you're talking about," I said, reasonably. "I just got back from out of state, I haven't talked to anyone—"

287

"You and Massimo," she hissed, "and *Tonio*, and *Lorel*, you're up to something, you're conspiring against me."

"I'm a student, I have better things to do than waste time *conspiring*—come on, Betta, please let this go, I don't know what you're talking about."

"IT'S MASSIMO," she shrieked.

I took a step back.

Betta balled her fists at her sides; her face was red. "He told them! He hates his family because he's *dating a fucking SCARPACI!*"

I stared at her. She seemed to recover after a moment—exhaled, flexed her jaw, and widened her eyes at me, like *Well? What 've you got?*

And I didn't say anything—I don't know that I'd have said anything at all, even if we hadn't been interrupted by a bellowing half-drunken voice behind me. People had frozen in our vicinity, shocked men and women I didn't recognize, a scandalized Serafina Di Natale—and Achille, who'd dropped his beer bottle and smashed it on the floor.

And Massimo, who looked like he'd just been shot.

There was a moment of silence before hell broke loose—a brief pause, the calm before a storm. Achille shattered it.

"TRAITOR!" He dropped his crutch and crashed into Massimo.

Both men hit the ground hard.

The girls danced back away from them, little screams, a flurry of glittering material and smashed bottles—clearing a space for Achille to straddle Massimo and hold down his head and aim a punch at my cousin's face.

Massimo caught his fist. He slammed his knee into the side of Achille's bad leg, inducing a litany of obscenities. He jerked his head free and twisted Achille's wrist back.

"MASSIMO!" Serafina pressed in beside me—Betta had disappeared—and she rang her hands. *"Madonna santa!"*

Achille pulled back and stumbled away, fought to get to his feet—his bad leg collapsed beneath him, he was on one knee.

Massimo leapt up.

"Massimo, stop! Stop it!" That was Serafina again, shouting over my shoulder, but he wasn't listening—he kept low to the ground, waiting. Because for all his composure and slick suits and mystique, Massimo was as unhinged as anyone, and I could tell he *wanted* to fight Achille, he was dying inside and he wanted to *feel* something.

Achille dove forward again and slammed his shoulder into Massimo's chest. But Massimo was ready this time, his hands were up, he grabbed fistfuls of Achille's suit and swung the other man around, let his momentum carry them both, and hit Achille in the face.

On the other side of the hall, the music faltered. There was a growing crowd now, yet no one was compelled to intervene.

There was blood—Achille had some on his chin, some on Massimo's fist. They were back on the floor. Achille grabbed at something to pull himself back up, found a tablecloth, and nearly pulled an entire buffet down on Massimo's head. Massimo rolled to the side and barely avoided the mess of smashing catering equipment—pasta spilled across Achille's pants, tea candles spluttered out in puddles of sauce.

"HEY!" someone bellowed from within the crowd. "HEY, what's goin 'on?!"

"Oh, Good Lord," said a voice behind me. Tonio shrugged out of his tux and pressed it into my arms. "Hold this, would you?"

I'd barely registered what he'd said before Tonio dove into the fray. He skidded through a puddle of tomato sauce and oil and crashed into Massimo before he could land another one on Achille.

Massimo fell against the table and scrambled for a footing. Tonio righted himself, held out his hands. "Massimo, I don't know if you've noticed, you're causing a bit of a scene—"

Achille got to his knees. Massimo dove around Tonio and slammed Achille back into the ground.

Tonio spun and grabbed his arm. "Massimo—hey—*stop*."

Massimo didn't stop. Achille's fist crashed into the side of his head and my cousin fell backwards into Tonio. He righted himself and lunged forward again.

"Idiots." I hadn't meant to say it aloud, but there it was—*idiots*.

I pushed my way through the crowd, away from the fight, back towards the dessert table.

No one was paying attention—all eyes were glued to the brawl, so a wall of backs hid me from sight. I reached the table and grabbed the candelabra from between piles of pastry dishes. I kicked the tablecloth aside and hooked my ankle around the cardboard box, dragged it out from under the table.

I dropped in the candelabra. Then I pushed back through the crowd and didn't look back.

I prayed to God I didn't see Betta. If I bumped into her again, I might hit her—I didn't think I'd be able to control it. I was so *done* with this night, I had lost my last ounce of sanity a long while ago, yet people insisted on pushing me over the edge, again and again and *again*.

Sure, there were fireworks fuses burning down behind me, but there were pipe bomb fuses in the warehouses, and it was all ticking down—tick, tick, ticking. And maybe Massimo was a grenade, maybe Tonio was dynamite, but I was a time bomb, and I could feel the silent countdown spiraling towards *zero*.

XV

Boom

i.

They said it was an accident—that during the fight, someone had bumped up against a table, and the tablecloth had slipped, and the candlesticks had somehow ended up in the box of fireworks meant for later that night. The people standing in its vicinity were blamed, but so was poor Oscar because he'd set the box there to begin with. He said he was sorry, it shouldn't have been possible—the box was *way* under the table, it wasn't even close to the fire—but the black marks on the ceiling and the hordes of panicked, angry guests were unrelenting.

Dora was sobbing and inconsolable with her mother and aunts and Francesco at her side, sobbing because Massimo and Achille and the stupid fireworks had ruined her party. Nicole was attempting to talk Gio down from calling the fire department. "It wasn't that bad, nothing's on fire, is it? We can save this."

My ears rang with the high-pitched shriek of rockets. I held my skirt, hands clammy, and pushed through the crowd.

I found Oscar and Massimo through a set of glass doors, off the back patio and across a dark courtyard. The space was boxed-in and overshadowed by surrounding buildings, sheer walls of brick and ivy, rusting trash bins in the corner. My cousin was on a concrete park bench between a potted tree and a still birdbath.

Oscar ran his hands through his hair—it was loose around his shoulders now. "Hell," he said, aptly.

Massimo slumped on the bench, elbows on his knees. He touched his lip and glanced at the blood on his fingertips. He wiped it on his ripped pants leg. "Hi, Pia." He had the guts to actually meet my gaze. Black eyes not flat like Tonio's, but the opposite, I guess—there was a lot of pain and hurt and feeling there, stuff I didn't have time for.

"I didn't think Betta would tell," I said.

"Neither did I."

I wished Oscar wasn't standing right there. "You didn't have to fight him, Massimo. You could have denied it." But we both knew that wasn't an option, because Betta's blabbing abilities were inexhaustible, and because the evidence was all there: Lorel was my roommate, I hung out with Massimo too much, and it was like Betta had said so long ago—the two of them ending up together was unavoidable and obvious. I rubbed my wrists and watched him, hunched over and spent with blood on his hands. "What are you gonna do?"

"I don't know."

Oscar dragged a hand down his face. "Oh, God, okay. Uh, I think we're all in a lot of trouble"—he didn't know the half of it—"but I can't stay long, I *think* I still have a job."

I crossed my arms. Even without the wind, it was cold. "Where's Tonio?"

"He went to get ice," said Oscar. "He shouldn't have jumped in like he did, he just made it worse. You should probably stay out here for a while," he told Massimo, "because Achille's pissed and I've seen him like this, when we picked him up in Chinatown this summer, he almost killed Raul getting him into the car. And since you're, uh…"

"A dead man?" Massimo suggested.

"Man, what's the deal? Your parents just don't like her, huh?"

"I wish it was that simple," I said.

"I don't get it. So no one knew? I mean, did *you* know?" Oscar looked at me. I nodded. "Well, man. That's gutsy." He rubbed the back of his neck, looked back and forth between the two of us. "That's your roommate, Pia, isn't it?"

"No," I said. "Not anymore. She's gone. If anyone asks, make sure they know that—she isn't around anymore."

"Right." Oscar looked like he knew exactly what I meant, and it made him uncomfortable. I felt sort of bad for him, because Oscar Hely was a pretty upstanding guy, and he'd been sucked into this dark undercover world of working security for my uncle, just because his dad knew Savino. That was the problem with this family: you didn't even notice yourself sinking until you were neck-deep.

"I've got to go," he said. "Mr. Moriondo's waiting." He faced me and nodded at Massimo. "You'll stay with him?"

"Yeah."

"Bye, Pia. Happy New Year." Oscar brushed past me; he disappeared back through the glass doors and into the party.

"What time is it?"

Massimo looked terrible—split lip, big tear in his sleeve, something in his hair that might have been sauce but easily could have been blood. "After eight."

"What time is it, exactly?"

He checked his watch. "Half-past."

"Oscar's leaving with Johnny." I needed to get that through his head—he didn't seem to understand what it meant. "They're going to get the truck, they're going to get the oil out of the warehouses. And"—I glanced over my shoulder, we were alone, but I still dropped my voice—"and they'll be back by midnight. They'll miss it. They can't find the bombs."

Massimo stood quickly. He swayed, and I held out a hand to steady him, but he kept his balance. "Where's Tonio?" His eyes were unfocused.

"He's getting ice—hey, how hard did you hit your head? Hey—look at me, focus on me—" He tried. His eyes kept sliding away. Maybe he just couldn't hold eye contact because he was Massimo Di Natale and a tragic hero. But there was also the possibility that he actually *couldn't* focus. "Do you feel sick?"

"Do *you*?"

"I'm serious—yeah, but—do you feel like you're gonna vomit?"

"I don't have a concussion, Pia."

I'd had a concussion in high school, playing soccer, gotten knocked around and had my head slammed against a goalpost. "What's taking Tonio so long?" I asked, with building dread. I couldn't do this without Massimo. He was the crazy genius who had gotten us this far, he was the renegade arsonist who'd burned down a warehouse and lit a fire under Diego Scarpaci.

"I don't know," Massimo said, "but look, I've got to stop them."

"*We* 've got to stop them," I said. "How?"

"I've got an idea."

"Does it involve blowing something up?"

He didn't say anything. He brushed past me, back towards the building—a faint limp in his walk, a dreamlike quality to his face.

I wanted to stop him. I wanted to backtrack and try to sort out this situation in a rational manner. But I couldn't make myself move. "Massimo."

He paused in the doorway and glanced back at me.

He looked so broken, like he could see the end and knew it was inevitable. Like he was ready to do something thoughtless and reckless, because Savino would be coming after him soon—the family knew, the secret was out, and Achille was right: Massimo was a traitor to the family business. I'd helped him become that. So maybe what I meant to say was *I'm sorry*, but that wasn't what came out.

"You're not Mario Mansi."

He raised his hand slowly and wiped the blood off his chin; his eyes focused on me for an instant before sliding away. "I think maybe I always have been, Pia."

293

He turned and slipped back inside, back into the party, where golden light and distant sobs echoed out into the night.

There had been a time not long ago that I might have cried, then. I might have gotten sick, I might have hunted around my apartment for a long-lost cigarette, something familiar and comforting—but there were no nerves, no fluttering anxiety spinning around inside me. I was too cold to feel anything at all.

I stood there in the dark courtyard, staring at the silver-rippled surface of the birdbath, and for some reason two memories resurfaced: one of Massimo that night in the kitchen after the fire, sitting across from me at the counter with a drink in his hand and moonlight on his hair and agonizing self-hatred in his eyes, the shadows stitched together around him like a funeral shroud. And I thought about Sabine, about the two of us sitting on the back step as night crept across the yard—the abandoned play-set, a pile of Papa's tools neglected and rusting in the coils of a garden hose. She'd held me while I cried. She'd handed me a token, a plan for the future, the first step down in a series of plummets from grace.

I stood there in the dark courtyard in my black Sunday dress, smelling of fireworks and smoke, and I was certain no one would ever hold me that way again.

Savino would. The idea came unbidden, entirely unwanted.

Savino would. Because he understood. Because they were right—my aunts, my cousins, everyone who'd ever said it to my face—they were perfectly right: I was like Savino, too much like him. In the same way that I knew and anticipated his motives, the next move in this life-sized game of chess he played, and hated him for it—he knew *me*. And he was possibly the only person alive who could say that.

"God, it's freezing out here." Tonio came up behind me. He'd lost the tuxedo—or, rather, I'd lost it in the crowd—and his sleeves were rolled up to the elbow; he gripped a sodden lump of brown paper towel in one hand. Ice. "I leave for one minute, and where is he?"

I didn't answer. I didn't know. *Savino would know.*

"Hey. Marzano." He peered down into my face, eyebrows pinched in the middle, almost as if he was capable of genuine concern. "What are you doing out here? Where's Massimo?"

"He left."

"He *what?*"

"He *left*. He said he had to stop Oscar and Johnny, they're getting the trucks, he said he'd stop them. He didn't tell me how."

"Oh, hell." Tonio dropped the chunk of ice and paper, kicked it into the shadows. "And you just let him leave? He's *drunk*."

"He's got a concussion."

"One or the other, he can't *drive*, Marzano."

294

I hadn't thought about that, about him taking the car. We'd taken Massimo's Lexus to the party, and he still had the keys, and by the time we got out to the valet parking, he'd already be gone.

"Pia."

I spun around.

Savino stood in the doorway. His shadow stretched out into the courtyard, covering us. He'd lost his tuxedo as well, or maybe he'd never been wearing one, maybe Savino treated every event like it was a casual olive oil tasting in his home office.

He nodded at Tonio. "Do you have your car?"

"Hmm? Oh, no." Tonio's hair had come unstuck from its gelled shell—he combed it back with an ice-wet hand, suddenly casual. "No, we took Massimo's car over, and I think he's gone home, so we're stranded. Figures. He means well, but he can be a right overdramatic *figlio di*—uh, you know."

Savino ignored everything else he'd said. He reached into his pants pocket and tossed something across the gap to Tonio, who caught it. "Drive us."

Tonio pocketed the keys. "Who?"

Savino looked at me pointedly.

I was too cold to think. *Leaving the party?* That hadn't been in the plan. Then again, Betta going rogue and Massimo bailing hadn't been in the plan either. "Where are we going?"

Savino turned back inside, beckoned for us to follow. "You'll see."

ii.

Savino would, I thought, as we shot through New York City in one of the Vitelli BMWs. Savino knew things. He knew everything, he knew the important stuff, the sort of thing that elevates a person. He had hands slick with green-gold oil, and it had made him untouchable.

He sat in the passenger's seat beside Tonio, pointed out turns in a hushed voice. Once, he looked over his shoulder into the back seat and fixed me with his steely gaze. "Did you both know about Massimo and the Scarpaci girl?"

I hesitated. Then I nodded. "But...you knew about her too."

"I *found out* about her," he corrected, "*after* Diego broke into you apartment." He faced front again, and I watched a muscle in his jaw twitch. "Your roommate, yes?"

"Yes. But she isn't there anymore—she left." Just in case he got it into his head to do a raid on my old apartment. "It isn't her fault. Or Massimo's."

"I think it's Massimo's fault that his brother is in a sling and Achille Salone caught a bullet."

My mouth was dry. The farther we got from the party, the more reality began to set in: explosives due at ten, Massimo tracking down Oscar with a concussion, Lorel was in trouble, and my mind was racing ahead too quickly to track down the source of the anxiety.

"I heard Achille started the fight," said Tonio.

Savino didn't reply.

I wasn't scared of driving at night. I'd heard that people with traumatic experiences sometimes avoided similar situations, like how Vince had refused to get in a car for a full week after the crash. But it didn't scare me. Maybe that was proof that I didn't believe the story: the deer, Papa swerving, man versus nature. Maybe that was proof that I believed divine or familial intervention must have occurred, in order to make him do something so stupid. I wasn't afraid of crashing, I knew how to drive in the dark, I knew because Papa had taught me.

He wouldn't swerve. Not for a deer.

Savino touched Tonio's shoulder. "Stop here."

Tonio pulled into an alley and threw the car into park. I hadn't paid much attention to where we were heading, but the spot seemed vaguely familiar.

"Okay." Savino unbuckled, opened the door. He spoke to Tonio. "Wait here. Johnny will be around in a bit, you drive him out to the *panificio*. Marco Biasi's waiting there. They'll do some business, then you take Johnny home, okay?"

Tonio's eyes flicked to me, so quick it was nearly imperceptible. "Why am I waiting for Johnny?"

"He'll be around with Oscar. Pia, come on."

"Why are you taking Pia?" But Savino shut the door on his question.

I turned to Tonio, who frowned at my uncle's silhouette through the glass. "It's fine. We have time." I fumbled in my pocket, tossed my cellphone into his lap. "Call Massimo."

The phone looked awkward in his hand, and normally he'd make some snarky comment about the monstrosity that is modern technology, but he barely glanced at it. "I don't like this," said Tonio.

I undid the buckle and opened my door. "Me neither."

iii.

It felt like a dream, like the scenery was frozen around us and I was simply walking through a memory, or someone else's story—faint traffic as a distant hum, the sound of my shoes on the pavement, fog-cloaked streetlights growing dimmer and fading to orange as we left them behind and descended into the shadows. My uncle and I walked down the alley side-by-side in silence, until it opened up into a concrete plot, and I

296

realized why the area seemed familiar—because I'd been there already once today, early in the morning, when purple shadows stretched across the tin roof and Tonio had parked around back to hide the car's headlights.

Did quicklime have a scent? I thought I reeked of it. "What are we doing here?"

Savino stopped by the door—a real door, not the rolling one Massimo had jimmied open that morning. He found the right key on his chain, inserted it into the lock. "Do you know what this is?"

Would he know if I lied? "Yes." *And we shouldn't be here.*

The door swung open. He leaned inside, flicked on a light, and motioned for me to follow. I did.

The room looked different in the light, stark and startlingly empty but for the crates—and, tucked away in the shadows, time bombs ticking, ticking, *ticking towards zero.* I stood in the doorway, my heart in my throat. We had an hour, I knew we had an hour, but still the inside of the warehouse was too warm, charged with electric energy. I wondered what it would be like, to stand in that warehouse when the bombs went off. I wondered if I'd know what had hit me.

Savino ran a hand over his hair, a strangely human gesture. He had his back to me when he spoke. There was a scar on the back of his neck, a silver crescent right above the collar of his shirt, and I fixated on it." You once asked Ida if we were safe."

I didn't remember that. "I did?"

"Mmm." He turned to the crates, ran his fingers along the slats, as if searching for a sign in the wood grain. Face tensed in concentration. "Last summer. After the show. You asked her—she told me later—you asked, and she said yes." He'd found whatever he was looking for and heaved the chosen crate onto the floor. He straightened and dusted off his hands. "You know why?"

"Why?" I wanted to sound bold, but it came out a hoarse whisper.

"Because of me." Savino crouched by the crate and pulled a switchblade from his back pocket. He set to work prying off the lid. "I take care of this family, Pia, and everyone in it. Before me, my father. And always, Valentino Marzano. And like I said yesterday: maybe someday, you." He paused. "They look at people like me and you. They think we're on a throne. But we're not. We're hanging on a cross. Call it honor, call it duty—it's a burden."

Nails rasped against wood, and the lid groaned open. Savino set it aside. Packed into the straw were black glass bottles, piles of them, with corks dripping silver sealing wax.

Savino looked up. "Come here."

I did, slowly. *Tick, tick, tick.* I paused on the other side of the crate and looked down into the straw. Each bottle was stenciled with a blue sparrow, a bird in flight, its wings spread like it was trying to escape the black-glass confines of its prison. *Oliveto Marzano.*

"This is our family's oil. You've tasted it. You know." He selected a bottle, dusted off the straw. "We bleed this stuff. There's always been talk of Italians with oil in their veins, divinities drenched in olive oil, the sacredness of an orchard. But for the Marzanos, and the Vitellis…it's true for us. It's the blood of this family. Sacramental. Do you understand?"

I did. But I shook my head, because I didn't want him to think we were on the same page. I didn't want to be here.

"You do. You get it. It stops flowing," he said, "and that's when we're really in trouble." He was working off the wax seal with his switchblade, eyes far away, frowning into the layers of bottles nestled in the straw.

I wet my lips. "Why am I here?"

"What would you do to protect your siblings?"

I blinked. Was that a threat? He didn't look at me when he spoke, but the words weighed heavily. "I…I don't know."

Savino paused with the knife. He looked up at me, and I'd thought at the beginning of the summer that there was something quietly dangerous about my uncle, but I'd been wrong. It was loud. "Really," he said.

I stared at him. He waited. My back teeth ground together and I swallowed past the dryness in my throat. *He'll know if you lie.*" Anything. I'd do anything for them."

"What's *anything*?"

Anything was arson and pipe bombs and putting my best friend's life on the line. *Anything* was setting off fireworks at Dora's engagement party, the peppery bite of olive oil in the back of my throat, wind stinging my cheeks while Tonio and I stood before a payphone and quarters filled my palms.

Savino stripped off the wax. He pulled the cork. "Think about that," he said. "It isn't theory, it's a daily practice. There's a reason this family does the things it does— the reason I do the stuff that needs to be done, to protect the way we live. That's why you're here."

Here meaning New York, or the warehouse?

Tick, tick, tick… An hour. A full hour. But I thought I smelled the quicklime, recognized it from the lab where Massimo had measured it out, and it seemed stronger than when we'd first entered the warehouse.

Savino rose to his feet, bottle in one hand and switchblade in the other. "We're going to Sicily."

I stared at the bottle—the blue sparrow, the golden liquid hidden behind black tinted glass. *Sicily.* "What?"

"We're going tonight."

I met his eyes. He was serious. "*What?*"

"You're going to meet your family. We're gonna talk to Valentino, in Sicily, on his turf. I told you yesterday—what happened before Christmas, we're dangling by the end of a thread. If he cuts off the Vitelli business, the blood stops pumping, and hell breaks loose."

I was cold. I'd been cold for a long time, but suddenly my fingers were numb and I couldn't feel my feet. "Sicily."

"But you're a Marzano, Pia. Remember that? What I said? You were born for this. You've had this power handed to you, you have a role that could save this family that would die for you. Look." He tilted the bottle, poured out a stream of gold—it slipped through his fingers, drizzled onto the concrete floor where it glowed green in the overhead lights. It splattered like a bloodstain. I could smell it from where I stood. "That's yours, and mine. It belongs to our family, it's in our blood, and we're gonna make sure we keep it. Valentino will listen to you, we're going to keep this family alive—the Di Natales, the Salones, your siblings."

I stared at the trickle of oil off his hand, frozen. "I can't go to Sicily."

His eyes were wary. "Why?"

I looked at him for a long moment, blinked away the vision of oil streaming to the floor. I thought about it—*why?* What would I become, if I went to Sicily with Savino Vitelli? I wouldn't be a prop, or a piece in his game. I'd be my own player. He was right, I had power, I could grasp it, I could propel the future of this family any way I wished, I could let the tide wash over me and refuse to acknowledge that the waves were full of blood. I could lean on Savino, choose ignorance, choose safety and simplicity and stability. I could go to Sicily.

But. "I can't leave the kids."

His gaze reminded me of the mirror—of stepping out of the shower and seeing my face through a cloud of steam and realizing I wasn't who I'd once been. How there was a lot less Marzano and a lot more Vitelli in my bones. He stood with olive oil on his hands, glinting gold on his scarred forearms and wrists. "The kid are why you've got to leave," he said.

It took me a second to understand what he meant. "Sabine won't bring them here."

"I don't need her to bring them to Brooklyn."

Cold fingers gripped my heart. I took a step back from Savino, towards the doorway—cool wind pressed into my back, ruffled my hair. *Get out. Get far away. Leave.* "Do you have people down there? In Augusta?" It smelled like quicklime, like smoke.

Savino looked at his oil-coated hand. His voice came from somewhere deep and far away." We have people everywhere, Pia. Don't make this difficult. It's really very simple."

I stood my ground, I wouldn't let him see me waver. "I won't go."

299

He lowered the bottle so it hung at his side. "You might not have a choice." He nodded in the direction of the road. "They're coming to load the oil. Oscar's going to drop us off with Valentino's guys, they're taking us over tonight. We'll be there by morning."

Some part of me was clawing to the surface—the part that wanted to fall into line behind my uncle. The part that wanted nothing more than for someone to hold me and take care of me and tell me that I could just be Pia—that would be enough—I didn't have to fight to keep my feet. Whatever sort of cross this was that I faced, Savino would help me carry it.

He waited, but I didn't speak. "I'll take care of you."

He knew exactly what to say, didn't he? Because that was all I wanted, was a person to lean on, someone who noticed when I was falling apart before I even knew, someone stronger than my cousin, because when Massimo and I leaned against each other, we both staggered.

His voice was soft. "I'm not going to hurt you, Pia—no one wants to hurt you, or your siblings, or Sabine. Sabine's a Vitelli, Vitellis don't get hurt."

I snapped back to the moment. *Sabine. Sabine and the kids. Family doesn't hurt family.* "What about Massimo? And Lorel?"

Get out, get out, run. The clock sped up in the back of my head. The timer ticked down to zero. We needed to get out of here, but I couldn't make my feet move.

Savino's jaw muscle twitched again. "We'll deal with that."

I couldn't *let* him deal with it. I couldn't leave the kids, or Massimo, or Lorel— what would happen when I turned my back? The oil stain on the concrete looked like blood. My heart skipped a beat. "What about Mario Mansi?"

An hour. I have an hour. Get out.

I knew I didn't have an hour. I knew it. Looking back, I smelled it—I sensed it— and I chose to stand there like my feet were planted in the cement. *A fixture in the Vitelli museum.*

He tilted his head. "How do you know about that?" His voice was gentle, yet something threatening lurked in his gaze, something that nearly shut me down, but the blood rushed in my ears and I wasn't thinking clearly enough to be scared.

"What about my parents?" I said.

He held my gaze. "A tragedy." As our family's blood dripped off his fingers, he said *a tragedy.*

"Did you know he was going to do it?"

"Who?" He voice was even, his expression betrayed nothing.

"You know who. Marco Vitelli. Did you know he would kill my parents, to have me sent here, or was it just convenient enough that you decided to ignore the truth?"

Somewhere, in Georgia, there was a dent in an oak tree, and it had been put there by a car, and my father had been behind the wheel, and I would never speak to him again. I

300

would never see my Papa, or Mamma, except in the eyes of Savino Vitelli and his sisters.

"I'm not going to Sicily," I said.

Savino nodded, in a resigned, faintly disappointed way. "I'm sorry you feel that way. I thought you cared about this family."

Rage boiled in my stomach. "I care about *my* family. I cared about my parents, who are dead, and I care about Cristine, and Carlo, and Vince. And you're right—they're all right, what people say, that you and I are alike. Because I would do anything to take care of them. *Anything.*"

"Which is why you're going to come with me."

I blocked him out. *Tick tock.* "Did you know?"

Why did I care? I shouldn't. I'd made him the villain in my head long ago, I'd known what he was for a long time, why should I question it now? *Did you know?* I wasn't that desperate, I didn't need Savino Vitelli, I didn't need to lean on him just because—because—

"You look a lot like her," I whispered. Because he had my mother's eyes, because he felt like everyone I'd lost, come back from the grave.

"I know," said Savino.

And somewhere, in the warehouse, water trickled through a slim plastic straw, into a compartment of quicklime. And the quicklime grew hotter and hotter, the temperature rose and the pressure built, until the walls of the metal pipe shook with the force. And Massimo Di Natale wasn't a genius, he was just a boy with too much ambition and illegal access to a lab and too many chemistry courses under his belt, a boy who made mistakes—God knows, he made mistakes—and his calculations were wrong, and so the time ticking down on his watch, wherever he was at that moment, was incorrect.

It happened in an instant.

The sound hit my eardrums—a rattling bang, like pots and pans clashing together, and I didn't know whether the sound or the fire came first, or the searing heat that hit my body like a wall, or the realization that life was hell, and I'd planted myself in the center of the flames.

They said the bulk of the shrapnel hit my uncle.

It made sense. Even in those last moments, Savino took the fall for me. He couldn't protect me from the fire, but his body acted as a wall—a human shield—and knowing that later, the expression on his face made even less sense.

Because I remember. Before he fell—before I hit my knees and before the world descended into a spiral of rapid images—I saw the flames reflected in his black eyes,

301

and he didn't look angry, or disappointed, and there was no pain in my uncle's dying expression. I could have sworn he smiled.

I wondered about that, later. I wondered whether, even as he felt his life bleeding out, his last thoughts were of protecting me. *Family*. And I wondered if that smile was for me as well—a reassurance.

Flames licked up the walls. Something inside me had stopped working.

There was pain, I didn't know where from, I didn't particularly care. The world grew hotter and the fire crept closer. The air was peppery and bitter, burning floral tones mingling with smoke.

I saw the smashed black bottle nearby. The blue sparrow flickered orange. Then the bird broke free of the glass, peeled away into the burning air, raining aquamarine feather shards onto the warehouse floor. It was gone.

I saw the ceiling reflected in a puddle of oil by my head. I saw crimson streams—mine or Savino's?—mingle with the green and gold, sacramental rivulets, and I thought *we bleed olive oil. He was right all along. We do bleed oil.*

iv.

Pounding footsteps rang in my ears, near my head, like claps of thunder and beating wings.

"Pia. Pia!" The voice was distant. It grew louder. A hand on my shoulder. "Pia!"

I'm alive, I wanted to say, only I didn't know if that was true. I didn't feel alive. I didn't know what I was feeling, it was a lot of pain and numbness, a deep-seated ache swelling in my chest, in my stomach. My eyelids fluttered—I saw red through my lashes, flames. I inhaled a lungful of burning olive oil in the air. I saw Odysseus emerging from the sea, burning waves of golden oil.

Liquid gold.

I was moving. Everything hurt. And then it hurt worse, because someone was carrying me, and whoever was doing it was running, and that made the pain worse. I left the fire behind, yet the heat clung to my skin; it seared my flesh, it burned in my muscle and bones.

They set me down at last, and a door slammed, and the only sound was a high-pitched scream in my ears—a perpetual tone ringing in my head, which made it hard to think and breathe.

But I had to breathe, if I was actually alive. I was alive. I was alive.

Another door slammed. I flinched.

The car started. I was in a car. I wasn't dead, but the warehouse was burning and the oil was burning and I was thinking about that half of a black-glass bottle with a blue sparrow stenciled on it, its wings broken off from the impact of hitting the ground. I remembered that I'd considered myself on the edge of a precipice, about to fall into an abyss and drag everyone I loved down with me, and how that's how I must look, at the bottom—like that shattered sparrow surrounded by green oil and flames.

Greek fire.

Something pressed into my stomach. It hurt. A sound escaped my throat, but I didn't hear it, just louder ringing, and the car jerking into motion, and a voice cutting through the tone in my ears—

"Hold on, Marzano. Don't die on me."

I drifted in and out of consciousness. There was less pain when everything was black—less feeling, less noise. I'd come back to the jolting of the car, pressure on my stomach, pain drilling into my skull, and a voice repeating over and over "Stay awake, focus—hey, Marzano—Pia, hold on, just hold on—"

My eyes opened at one point. My mind couldn't really make sense of what I was seeing—Tonio in his undershirt with one hand on the wheel, the other reaching across the console and applying pressure to my abdomen, shooting through traffic, the city lights and neon greens casting weird shadows across his frantic face and the car's interior. It was a fevered dream.

"Hold on, we're almost there, hold on"—he glanced at me, saw I was awake, I'd never seen genuine fear on Tonio's face, but there it was and it chilled me—"Pia, don't close your eyes, talk to me. No, don't look down—"

His dress shirt was balled up, streaked with black and soaked with red. I didn't think Massimo or Achille had bled that much earlier. I couldn't figure out how he'd have gotten so much blood on his shirt. And what was it doing here, wadded up, pressed into my gut like that?

"Pia, eyes on me. Focus, Marzano. Look, tell me about Vince, right? Talk to me about your brother, tell me about him, how old is he?"

Vince. Sweet, baby Vince, with his sad eyes and wide smile, the way he threw his entire body into a hug, how his face lit up when he saw me come home. I loved him so much it hurt. I wanted to go home.

"How old, Pia, huh? Come on, you don't know your own brother's age, is that it?"

"Ten."

"Is he?" He sounded relieved. "He's been ten a long time, are you sure? When was his last birthday, what did you do for his birthday?"

He was trying to distract me. I wanted to shut my eyes and slip back under.

"Don't. Hey, listen, listen to me, focus. Look at my face."

I did. I wished, in a distant sort of way, that he'd focus more on the road and stop looking at me to make sure I was looking at him. There was blood on his undershirt, too. There was some on his face. His eyes were wide, teeth clenched, like he'd seen a ghost and he was trying to keep his composure, like I might die at any moment.

"Okay, Vince is ten," he said. "What about the other two? What are their names?"
Cristine. She was too young. And Carlo, too old.

"Pia, listen, you know what Massimo did? The fool went off and he found Oscar and Johnny, in their truck—big fucking truck, and him in his Lexus— rammed his car right into the shipment truck, wrecked them both. That was his plan, him concussed—it was a concussion after all, not drunk, although it's always safe to assume Massimo's a bit drunk in any scenario. Are you listening? Pia. You should get a real kick out of this, I used the damn phone. I used a *cellphone.* I called Massimo, he was banged up pretty bad but he got away before the cops arrived, before Oscar and Johnny could stop him— just ran off into the streets like a madman, he told me what he'd done. And then I called your 'roomie', which—really, Marzano? That's what she's called on your phone? That isn't a real word, *roomie*—but I called her and she picked up her idiot boyfriend, if that's still what they are anyway. Are you still here? *Marzano.*"

The next thing I knew, I was being tossed around between people—shouting, doors slamming, and then footsteps echoing around a closed space, and words—an assortment of words selected at random—floating to the surface: *fire, Massimo, Savino, warehouse, Marzano, shrapnel.*

I didn't hear Tonio's voice anymore, and somehow that was the worst part, feeling suddenly alone in this half-conscious world where shapes were fuzzy and sound came in bursts.

Memories crept back slowly, in the space between pain and blissful forgetfulness.

I remembered hitting the floor in the warehouse, my head making contact with the concrete, everything snapping in and out of focus as flames sprang to life along the walls.

I remembered my mother's eyes, black reflecting orange flames, and a finger tracing a cross on my forehead—up and down, practiced yet unsteady. *Be careful. Be safe.*

And I would have suppressed that part, I would have chalked it up to hallucination, if not for what Tonio told me later. That when he'd found me in the burning warehouse, covered in mine and my uncle's blood, metal shrapnel studding my stomach and arms, there had been a cross on my forehead, painted in blood and oil.

Maybe it was a curse. Or maybe it was forgiveness from Savino Vitelli.

XVI

Mercy

i.

"Shhh, she'll wake up." That was Massimo's voice.

"Well, she needs to wake up," Tonio murmured, "we can't stay here forever, they'll kick us out at some point."

"No, they won't, she's Pia Marzano." *Lorel.* "But they might kick *us* out. Me, specifically. And Massimo."

"The chloroform will wear off soon," said Massimo.

"Mister chemist with the ill-timed explosives knows a lot about chloroform, does he?"

"Tonio—"

"Alright, fine. Fine."

I opened my eyes. I wasn't in pain, but everything felt numb and fuzzy, and the room spun—too bright—until it halfway settled into place. They were lined up in folding chairs beside a pile of medical equipment: Tonio in his bloodstained undershirt (my blood?), arms crossed, slumped in his seat yet high-strung and restless as he glared at his shoes; Lorel, gnawing her lip, leaning heavily against Massimo, who sat upright and stared across the room with sad, solemn eyes.

"Well, hi, Marzano." Tonio straightened. "Welcome back."

"Pia!" Lorel rose and crouched beside me. I was on a bed—a cot, really. She looked like she wanted to touch me, comfort me in some way, but didn't know how. "You're gonna be alright. Angelo's an EMT, he patched you up, did a blood transfusion, you've got a slight concussion but you'll be okay. How do you feel?"

"Who's Angelo?" My tongue felt thick.

"Angelo Scarpaci," said Massimo. "Lorel's uncle."

I narrowed my eyes at Tonio. "Where did you—?"

"Scarpaci casino." He shrugged. "I wasn't sure where else to take you, they'd have looked into it if we'd gone to the hospital, and I figured you wouldn't want that."

"You can sit up, if you want," said Lorel. "You've got some burns, and some stitches from shrapnel, but it—it could have been worse. And we found you some clothes, Sara keeps a change in her work locker."

I sat up, stretched out my legs under the sheet. My skin felt raw. I was hollow inside.

I wore sweatpants and a tattered NYU shirt, and below the sleeves my forearms were a patchwork of angry red burns and swatches of gauze. I stared at them for a long moment, transfixed, chest tight. I thought about the first time I'd seen Savino, when he'd walked through the door of the Vitelli house, and I'd seen him and I'd known who he was right away—not because he looked like me and Mamma, not because of the authority in his gaze, but because of his arms—knotted, scarred baker's arms, crossed with burns and cuts—arms that said *I worked for this, I earned this*. I did this to myself.

"Pia," said Lorel. "You're gonna be alright. It looks worse than it is."

I didn't care. I couldn't explain it to her. There wasn't a soul in this world who understood what was going through my head. I couldn't fucking breathe.

I pulled up my shirt—Mamma's medals clinked together on their chain. There was a bandage on my midriff, and a collection of cuts and splattered burns surrounding it.

"That was the biggest one," said Lorel. "What was it, twelve stitches?"

"Seventeen," said Tonio. "You're drugged up, by the way."

"What?"

"If you feel dizzy," said Lorel, "it's just because Angelo put you on codeine, or morphine, or something like that—he said it would wear off in a few hours, but Tonio's got more when you need it."

I dropped my shirt, exhaled. Bandages felt like the least of my worries right now. I was in Scarpaci territory; I'd had bad experiences with that, and I wasn't slow enough to not be alarmed. "Is your dad here?"

"Mom kicked him out, told him to stay away till you were stable. My brother Lucio's off distracting him. We snuck Massimo in, but..." Lorel looked back at him.

I looked too. Massimo clasped his hands in his lap, stared at them for a moment before he met my gaze. "We're leaving, Pia."

I didn't have to ask who *we* included. I wasn't shocked, either, so I was surprised by the sudden stinging in my eyes. "When?" Was it my fault? I should have told the Vitellis sooner, that I was the one who'd put together the explosions—I should have told them before they could assume it was Massimo or the Scarpacis. *My fault.*

Lorel squeezed my hand. "We're leaving tonight, getting out of New York before the sun rises. We have to leave before your family realizes what happened. We just wanted to wait till you woke up and we could say goodbye, and Angelo says you're in decent shape, you'll be okay. So I'm finishing school online. I called my cousin Maria in Chicago, we're going to stay with her for a while and then we'll work our way up north."

"Montana?"

Massimo smiled a bit. "Maybe. Somewhere far from the city."

My two best friends, my cousins, running off together. How romantic. How lonely. I felt real pain in my chest, like someone was twisting a blade above my heart.

I wondered if Lorel knew about the ring. I wondered if she knew what she was getting herself into with Massimo, and whether Massimo would ever feel like he was good enough for Lorel, and I wondered how long it would last, which were all horrible thoughts to have in that moment when they were searching for a soft place to land.

I squeezed Lorel's hand back. "I'm sorry."

Her eyes shone, but her voice was steady. "I'm not. We're going to be fine, Pia, all of us. We're gonna be happy."

I desperately hoped they would be. I didn't know about myself.

They slipped out quietly—I wouldn't have known they were fleeing the city, they were so casual about it. A simple, "Bye, Pia," and a quick hug from Lorel, and then they were gone, and they shut the door behind them. I didn't know when I'd see them next, or if I'd see them at all—Massimo with his calm eyes, carrying a can of gasoline into the apartment, drinking sambuca out of a coffee mug—Lorel with flowers in her hair, aggressively optimistic, eating stale scones over the kitchen sink. They left, and I don't think either of them realized how much that hurt to watch them slip away, to watch them turn their backs on me and walk out the door hand-in-hand.

It felt like waking up into a harsher reality. I looked at my arms, ran a hand down the bandages and throbbing pink burns. "He's gone."

Tonio watched me, his black eyes following my hand. "Yes."

"He's..."

"Savino is dead. I saw him. He's dead."

When would it feel real? I flipped over my hands and stared at the palms. Blood was crusted under my nails. Slick traces of oil in the cracks of my hand. "He's—he was the heart."

"The what?"

He wasn't dead. People like Savino didn't die. They couldn't. He couldn't. "He said if the heart stops, the blood stops pumping, and the blood of this family is oil. And Savino"—it hurt to say his name—"he was the heart." I looked up, I felt tears building. "Do you remember"—my voice cracked and my face burned—"*Macbeth*, Lorel stood there on stage and she scrubbed her hands, scrubbed them over and over again and— she still saw blood, she couldn't clean it off, it just stayed forever?"

Tonio nodded. I spoke of blood, but there he sat covered in mine.

"Who's fault was it?" I asked.

"Well." He tilted back his head to the ceiling, took a deep breath. "I don't think there's an answer to that question—not one that satisfies, anyway. It's a culmination of good intentions and the fact that humanity is deeply, tragically flawed. Maybe it's Marco's fault, for killing your parents, or your aunt's for sending you here without thinking, or Savino's for manipulating everyone and...placing olive oil on an altar right beside God Himself." He focused on me, eyes tired but still sharp—ever-sharp, Tonio was, always quick. "Maybe it was my fault...because I've played spectator for so long, I never once tried to stop any of it from happening. Or Massimo's fault for not thinking before acting, for miscalculating the time bombs, or Betta's fault for being Betta, or Achille's for being Achille, or any of the parents and aunts and uncles for watching decades of crime and manipulation and never speaking up, never trying to stop it."

"Or mine," I said.

"Or yours." Tonio held up his hand so I could see his palm, see the creases and calluses lined with rusted red. "We've all got blood on our hands, Marzano."

I didn't feel forgiven or soothed—but at least, if only in a small way, I was understood. I shoved the sheets back and swung my legs off the bed. I smelled quicklime. "I have to get to the kids."

"Why?"

"Because they'll know it was me. Do they know he's gone? Marco Vitelli knows where we live in Augusta, Savino says he has guys there, he'll either kill the kids or he'll try to use them against me and Valentino—" Cold fear gripped my heart, I felt sick, I thought about Vince and Carlo and Cristine, and poor Sabine, and I thought about my parents 'car smashed up against a tree, and we couldn't do that again. Never again. I'd said I'd keep them safe, and I couldn't let Marco Vitelli have the last word.

"They don't know it was you," said Tonio.

"They'll put it together." I rose to my feet, slowly, the movement pulling at the stitches. "Even without Savino, they'll figure it out. I didn't get the chance to tell them, but they'll know."

Tonio stood. He held out a hand, as if to steady me if I lost balance. "They won't put it together, because I told them it wasn't you or Massimo."

"When? Who did you tell?"

His voice was low, almost casual. "I slipped away at the party and left a note at the Vitelli house, told them what I was planning."

I stared. My mind struggling to wrap around what he'd just said. The world was still tilting, fuzzy around the edges, and I didn't fully trust anything I was hearing. "You—"

"I actually phrased it like a suicide note, they might think I'm dead for a while—not intentional, but I suppose that's a fringe benefit."

He said it so evenly, as if he didn't care, as if the idea of being estranged from his parents, his brothers and Ida, from the Vitellis and Di Natales, was a simple decision. A hint of amusement came back into his eyes, perhaps at my reaction.

"You took the blame." I couldn't believe it. "Why?"

Tonio shrugged. "I've got nothing to lose. What have I got? A couple of cars and a nicotine addiction. But Massimo, and you with your family, you have people to look out for. The Vitellis can't really hurt me."

"But it was't your fault."

"Yes, so I *lied*, Marzano." He smiled thinly, and I had a startling flashback to last year, the beginning of the summer, when things were simpler and I had no battles to fight.

I shook my head. "The whole family will be after your head. They'll think you killed him. On purpose. And not just the Vitellis in Brooklyn, but Marco too, and maybe Valentino."

His smile faded quickly. "So, we'll go."

I put a hand to my stomach. "Go where?" The dull pain wasn't from the shrapnel, the stitches—it was a deep ache that echoed through my chest, coiled around my throat. *He's gone. Savino's dead.*

"Augusta, like you said, we've got to get you back to your family. I've got a car, so we'll go tonight and we'll arrive tomorrow. No one will even notice we're gone."

"They'll notice eventually," I murmured.

Tonio spread his hands, palms up. "Well, yes, eventually, when no one sets off fireworks in the middle of the next party. But we'll be far enough away by then."

I ran a hand down my arm, down the tingling gauze-wrapped skin, and I rubbed the oil from my knuckles. I'd come to New York because of Savino, I'd come because Sabine had sent me into her brother's waiting arms. And even with all the turmoil—the kidnapping, the fire, late nights taking in oil shipments and busting up casinos—I'd always known nothing really bad would actually happen to me, because Savino was watching.

No more. On my own. I wondered if the burns would scar.

"You've got two cars," I pointed out.

Tonio nodded. "That's true."

My heart-rate was through the roof, my eyes pricked. The floor tilted. "Why the *hell* would you have two cars?" My voice was small and tight.

Tonio held out a hand to steady me. I took it. "Because I'm a pretentious bastard, Marzano, we already know this."

ii.

When we stepped out of the room, into the carpeted hallway, I found it vaguely familiar—same dark green wallpaper, flickering overhead lights, colorful abstract paintings lining the way down towards the stairwell and elevator. And, in the other direction, a fire escape.

I'd been duct-taped and held for ransom in one of these rooms. I rubbed my wrists, nervous, as Tonio closed the door behind us.

"He isn't here," said Tonio. *Diego.*

No one was here. Massimo and Lorel—they were gone. It was just the two of us and the hum of the city and the distant crack of fireworks in the night.

We went out a back door. I caught a glimpse of the casino lobby—bright and bustling, flocks of tourists and New Yorkers going about their business without a care in world.

Tonio led the way back into an employee's corridor, still and quiet, where our footfalls echoed off the narrow walls. "They have a car to take us to the apartment, we got rid of the BMW so they can't trace any of this back to the Scarpacis." He shoved open the heavy exit door, held it with his shoulder and nodded me through.

I'd been in this alley before. I craned my head back and followed the zig-zag of fire escape climbing the side of the building, the place outside one of the upstairs windows where a body had lain beneath a coat, and I'd never thought about it too much, I'd never bothered looking into whether Savino had actually killed that man, because I hadn't wanted to know.

Instead of Tonio's convertible skidding around the corner, a gray SUV sat in a cloud of billowing exhaust. Matty leaned against the hood, arms crossed, speaking to a short blond woman in a parka. They both looked up when the door clicked shut behind us.

The woman put a hand on Matty's arm. "Get them out of here."

Matty nodded. He rounded the front of the car, eyes fixed on me as he slid into the driver's seat and slammed the door.

The woman stopped in front of us. She felt vaguely familiar, but I quickly realized it was only because she looked so much like Lorel—large pale eyes, pointed chin, lips pursed in apparent disapproval. Her short hair was streaked with silver at the roots. But I didn't see any of Papa in her.

"You should leave," she said, "and not come back. Okay?"

I nodded.

The famous Calpurnia Marzano pulled her coat closer and sniffed. She looked me up and down, but her expression was inscrutable. "You don't look much like Leo," she decided.

"Neither do you."

"No. I look like my blessed mother. The saint, Devota Maria." She sounded bitter. "You stay away from the Vitellis, and the Marzanos. You get far away from both, and don't look back—that family is poison, they're just street thugs, all of them."

"Your husband kidnapped me."

She rolled her eyes. "I am not responsible for everything Diego does! He's rash, and his brothers encourage him. We also stitched you back together though, you have Angelo to thank for being alive." She waved a hand at the car. "Go. Matteo will drive you. Get out of the city, tonight."

Even from that short exchange, it was clear to me why Lorel didn't get along with her mother. Calpurnia stood on the back step and watched the SUV until we rounded the corner, and she was cut off from sight.

We didn't talk much, we just moved. The looming threat of morning hung over me as I threw stuff in my suitcase, repacked everything I'd unpacked just a few days before, and dragged it out into the living room. Tonio was banging around in his room, so I slipped out onto the balcony, shut the door gently behind me and lit a cigarette.

The smoke was heavy in the frigid air. Bitter in my throat. I leaned against the railing, stared out at the city: crawling traffic, flashing lights, darkness hanging over New York without a promise of sunrise to come. I was reminded of the nights we'd stood on this same balcony, a drink in Massimo's hand, ice clinking against his teeth. Tonio exhaling long spirals of gray smoke into the neon-tinted night. Rubbing oil out of my palm, smoking one of Tonio's cigarettes and taking drinks when my cousin offered them. I was reminded of last night when we'd stood in the courtyard outside the ballroom, blood on Massimo's face and acrid smoke in the air. Ice water dripping from Tonio's hand. And a shadow in the golden light spilling from the doorway.

I missed Lorel, and Massimo, and the people we'd once been. Though maybe we'd always been the people we were now, just buried beneath layers. Regardless, I thought Mamma and Papa wouldn't recognize the girl standing here now on a dark New York balcony, smoking one last cigarette, blood and oil in the creases of her hands.

I hadn't meant for anyone to die. It wasn't malicious. It was desperation and vaguely noble intentions. It was fear.

Sometime today, Ida Vitelli would realize she was a widow, and her children were fatherless, and my aunts had lost their baby brother. I'd killed Savino, who was untouchable. I'd killed a god. I hadn't meant for us to be in the warehouse at that time—yet it was still my fault. Maybe no one else would ever know that, but I would. I would. Because as much as I'd tell myself in the months and years to come that it had all been accidental—that I couldn't have known—

I knew.

311

I knew in those final moments, standing in the middle of the warehouse. I knew as the smell of quicklime grew pungent and heavy in the air, as the clock ticked down in the back of my mind, I knew I should get out. I knew we should both get out. I'd known Massimo wasn't perfect, that there was room for error, that nothing about this oil was predictable. Yet I'd stayed, I'd even stalled. I'd looked Savino in the eye and asked him things I'd never dared to ask before, because I'd known we had reached the end of something. I knew.

One hand on Mamma's medals, the other on a cigarette like Papa. I leaned out into the night. "I'm sorry," I whispered.

The glass door slid open behind me. "You keep smoking those, they'll kill you."

It was almost the same thing Sabine had told me, ages ago, on the back step. If I were Massimo, I might have responded with something like "Well, would that be so bad?" But I was Pia, and I remembered that I had people to take care of, people who were relying on me for safety and security—that, in a chilling, poetic way, I was someone else's Savino Vitelli, like it or not. I always had been, and I always would be.

"He wanted to take me to Sicily," I said. "Tonight. Use the kids to make me vouch for the business to Valentino."

"Ah. *Sicilia.*"

I turned to look at him, framed in the doorway—a fresh change of clothes, careful slicked-back hair, the perfect picture of Tonio Salone as I'd always known him. Yet there was something different, maybe in his gaze or in the way he stood.

"I don't make plans," I said, suddenly," because I don't want them to fail." I let the words hang there. I waited for him to jump on them and give me grief, slither in and exploit the moment with sarcasm.

He just shrugged. "I've never moved away," he said, "because the world is too wide for me to understand everything properly, and that scares me."

I couldn't imagine anything shaking Tonio. But then I remembered his voice earlier in the night as I bled out in the car—and I hardly remembered what he'd said at the time, but I recalled his voice.

"That doesn't mean I shouldn't do it," he said.

I pushed back my hair and exhaled. Tamped out my cigarette on the railing. "I'm gonna do it. The kids need me to do it, I've got to get them out of there. We'll run. If one thing doesn't work, I'll try another, and I wish I could give them something stable and consistent, but that's just not how it's going to be, the Vitellis ruined that when they...killed Mamma and Papa." I put a hand to my stomach, over the stitches, and breathed in deeply—city and smoke, the lingering scent of candle wicks and espresso drifting from the open door. Pain." It's gonna be a mess, Tonio. But you don't have to be there for it. I can't drag you down with me."

"*Drag me down.*" He stuck his hands in his pockets. He thought about that as he stared out over my shoulder, his eyes reflecting the night—gray moonlight and neon. "I've been dragged down for a while, Marzano. Most of my life. This mess is an impermanent thing, plastic, the plans are unfixed and fleeting. That's what I was trying to tell you, last summer at the park."

It took me a second to recall the memory. "I remember you lecturing me about academia."

"Yes, and you eloquently suggested I shove it up my ass. But listen, Marzano—has anyone ever explained to you, that you don't have to have it all figured out? No? You don't have to decide, right now, what you're gonna do with the rest of your life. You're gonna grow and learn, you'll go places and meet new people, you'll have different interests and jobs and studies. So while you're sitting here agonizing over what the rest of your life is going to look like...your time is ticking down, it's passing you by." He nodded at the sky, void of stars. "We're in the gutter. But it would be a pleasure to wade through it with you."

iii.

We drove through the early morning and the day. And I knew the kids would be home, because it was the new year, but nothing prepared me for that moment when I knocked on the front door and the curtain rustled at the window and, a moment later, Vince threw open the door. Nothing prepared me for how good it felt to hold my little brother and cry into his shoulder, and know that no one would take him away—no one could take my siblings, no one would hurt them—because I'd do anything to keep them safe. I knew that now—I'd do anything. That meant Marco Vitelli couldn't hurt them, Valentino Marzano couldn't use them, because they'd have to go through me, and I wouldn't budge, not an inch.

I could take the shrapnel in their stead.

Sabine didn't understand. I couldn't make her understand—that Savino was dead, that the family would come for me and the kids eventually, because they needed Leo's and Carla's children in order to keep the business alive. We stood on the back step for a good hour while I forced her to listen, and laid out my plan, and endured sixty minutes of her shaking her head and saying, "no, *cara*, oh no," until I couldn't stand it anymore and I pulled up my sleeves, I showed her the stitches.

"This family bleeds oil," I said, hearing Savino in my voice—even, undaunted, matter-of-fact as I handed her this monstrosity to wrestle with. "We can't live like that."

I sat my family down in the living room like I had all those months before, the night Mamma and Papa died—I sat them down and I told them we were leaving. They deserved to know everything. They deserved to hear why their lives were being uprooted and stripped away. I told them as best I could, while Sabine stood in the back with a hand over her mouth, and Carlo's jaw dropped, and they all openly stared at Tonio, who sat back in an armchair with his eyebrows raised and a faint, immortal smile on his lips—because, like Lorel, Tonio Salone was fully aware he was living a story, and he was painting this scene into a median chapter.

I skimmed over the last part. I told them someone had planted bombs in the warehouse, without including the part where Massimo and I spent twelve hours in the Fortuna laboratory. I told them Savino was dead, and people would come looking for us soon enough and we needed to disappear.

Cristine didn't speak—her brows were drawn, intense while she listened, digesting everything. Carlo wanted to see my burns, but I wouldn't show him right then, not in front of the other kids. And Vince just looked back and forth between me and Tonio, and finally he whispered, "Where will we go?"

I didn't tell them. Because I couldn't tell Sabine.

I asked her if she'd come with us, but I didn't push her. I knew she loved us, but she also loved her freedom, and we both knew that if she ran off with the Marzano children, she'd have to hide from her family forever.

"I can't tell you where we're going, then."

I stood out behind the house, barefoot, toes digging into the brittle grass. It was January and it was cold, and it wouldn't rain any time soon; I knew by the smell in the air, the way the plants had dug their roots deep into the sandy soil. That was me, I thought: roots reaching deep into this place, planted like I'd never budge. If I uprooted, I might leave part of me behind—the play-set, already rusting; the creaky step on the stairs that reminded me of Papa leaving for work in the morning; the loose baseboard in my parents' closet. This house was steeped in their memory.

But Massimo had said I was a symbol of the Vitelli-Marzano union. Me and my siblings, we were taking Leo and Carla with us. We'd forget Augusta and the house someday, but we'd always look back at each other and remember our parents. They'd left behind more than a house and fleeting memories.

Sabine twisted her bangles, spun them around with red-painted nails. She glanced at the back door, wide eyes distracted and frightened. The kids were banging around inside, packing, but only the things we could fit in Tonio's car. "Pia, come on, I need to know that you're okay—I know you can do this, I know you can take care of the kids— I don't know about that Tonio, he gives me bad vibes"—*didn't* he—"but I trust you, *cara*. I need to know you're okay, I need to be able to contact you—"

"If you knew," I said, "you could tell other people, and that would put you in danger."

"No one's going to hurt me, I'm a Vitelli, Savino would—" She stopped.

I saw it on her face. It felt like a punch to the gut. "I don't know what they'd do," I said, "that's the problem."

Her eyes were tragic. "What will *I* do?"

"You..." I swallowed. "Sell the house, if you want. Don't go back to Brooklyn. And if they come looking for us—"

"Who?"

"—your father, the Marzanos or the Scarpacis, Gio Di Natale or the Salone brothers—pretend you don't know anything. And they'll leave you alone."

Sabine barked a laugh. It was perhaps the first time I'd ever seen her truly rattled, like the ground was disappearing beneath her feet. "But I *don't* know anything, you're not telling me anything."

"That will keep you safe." It didn't feel like my voice. I stared down at my feet in the dead grass, because I couldn't meet her eyes.

"And who will keep *you* safe, *cara*, huh? Not that Tonio guy, not Cristine and the kids, and I won't be there. Who will take care of *you*?"

No one. That was the truth of the matter.

There was no healing where I'd come from. I'd have to go find it.

Me and Tonio were unsteady. But we could lean on each other and maybe—just maybe—stay upright. And perhaps Mamma and Papa were watching me from heaven, where they were partying with the saints, if they even still recognized their daughter. But there was no one else to keep me safe where I was going, no one to shelter me from my plans and choices and from the fact that wherever I went, I was Pia Marzano, and there was something intrinsically tragic and treacherous in the name.

EPILOGUE
Fragments

I've thought a thousand times about how things might have ended differently: if I'd never gone to New York, if I hadn't been in the apartment that day Massimo arrived smelling of smoke, if the night in the warehouse simply had not been. The thoughts circulate and splinter off into shrapnel, showing me what might have been, who might still be alive, where I might be now if not for the choices I'd made.

I close my eyes and imagine that night, and all the nights leading up to it—stagelights and fire, moonlight breaking through a stained-glass sparrow, smoke on the balcony and smoke in a ballroom—all leading up to a pivotal moment. *Blood and oil. It's on both our hands.*

I think about it when I lock up the apartment at night, with the kids and Tonio safe inside, when I draw the curtains. I wonder if we'll find a permanent place to land someday. Tonio was right, the world is big, and it's gotten bigger since we've moved out west—all sprawling deserts and sprawling plains, towering redwoods and orchards stretching as far as the eye can see. It's impossibly big, yet somehow I know that it will never be big enough to put distance between us and our family.

I think about it every time I change my phone number and email address, every time I reject a call because the number feels familiar. When the lawyer finally got through and told me Savino Vitelli had left a certain *Panificio Zeppole* to my name, I almost threw out my computer. I was shaking and sobbing in the kitchen at 1:00 AM, quietly so I didn't wake the kids, furious that no matter how far we fled, it always found a way back to me. Furious that I'd killed Savino and he'd given me the bakery in return—one last ploy to keep me in New York, because if Luca Catenacci wouldn't do it, the bakery surely would. Because even in death he knew me, and my scarred and damaged arms, and the way I couldn't get it out of my head.

I dreamt about it, all the time: *standing in back of the* panificio, *gentle with the focaccia dough, only I was tense because I knew he was watching. I dipped my hands into the green-gold oil, and it burned on my skin, and the kitchen was on fire around me, and I knew ghost flames would chase me into wakefulness, but in that hallowed moment all I saw was the slick shine of oil—and in the orange flames, I thought it was blood.*

"What would you do for your family?" Savino asks. *"How far would you go?"*

Because he's done more. He's spilled oil and blood for this family, and sometimes I wonder if they aren't the same thing.

I've thought a thousand times of how things might have ended differently, if they've ended at all.

I put the kids in school. Tonio finds a job teaching English and Literature. I tell the lawyer to give the *panificio* to Ida—I don't want it, maybe once I would have, but not anymore. I give the bakery to Savino's widow and I take up Kyle Litwiller on his offer, I find the men who run the olive orchards, and all day I work in the dirt with the California sun on my face and the wind lifting sweaty hair off the back of my neck.

I crouch in the branches of a tree during harvest, I take fruit and soil samples and I watch the mills turn hard green olives into an oil people will take and dilute like *lampante*, like something used to burn in a lamp, like it isn't a sacred chrism.

I taste it, with the peppery bite and the bitter aftertaste. The undertones change with the time of harvest and the cultivar, with the season, with the year. The oil is always changing, but it's the same entity. It echoes ancient tradition—Odysseus bathing on Scheria; Savino Vitelli pouring out oil through his hands, onto the warehouse floor; Valentino Marzano locked away in his orchard fortress, playing a game of destruction and manipulation from lofty heights. I feel their eyes on me, and sometimes I hear their voices in the rattling leaves.

"What would you do for your family?" asks Savino—a fleeting shape in the shifting light, the memory of his voice on the wind.

So I stand in the shadows of olive branches, and I plan the road ahead. "Watch and see."

Acknowledgments

This story took flight one evening when I decided to write the book I wanted to read: a book about a bakery, olive oil, the mafia, and morally-gray characters making bad decisions. The story wouldn't have gotten much further than the first chapter, however, if not for my sister Claudia, who encourages my own bad choices by way of her insufferable enthusiasm. I spent months reading aloud the chapters as I wrote them. She listened patiently and egged me on when my energy flagged. This book wouldn't have been possible without her help and encouragement.

More thanks are due to:

Katrina Leonard: for nearly ten years of the best friendship, innumerable escapades, and many a pasta night. Here's to many future adventures.

Sarah Tharpe: for the gorgeous cover art, the endless enthusiasm, and for providing the skeleton wine glasses; you have been a wonderful friend and one of my biggest supporters through this self-publishing journey.

Lisa Coughlin: for cheese, stellar author pictures, and writing nights at the treehouse.

And of course, none of it would have been possible if not for my family—the Boassos and the Edwards; the grandparents, uncles, aunts, and cousins. Daddy: my harshest critic, which makes it all the better when he says it's a job well done. Mommy, who read it second, provided the sambuca, and seriously shipped Tonio and Pia until the very end. Marina, for all the Target excursions and nights binging Community. And Sam: I finally found you a new book to read; it's this.

For all the burgeoning writers, bookstagrammers, and indie authors who have followed along on this rocky road to publishing—it is a beautiful, supportive community, and our legions are ever-growing.

For all the baking experiences and family mafia stories, olive-oil tastings and evenings in the theater, nights writing by candlelight and nights reading aloud in the silence of a sleeping house. Our lives are stories, and I'm writing this one into a median chapter.

Made in the USA
Columbia, SC
07 December 2021

50610060R00202